RHYS LEWIS

The Autobiography
of the Minster of Bethel

About the Author

Daniel Owen was born on 20 Oct 1836 in the market town of Mold, in Flintshire, North Wales. He wrote *Rhys Lewis*, the first significant Welsh novel, and went to become Wales's leading nineteenth-century novelist.

He was brought up in poverty after his coal-miner father was killed when the Argoed pit flooded. He had little formal education and was apprenticed to a tailor in 1848 aged twelve. He developed his reading and writing in the Sunday School of Bethesda Chapel, in New Street, Mold. In 1865, aged 29 he went to Bala College intending to become a minister, but had to abandon college when his mother and sister fell ill. He returned to tailoring in Mold, and became a part-time preacher. He took up writing and, after publishing some shorter works, wrote the first 25 chapters of *Rhys Lewis* as a serial in a Methodist magazine. This material, with 17 additional chapters, was published as a subscription novel by Owen's neighbour on New Street, stationer John Lloyd Morris, in 1885. It was then taken up by Hughes and Son of Wrexham and has never been out of print since. Owen went on to write other best-selling novels, including *Enoc Huws* and *Gwen Tomos*. He died on 22 October 1895 and is buried in Mold Cemetery.

About the Translator

Dr Robert Lomas has worked on cruise-missile guidance, fire brigade command-and-control systems and the early development of personal computers. He is a Visiting Fellow in Operations Management at Bradford University School of Management and has written best-selling books on Freemasonry and science, including *The Hiram Key, Turning the Hiram Key, The Secret Science of Masonic Initiation, The Man Who Invented the Twentieth Century* and *The Lewis Guide to Masonic Symbols*.

www.robertlomas.com
twitter:@Dr_Robert_Lomas

RHYS LEWIS

The Autobiography
of the Minster of Bethel

by Daniel Owen

Translated by
Robert Lomas

Translation and Preface © Robert Lomas 2017
Foreword © Dr John Hywel Roberts 2017

The right of Robert Lomas to be identified as the Author of the Work has been asserted by him in accordance with the Copyright, Designs and Patents Act 1988.

The right of John Hywel Roberts to be identified as the Author of the Foreword has been asserted by him in accordance with the Copyright, Designs and Patents Act 1988.

This translation published 2017
by Dowager Books

All rights reserved. No part of this publication may be reproduced, stored in a retrieval system, or transmitted in any form or by any means without the prior written permission of the publisher, nor be otherwise circulated in any form of binding or cover other than that in which it is published and without a similar condition being imposed on the subsequent purchaser.

ISBN-13: 978-1546721574
ISBN-10: 1546721576

Published by
DOWAGER BOOKS
www.dowager.com

Dedicated to
My *Nain* – Sophia Woodcock, née Blackwell, of Pownalls Row, Mold –
who met Daniel Owen as a child and introduced me to his writing.

CONTENTS

FOREWORD	1
PREFACE THE PUBLICATION HISTORY OF RHYS LEWIS	8
FOREWORD TO THE J. LL. MORRIS EDITION	10
INTRODUCTION	11
CHAPTER 1 THOUGHTS ABOUT BIOGRAPHY	12
CHAPTER 2 MY BIRTH	14
CHAPTER 3 MY EARLIEST MEMORIES	16
CHAPTER 4 EVAN JONES GWERNYFFYNNON	19
CHAPTER 5 THE CHILDREN'S SEIAT	24
CHAPTER 6 MEETING THE IRISHMAN	29
CHAPTER 7 THE TWO SCHOOLS IN MOLD	33
CHAPTER 8 UNDER INSTRUCTION	38
CHAPTER 9 CHURCH MATTERS	44
CHAPTER 10 THE SUBJECT OF EDUCATION	51
CHAPTER 11 WIL BRYAN ON THE NATURE OF A CHURCH	57
CHAPTER 12 DISCUSSIONS BY THE HEARTH	65
CHAPTER 13 SETH	71
CHAPTER 14 WIL BRYAN	80
CHAPTER 15 THE BEGINNING OF OUR TROUBLES	87
CHAPTER 16 THE DAY OF BEREAVEMENT	95
CHAPTER 17 FURTHER SUFFERINGS	104
CHAPTER 18 THOMAS AND BARBARA BARTLEY	111
CHAPTER 19 ABEL HUGHES	117
CHAPTER 20 THE VICAR OF THE PARISH	125
CHAPTER 21 THE CONVERSION OF THE BARTLEYS	132
CHAPTER 22 A VISIT FROM MORE THAN ONE RELATIVE	141
CHAPTER 23 BOB	150
CHAPTER 24 COMFORTING AND SOMBRE MEMORIES	158
CHAPTER 25 AN ELEGY IN PROSE	167
CHAPTER 26 THE SINNER AND THE SPECTRE	174
CHAPTER 27 MY DAYS OF DARKNESS	183
CHAPTER 28 MASTER AND SERVANT	192
CHAPTER 29 HELP FROM A CLEANER OF CLOCKS	202
CHAPTER 30 THE POACHER	212
CHAPTER 31 DAFYDD DAVIES	223
CHAPTER 32 AN ABUNDANCE OF ADVISERS	232
CHAPTER 33 MORE OF WIL BRYAN	242
CHAPTER 34 THOMAS BARTLEY ON EDUCATION	251
CHAPTER 35 TROUBLED TIMES	261

CHAPTER 36 A WELL- KNOWN CHARACTER	**271**
CHAPTER 37 THOMAS BARTLEY'S VISIT TO BALA	**283**
CHAPTER 38 A FORTUNATE ENCOUNTER	**298**
CHAPTER 39 WIL BRYAN IN HIS CASTLE	**307**
CHAPTER 40 THE ADVENTURES OF WIL BRYAN	**318**
CHAPTER 41 THE FIRST AND THE LAST TIME	**326**
CHAPTER 42 THE MINSTER OF BETHEL	**335**
TRANSLATOR'S POSTSCRIPT WHY TRANSLATE A VICTORIAN NOVEL ABOUT MOLD?	**339**

Caroline, Joseph, Teddy and Sophia Blackwell in Pownalls Row, Mold, circa 1898. The little girl on the right is the one to whom this translation is dedicated.

FOREWORD

by Dr John Hywel Roberts

Daniel Owen's semi-autobiographical novel *Rhys Lewis* of 1885 was not published in a political or cultural vacuum, nor was its author uninvolved in local affairs. The issues that attracted his attention – from political and social reform to religion, language and education – were part of an established and vigorous debate about entrenched principles. The novel was written In the context of a distinctive vision of Welsh identity that reflected the desire of religious leaders, civic dignitaries, teachers and most of the adult population to influence the conduct of rural, urban and industrial life throughout Wales for the better.

As E.G. Millward observes in his introduction to the 2002 edition of *Rhys Lewis*, by Daniel Owen's time Wales had an abundance of Welsh-language newspapers and joumals. Since the beginning of the nineteenth century these had been significant influences in disseminating ideas on the shaping of people's lives. Between 1832 and 1884 one of these was the impetus for reforming the electoral system, which increased the political power of the lower classes. In addition, with the rise of Chartism, a drive to establish greater authority for trade unions took shape. Gradually, restrictions on union activities were relaxed, and in 1868 the Trades Union Congress was founded. At the same time, the passing of the first modern Education Act for England and Wales in 1870 gave the state a much more influential role in the education of the children of the poor. In addition the power of Nonconformity was evident in the religious revival in Wales in 1859 and in the boost to the temperance movement when the Welsh Sunday Closing Act came into force in 1881. Finally, the National Eisteddfod of Wales, after a period of decline, was slowly beginning to regain prominence; it offered prizes for works of fiction and began encouraging writers of Welsh fiction to take the novel seriously.

The tradition of writing in Welsh dated back to the tales of the Mabinogi and the poetry of Aneirin, Taliesin and Dafydd ap Gwilym, to the Middle Ages, when poets and prose writers received valuable patronage from Welsh princes. Gradually this responsibility passed to members of the landed gentry and the monasteries. After the invention of the printing press, books written in Welsh were becoming available by the middle of the sixteenth century, and the appearance of the first full translation of the Bible into Welsh by Bishop William Morgan in 1588 was an important and influential achievement. Over the next two hundred years many Welsh-language tracts, sermons and books on theology, politics and antiquarian studies were published, and poetry framed in strict metres continued to appeal to scholars. But little serious attention was given to writing fiction in Welsh, and it was not until the nineteenth century that a new interest in fiction began to appear. Why? In part, because of three important and interrelated factors – education, religion and language – that from the late Middle Ages onwards helped to change the pattem of Welsh culture in general and and that of communities like Mold and its hinterland in particular.

The roots of an education system for England and Wales ran deep. Schools had been established in a number of monasteries and cathedrals during the early Middle Ages. Their chief aim was to educate boys and train them to become servants for church and state. With the Reformation the supreme authority of the Roman church was shattered, and Protestantism became a dominant force. The Tudors saw its vital importance in preserving and extending the powers of the monarchy, and sought to turn this to account in part by using education as a way to defend the realm. However, until the last years of the seventeenth century little attention was given to providing formal schooling for the children of the mass of the population. Change here began in 1698, with the establishment of the Society for Promoting Christian Knowledge (SPCK): one of the earliest nationwide efforts to organize some sort of schooling for the children of the poor. The intention was to preserve a stratified society but also to rescue the poor from extreme poverty by teaching them some of the rudiments of reading and writing as well as religious instruction. The aristocracy and middle classes, with a touch of refined cynicism, found this a good way to display their humanitarian sentiments and pious ideals. It is hard to gauge exactly the success of these charity schools. Some of them became pawns in political disputes, and critics feared that their work might eventually undermine the highly stratified classes of society that then existed. At the same time – and only in parts of Wales – additional impetus came from the Rev. Griffith Jones of Llanddowror, Carmarthenshire, who launched a crusade against what he saw as the apathy of the clergy and the ignorance of the peasants. He set up a system of peripatetic schools and itinerant teachers to guide pupils to read in Welsh, aiming not only to save as many souls as possible from the evils of the period but also to raise the level of literacy in the Welsh language.

Indirectly, the charity schools prepared the ground for the spread of Methodism. And Methodism's emotional appeal was to have a significant effect. The attitudes of workers changed. Drinking and debauchery were checked. Sunday School class meetings gave some training in democratic methods, and the poor awoke to the need for self-improvement. But, if the Methodists reacted unfavourably to the state-sponsored prvileges of the Anglican Church, they certainly did not reject the basic concept of the eighteenth century's stratified society. Methodism's full potential in an educational context, did begin to become apparent by the latter stages of the eighteenth century, however, in particular with the advent of Sunday Schools.

When the Rev. Thomas Charles settled in Bala in 1784 he became increasingly concerned about the education of the peasantry and, in spite of initial doubts, he began to develop Sunday Schools. Catering not just for children but also for adults, the growing middle class and the peasantry, these taught reading (though not writing) using Welsh and English and quickly became an important part of Wales's cultural and educational life.

They also helped the Welsh Calvinistic Methodists to break away from the Anglican Church in the early nineteenth century: something that had important consequences. Methodism became the strongest denomination in north Wales, and its actions helped to strengthen the membership of other dissenting groups. Above all, it helped to widen the breach not only between Anglicanism and nonconformity but also between conservative, anglicised landlords and radical Welsh tenants. These factors, in due course, were to influence the growth of educational provision.

In retrospect we can see that efforts to educate the poor up to the end of the eighteenth century sprang from philanthropic and religious motives intermingled with pity, fear and altruism. The nineteenth century, though, brought a remarkable change in interpretation and provision. This began slowly and spasmodically, and earlier aims and motives were by no means abandoned completely until the latter part of the century. The growth of the factory system and industrial towns, along with the rapid increase in population, focused attention on society's inadequacies. A variety of remedies for social problems was suggested during the first half of the century – population reduction, more stringent legal measures, currency reform, the expansion of free trade, consolidation of class differences and state legislation – and against this confused background new ways of educating the children of the mass of the population were explored.

Satisfactory expansion of education seemed to be unrealistic without both adequate financial support and an abundance of teachers. This need led to the founding of two voluntary philanthropic societies backed by churches and chapels, both Anglican and Non-conformist. The National Society was founded in 1811 by Andrew Bell under the patronage of the Church of England, and the Royal Lancasterian Society was set up by Joseph Lancaster in 1808 with support from Methodists, Baptists and Independents; in 1814 it changed its name to the British and Foreign School Society. There were small differences between the teaching methods of the two societies, but the methods of both were based on a practice that came to be known as the 'monitorial system': under the supervision and control of adults, children were set to teach children. Bell summed up the approach when he said, 'it is in school as in the army: discipline is the first, second and third essential'. At first, most of the teaching concentrated on drilling in reading, writing and arithmetic. As the century advanced other subjects crept in, and central government began to provide financial assistance for the schools. By the 1860s increasing costs led to the introduction a system that became known as 'payment by results'.

The process was disturbed in 1847 by a report produced by English university professors Lingen, Symons and Vaughan Johnson on the state of education. This heaped criticism on Welsh schools, not entirely without cause. While some of the monitorial schools were bad, private-venture schools – like that run by Robin the Soldier which Daniel Owen describes in *Rhys Lewis* – were worse. Unfortunately the report writers were English and understood little about what they heard, but they went on, notwithstanding, to condemn the cultural, religious and moral life of the people of Wales. Swift, volcanic reaction followed, and this helped to turn education in Wales into a burning public issue for the rest of the century, especially among the Non-conformist bodies. Non-conformists began to dominate the press in north Wales, and, inspired by Denbighshire journalist Thomas Gee, they helped to transform Methodism from a conservative force into a strongly radical one. So now there existed in Wales a population whose ideals were shaped by cultural meetings and political discussion, and whose press and chapels recognized the value of education for intellectual and social advancement.

Paradoxically, though, the average Welshman of the time did not seem to be very concemed about his language. English was the language of the schools, and under the Education code of 1862 Welsh was not recognized for government funding purposes. Few people objected to this, because they wished their children to learn English, and teachers had to use a variety of methods to prevent pupils from speaking Welsh on school premises. The most common one was the 'Welsh Not': a block of wood placed around the neck of a child heard speaking the language in school. By 1888, though, central government was beginning to recognize the futility of the language regulation, and it agreed that Welsh could be included as a specific subject in the school curriculum.

One institution that might have been expected to be strongly protective of Welsh was the National Eisteddfod. However, the Eisteddfod and some of its supporters were rather lukewarm towards the language, according to historian Hywel Teifi Edwards, who quotes H.A. Bruce (later Lord Aberdare) in 1851 as seeing Welsh 'as a serious evil, a great obstruction to the moral and intellectual progress of my countrymen'. In reality, until the middle years of the nineteenth century the strongest defenders and protectors of the Welsh language were the Welsh chapels. Later, added impetus came from the growing power of the Welsh press, led in north Wales by journalists such as Thomas Gee and Gwilym Hiraethog. And such men saw newspapers and journals not just as protectors of the language but also as vitally important organs in the process of the education of adults.

And here lies the importance of Daniel Owen. Beginning with *Rhys Lewis*, and continuing in his later novels *Enoc Huws* and *Gwen Tomos*, he brings to life a range of characters and personalities that were recognizable to the people of Mold, his home town, and other communities in north-east Wales. He places them in the context of the politics, religious controversies and industrial disputes of the time, along with the influence of educational developments over a long period and the social patterns and conventions of the day.

– o –

Twenty-five years ago I began seriously to delve into my family's history. In one sense I had already been doing this for decades: as a small boy I can remember being told about some of my ancestors, although the information was often quite sketchy. Nonetheless, it stuck in my mind, and I carried it with me through my teenage years and into adulthood. Eventually I decided that I had to take some decisive action to retain the data. I had to stop memorising it and stuffing it into my head; I had to get down to some real work and codify the material. That's when the problems started.

My family was a scattered one, like that of Abraham Wood and his retinue of gypsies, hanging out not just in Wales but also in England, Scotland, Ireland, Canada, the USA, Australia, New Zealand, South Africa and South America. Tracing their whereabouts, delving back many centuries, raiding libraries, archives and museums became an obsession. But I had one advantage over many others who have done the same sort of thing. The roots of my family were very firmly Celtic – and not just Celtic but Welsh. So, as Welsh is my first language, I needed no help when delving into source material written in Welsh. And what a boon that was to me!

And that is why my admiration for what Robert has done with *Rhys Lewis* cannot be measured. Like many with Celtic ancestry, he got to know about some of his family from a young age and was able to visit the part of Wales that they came from. But there was one thing he could not do very efficiently: learn the Welsh language. He is clearly very proud of his Welsh ancestry, but speaking the language fluently is something that has eluded him ... so far anyway. And I'm not really surprised. Welsh is one of the more difficult European languages — not quite as hard as Finnish or Hungarian, but it is still pretty difficult for a non-Welsh speaker to grasp its complex rules of grammar and make sense of much of its pronunciation. Just think of those words that have double letters — like 'll' or dd` (or even 'ddd') and 'ng' or 'th'.

But what does Robert do? He decides he would like to read Daniel Owen's *Rhys Lewis* in a good English translation, and then that he will do that translation himself. But which version of *Rhys Lewis*? Now, like other European languages, Welsh changed gradually over many centuries, and without having any really strict codes of grammar to control the process. (Oral versions of languages do this sort of thing.) But the time comes when philological scholars decide that certain standards have to be set, lest a language deteriorate and end up as a meaningless collection of raggle-taggle sounds. Scholars today can be found berating what they fear is a kind of slovenliness creeping into English speech. They complain about the way conventions and rules of grammar are ignored; in response, others dismiss these criticisms and call their opponents finical, desiccated pedants. But this is nothing new. The Welsh language went through a similar phase from the end of the nineteenth century. An illustration of this was the purification exercise applied to Daniel Owen's last three major works — *Rhys Lewis*, *Enoc Huws* and *Gwen Tomos* — with spelling, grammar and sentence construction all revised. But when Robert decided to translate *Rhys Lewis* into English he took as his Welsh source material not the 2002 revised edition but the 1885 presentation version, printed for just two thousand private subscribers. (That early version, produced by a local printer in Mold, had not been professionally edited, as the later Hughes and Son edition was. It contains many quirks of local Welsh spelling, which add to the problems of translation.) Did Robert realize what he was going to have to do? If you go his translator's postscript on p. 349 you will see his explanation of the method he used to overcome the problem of working from a somewhat unfamiliar language and of needing to make sure that his English version was intelligible and easy to follow. Has he succeeded? Judge for yourselves when you have read his work.

Looking back over many decades I see that what Robert has done is characteristic of him. You will know from his translator's postscript that he has suffered a serious level of dyslexia, which affected him through his schooldays and beyond. But it is clear that there is — and has always been — an element of stubbornness in his nature, and he can call on this when required. Without such stubbornness (in his case, a valuable creative force) he would not have made the strides he has.

He would not have gone from a non-selective secondary modern school to university, graduated with first-class honours, completed a Ph.D, established a computer business, and become a university teacher and a recognized authority in his chosen academic field with a very substantial body of research and publications behind him. Nor, in addition to all that, would he have managed to learn to read music and play a variety of musical instruments, as well as translating articles and books into English from difficult languages such as Russian and Welsh.

In my academic career I have come across a small number of highly intelligent and bright students, with an occasional brilliant one. I think I would put Robert at the top of the list. But I do have one question for him: 'Robert, what next?'

John Hywel Roberts
March 2017

PREFACE

The Publication History of *Rhys Lewis*

It is not widely known, that the first complete edition of Daniel Owen's novel *Rhys Lewis* was published by J. LL. Morris of New Street, Mold, and not by Hughes and Son of Hope Street, Wrexham. Morris's edition, funded by subscription, appeared in April 1885 at four shillings; that of Hughes and Son followed in October at two shillings and sixpence.

The first twenty-five chapters had already appeared between 1882 and 1885 in the Holywell-based magazine *Y Drysorfa*, run by P.M. Evans, a printer active with the Calvinistic Methodist cause. The magazine was edited by the Rev. Roger Edwards, the minister of the Bethesda Chapel, in New Street Mold where Daniel Owen worshipped. Evans and Edwards turned *Y Drysorfa* into the leading Calvinistic Methodist journal with a wide circulation throughout Wales.

But, that serialization might have been the end of the *Rhys Lewis* story, had a new business not opened opposite Daniel Owen's tailor's shop in New Street, Mold. John Lloyd Morris, who also worshipped at Bethesda Chapel, set up the Mold Printing and Stationery Company, in the premises currently occupied by *Siop Y Siswm*, and the 1895 local trade directory lists his business as Booksellers, Stationers, Toy and Fancy Goods Dealers, and Advertising Agents. Morris was agent for the Denbighshire Building Society too and an accountant and commission agent for Beresford and Company, estate agents. Keen to become a publisher as well, he also invested in a modern printing press.

Daniel Owen thought the story of Rhys Lewis finished when he delivered instalment 25 to *Y Drysorfa*. It closes with a clear ending:

> As I write this Thomas and Barbara Bartley have grown old, but they still speak of thee. Barbara yet has only a grip of the letters, same as Thomas, but on Sunday afternoons she puts on thy spectacles and turns over the leaves of thy old Bible, as she seeks to imitate thee.

But John Morris had bigger ideas. There were unfinished threads in the tale. What happened to Wil Bryan? Did Rhys succeed as a Minister? What became of the Irishman and Rhys's father? I strongly suspect Morris suggested that, by adding a few more chapters, Owen could not only round off the story but also sell it as a full novel. And who better to publish it than J. LL. Morris of New Street, Mold?

Morris described what he proposed as a *Cyfrol ddestlus*, 'a neat volume' to be reasonably priced. He had the contacts and the marketing skills to create a subscription list of individuals who wanted to read the rest of the story and own a limited edition of the complete novel. To add value to the proposition he offered to print a full list of the names and addresses of subscribing patrons at the end of the book. His idea worked: that appendix shows 978 copies sold to confirmed subscribers before the book was printed. That guaranteed revenue of £195 12s to cover the cost of the printing and binding. And John Morris soon managed to sell out the entire print run of 2,000 copies: as Daniel Owen wrote to a friend:

> It [the extended subscription edition of *Rhys Lewis*] has been completed; we have published a limited edition at four shillings and sold two thousand copies in six months.

Between them Morris and Owen cleared £400 on the deal, but the success of the venture caught the interest of a larger, more established publisher, and Daniel got an offer from Hughes and Son of Wrexham to produce a mass-market edition retailing at half-a-crown: just over half the price of the Morris edition. This put paid to John Morris's ambition of turning Mold into a publishing centre to rival Wrexham; the only acknowledgment of his edition in the Hughes version is the subtitle above Owen's foreword, 'Preamble to the First Edition', which could suggest that Hughes's was the first edition – as I believed it to be until I discovered a copy of Morris's earlier one.

The Morris volume is bound in better quality board, printed on better quality paper and takes up 436 pages of text for the story with a list of subscribers' names and addresses added as an appendix. The Hughes and Son edition has a plainer font, 432 pages of text and a series of illustrations attributed to B. Lewis (probably an alias for Daniel Owen himself).

If I was going to translate *Rhys Lewis* I decided to make sure I worked from the earliest version I could find: the Morris Edition. I haven't compared the Hughes's edition with Morris's, but as I passed my translated chapters over to John Roberts to read and comment on, he picked up a few changes in the names of characters, and asked me to check against the Hughes edition. They were changed in the popular edition, perhaps to avoid libelling a real Mrs Powel and Mrs Peters (to mention only a couple). I don't know if other changes were made; to find out I would have to translate and compare both editions, and I'm not that curious, now I have realized my ambition to read and translate *Rhys Lewis* the way Daniel Owen first wrote it as a 'neat volume'.

This modern translation is my retelling of Daniel Owen's story in the modern English I normally write. To echo Daniel Owen: 'If you find sections offend you, then that was not my intent. I wrote it for you to enjoy reading it, and if you do not, then I regret inflicting it on you.'

Robert Lomas
Gorwel, 3 January 2017

FOREWORD TO THE J. LL. MORRIS EDITION

To the Reader

If an unsung author sets out to publish a book in Welsh, at a price of four shillings a copy, and if it has previously been widely circulated as a monthly serial, you may expect him to come to grief. I did not think of turning the serial *Rhys Lewis* into a book, as I thought there would be no interest. Then I was surprised when people asked for one. A great list of people subscribed to cover the costs of printing this extended edition of The Autobiography of Rhys Lewis, and I would like to thank my fellow countrymen for their incomparable support for both Welsh literature and myself.

If I told you how hard I found it to write this book, you might think I was just trying to dodge criticism. However, offering it for sale will produce a true opinion of its merit. I do not expect any special treatment from my readers, and if they do criticize it then, as Wil Bryan would say, 'Fire Away!' No one will find more shortcomings in it than I have already seen. But I am not trying to appeal to sophisticated academic readers, rather I write for the common man.

If there is any merit in this book it must be that it is totally Welsh in its characters and literary ideas. It owes nothing to any foreigners. But if you find sections offend you, that was not my intent. I wrote it for you to enjoy reading it, and if you do not, then I regret inflicting it on you.

Author [Daniel Owen]
Mold, April 30, 1885

INTRODUCTION

The Minister of Bethel has been lying peacefully beneath the turf of our valley for some time now. He always seemed to be a wise and unassuming man. However, those who knew him maintained that there was more to him than showed on the surface. He never made a show of himself but he wasn't a popular preacher, for he couldn't sing. His lack of musical tone was a great drawback, but his preaching was always worth a listen. Men of mature judgment say his sermons compared favourably with the best heard from any Welsh pulpit. He occasionally wrote, anonymously, for a journal called 'The Tradarian'. People read his articles with respect, but I doubt they would have bothered if Rhys Lewis had signed his words.

His ministry was mostly successful and happy, as most of his congregation had a good measure of common sense and some Christian feeling. He was good-natured and sociable in company but preferred the peace of his library. If he overindulged his love of solitude and forgot his public duties, his church deacons would remind him. Now and again he was low in spirit, as though something weighed upon his mind, but what that might be even his closest friends never knew. Some said he had a disorder of the nervous system, but if you read this history, you may gain a different insight into the questions that worried him.

He died young, in the midst of a useful career and without a stain on his character. However, when his executrix asked me to arrange his books and prepare them for sale, I came upon a bulky manuscript written in his own hand. It was an autobiographical journal, and it looked interesting, so I asked permission to study it. It was obvious that he had written the manuscript to clarify his thoughts, not for publication. It was so thought-provoking that I asked his executrix for permission to edit it for publication. She allowed me to do so, and this book is the result.

Whilst apologizing for its frankness I hope readers will enjoy it, even though the opening chapters are childish and frivolous. Nevertheless, the story grows in strength, offering forthright accounts of remarkable old characters, both worldly and religious. In the interests of prudence, I have changed the names of some individuals, but I have not made any other changes to the text. So if, dear reader, you meet with things in these pages which are not quite to your taste and find a freedom of expression that sometimes borders on the profane, or an inordinate obsession with detailed description, I ask you to remember that the author did not write this work for publication.

CHAPTER 1

Thoughts About Biography

I have read many biographies over the years and both enjoyed and learned from them. There is as much virtue in biography as in any other writing if the author knows his subject. This is not true of all writers and all topics. No matter how faithfully a biographer describes the public persona of his subject, he cannot know his subject's inner thoughts. If a writer could pose questions to his subject, even beyond the grave, we might learn more. Here, autobiography has a great advantage, though it is not as trustworthy as a life history written by an impartial observer.

I have available facts and feelings, as I write my own life, that no one else knows. But, if I write my own story for publication, I am afraid that readers will think I overestimate myself. And I might fail to claim for myself the character and station which a less partial author would give me.

All the biographies I have read took the great and the good as their subjects. They were about people who moved in circles I will never know, and they were always remarkable in some way. Often these notable individuals lived lives I find quite strange. Their differences make their memoirs worth reading, but I think it would be more interesting to read the story of an ordinary man, one who moved in my circles and had experiences like my own. What a pleasure to read an accurate memoir of the life of an ordinary soul like me.

Most writers ignore basic thoughts and feelings because they are commonplace. We see them everywhere, so they remain unnoticed. It is not for any lack of beauty that the daisy does not attract the attention of the florist or inspire the spirit of the bard: it is because daisies are in every field and trodden upon by every cow. If the robin redbreast and the goldfinch were to sing of the beauties of nature, the primrose would attract their praise, even though it thrives only in neglected hedgerows.

All men born of women have interesting life histories. Every life contains events worth writing about, and everyone thinks thoughts that no one else has thought before. However, the difference between a common and an uncommon person is that the former will not write these thoughts down. The latter are uncommon in expressing what they think and feel.

When reading a well-known author or listening to a famous preacher I often feel that they say nothing that is new to me. They only put into words ideas I feel but cannot express. They **articulate** heart-secrets that I struggle to spell out. The thoughts and feelings sleep within me, and these masters of words knock on the door of their sleeping apartment. My secret beliefs rub their eyes and come alive in my mind.

I want to understand myself. That is why I have to write this history of my life. It is not for others to read. I write it for myself. If I do not write my own biography now, while I can, no one will be able to write it once I am dead. A hundred years from now it will be as if I had never existed. Like thousands of my contemporaries I will dwell in the forgotten oblivion of silence. I dislike this thought, even though it is the fate of common people. Neither remembrance nor forgetfulness can do me good or evil once I am dead, so why should I care if my name dies with me? The dead do not derive satisfaction from their gravestones. The markers are for the comfort of their loving friends; their bones do not lie any easier under a memorial. What value has life eternal if I am forgotten?

This is why I write my own history. It is for my own peace of mind, not to get it published. If I write for a publisher I will not be able to tell the truth, the whole truth, and nothing but the truth. I will have to think about my readers and their opinion of me.

Rhys, I ask myself, what have you to say for yourself? You must be sure to tell the truth. This I promise myself I will do. Should anyone discover my secret writings, then know that my words are true and I would not change a one.

CHAPTER 2

My Birth

I thought, when I decided to write my autobiography, that I would be able to do it without help. Then, as I started, I realized how foolish I was. I must depend completely upon others' memories to recount the early stages of my life. I am determined to be truthful, so I must admit I remember nothing about how I came into this world.

I rely completely on the testament of my mother. She said I was born by the faint light of a halfpenny candle, between two and three o'clock in the morning of the twentieth of October 1856. It may have been the poverty of my surroundings or the dimness of the light that upset me, but Mam tells me I was so cross that I yelled and screamed the house down. The neighbours, who helped her, say I was an inconsiderate, unfeeling little wretch for making such a commotion. Surely, they say, 'You must have been aware that your birth almost killed your dear mother?'

Nobody consulted me at the time. Perhaps that is why I was so bad-tempered and unreasonable. But this is a guess that I cannot state as a sober fact. If I were not completely sure that Mam never lied to me, I could hardly believe that I began bald-headed and toothless. She said I had a nose that was not only flat, but like a new moon with its two horns turned up. I was so fleshy there were no dimples to mark my elbows and knees. Now all I can show are protruding bones.

I cannot remember not being able walk, but Mam told me that once I did nothing but lie on my back, crying and kicking, waiting for someone to carry me. I remember none of this but still feel guilty about such bad behaviour. I remember nothing of the first three years of my life but those who knew me then make bad accusations against me. I believe they tell the truth, but I do not recall anything of this time. I was but a living lump of clay. So when did I develop reason, memory and the other attributes of a real person?

Mam tells me that I quickly developed a spirit of mischief. It is something that I still sometimes give way to. I broke many things. I smashed the few ornaments my mother owned. I scratched faces and pulled the hair of family and neighbours alike. I tugged one young girl's earring so hard that I ripped her ear lobe, and the blood streamed down her shoulder. Among my cruelties, I squeezed the life out of three young kittens. Nevertheless, I cannot feel guilty about these acts, as I do not remember them.

Everyone acted as if I were a blessing and seemed to like me, whilst I was nothing but a source of worry and trouble. Mam lost so much sleep over me that she often had to get up in the middle of the night to make me a cup of cinder tea. She would place ashes from the fire in a cup of hot water, put some of the mixture in a clean cup with warm water and sugar. Sometimes it would cure my wind, but if it failed I would cry for hours at a time. As I could not yet speak, no one knew what troubled me. However, even when I screamed my loudest, Mam said she wouldn't give me up for the world.

I grew into a great fat lump who lived entirely on milk. Despite my weight, the neighbours would argue about who would carry me. I must have liked not having teeth, because when they began to grow I was upset and lost weight. I had such fits of bad temper about my new teeth that I drove myself into convulsions. What a fool I was. Would that I could grow new teeth now. However, as I am again toothless, no one can knock my teeth out.

Now I have written enough about a time of which I remember nothing and it will be better to write about times I know something about from my own memories.

CHAPTER 3

My Earliest Memories

One of the first things I remember is going to chapel with my mother. I am glad my earliest recollections are of our dear old chapel. Chapel has given me so many memories and twinges to my conscience over the years. Perhaps the first, second or even the twentieth times I went to chapel have merged to create this childish impression within me.

I remember holding my mother's hand to walk the endless distance to chapel. It was such a long excursion that I demanded to be carried most of the way. I think it was winter, for I remember feeling cold.

It must have been a Sunday night, because the chapel was packed. Glittering candles lighted its winter gloom. The light was frighteningly and flickeringly different from the bright and steady gaslights we now have. I was so frightened when I glimpsed a massive intimidating crowd looming out of the shadows that I burst out crying. The noise embarrassed Mam, so she stuffed her hand into my mouth, to reduce my volume. She nearly smothered me. Then a kind soul popped a sweetie into my mouth. Sucking on that glorious Nelson ball was such a comfort I stopping wailing at once. Oh, what has happened to those fantastic sweetmeats? There is nothing like them these days. Either my tastes or modern sweets have changed.

When I first saw the ground floor of the chapel, it was different from how it is now. It had many rows of backless benches running across it, with a few deep seats ranged around the walls. In the centre of the floor was a large stove, which always attracted crowds of children, their faces red as cocks' combs in the fire's warmth.

Near the front, there was a Big Seat for the preacher, although I didn't know what a preacher was then. To the left of it was the Singer's Seat for the choirmaster. Under a high box that Mam called the pulpit there was another special seat. In it sat an old man with a velvet cap. Every now and then he stood up and snuffed out burnt-down candle stubs to replace them with new ones. I would later know him as Abel Hughes. The pulpit, which was high against the wall, reminded me of a swallow's nest up under the eaves of our cottage. I was puzzled how the man in the box managed to climb so high and why he wanted to. Would he fall when coming down, as I usually did on our stairs? Or would the old man in the velvet cap carry him down, as my big brother Bob used to carry me?

Only the man in the box was speaking. I didn't understand why everyone else was so quiet. I didn't understand much of what he said.

The only words I recognized were 'Jesus Christ'. At first, I thought the man must be that Jesus Christ that mother kept telling me about. I kept expecting him to finish soon, but he kept going. He must have been speaking for a few hours when his face went fierce and flushed red, and he shouted at me. Then I knew he wasn't Jesus Christ. I don't know why he was telling me off but he kept looking at me and yelling at the top of his voice. His shouting made me cry again, and Mam half suffocated me for a second time. Then the friendly woman in the next pew gave me another Nelson ball so I stopped wailing and concentrated on sucking the sweetie.

As I calmed down, I took more interest in the room, both upstairs and down. I was surprised there were so many people upstairs in the gallery. Did they sleep there? Had they beds enough? Then I felt the chapel darkening, and the man in the box growing smaller, and moving farther and farther away from me, even as he shouted, louder and louder. Mam gathered me into her arms, and I fell into a deep sleep. I don't know how long I slept, but I dreamt of the singing of the congregation without properly waking, even though I liked singing much better than shouting.

I woke up as the man in the pulpit stopped speaking. He stood up and wiped the sweat from his brow with a great cravat, tied loosely about his neck. Abel Hughes stood up and started to climb the pulpit steps.

He's going to bring the man down on his back, I thought, just like my brother Bob brings me downstairs at home.

I was disappointed when Abel stopped halfway, turned around and started to speak. Now, with my mature insight, I know he was announcing the chapel programme for the next week. When he finished most of the congregation stood up and left. The chapel doors closed, but my mother and some others stayed behind.

'We're never going home,' I thought, and began crying again.

'Hish, Hish Rhys *bach*,' Mam said. 'We'll go home soon.' That pacified me a little.

The man who had been shouting at me, come down from the pulpit. I watched him warily, expecting him to trip on the steps but he got safely to the bottom. Then Abel Hughes lifted a linen cloth off something in front of the Big Seat. He folded the cloth neatly, and put it aside and held up a lovely cup. The shouty box man walked towards Abel and said something about Jesus Christ. Then he started to eat from a plate of bread pieces that Abel had put near the goblet. He took a bite, followed by a small sip from that beautiful cup and set the plate aside.

'He's having his supper,' I thought, 'but now he's tried it, he doesn't like it.'

Then to my great surprise he picked up the plate of bread and started to offer it round. I was hungry so I decided that even though he'd been shouting at me, he was a decent chap after all. He came to Mam and she took a scrap from the plate. I held out my hand, but he refused me, abruptly pulling the plate away. The man obviously had a grudge against me. For the sixth time that night, I burst out crying.

Mam struggled to sooth me. Then the man came around with the cup. I hid my face under her cloak. I didn't want to look at him. I wasn't going to give him a chance to refuse me again. What with the cold darkness of the winter night and the insults of the preacher, I was so grumpy and truculent on the way home that my poor mother had to carry me all the way.

I'm glad I am not writing this history for a publisher. If I were I wouldn't have been able to say how I really felt, so simple and so childish, yet so completely true. Simple honesty might be new to literature, but it is well within the experience of most people.

CHAPTER 4

Evan Jones Gwernyffynnon

Thinking back to back to my childhood, I'm amazed that I'm still the same person, despite so many changes in my thoughts and ideas. How different is the child from the man, and yet how similar? I wouldn't want to change my personality, or swap my mind for another.

I have often stood where the river Alun loses itself in the Dee and felt an upwelling of pity. How brave, bright and beautiful the Alun looks as it rushes down from Llanarmon-yn-Ial past Cilcain, through the Belan, and along the Vale of Mold. As it nears Holt its face changes, and I feel the sorrow of its impending absorption into the Dee. As it flows on towards the sea, the little Alun becomes only a small part of the great Dee.

I feel the same sorrow for the child I once was, as he had been absorbed into the man. I don't know how others feel, but I think I am still the same person and I wouldn't want it otherwise. I feel the child, deep inside me. He and I are still me. To think otherwise is the way to madness, for don't we say, 'He is beside himself,' rather than 'inside himself', when we speak of one who has become insane?

When I review my life with all its epochs, circumstances and prospects down to the present, I'm happy that I am the same person. I also think that when I move into that great world of eternity, I will still be me. My identity was not lost as I grew. I was not absorbed, like the poor river Alun, into the mighty river of humanity. It's wonderful to know that, even after a thousand ages in the sight of the Almighty, I will keep that same consciousness that I knew whilst holding my mother's hand to chapel.

If I tell the truth, I must confess that I didn't always like going to chapel. The service was too long, especially when I couldn't manage to sleep through it. The singing pleased me, but when the preacher talked on and on, I would develop an intolerable pain in my legs and have to kick them about. How Mam struggled to keep me still and soothe me.

Mam was the most Methodist of Methodists, blessings be on her. She clung fast to the faith and traditions of our fathers, and her most sacred belief was that we observe the Sabbath most strictly. On Sunday, Mam wouldn't let me even speak of play, let alone look at a toy. I had to sit still and look serious all day. As a child, I couldn't tell one day and from another. Yet if I became restless or playful on the Sabbath, mother would insist that Jesus Christ was angry with me. She told me shouldn't go to Heaven. She said I was risking burning in the eternal fires of Hell. This was hard for me to understand. If Jesus was fond of little children, as Mam said he was, why would he be angry if I played on a Sunday? I came to hate the coming of the Sabbath. I was sure was I would offend Jesus again and so be cast into the fires of Hell.

'What sort of a place is Heaven?' I asked mother.

My face fell when she said. 'A place where everyone keeps an everlasting Sabbath.'

'I don't want to go there then,' I said at once.

My words hit her like a blow. Her face darkened and tears welled up in her eyes. I threw my arms around her neck. 'I'll go to Heaven if you want me to,' I said. 'But I hope Jesus Christ will let me play just a little when I get there.'

Poor Mam. For all her good intentions, she approached my religious training in an awkward way. Yet my dear old mother, ignorant and uneducated as she was, was the best mother in the world. The Almighty always answered her prayers on my behalf. What would I not give for one more look at her face, for one more chance to soothe her pain at my thoughtless words, to say how sorry I am for my disobedient ways as a child? But my disobedience and wickedness never lessened her love for me. I have had many trials and temptations since I carried her to the cold churchyard. I have had many faithful friends since, but none who loves me like her. She loved me more than she did her own life. Without her, my world is cold and strange. Without her, there is no one who understands me, or fully knows my feelings. (Forgive me, but before I write more, I need to visit the rough stone above her resting place, with its incised lettering, to stand a few moments to respect her memory.)

My recollections of Sunday School are confused and muddled. Nevertheless, I am sure of one thing. I did not learn my letters there; I knew them before I first went. Perhaps I knew the alphabet intuitively, for I cannot remember ever not knowing my ABC, but Mam may have taught me when I was too young to remember.

Evan Jones from Gwernyffynnon was my first Sunday School teacher. He was a smallholder with only a few acres, and some cows he worked for himself. Sunday School took place in the high gallery while the service was in full flow in the main chapel. Evan taught us from a little book, called a Primer. After the lesson, I would rush to tell mother what he had shown me.

Evan Jones was a decent old fellow. On Sundays, he'd put on his best blue coat with bright buttons, and breeches with grey leggings. There were six or seven of us boys in Evan's class. He would take one boy upon his knee and give him a lesson, whilst the rest played about.

Once every boy had had a lesson, Evan felt had done his duty so he took a nap.

When he slept, his chin sank deep into his vest, and the big collar of his coat came up to the crown of his head. To amuse myself I used to count the buttons on his clothing, over and over. Even now, I know their exact number. There were seven buttons on each legging, five on the knees of his small clothes, four on each side of his coat, with two behind, and seven upon his waistcoat. As I write this, I see him quietly snoozing after he had fulfilled his obligation to the Sunday School.

Evan had an enormous watch that we called a timepiece in those days. He kept it in his breeches pocket.

'Why does Evan not wear his timepiece in his waistcoat pocket like the gentlemen at the Hall?' I asked Mam.

'It would be a great sin to wear his watch in his waistcoat pocket. No one but those who have not felt the rope would ever wear their watch on their waistcoat,' she said.

I didn't know then what 'feeling the rope' meant but guessed it must be a tremendous way to make a man good. After that, I was proud Evan Jones kept his watch in his breeches pocket instead of his waistcoat.

Evan had tied a bit of black ribbon to his watch and from it hung a white shell, an old coin, and a red seal. All the boys in Evan's class had a burning desire to get a closer look at his watch. One warm Sunday afternoon, after he had finished his lessons and fallen into a deep sleep we saw our chance to get hold of it. We knew Evan was sound asleep because he was snoring loudly. Now was our chance. My pal Wil Bryan, who was the eldest, offered to do the deed, and no one objected. He carefully sneaked the watch out of sleeping Evan's pocket, and handed it round for us all look to see. We each took turns to put it to our ear. We took our lessons in the highest corner of the chapel loft. It was so high we called it Gibraltar. We were well out of the way and were not disturbed. I had Evan's watch in my hand, it had been twice around the circle already and we were wondering how to get it back into his pocket. Then a great voice thundered around us.

'What are you up to here?' it roared.

I jumped with fright and dropped the watch. Its glass smashed to bits. Evan, our dozing teacher, jumped awake as if stabbed in the back. The velvet-capped head of the superintendent of the Sunday School, Abel Hughes, peered angrily over the top of a seat. Evan was so shaken and surprised he didn't notice what I had done to his watch.

'Evan Jones, is it sleeping you are?' asked Abel, in his severest voice.

'No, look you. I was ... I was ... meditating,' came Evan's hesitant reply. Even to my childish ears, he sounded sheepish,

'Meditating indeed! Meditating? While your class plays with your watch, were you? I will bring your behaviour before the Teachers' Meeting, sir, and see what they have to say about you meditating,' Abel shouted as he stalked away in high dudgeon.

The watch lay smashed and disregarded at my feet. I began to cry. I was good at crying. Evan looked first at the damage and then at me. He picked up the broken watch, wrapped it in his handkerchief, and placed it in the breast pocket of his blue coat. Seeing how upset I was, he took me upon his knee and even though he thought me guilty of the whole thing he spoke soothingly, 'Never mind, Rhys *bach*, it's not all that bad.'

It must have been his fellow feeling of guilt that made Evan speak so kindly. But his kindness only made me cry the more. I got home with my eyes so swollen that I couldn't hide my distress from Mam.

After listening to my tale of woe, all she said was. 'Well, we'll see what's what tomorrow.'

She was as good as her word. She spoke to Evan and saw what was what. She saw but I felt. Her solution was to spank my backside until her hand hurt, but not as much as my backside did.

I don't know if the tale of Evan Jones Gwernyffynnon being caught napping was discussed at the Teachers' Meeting, but I suspect it must have been. Always after that, whenever Evan settled down for a rest, he would ask us keep a lookout, and wake him if Abel Hughes came near. This we did willingly. As a class, we were on his side. We didn't like Abel persecuting him for taking a nap after he had given each of us our lesson. It wasn't fair. And we liked our freedom to play while he dozed.

If I were writing this history for publication someone might be tempted say, 'How much better the teachers and the Sunday Schools are now than they were then,' and they might be right. Evan Jones was only one of among many such teachers, but he was as good a teacher as most and better than some.

I was still young when Evan died, but I still have a great fondness and respect for him. He improved my reading, and I know by heart many of my mother's adages about him.

'Evan is a man with the root of the matter in him,' she would say. 'Evan Gwernyffynnon is greater on his knees than he is standing up. Evan knows well what it is to feel the rope. A man of secrecy is Evan Jones. Had Evan as much learning and money as he has grace, he would be a Justice of the Peace by now, and the owner of the Hall would be but a beggar in comparison.'

I didn't understand these remarks, and others like them, when my mother first made them but came to understand as I grew up. Evan Jones, for all his faults, was a fine man and one who loved our religion.

Whilst I was in his Sunday School class, I thought his habit of sleeping through part of his lesson time more a virtue than a vice. It gave us children a chance to play. He worked hard for a living, had felt the rope of many a farm beast in his time. He got up at five every morning to milk his cows. I pardon him sincerely. If I get to Heaven, I will seek him out and thank him for the good he did to me. I know it's silly, but I keep thinking of Evan in Heaven, in breeches, grey leggings and blue coat. I cannot imagine him dressed any other way, and I'm sure my memory of his button count will be still be accurate.

CHAPTER 5

The Children's *Seiat*

During my boyhood one of the most important religious institutions of our chapel was the Children's Meeting, or as we called it in the Welsh tongue, the Children's *Seiat*. The *Seiat* met weekly, summer and winter, and every boy and girl, whose parents were church members, had to be there unless they were ill. No one could miss two meetings in succession without a good excuse. At the next Church Meeting, or full Chapel *Seiat*, Abel Hughes would call upon the parents to explain their children's absence. Unless their parents gave a satisfactory reason, he would give them a public rebuke for their neglect. What a falling off there has been in such things since then. Now I find it impossible to get children to attend *Seiat* regularly for even a few weeks in the winter.

I dare not publicly rebuke parents for not sending their children to *Seiat*. The children of Mrs Powel, of The Shop, do not come to one in four of the meetings. But if I tried to reprimand her, she and her children might never come to chapel again, let alone to the *Seiat*. However, if Abel Hughes were alive now, he'd call Mrs Powel to account and many another too, no matter what the consequence. He would tell them that the Church of England was more suited to their ways, and the sooner they moved there the better. Has that race of honest elders completely died out? Many were outspoken to the point of rudeness, but, for all that, they had a sincerity that stands in favourable contrast to that of the present bland generation of religionists.

As soon as I could recite the verse 'Remember Lot's wife' I was sent to the Children's *Seiat*. I went in the care of Wil Bryan. Wil was a few years older than me, and he played a large part in my history. I mention him often in this biography, sometimes with great pain. I once thought he had no equal in the world, but later thought it would have been better if I had never met him.

Wil could absorb his verses quickly whilst I was slow to learn. I often had to rely on 'Remember Lot's wife,' which I knew well. My mother knew nothing about this, as she would teach me a new verse for each meeting, but by the time I got there, I had forgotten it. I would fall back on the trusty 'Remember Lot's wife.'

More than once I would start a new verse saying: 'This is a faithful saying, and worthy ...'Then I would break down, and have to resort to 'Remember Lot's wife.' I was such a small boy that for a long time my shortcoming was overlooked. It was not until the other children began to call me 'Lot's wife' that I stopped mentioning the lady.

My constant repetition of this single verse made sure that the leaders of our *Seiat* spent a lot of time discussing it. I soon knew as much about Lot's wife as there was to know. By the age of five I had firm views about the Sodomites, the angels, the fire, the brimstone, Lot and his family, the pillar of salt, and the plain of Zoar which stay with me still. I learned a lot of scriptural history without realizing it was happening.

Biblical knowledge was more widespread when I was young than it is today. I recently asked Solomon, the fifteen-year-old son of Mrs Frederick Powel of The Shop, 'Who was Jeroboam?'

'He's one of the apostles, ain't he?' he answered.

It makes me sad to think that many children of religious parents nowadays, are no more knowledgeable about the first king of the northern kingdom of Israel than Solomon Powel. Indeed, know-ledge of biblical history and characters is sadly lacking in the young now, unlike in my days at the Children's *Seiat.*

John Joseph and Abel Hughes, who led the *Seiat* in my childhood, were devoted to teaching us children. Abel was already an old man when I first knew him, but he took his duty to teach seriously.

Joyful John Joseph loved showing us how to sing choral chants such as 'O, that will be joyful,' and 'Never-ending shall the sound be of those glorious harps of gold.'

Abel Hughes was serious and sober as he listened to our verse recitations. He commented upon them as earnestly as if the Day of Judgment were about to dawn. He was a complete contrast to John Joseph. We children liked John Joseph better than we liked Abel Hughes. If Abel couldn't come to *Seiat*, John would take out his tuning fork, strike it against the stove, place it to his ear, shut his eyes, set his neck awry to catch the sound, and hum two or three notes before leading us in jolly songs of praise. We didn't know what high and awful purpose these tuning fork rituals served but we did know that Abel Hughes would stop John Joseph performing this ceremony if he were there. If John went to pull out his tuning fork, Abel would say to him. 'Put it away. Such things are not in keeping with The House of God.'

How lucky it is that Abel is not alive to see the man in the Big Seat announcing. 'The next hymn is in the key of Lah.' To be followed by two dozen of the congregation shrieking each against the other, 'Doh, soh, doh, soh?' I don't know what he would have said about such behaviour; I fear it would have quite unsettled him. 'Religion is going to the dogs,' he might have said.

Oh how things change in less than a generation.

Abel Hughes was always punctual when starting and ending the Children's *Seiat*. We knew to the minute when he would walk through the chapel door. So Mam was pleased that Wil Bryan would call early, to pick me up. How she praised Wil for collecting me in such good time. Little did she suspect that the reason Wil came early was so we would have time to play hide and seek in the chapel gallery before Abel arrived.

Wil was a sharp lad, and he'd noticed that Abel always began the meeting by looking at his pocket watch, and finished it by looking at the time on the chapel clock. One night, as we waited for Abel to arrive, Wil announced. 'I'm going up to the gallery to move the clock hand half an hour forward.'

He was as good as his word, and off he went up the stairs. The rest of us were afraid that Abel would come and catch him. Wil had just reached the clock seat and was reaching towards the minute hand, when Abel walked in. He was bang on time. Wil dived down at once. Our hearts jumped into our mouths, for we knew that Abel Hughes was not a man to trifle with.

Abel began the meeting by offering up a prayer. He closed his eyes tightly to pray. We scholars took the chance to open ours and looked what was happening around the clock seat. We watched Wil move the minute hand, and then coolly rest his elbows on the balustrade. He gave us all a broad wink. His daring astounded us.

While Abel prayed on, hands together and eyes closed, Wil fumbled in his pockets, and took out a handful of crumbs. Slowly and deliberately, he dropped them upon old Abel's head. Either Abel was fully absorbed in his prayer, or his velvet skullcap protected him, but he didn't seem to notice the outrage.

John Joseph was not there that evening and I always found the meeting rather flat without singing. None of us was much good at reciting our verses. We kept sneaking a glance at the chapel loft where Wil Bryan was hiding. He would pop into view and grin at us every now and then. He was the only one whose heart was not quaking with fear, and he was enjoying himself immensely. Abel kept telling us off for our indifferent recitals, and for clock-watching. He didn't know that we weren't looking at the clock but at the top of Wil Bryan's head. At last, Abel Hughes grew tired of trying to direct our minds to the lessons. He looked at the clock.

'How quickly the time has flown this evening,' he said.

At that moment the chapel door opened, and Margaret Ellis, the caretaker came in. She'd come to complain to Abel that the children came early to chapel, to play about. And about the frightful noise that they made when they did.

'Can you name the culprits?' Abel said.

'Hugh Bryan's son's the worst of the lot,' she said. 'And he's been more than usually bad tonight.'

'My good woman,' Abel said, 'You, like me, are getting old. Wil Bryan hasn't been here tonight. I find that somewhat odd, for he is usually a good attendee.'

'Abel Hughes! Do you think I don't know what I'm talking about?' Margaret said. 'Didn't I see him with my own eyes? Didn't I hear him running up and down the chapel?'

'Rhys,' said Abel sternly, looking me straight in the eye, 'did Wil Bryan come with you to *Seiat*, tonight?'

I couldn't stop myself looking towards the clock seat where Wil stood. He shook a warning fist at me. I didn't want to split on him. Then, luckily, the caretaker saw his head as he ducked back into hiding.

'Abel Hughes,' she said. 'He's in the clock seat. I saw him this minute.'

We all trembled with fear as Abel, stood back against the Big Seat and stared at the gallery, but for the life of him, he couldn't see Wil.

'Bring that bad boy down, Abel Hughes. I know he's up there,' Margaret said.

Abel Hughes was seriously annoyed, He moved towards the gallery. I felt my heart in my mouth as I watched him close in on the clock seat. However, before he could reach it Wil jumped into an adjacent row, and then into the next, and by jumping quickly from seat to seat, got to the top of the stairs. Down he leapt at a single bound. Margaret tried to grab him, and he nearly knocked her over escaping through the chapel door.

Wil was halfway home before poor old Abel, had turned around. Margaret Ellis the caretaker was forthright in giving her opinion of his character. Our dear old teacher did his best to regain his self-control, but he was so shocked that he sent us away without a closing prayer.

'Go home quietly, like good children,' he said. 'And don't follow the example of William Bryan.'

When Abel used Wil's full Sunday name it did not bode well. Sure enough, Abel went straight to Hugh Bryan to complain about his son's bad behaviour. The following morning Wil told me that his father gave him a beating such as he'd never had before in his life.

This episode is so childish as to be only worth the telling for myself. Yet I can remember I used to look upon the events of that night with as much seriousness as when Wellington reflected on the Battle of Waterloo. It was a big night in my young life. In my childlike simplicity, I admired Wil Bryan's pluck and daring. I honestly believed the world was too small to hold him. Now, however, I cannot help thinking that out of that seed of bad behaviour grew a massive tree.

What a pity it is was that Wil didn't listen to the advice of Abel Hughes and John Joseph at the Children's *Seiat*. If only he'd remembered how Abel advised us to keep from even an appearance of evil, and warned us about us the peril of walking in the ways of the ungodly. If only he'd thought how earnestly Abel prayed for us, and committed us to the care of the Good Lord who was such a Faithful Guide and Great Saviour. Had he done so, things might have turned out so different. If Wil did remember, then his reflections cannot have been pleasant.

CHAPTER 6

Meeting the Irishman

I have found it more difficult than I expected to discover my own beginnings. My experience must be similar to anyone who tries to trace the beginnings of things. For example, I don't know when I first realized I was closer to my mother than to any other woman. I'm not sure when the idea of God first formed in my mind. And when did I first realize I was a separate person? Or appreciate the notion of sin, personal responsibility and the world to come after death?

When I try to pin down the starting point of a notion, I often find I am mistaken and its source is farther off than ever. When I follow up, I get lost in the great unknowing that existed before my memories begin. Why is this, I wonder? Does my memory never register anything starting? On the other hand, do all the beginnings happen before my memory creates an impression of them? Or are a beginning and the memory of the event simultaneous? Or has every idea I have ever had been planted in my soul at its creation? Do circumstances awaken the idea from its torpor? Does my soul have the flexibility to take in impressions and with constant repetition deepen them into an idea?

These thoughts occurred whilst I was trying to recall how I came to be aware of the nature of my family. I must have been about six years old, and my brother Bob about eighteen. Bob was a great strong man who could carry me on his back without effort. He was a miner, and no one ever admired a brother more than I did mine. When I saw him coming home, clogs on feet, lamp in hand and face as black as the chimney back, my heart leaped with pride. At first I did not know where the money that kept Mam, Bob and I came from. Then I learned how all the good things of this world have a price. This is a truth that to my sorrow I have since proved a thousand times.

As a child, I was always asking Mam for this or that. Her answer was always that she had no money to buy it. The highlight of the week was when Bob brought his wages home. We three would sit around the fire as Bob emptied his cash into mother's apron. She would count the money and check it many times. To my child's eyes there was so much that I couldn't see why Mam kept saying she had no money. While she was counting it, she sometimes looked pleased, sometimes serious, but always thoughtful. Poor innocent that I was, I thought she was amazed to find herself so rich. Had I but known it, she was debating how to pay everybody their due and use the remaining coppers in her apron to best advantage. What a splendid Chancellor of the Exchequer

She would have made. She coped so well on the trifling amount that Bob was paid.

After the counting, Bob and Mam would have a quiet chat and I would hear the words 'rent' and 'shop'. I looked forward to pay day because when she had money Mam would go to the shop and buy food. For that day at least, we ate. What a rare and simple pleasure it is to have enough to eat. Few appreciate that pleasure except those who have gone as short of food, as I have. Short, did I say? At times, we were so short that we had nothing, but that is something which I will come back to later.

Wil Bryan was my best friend. Remembering hunger has stirred up thoughts of Wil. How I used to envy Wil Bryan. His father kept a large shop where there was everything in abundance. Wil had potatoes and meat for dinner every day. I had bread and milk, if I was lucky. Wil often had new clothes. I had my brother Bob's old ones remade by mother. Wil had a penny to spend every Saturday. I only saw the colour of copper when Bob emptied his pockets into mother's apron.

I thought Wil the happiest lad in the world because he owned a real live little mule. There was nothing else in the whole wide world I wanted as much as a little mule like Wil's. I was not the only one who envied Wil. The feeling was common amongst his friends. Wil was aware that this accident of ownership made him superior to the rest of us. If we happened to offend him, his worse punishment was to prevent us going anywhere near his mule. Usually this was more than enough to make us apologize at once. Wil used that little mule to tyrannize us unmercifully. Once, when somebody happened to stray from the subject, he gave orders that nobody without his permission, was to say a single word that was not about the mule and we had to do it. When I reflect on it, I realize how many people I have known, of every age and station, who have made capital out of their little mules.

I mention Wil Bryan's little mule because it posed a question in my soul. When I thought about Wil's happier lot and his advantages, I wondered what the difference was between us. Eventually I realized that Wil had a father, while I did not.

'Why don't I have a father?' I asked my mother. Tears welled up in her eyes. She was upset and tried to distract my attention.

'Is my father dead?' I said, determined to press the question.

'Yes poor child,' my mother said. 'Your father is dead in sin and transgression.'

Mam often used scriptural similes but I didn't understand this one. I didn't dare ask again, so I accepted her answer. I decided she was afraid to tell me that my father lay in the black hole of the grave. The idea that my father was dead made me sad for a while, but Mam soon distracted me, so my gloom lifted.

MEETING THE IRISHMAN

Sometime after this, we three sat round the kitchen fire. I was happy, though I cannot speak for mother and Bob. It was pay night, so my mother had been to the shop, and we had just finished a good supper. Mam let me stay up later on Bob's pay nights. This gave me a great deal of satisfaction. Oh, what little things brought me happiness in my boyhood! If only I could have stayed a boy forever!

We were huddled up to the fire because it was winter and the night was cold and stormy. I sat on my own little stool listening to the wind as it roared down the chimney and whistled through the keyhole. I was feeling sleepy, but was fighting not to close my eyes. I was afraid that Mam would send me to bed, and I would miss out on staying up late the following week. I was almost nodding off, when a loud knock came on the door. I woke up at once.

A repulsive looking man stalked in, slammed the door and walked straight to the fire without speaking. He didn't wait for an invitation to come in. As soon as I saw him, I thought him a bad man. He was ragged and dirty, and his clothes stank so he flooded the house with his unwelcome stench. He spoke in Welsh but his accent was foreign and he sounded like an Irishman. All dirty, ragged folk were Irish. My brother Bob leapt to his feet. His face was white with anger and his limbs trembled with rage. He went to grab the intruder, and throw him out. The Irishman was puny and weak so Bob could have done so easily, as he was supple, strong and well built. However, I was shocked to hear Mam begging him to hold back. The tremor in her voice frightened me.

I had never seen such a dirty ugly lout as this stranger. I was shocked at his rudeness in walking straight into house. I could see Mother was upset but making a strong effort to control herself.

'James,' she said to the Irishman. 'I have told you many times you are not to come here. I never wish to see you again.' Her voice was firm and resolute.

The stranger pretended not to hear. He knew my name because he spoke to me and tried to make friends with me. I wondered how he knew me, and tried to pull back from him as I would from a viper. He grabbed me and tried to force me to sit on his knee. I struck at his face with my little fists before Bob pulled me out of his clutches.

'James,' Mother said. 'I've told you not to come here. Please leave now.'

The Irishman refused. Once more Bob jumped to his feet to throw him out, but again Mam stopped him. I was angry with her for not letting Bob throw this offensive intruder out of our house.

The Irishman asked for food, and to my surprise, Mother put some in front of him. He ate so quickly and greedily that I thought he wouldn't stop until he had eaten all we had. I begrudged him every bite as did

31

Bob. Bob had sat me on his knee, to comfort me, and I could felt his legs trembling with anger.

When the Irishman had finally done eating, he drew himself up to the fire as if he meant to settle for the night.

'James,' she said. 'I have fed you. Now leave this house I beg you.'

'I need money, 'the Irishman said. 'I don't intend to leave until you give me some.'

To my utter amazement, she handed him some coins. Bob flew into a rage, his voice angry.

'You're mad,' he said to Mother, 'I don't go down the mine to toil and sweat, for my hard earned wages to be given to this drunken thieving scoundrel.'

I too, was annoyed that Mam had given so much of Bob's money to the Irishman. She had given him enough to buy me a little mule like Wil Bryan's. Yet young as I was, I was sorry for her. I guessed that the stranger had some secret influence over her, and she couldn't help herself. She had to do what he said.

Bob's outburst didn't bother the Irishman. Even though he had taken our money, he lit his pipe from the fire and began to undo his boot-laces. He seemed set to stay the night.

Then Bob lost patience. He sprang to his feet and opened the door wide. He took the Irishman by the scruff of the neck and flung him out into the street as if he were rubbish. Then he barred the door. All this took less than a quarter of a minute. I clapped my hands in joy, before I realized that Mam had fainted. I started to wail with grief; I thought she was dying. Bob sprinkled water over her face, and she came to and began to cry. Bob and I mingling our tears with hers for some time.

Finally, after drying her eyes, she spoke quietly with Bob. I could just make out that they were talking about the Irishman, who they referred to as 'He'. I tried to ask them who 'He' was, but all they would say was that he was a bad man, and that I must not tell anybody about him.

It would have been far better for me if I had never learned anything more about him, but Providence ordained otherwise. This 'Irishman' became the bane of my existence and dropped wormwood into my sweetest cup. How different my history might have been but for him. While my friends thought me blessed and happy, he like some evil spirit blighted my enjoyment, and hounded me like a nightmare so that I had no rest.

CHAPTER 7

The Two Schools in Mold

Everyone has an opinion about themselves, true or false. They know how they feel about their personal appearance, their physical and mental abilities and their social status. To put it another way, we all have an idea about our own importance, although it is not often that we tell others what it is. As a rule, we keep it to ourselves.

It makes sense that a man knows himself best, and he can form a correct judgement. If he is a man of parts, he daren't admit it, to avoid lowering himself in the eyes of others. He wouldn't want to appear smaller to their minds than to his own. Only one in a million has the confidence of the Apostle Paul, to fearlessly tell of their superiority to others, although the proportion who think themselves superior is far greater. So brightly does the beauty of humility shine before men that even honesty has to veil its eyes in her presence. How great was our Saviour that He could make such revelations and claims for Himself without tarnishing either His meekness or His modesty?

Many people think that greatness and humility ought to go together. But what men call humility is only a strategy. Picture to yourself, Dr Somebody, speaking to an audience. You are saying:

'Well, my dear brethren, you know I am greater than any of you. I can write a tract or compose a sermon better than anyone here. I am as good as any dozen of you for culture and natural ability and better than the two best of you working together.'

How would the brethren respond? They would stare at each other, and their looks would suggest that you were off your head. Yet, who knows better than you that the words I have put into your mouth are true. Even if you would not dare say so for the world. A great man knows he can leave it to others to form an opinion of him without any guidance from himself. Most likely, they will rate him too highly, but he would prefer that they err in this way rather than the other. There is never much readiness in a man to set right those who show a tendency to value him at more than his proper worth.

From my own experience, I know that awareness of my inferiority is uncomfortable. This might be why a small man always tries to show himself to best advantage. I have seen this in other animals apart from man. The other day I saw two cocks on a dunghill. One was a large Cochin China, well rounded, long-shanked and high-crested, the other a pert little Bantam. The Cochin looked listless and easy-going. The other thrust out his breast and stood a-tiptoe, his head and tail held so high that they nearly touched each other. With a clear voice, he crowed and crowed. He wanted to pick a fight with the Cochin. Round and round he circled, saying. 'Look at my breast and tail. You don't have as fine a tail as me.'

The Cochin tried to ignore him, but the bantam persisted until the Cochin finally crowed back. His crow was more a groan and he sounded to be sympathizing with the bantam for his size. I don't know if chickens imitate men, or men imitate cockerels but they act the same.

Having thought this through, I feel I must ask myself: 'What measure do you take of yourself, Rhys? There is no one listening, so you can answer honestly. No one will think you conceited or hypocritical. You are a preacher, the pastor of your flock, and yet you sometimes write poetry and articles for periodicals. How do you see yourself?'

I will put my foot on the neck of my pride and try to answer honestly. There's no point in deceiving myself; nobody can hear my thoughts.

The Great Lord, who knows everything, knows that I should be an example in religion and the proof of things spiritual. Yet, He also knows I am painfully insignificant. The more I engage with matters Divine, the more I feel temporal matters holding me back. The promises of Holy Scripture, which are so emphatic about the power and grace of our Saviour, are all that stop me sinking into despair under the weight of my guilty conscience. From the depth of my heart, I pray that He may strengthen me in the Faith.

I am not good-looking and I wonder why some people hold me in tender affection. I have envied the charm of manner possessed by the poet and writer Thomas Jones, known by his bardic name 'Glan Alun,' who made everybody overlook his plain aspect by brilliance of his mind. Dear man, I prefer thee to a hundred comely and smartly dressed, soulless individuals. I like to think that I am not repulsive in appearance, but I might be mistaken. Nevertheless, I would be pleased if I, like Thomas Jones, possessed a remarkable soul. I try to present a commanding presence as a preacher, for anyone who climbs a pulpit without one will be marked down.

I exceed some of my brethren in my natural tendencies, and I dare to say that because nobody is listening. Not for the world would I tell anybody this. Were anyone to suggest it to me, I would most certainly protest, and that maybe because of the humility in me.

The extent of my knowledge is not great. Indeed, many youngsters in my congregation know a good deal more than I do. I struggle to stop them understanding too much, too soon. Consider geography. I know little of that subject and if some youngsters ask about it, I must hide my ignorance. It would never do to let them know how uneducated I am, because those boys believe I know everything. I have ways of getting out of such difficulties.

When someone asks a question and I do not know the answer, I redirect it to a boy in the class who I think can answer it. If I fancy he has given a correct answer, I reward him with nod of approval. However, if neither I, nor anyone else in the class can answer a question, I tell my scholars how important it is that they investigate for themselves. I tell them that the knowledge they obtain will be of greater value to them than any they might take by me answering the question for them. I also promise to carry the question over to the next meeting, by which time I will expect every one of them to be able to answer it. In the mean time I search out the answer for myself. Of course, I tell no one about this technique, but I am sure that the wise elders would not blame me even if they knew. If I were I to admit ignorance before the boys, it would greatly diminish my pastoral value.

I have written a long preface to this present chapter because I want to explain how much I feel my lack of advantage in education from my early youth. This is a serious shortcoming for a preacher. I am always tripping over something I should have learned in school. I can never aspire to match the position and value of those who had a thorough training in their childhood.

When I was a boy, there were only two day schools in Mold, where I was born. One was run by a gentleman by the name of Mr Smith. Mr Smith was the great sage of our town. People looked up to him with a veneration that was close to worship. He was fluent in seven languages, and could speak words no one could understand. Mam told me that Mr Smith was up there with the self-taught linguist Robert Jones, who was known as Dic Aberdaron on the title page of the great dictionary of St Asaph. Together they were the two greatest scholars the world had ever seen. I believed her. I would stop in the street to stare at him with admiration. He was a tall, thin, grey-headed man who wore black clothes and spectacles. He was the only man in Mold who let the hair to grow under his nose. His school was a superior institution, to which only the gentry and the well-off sent their children. His scholars carried their books to school in green bags. Green bags of books retain their ability to impress me to this day.

Mam did not think of sending me to Mr Smith's school, even if she could have afforded to. She thought him irreligious. He went to Top Church on Sunday. To attend the Church of England instead of going to Chapel didn't impress my mother; the Church of England and Religion were words very far apart in my mother's vocabulary. And, to make matters worse, he was in the habit of taking a stroll on Sunday afternoons. Mam thought he should have been at home thinking about the Word and the Doctrine.

My mother heard from an old maidservant of Mr Smith's that he kept in his house what the maid called a 'Devil-raising Book'. She claimed he always read it 'after dark'. My mother had no doubt about the correctness of this story, because one night when Mr Smith left the book open upon the table and the maid saw it next morning. She went over and tried to read it, but not a word could she read except 'Satan,' for she didn't know a word of English. When she visited the room later, the book was gone. Mother also remembered how Mr Smith went with Parson Brown to visit the haunted house of Ty'n Llidiart. The two gentlemen laid the spirit, which dwelt there, and shut it up in a tobacco box. My mother assumed that if Mr Smith, who was not a parson, could assist Parson Brown, who was a priest, in the task of laying spirits, he must know how to raise them as well.

Mam's main reason for deciding Mr Smith was irreligious was that he wore a moustache. Nobody could persuade her that a man who knew the great things of religion would allow hair to grow on his upper lip. She never took anyone who wore a moustache to be a good Christian. A wisp of hair near the ear was acceptable but even such great preachers as Mr Elias and Mr Rees would not have been taken for Christian if they had worn moustaches. These were insurmountable obstacles to me going to Mr Smith's school even if it had been free, which it wasn't. Besides which, my mother didn't believe in higher education. I often heard her say:

'No good will come from over-educating children. Too much learning has led many a man to the gallows. And as for the children of the poor, if they are able to read their Bible, and know the way into the Life eternal, that is quite enough for them.'

The other school was kept by Mr Robin Davies or, as he was usually known, 'Robin the Soldier'. He was an older, fleshy, well-set sort of man, who had spent the prime of his life in the British Army. He had distinguished himself as a brave and stalwart warrior. When he came back to his native Mold, he left his right leg in Belgium where he had been campaigning against 'Bony'. It was a pledge of his zeal and fidelity to his country. Robin made up for this loss with a wooden leg, made from foreign wood. He had shaped it with his own hand and tipped it with an iron ferrule. When he left the army, in recognition of his service and as compensation for the loss of his leg the Government gave him a pension of sixpence a day for life. In honour of this endowment, Robin called his wooden leg 'Old Sixpenny'.

In the first weeks after his return from the army, his friends asked him out to supper to listen to the tales of his battles and adventures abroad. Over time, his stories grew stale, and Robin wore out their hospitality. At last, the only place they he could still tell them was in the taproom of the Cross Foxes. He became a regular there.

The wages paid by his wooden leg were barely enough to pay off his weekly slate at the Cross Foxes, so the old soldier found himself struggling. But relief was in sight. He found an opening as a tollgate-keeper, and he fared sumptuously for a season. He grew sleek and self-satisfied. This state of affairs would doubtless have continued, had not the turnpike owners discovered that it was not Robin who kept the gate, but the gate that kept Robin. After meeting in solemn conclave, the authorities decided that this was not the purpose of the turnpike trust. Indeed, some members were so hard-hearted as to insist that the trust dismiss Robin from the job.

Parson Brown was always kind and charitable towards those of his parishioners who he considered orthodox. The old soldier was one of his dearly beloved brethren and a devout man by the standards of Parson Brown. Robin went to Top Church every Sunday morning, to his bed every Sunday afternoon, and to the taproom of Cross Foxes every Sunday evening. This was enough religious devotion for Parson Brown to take an interest in his welfare. He suggested to Robin that he should set up a school. Mam told me the story.

'Robbit,' said Parson Brown in what my mother parodied as his usual broken Welsh. 'Robbit, you a scholar, you able to read and write and say catechism. You start school in old office empty there. Me help you. Many children without learning hereabouts, Robbit; you charge week penny, make coin lot, live comfortable, me do my best for you. You, Robbit, have for the country been fight; me for you fight now.'

Good for Parson Brown! He had a warm heart. He didn't rest until he'd set Robin on his feet, or rather his foot, in the matter of starting a second day school in Mold.

Soldier Robin started his school long before I was old enough to go to it. Why my mother sent me there I cannot remember. I had no burning desire for an education, and it wasn't because my mother admired Robert's religion devotion. I think Parson Brown must have influenced her. Although Mam never believed Mr Brown knew what she called 'the great things of religion,' she always had a high opinion of him as a philanthropist and neighbour.

I resigned myself to the idea of going to school once I realized that Wil Bryan was already a pupil there. I thought it a great sacrifice to go school, and I hoped Wil would recognize my self-denial.

I have noticed whilst reading biographies that they rarely tell of their subject's first day at school. This is not surprising, as only the subject would know about the matter, and the author could not. My first day at school is fresh and alive in my memory. I have decided to write down its events, not for other people's amusement, but for my own. I am probably the only one who will find it interesting but, because I do, I have decided to devote another chapter to what happened that day.

CHAPTER 8

Under Instruction

If, when I rest in my grave, my friends find this biography, and if they bother to read it, they will wonder why I have rambled on for so long about unimportant things. 'Why did he take seven chapters to get from his birth to his first day at school?' they will ask in amazement. 'If he had sent this great tome to a popular magazine the editor would have lost patience and told him to get on with it or stop bothering to write it.'

Being able to dwell on ordinary things is the advantage of writing for myself, rather than for the public.

A man sent on an errand walks straight. He takes the shortest road walking at his best pace of some four miles an hour. He keeps looking at his watch so as not to waste any time. However, if he takes a stroll along an old country lane he doesn't time the passage of milestones. He climbs hedges, wanders around bushes, goes bird-nesting, collects nuts and blackberries, sits upon the mossy boulders and lolls by the river bank. He forgets that he has a watch in his pocket.

Who is the happier? I would say the man on the stroll – and, like him, I am free, with no one to take me to task for indulgence even if I write a preface to every chapter. No one tells me to recast sentences that are a little clumsy, and I don't have to bother what a reader might think about what I write.

Earlier this evening I was thinking of Dafydd Davis who is an elder of my flock. He is a God-fearing man, but also an oddity. He belongs to the old school faithful who will not deviate from the rules of our fathers. He will not even brush his hair back from his forehead. I hold both his good sense and prejudices in great respect. I have heard that Dafydd Davis holds a high opinion of me. That might be why I think so highly of him. Indeed, the more I think about it, I see this is a rule I often use to take the measure of my brethren. If I find that so and so happens to think well of me, I decide there must be something special about him. On the contrary, though, I once thought highly of the brother who keeps the Post Office. Then I found that he didn't hold a similar opinion of me, so he fell in my estimation. I am not proud of this, but it is the truth.

What would Dafydd Davis think if he knew that tonight I am writing the childish story of my first day at school? I suspect I would go down in his eyes. Fortunately, he doesn't know. I often find myself doing some things, and not others, for the sake of Dafydd Davis. When I talk to him, I am tempted to crack a joke, but out of respect for the old man I do not. I once fancied I might let the hair grow on my upper lip, but then I thought how upset Dafydd Davis would be. I have shaved regularly ever since. Because Dafydd Davis does not know that I write for my own amusement I can give a full account, hiding nothing of how I first went to the school of Soldier Robin.

One cold dark winter Monday Wil Bryan called for me to take me to school. 'Take good care of him, Wil *bach*.' Mam said.

'I will indeed, Mrs Lewis,' Wil said, grinning at her, but as we walked down the High Street, he revealed that I might have to fight one or two of my new schoolfellows.

'It's not a pleasant thing to have to fight,' Wil said. 'But it's the custom of the school with a new scholar, to see what he's made of. But don't worry, I'll take care of your back and see that you get fair play.'

I knew that my talents did not lie in fisticuffs, so I was not consoled. Then I found something else to worry me. What if Mam found out? Even worse, what if Abel Hughes, told me off at Children's *Seiat*?

I couldn't admit having qualms in front of fearless Wil Bryan. He rode so high in my estimation that I would not have disappointed him for anything. 'I'll do what you say,' I said.

The room where the old soldier held his school was long and narrow. Round its wall was a desk with a rough, crooked bench attached to it. Scholars had carved some kind of picture, or their name, on every square inch of it. At the far end, close to the fire, was the master's desk. Through the base of it, Robin had drilled a good-sized hole. I later found it was to house his wooden leg. When he sat down, he would push the ferrule through this hole.

As we went into schoolroom, we saw a strange and wondrous sight. Boys were standing on the desk, and boys were mounted on other boys' backs. They were playing horses and galloping about the room. Other boys, squirming about like eels in mud, were in a great heap on the floor.

One lame boy, who walked with a crutch, was pretending to be the master. He sat at the front desk with his crutch thrust through the hole as if it was a wooden leg. He yelled for silence but everyone ignored him. All the boys were shouting at the tops of their voices. Just one stood on the desk near the window. He was the look-out. He divided his attention between the horseplay and watching for the arrival of the master.

I felt odd that Mam let me go with such wicked children. If she'd known what sort of boys they were, she would have stopped me at once. Although I sensed that this was the best place to have fun that I had ever seen, I felt a deep shyness in me. Wil had abandoned me to join in the play. Then the lad who was acting as lookout put two fingers to his mouth, and gave a piercing whistle. Every boy rushed to his proper place in an instant. They left me looking foolish, standing like a lonely statue near the door as the Teacher came in. He stumped past me without acknowledging me at all. He seemed agitated and looked around with a fierce look on his face. I guessed the guard had not been quick enough to give the signal, and the master had heard the racket. He walked over to his desk, and drew out a long stout cane. Each lad, well knowing what was coming, shrugged his shoulder as the old soldier went round the school, caning each one in turn. His blows were cruel and indiscriminate.

I was the only one to burst out crying even though he didn't beat me. His process of mass punishment terrified me. The other boys weren't bothered as they were used to the procedure. Once the last boy had received his caning, the master stumped back to his desk, put his hands together and said in a pious voice. 'Let us pray'.

He slowly recited The Lord's Prayer. The boys were supposed to copy him, but I heard some wicked ones using words very different from those usually said in the prayer. I was shocked at their disrespect and even more by the ripples of low laughter that came from those who heard the profanities.

The prayer over, the old Soldier assumed a voice of command:

'Rivets, my boys, rivets,' he cried. Apparently, he said this every Monday morning. It meant, 'Pay up your pence'.

One lad had come without money. He had to hold out his hand and receive the tingling imprint of the Soldier's cane. He danced back to his seat, clutching his fingers between his knees, under his armpit, putting them into his mouth, and shaking them as if he had pulled them from a raging fire. Wil told me later that this performance always followed a stroke of the cane, especially if the boy hadn't had chance to spit on his palm, and place two crossed hairs on it.

All the boys held a steadfast belief that spit and crossed hairs would protect against the smarting. I carried out many trials and I found it didn't help at all. Few boys cried after a single stroke on the hand. If given two or three strokes, a boy could howl without the rest calling him a coward. I always cried after the first stroke, but I was known as a crier and couldn't help it.

Wil Bryan took me up to the master who took my penny and entered my name in the register. The penny, as I handed it over, was hot from the tight grip I had kept on it, for fear of losing it.

'Go to your seat boy,' the teacher said. 'You will sit between Wil Bryan and Jack Beck. Be ready to attend to your lessons.'

As I sat down next to Jack Beck who whispered. 'Have you got a halfpenny?'

I whispered back, 'No I haven't.'

'When can you get one?' Jack Beck demanded. 'I know a shop where there are heaps of things to be had for a halfpenny. I know the shop wife, you'll get as much again for your money if I come with you.'

'If you don't shut up you'll be sorry,' Wil Bryan said. 'Rhys here will give you a good thrashing.' Little did I know what a cunning young rascal he was.

'He can't thrash me,' Beck said.

'Are you afraid of Beck?' Wil asked me.

Although I felt just the opposite, I put on a bold face. 'I most certainly am not,' I said.

'Very well,' said Wil, and within a matter of minutes, the news spread into every ear in the school. 'There's going to be a fight between Rhys Lewis and Jack Beck'.

My conscience was deeply troubled at the thought of fighting, but I wasn't going to let Wil down. He was bubbling with excitement and telling me the best way to prepare for the bout. I couldn't help thinking that my mother at home and Abel Hughes at the Children's *Seiat* had both taught me that fighting was a sin.

I didn't want to punch a boy who had never said a bad word to me, and with whom I had no quarrel. If my mother heard of the battle, she might be a little lenient because Jack was a Church of England man. I knew she didn't have a high opinion of Church people. Perhaps she might view the contest as a sort of accidental collision between Chapel and Church.

No work went on in the school for the next hour. The old Soldier kept his head down at his desk, either reading or writing. The boys' books were open in front of them but they kept up a continuous muttering. I knew they were talking about Jack Beck and me.

If the talk became a little loud the master, would shout 'Silence!' For a few minutes, the room would quieten down, and then the murmuring would start once more. At a quarter to eleven, the master told us we could go out to play. The class jumped to their feet and pushed out like a herd of sheep rushing a gap. My heart was thumping in my chest for fear of what was to happen. The crowd swept me out into the yard in a blur. I found myself standing facing Jack Beck. I closed my eyes and flailed my fists, but don't know what happened because I couldn't see. I kept my eye closed, not to protect them from my opponent's blows, but because I was terrified. Luckily, the battle didn't last long. I was astounded to discover I was the winner. To this day, I think that Wil Bryan helped me. I don't know which made me prouder that the fight was over, or that I had won and kept a whole skin.

Then I heard the stern voice of the Soldier, calling us into school. It struck terror into my heart. He had seen everything that had happened. I heard several of the boys saying that it was a boy they had nicknamed the Skulk, the son of the woman who cleaned the English church, who had told the master. They were all angry and aimed a legion of threats at his head.

We trooped back into the schoolroom where the master called Jack Beck and me up his desk

'Explain your behaviour,' he roared.

At this fearful moment, Wil Bryan rushed to my aid. He came up to the Master's desk and without flinching, asserted that Beck had confronted me and struck the first blow. Beck denied this so emphatically that the master called another witness. This boy was an enemy of Beck's so naturally he confirmed Wil's evidence.

'Rhys Lewis,' the old Soldier said. 'Because this is your first day at school, I will let you off.'

He gave Beck three strokes with the cane. The first for fighting without good cause. The second for taking a beating from me. And the third for denying the accusation brought against him.

I sympathized with Beck. Soldier Robin had him hoisted on the back of the sturdiest lad in school. He then pulled down Beck's trousers to reveal a part of his body I did not care to see, and do not care to name. All I will say is that Beck received his punishment on naked flesh.

As he brought the cane down the old Soldier emphasized the justification for each stroke.

'This is for fighting without good cause' – whack.

'This is for losing the fight' – whack.

'And this is for denying the truth of the accusation against you' – whack.

I can repeat that formula so easily because I heard it so often during my time at the Soldier's school. The beating ceremony was a regular feature of the old Soldier's regime, and it never varied. Every scholar in the whole school who endured the punishment would dance and shout after the cane's impact, every boy but one. The boy who never cried out whilst being beaten was Wil Bryan. However hard the old Soldier laid on the strokes, he could never make Wil cry out. Wil was the very embodiment of bravery and a hero in our eyes.

The class enjoyed seeing poor Beck flogged. I thought this cruel, particularly as no one knew who would be the next to feel the cane.

Little more happened that afternoon at school. That first day in school, I got only one lesson in spelling. The others didn't get any more. We all got more canings than lessons. Nevertheless, one thing happened that day which soothed my conscience a little. In the middle of the day, I went home for my dinner and a kind neighbour gave me a halfpenny for my courage in going to school.

That afternoon I told Jack Beck that by chance I had come by a half-penny. I made peace with him and he duly escorted me to the shop. Indeed, we did make an exceptional ha'porth purchase. I gave him most of the proceeds, not wishing the sun to go down on our anger.

In my innocence, I fancied that things having ended so happily, there was no need for me to pray for forgiveness before going to sleep. Therefore I did not, but I was glad that neither my mother nor Abel Hughes ever found out about my fight.

These, as far as I can remember them, are the events of my first day in the school of Soldier Robin.

CHAPTER 9

Church Matters

Recently I visited the local British School, here in Mold. It has good organization, strict but easy discipline, a clean and happy appearance to its children and imparts useful instruction. The school impressed me. It couldn't have been more different to Soldier Robin's school. My blood boils still when I think of that old soldier's stupidity, laziness, hypocrisy, and cruelty.

To complete the story of my education however, I must write more about him before I turn to matters of more importance. I would be pleased if I could forget him forever. When the Almighty calls me to give testimony against him in His Higher Court, I hope I will find it in myself to plead forgiveness for Soldier Robin, even as I expect the Good Lord to grant forgiveness to me.

The most important part of his job, in the view of the old Soldier, was to take our pennies. His next care was to break at least one stout cane a week on our backs or hands. Our parents knew about his rough ways, but they believed it contributed to our improvement. We in turn accepted harsh discipline as regular as meal times, but with less appetite. No one was interested in learning, and our teacher was the least interested of all. It gave him more pleasure to see us fail to learn, than to help us succeed.

Failure gave him reason to punish us. He expected us to learn without any guidance from him. His disappointment showed if we chanced to master a lesson in spite of him. He didn't try to stimulate love of knowledge in us or inspire any ambition to excel. He imparted a dislike of all learning, and an urgent desire in every boy to grow strong enough to thrash him. That pleasure, I also anticipated with relish.

As I sat in class, feeling the throbbing of my back and the heaviness of my heart after yet another painful beating from him, I would look at his wooden leg. I wondered how many Frenchmen he had killed whilst fighting Napoleon. Jack Beck said he'd killed three hundred Frenchies, but Wil Bryan reckoned it must be more because, as he said, 'he enjoys killing. Nothing would give that old warrior greater satisfaction than to kill the lot of us. He would too, but he's afraid he'd hang for it.'

We agreed with him. It was easy to believe. Soldier Robin's diabolical rage showed on his face every time he thrashed a boy. The veins of his forehead engorged and turned black, his jaw distended and his expression became horrible to see. Yet if Parson Brown paid him an unexpected visit, the old soldier would change his aspect in an instant. It was miraculous to see his transformation.

The Parson was plump, pudgy, easy-going and kind. He never thought ill of his neighbours, particularly if they attended the church of St Mary at the top of the town, which we all knew as the Top Church. I saw him come into school whilst the old Soldier had a fit on and watched the soldier's expression instantly take on an almost heavenly aspect. The old hypocrite would call a boy out to the front of class to repeat a Collect or the Catechism. When the boy did, he would stroke the lad's head in a show of false affection. The trusting Parson Brown would then congratulate him on his efforts and our successes.

'You do deal of good here, Robbit,' he would say in mangled Welsh. 'You will be paid for all this in a higher place.'

None of us dared look displeased when Parson Brown was there. We knew better than to give him any sort of hint that we were anything but perfectly happy. Should we do so, we well knew the matter would go badly with us as soon as the good parson's back was turned. The old Soldier must have really struggled to pretend to be gentle and benign. The titanic struggle he made to subdue his villainous inclinations while Mr Brown was there always caused a reaction later. Once the Parson left, his temper would be worse than ever.

Sometimes a bold parent might complain to Parson Brown that the Soldier behaved cruelly towards the boys. Naturally, the reverend gentleman would come at once to the school, and talk the matter over with the master. Soldier Robin would call up any lad whose parents had accused him of being cruel, and in front of Mr Brown, ask his victim. 'Am I not a kind master?'

His eye gave a plain indication of the answer he expected. The boy felt he must agree, and so Mr Brown went away satisfied that the complaints were idle gossip.

There were some advantages in attending Soldier Robin's school – at least so I thought. Every Friday afternoon the old trooper would pick two boys to be his servants for the coming week. The servants' duties were to light the fire, clean the schoolhouse and run errands. The errands included trips to the Cross Foxes to fetch beer. The soldier didn't send any money with this demand.

I never liked that job. The alewife, Mrs Tibbet, was old and fat. Her body was the same thickness all the way, up like a pillar, and was crowned with a face that was perpetually purple. People said she was that colour because she drank too much. She said she never touched a drop but no one believed her.

When Wil and I asked for a jug of beer, to take to the old warrior, she would shout and tell us off for bringing no money. She'd show us a long list of the old Soldier's arrears, which she kept chalked up on the back of the cellar door.

I was delighted to find an adult who shared my view of the old Soldier's character. She would list his failings, with great passion. Pointing at the reckoning on the cellar door, she would say, 'He'll never be able to pay that off.'

'And he has another much larger reckoning that he will also never be able to pay,' Wil said to her, suggesting that Robin would be judged for his sins in heaven.

'What!' said the old woman in great alarm 'has he got another account somewhere else, then?'

'Mrs Tibbet,' said Wil. 'I am referring to the great reckoning at the Day of Judgement'.

'Oh well, that's between him and his maker,' she said, calming down at once. 'We must all of us go to our answering, and then all will have justice. If he pays me what he owes then he may take his own chances with the Almighty.'

The most unpleasant duty of the soldier's servant was to light the schoolhouse fire. We had to find our own kindling, as the hedges round about clearly showed. One morning Wil and I were without a scrap of wood to start the fire.

'Do you know if the master takes his wooden leg to bed with him, or does he leave it where we could steal it?' Wil asked in all seriousness.

'I don't know,' I said. 'Why?'

'Ah,' said Wil, 'what a beautiful blaze it would make.'

As I write, I can see his face brightening at the thought of the jape. Poor old Wil never got the chance to put that idea into practice.

Being the weekly servant had advantages. I did not have to look at a book, and was exempt from all punishment, no matter what mischief I did. In addition, it was said in a whisper, that the master had once actually smiled at a servant but I cannot vouch for the truth of this. I never saw him smile, unless Parson Brown called.

Because of the great benefits of being a servant, every Friday afternoon saw us waiting like mice to hear who would have privilege the following week. The honour did not often come to Wil Bryan or me. Perhaps this was because we hardly ever went to Church, our parents being chapel folk. We did, however, always go to St Mary's when there was to be a holiday distribution of cake after the service.

It was a just such a cake-motivated visit to Top Church one Good Friday morning that ended my time as a scholar in the school of Soldier Robin. Once I have described what happened I hope to forget this particular tyrant forever.

I struggle with my feelings about the incident I am about to describe. I have a guilty conscience about the mischief, but I can't suppress an inward chuckle when I remember my part in it. If that is sinful, I hope to be forgiven, but I cannot gloss over this tale of my wickedness. It had an important effect on my life and was why I stopped attending day school.

My story begins on Good Friday morning. There was no service at chapel, and the weather was too wet to play out so Wil Bryan suggested we go to Top Church with the rest of the boys. I had no idea that he had any hidden intent, and he didn't mention anything as we walked up the town. Perhaps he was afraid that if he'd told me what he intended to do, I would not have gone with him.

Soldier Robin's scholars had a great square, deep-seated pew set aside for them in Top Church. It could hold twenty or more boys and was so deep that the congregation couldn't see us and we couldn't even see Parson Brown in the pulpit.

The pew behind was long and narrow. The Soldier sat alone in this seat. His purpose was to overawe us and keep us in order. For his comfort, Parson Brown had had a hole bored in the partition. Soldier Robin would shove his wooden leg though this hole as he sat down. This was not just for his comfort, the wooden leg stuck into the boys' pew so we would see it. This was to remind us that the schoolmaster was near, even if we couldn't see him. He was supposed to make sure we kept within the bounds of decency.

As the service began I saw Wil looking closely at the end of the wooden leg. Out of his pocket, he took a length of thin, strong cord with a running knot tied in it. His careful preparation told me what he was up to was pre-planned. He went down on his knees and slipped the knot around the tip of the ferrule. Then he handed the other end of the cord to me.

'When you feel a bite, keep tight hold of the line,' he whispered, speaking of the leg as if it were a fish.

I didn't dare disobey Wil and before long, I felt a tug. As is the custom in the English Church, the congregation stood up at that point in the proceeding. The Soldier tried to do likewise. The tight cord trapped him and he fell back in his seat like a lump of lead. There we held him for the rest of the service.

He bellowed and roared like a bull in a net, but the mighty tones of the organ drowned his noise. Wil and I held the cord till we were blue in the face. None of the other boys gave us any help except Jack Beck, who rolled up his sleeves and seconded us splendidly. We didn't have to ask him. Most of the others enjoyed our mischievous trick so much they had to hold their sides with laughter, and stuff their handkerchiefs into their mouths to prevent themselves from screaming aloud. A few watched in fear and trembling being, frightened at the inevitable consequences. Only the Church cleaner's son seemed honestly displeased. As the service was ending. Wil told John Beck to take his knife and cut the cord within a foot of the leg.

Once Beck had done this, Wil whipped the remainder into his pocket, saying. 'There he is now, like a hen which doesn't come home to lay.'

He was alluding to the custom of tying a string to a hen's leg, so that her owner could tell where she laid her eggs.

'Walk out normally and keep your faces straight,' Wil said. We paraded slowly and seriously according to his instructions. Glancing back, I saw Parson Brown looking over the edge of the Soldier's pew as he made his way to the vestry

'Hullo! Robbit,' he said, mangling his Welsh, as usual. 'I thought you not in Church today.'

We didn't wait to hear any more. Wil Bryan assured us later that he saw the reverend gentleman pressing his handkerchief to his mouth, the nape of his neck and his ears going red from laughter on seeing what had kept the Soldier out of sight. I think this quite likely, for Mr Brown was a merry old character.

I wasn't looking forward to Monday morning. When the extent of the atrocity we had inflicted on our teacher dawned up on us, we were quite sure that the 'Skulk', the Church cleaner's son, would pass onto the master every detail of what had happened. Over that Easter weekend Wil Bryan, Jack Beck and I spoke many times. Try as we might, we couldn't see any way to dodge the punishment we had stored up for ourselves. Monday came, and we had to go to school. Wil was eager to go, and he called for me earlier than usual. I think he wanted the business over and done with. Alternatively, I wondered if he had in mind some ruse to evade the inevitable penalty. He was quiet and thoughtful as we walked up to the school unlike me who was so terrified that my legs would hardly carry me. The look on Jack Beck's face showed he shared my dread.

Wil could see we were both frightened so as we came to the schoolhouse door so he tried to jolly us along. 'Cheer up, boys,' he said. 'It'll turn out better than you fear.'

I didn't see how he could believe this, but his words encouraged me to think he had a plan for our salvation. All the other boys other were already in school. They sat still and silent. They looked anxious as we arrived. We went to our seats silently, Wil stared straight into the Skulk's face for a long time. The Skulk blushed to the roots of his hair and looked away. We all knew what that meant, but nobody said anything.

The silence seemed to go on forever. Then we heard the sound of the Soldier's wooden leg, its tapping getting louder as he pegged his way towards the schoolroom. The boys stared at Bryan, Beck and me. Their faces showed pity and concern. I cannot describe the extent of my fear as the fierce face of the master appeared round the door. He looked straight to where Wil and I were sitting. I hoped desperately that Wil Bryan had a plan of escape.

The old warrior went to his desk and said prayers as usual. The responses of the class were weak and half-hearted. No sooner had he said Amen than he took up a stout new cane. He turned up the cuff of his coat-sleeve, spat on his hand, and glared like a tiger. He limped towards Wil Bryan. Wil jumped to his feet. The Soldier stopped. He spoke to the Skulk. 'Lock and guard the door boy.' The Skulk rushed to do his bidding and stood guard by the door.

I could see that Wil wasn't going to run. His lips were white and trembling and his eyes burned as he stared at the Soldier. His defiant attitude made the master hesitate. Robin's face turned ghastly with rage and he moved slowly forward, lifting the cane high preparing to bring it down with all his strength. Wil stared steadily at him, showing no fear.

Before the Soldier could strike, Wil jumped up, grabbed his wooden leg and yanked it from the floor. At the same time, he butted the schoolmaster in the stomach with his head. The old man hit the ground like a felled tree. The dreadful crack of his skull hitting the stone floor echoes still in the ears of my memory as I write.

Wil turned on his heel and walked purposefully towards the door. The Skulk trembled and stood aside. He handed Wil the key. Wil beckoned us to follow. Jack Beck ran for dear life. I froze. Hundreds of times since have I regretted that I didn't follow him, but I was shocked. For the first time, I saw that Wil, even though he was my best friend, was a really bad boy.

The Soldier lay dazed and stunned for some time. However, he wasn't totally helpless. Never before or since I have had to watch a man with a wooden leg trying to get up from the ground. He made a stupendous effort. I was amazed that old warrior got up without help. He rose like an ox that a butcher has failed to stun completely in the abattoir. As he got to his foot, he snorted loudly through his nostrils. Too late, I saw the folly of not going with Wil and Jack. I jumped up and made for the door but I was too slow. The master's cane knocked me down and as I lay on the floor, it cut and slashed from every direction, over my head, neck, back, hands, legs, and the rest of my body. There was no escape from the rain of blows of blows and pain was endless. I feared I was going to die as darkness rose up through my agony and swamped me. I sank into terrified swoon.

I came to my senses in the midst of a dream. I was on the ground and couldn't move. The school looked empty, but I could hear moans of agony. At first, I thought it must be me groaning and that I had been left to die. I made a desperate effort and turned my head. A group of boys was standing terror-struck near the open door and among them was Jack Beck. I screamed out to him. He ran over and helped me sit up. Every joint and each bone of body shrieked with the pain.

Then I saw the old Soldier stretched on his back, his face pallid, he was gurgling and moaning. Kneeling on his chest was a black faced demon and it was choking the life out him. I thought the Evil One had come take the Old Soldier for his own. The Devil's face was as black as the chimney back. His white teeth showed in a vicious snarl and his eyes bulged with anger. I screamed in fear as the Old One looked directly at me.

Only then did I recognize Bob, my elder brother. He was kneeling on Robin's chest and throttling him. He was in his working clothes with his face as black as coal. As I have vowed to tell the truth, I must admit to my shame that I used all the strength I had left to shout. 'Give it to him, Bob.'

As I cried out, Bob dropped the schoolmaster and rushed over to me.

'I thought you were dead,' he said and began to cry.

When he saw I couldn't walk, he lifted me on his back, and took me home. We left the Soldier on his schoolroom floor to recover as best he could.

I found out later that when Jack Beck made his escape, he waited outside the door to see how I got on. He soon realized that I was being badly beaten. Then he saw my brother Bob, making his way home after the night shift.

'The old soldier's killing your Rhys,' Beck shouted.

Bob rushed into the schoolroom and saw the master beating my insensible body as it lay at his feet. He sprang on Robin and dropped him to the floor again. Then he grabbed him by his throat and jumped on his chest. That was what I saw as I came to.

That was not the end of the business. Bob, Wil Bryan and I were all members of the Children's *Seiat*, and the elders reported these events to the meeting. I shall need another chapter to tell what happened there, and what our elders did about this matter. If I were writing for publication, I would have to add more detail about Soldier Robin's school, so that today's boys could see the enormous improvements that have taken place in schools and schoolmasters in half a generation. But, as I write for myself, I will close now and abandon the subject of Soldier Robin, for I never went back to his school.

CHAPTER 10

The Subject of Education

**As Bob carried me home after that merciless beating, I was afraid I would get another from my mother. She was not going to be pleased about my wicked behaviour in church.

'Do you think Mam will beat me too?' I asked him, 'For what I did in church?'

'I'm sure you won't need another beating for at least a twelve-month,' Bob said.

Every little jolt of my body made me ache, but, sore as I was, the thought that my punishment was over cheered me up. Then I remembered Bryan and Beck, the poor fellows. They still had their hidings to come. If the Soldier didn't beat them then their parents would most certainly take the stick to them. I might have been their scapegoat in the schoolroom, but it wasn't the end of the matter.

As Bob carried me into the house, Mam gave me a hard look and said. 'What did you do to earn such a beating?'

I never lied to Mam, so I told her the whole story of tying off the Soldier's wooden leg in the Church. I couldn't help noticing that Bob seemed to be enjoying my tale but I could see Mam wasn't. Once I finished Bob had to plead hard, on my behalf, to save me from a further beating.

'Just look at how badly Rhys is lacerated' he said to Mam. She looked at the state of my body. She saw the great red weals the Soldier had inflicted, her tone softened, and I saw tears well up in her eyes.

'Rhys,' she said through her tears. 'You have been a very naughty boy.'

At the time I thought she was weeping for my wickedness, although now I think it was for my injuries.

'I know that Robin is a soldier, and is used to hard discipline,' Mam said. 'But he should know the difference between beating a child and battling that awful Bonaparte.'

She shot a quick look at Bob. 'That said, a wooden leg is a wooden leg after all' she said. 'And he lost his fighting for our country.'

I saw that my scars had awakened my mother's sympathy but I wondered why she still made excuses for the Soldier. Now I think she wanted to emphasize that I merited my beating and hoped I would learn a lesson. Then she startled me.

'I think you have had enough of schooling, Rhys,' she said. I was overjoyed, as I had been going to school for nearly a whole year. 'It's high time that you did something useful.'

As Mam believed that too much learning spoiled a child and could lead to the gallows, I wasn't too surprised. Now she went on to justify her decision to Bob, who was not looking pleased.

'I never had a day's schooling myself, save at Sunday School,' she said, staring at Bob.

'And your Nain and Taid never had a penny spent on their education but they knew what was what,' she said. 'They found the Truth, they were blameless throughout their lives, they were respected by their neighbours and they died at peace.'

Mam had strong feelings, and always spoke her mind. She had an excellent memory. She would often emphasize her points by quoting a passage of Scripture, a verse of Vicar Pritchard's, or perhaps even something from the Bard of Nant. However, she always qualified anything the bard said with, 'It is a great pity that Twm o' Nant never found grace.'

She looked distracted and worried, and then she seemed to make up her mind.

'I have to go out,' she said. 'And while I am gone, Rhys, you should read the Proverbs of Solomon, where he says, my son, if sinners entice thee, consent thou not.'

She put on her cloak and bonnet and went out.

Bob watched to see which direction she walked.

'Rhys, Mam's going over to put the old Soldier through his drill,' he said. 'While she's gone tell me that story of the wooden leg again.'

I found it much easier to tell the story without my mother listening. I had hardly finished when she came back looking calmer but more serious and troubled. She took off her cloak and bonnet, sat down and wiped her eyes with her apron, and spoke in a serious voice.

'Bob,' said she, 'Apart from the trouble I have had with your father, this is the saddest day I have lived to see. I hoped for better from you. I hoped you would find salvation. I thought you would have been a support to me. I fancied that my good seed had prospered, but I see tares appearing. Our Old Enemy has done this.' Mam liked to use scriptural idioms and by the Old Enemy, she meant the Devil.

Bob was squatting, collier-fashion, by the fire. He was on his haunches leaning back against a support of the mantelshelf.

'Well, Mam, what's wrong now?' he said. 'Satan is always troubling you. From what you say, I might think that the old fellow never found time to bother anybody but us. Nothing ever happens to us without you seeing the devil's hand in it.'

He sighed and looked into the fire.

'For my part,' he said. 'I think it's about time he gave somebody else a turn. I have no great liking for his company, and I don't care if he hears me say so, either. But I can't see why our family merits so much attention from the Devil. He must neglect a good deal of his business with other people to plague us so much. For, clever as he may be, he's only finite.'

Mam looked shocked. She used her apron to slowly wipe a tear from her eye before she spoke.

'Bob,' she said. 'I'm sad you speak so lightly of such weighty matters. We're not without knowledge of the devices of he who goes about like a roaring lion seeking to devour us. What I have feared for so long has come about. I have told you repeatedly that reading newspapers would be your ruin. You fill your head constantly with tissues of lies instead of reading your Bible. When I was a girl, we never saw a newspaper. Only the folk at the Hall, and the uncircumcised, idle, pleasure-seeking, fox-hunting Saxons bought them. No one who set store on his soul ever thought of reading anything but the Bible. Now, everybody reads newspapers and English books. What's the result? We have a generation of people who don't hold the fear of God before their eyes. They are proud and ostentatious. They think more of finery than of salvation. They know little of the Death that brought life unto the world. Those are the fruits of reading newspapers I warn you Bob.'

'You're mistaken, Mam,' Bob said. 'Those are not the fruits of reading newspapers, but the fruits of a depraved heart. Remember what St Paul says, give attention to reading.'

'So he does, my son,' Mam said. 'But to reading what? Not to reading newspapers, but the Holy Scripture, so we might be wise unto salvation. The Apostle also says, whatsoever things are true, whatsoever things are honest, whatsoever things are just, whatsoever things are pure, whatsoever things are lovely, whatsoever things are of good report, if there be any virtue, and if there be any praise, meditate on these things.'

She looked him in the eye. 'How is it possible for you or anyone else to pay due attention to the Word of God if you have your nose everlastingly in a newspaper? Beware, my boy, beware.'

'The world goes on, Mam,' Bob said. 'It's no use thinking that things should remain as they were when you were a girl.'

'Goes on!' said mother, now raising her voice. 'Yes, fast enough, but whither, pray does it go? Does it go nearer heaven? I don't think so. Are the means of grace better known than they used to be? Is there more listening to the Gospel, and following the ministers of God's Word? Do you see the people in harvest time leave their labour in broad bright day to go and listen to the Word of God? They'd much rather go to a concert or an *eisteddfod* to stamp their feet and shout hooray. Or shout encore after some comic song when they should be going to hear a sermon and shouting Hallelujah, or Glory to God.'

Her face was stern as she went on. 'If that is what you call going on, then I'll settle for going back, Bob.'

'You talk of when the Gospel was new to Wales, so people naturally took a greater interest in it,' Bob said. 'Now we are long accustomed to the Truth, but there is no less real religion in the land.'

'New! What are you talking about, new?' said Mam letting her temper show. 'Is the Gospel not as new today as it ever was to those who feel its need? Will some new virtue in that Dear Death ever become known? The Gospel is glad tidings of great joy, and always will be. Goodness help us if at the end of a thousand ages, it is 'long accustomed' we are. I'm shocked to hear you speak like that – you, a lad who has read so much. The Gospel was never a new subject. Wales was acquainted with it time out of mind. But through reading the Word, the people got a new heart, new spirit, new relish for prayer to God and an outpouring of the Holy Ghost. Now people read the papers in place of their Bible, and have a greater taste for concerts and *eisteddfodau* than the means of grace. There is no room to expect a blessing and an increase in the ministry while things are such.'

'You must admit, Mam,' said Bob, 'That we have more chapels and opportunities for religious practice and more preachers of the Gospel now. There is are more opportunities to hear the Word. At the time you speak of, there were just a few poor folk connected with the Cause. The preachers were but plain men, ill-informed, and uneducated. Nowadays our most respectable people are religionists, and our ministers are men of refinement and culture.'

'What you say is true, Bob,' mother said. 'We should be thankful there is more chance to hear the Gospel, but is there more believing? I fear religion has become more a fashion than a way of life. Many come to chapel, not to seek our Saviour but to be seen by others. Our congregation is more like a flower-garden than a gathering to hear the Gospel.'

She was pleating her apron in her lap, as always did when agitated.

'It was poor folk who first joined The Cause,' she said. 'I have often heard your Nain say so. Nevertheless, look you, they were rich in grace, and heirs to the life eternal. How many of those spectacle-wearing, book-reading, people can you name who are noted for grace and piety? Are they a terror to the ungodly of the town? You don't see the drunks and the idle skulking off to their holes when a spectacled one comes in sight. They did before the God-fearing poor folk of old. These fine chapels are very convenient, I admit that. But there will be more rejoicing in heaven over a barn full of believers than over fine buildings full of spectacle-wearing, newspaper-reading sceptics.'

She stopped fiddling with her apron and stared at Bob. Her face was calm and composed.

'You upset me, Bob,' she said, 'when you spoke so slightingly of the old preachers. Like so many these days, you think ungenerously of God's servants of old. Plain and uneducated they might have been but they had the Holy Spirit. It will be better for you if you don't call them ignorant in my hearing. They knew the way to heaven, Bob, and they knew their Bible word for word. Tell me, where can you find their equal these days?'

'I didn't mean to distress you, Mam,' said Bob, 'or to disrespect the old preachers. They were pious, holy men but they wouldn't do for these days. Education has made such strides, and congregations are so much better informed than they were then.'

'Wouldn't do?' Mam said, raising her voice again. 'Wouldn't do for whom, do you think? They did for God then, and they ought to do for us now. Wouldn't do, indeed! Nothing would please me better than to see them get the chance. Were old Llecheiddior to visit us you'd see what a racket there would be. You know what? Those old preachers could set a congregation afire, spectacled folk and all, in the time it takes a whole wagon-load of students to fumble for their pocket handkerchiefs.'

'You've never liked students, or any sort of learning, Mam,' Bob said. 'But the best men we have are splendid scholars, and do all they can for education, particularly the schooling of preachers. What would become of us, but for our learned men, some of whom you yourself rate highly?'

'I'm not against learning. Bob. No, in the name of goodness,' Mam said. 'But it's not necessary to give a lot of education to poor children. It's not learning that makes a great preacher. If learning were all that mattered than Dick Aberdaron, would been the world's best preacher. But, goodness help him, what with his cats and his filth, his scholarship didn't help him. Education is well enough if sanctified by grace; otherwise it's just a curse, because it doesn't make you sensible or holy.'

'St Paul, your great friend was a great scholar,' Bob said. 'And he would never have done what he did unless he had been.'

'You can't prove that,' Mam said. 'Just because he sat at the feet of the teacher Gamaliel doesn't make him a scholar, let alone a great one. Don't think that because you understand politics, you know your Bible better than your mother does. It was that conversion on the road to Damascus, which made Paul great. Before that, he was nothing but a great persecutor, and we would never remember him for that. And I'll tell you another thing. Paul didn't value worldly knowledge. Had the people wanted to make him a Doctor or a Master of Arts, he'd have told them he was only interested in knowing Jesus Christ crucified. The title Paul, servant of the Lord, is a thousand times better than Doctor Saul of Tarsus.'

I could tell Mam was agitated, for she was again frantically pleating and unpleating her apron. She was trying to control her temper.

'Do you know what?' she said not quite managing to keep her anger out of her voice. 'I have no patience listening to you and your be-spectacled friends talk of education, education and more education as if it could make seas and mountains. Education is no substitute for the grace of God. Education teaches people not to respect their elders. The grace of God does nothing of the kind. I do know that.'

'I don't understand what you mean,' Bob said, not looking at her.

'You well know what I mean,' Mam said, her eyes glistening with tears and her voice bristling with anger. 'Was it reading newspapers and English books that educated you to assault an old man who lost a leg fighting for his country? I'm shocked that you, a boy who never had a day's schooling, should bring such disgrace upon the Cause and shame to your mother.'

Mam squared up to face Bob.

'Go at once, and ask the old man's pardon for shame on you.'

Bob looked back at her, and his face reddened.

'I'll never ask his pardon, never,' he said. More tears were welling in Mam's eyes and Bob looked at the floor.

'Even if I was a little hasty,' he said. 'I only did my duty, and if ever again I see that old Soldier or anyone else, even if he be as big as a house, beating Rhys as mercilessly as I saw him being beaten today, then I will defend him if it is in my power. I would not be his brother if I failed to do so.'

Mam seemed to shrink back at this expression of brotherly loyalty but she wasn't finished yet.

'You shouldn't let a depraved nature rule you, my son,' she said, her voice mournful. 'The Word says you should be not strike out in anger.'

'That is a verse for a bishop, not for a collier, Mam,' Bob said.

'Your heart is hard, Bob,' she said. 'These English books and newspapers have changed you. But I'm glad that I went to see Abel Hughes to tell him the story before anyone else did. I have asked him to speak to you at Chapel tomorrow night. If others wish to conceal their children's disobedience and wickedness, I do not. Pray for grace, my son.'

With that she buried her face in her apron and began to cry. This put an end to the controversy, as far as Bob was concerned.

Although it was still broad daylight, Mam sent me to bed to heal my wounds. I couldn't sleep so I fell to pondering over something mother had said to Bob. 'Apart from the trouble I have had with your father.' What could that mean?

CHAPTER 11

Wil Bryan on the Nature of a Church

Even though Mam made me stay in bed for a day and a night, I didn't feel much better when I got up. My body felt as if I'd been soaked in starch which had set hard while I slept. All my limbs were so stiff that every move hurt me. But, knowing I'd finished my schooling made the pain worthwhile.

Mam looked downcast, and sighed frequently. I was convinced that my wickedness was worrying her. I was troubled that I had brought her so low. She didn't say anything but she looked serious all the time. She didn't ever ask me how I felt. I guessed this was because she didn't want me to think my whipping was anything but richly deserved. I knew she wanted to know how I felt, but she wouldn't ask.

From being very young, I was quick to notice hints and signs, and I still have that talent. My mother would speak in parables if a neighbour called at our house. She'd say to her friend, 'little pigs have big ears'. She thought I couldn't tell what she meant, but I knew I was the little pig, and my long ears could follow what she said, although she hoped it would sound as confusing as Latin to me.

As she tended to my welfare while I lay in bed after the beating I noticed her furtively watching me if I tried to move. I could read her heart as if she carried it in her hand. I felt unworthy of all the care and love she gave me. I didn't know it then, but what weighed most heavily on her mind was the knowledge that the chapel was bound to discipline her sons.

Once I was out of bed, I saw Wil Bryan and Jack Beck hanging around the house trying to see me. While Mam was looking after a loaf in the oven, I sneaked out into the garden and had a long confidential chat with them.

They told me the whole town knew about our antics in the Church and the consequent events at school. Their parents had thrashed both Bryan and Beck, but they said their beatings were not in the same class as mine from the master. This made me think I had suffered so much I was a bit of a hero. Neither of my friends had been to school that day. Jack Beck had his father's permission to stay home until he had spoken to the master. Wil Bryan had no such permission. He was just keeping out of the soldier's way.

Two things I said had made a great impression on the boys. The first was that my mother had said that I had done with schooling. They stared at me enviously, as if they couldn't possibly comprehend how such happiness could befall any human creature.

'Rhys! I wouldn't complain if the old Warrior were to tie my hands behind my back, make me stand an hour on one leg, and then to break a new cane across my shoulders, if the gaffer there (meaning his father), would offer me the same,' Wil Bryan said.

Jack Beck agreed that it was a wonderful thing not to have to go to school anymore, but he was confused when I told him that Bob's case, my own, and Wil's would be brought before the *Seiat* that very night. Beck, being a Churchman, didn't understand about the *Seiat*, or what I meant when I said, 'it will be brought before the *Seiat*.'

Wil Bryan took it on himself to describe it to him. Wil had a special gift for defining anything that he fancied he understood. This is how he explained the nature and object of the *Seiat*.

'You see, Jack,' said Wil. 'The *Seiat* is where a lot of good folk, who think themselves bad, come together every Tuesday night, to find fault with themselves, and run each other down.'

'I don't understand you,' said Jack.

'Well,' said Wil, 'look at it in this way. You know old Mrs Peters, and Rhys's mother here, and it's not because Rhys is here that I say it, but anyone will tell you they're a couple of good, pious women. Well, they go to *Seiat*, and Abel Hughes asks what's on their minds. They reply that they are a very bad lot, guilty of I don't know how many things, Mrs Peters usually cries as she says it. Then Abel Hughes will tell them they're not as bad as they think. He'll give them some advice, repeat a lot of verses for them, and then move on to someone else. They will all carry on in the same way, and it goes the whole way around, until it gets to be half-past eight o'clock. Then we all go home.'

'There's nothing of that sort in our Church,' said Beck. 'We have no *Seiat*, and I never heard anyone run himself down.'

'That's the difference between Church and chapel,' said Wil. 'Church people think themselves good when they are bad, while chapel people think themselves bad when they are good.'

'You don't mean to tell me,' Beck protested, 'that all those who belong to *Seiat* are good people and that everyone who belongs to the church is bad?'

'All who take the Communion in chapel are good people,' Wil said. 'although they think themselves bad. And all who take the Communion in Church, think themselves good, while more than half of them are bad. There's the old Soldier. He takes Communion on Sunday morning, just to please Mr Brown, and every Sunday night he goes boozing in the Cross Foxes till he's too blind to see his way home. If he belonged to the chapel he'd be kicked out pretty sharp. But did you ever see anybody booted out of Church?

Jack kept quiet so Wil went on to explain what I meant by 'being brought before *Seiat*.'

'When anyone belonging to the *Seiat* does wrong, you see,' Wil said. 'Someone else goes to the elders and splits upon him. At the next *Seiat* Abel Hughes will call him to account. If he's poor, like William the Coal, Abel will make him come up to the bench before the Big Seat. But if it's a swell, like Mr Richards the Draper, Abel goes up to him.'

'And what does Abel do with him? Take him off to jail?' asked Jack.

'No way,' said Wil. 'Abel will ask what went on, and then invite one or two of the others to say a few words. If the sinner repents and, like William the Coal, lays the blame on Satan, and says he won't do again, they forgive him. But if he's stubborn, like Mr Richards the Draper, and won't say anything at all the *Seiat* will refuse him Communion for three months or more. If it's something really bad they'll chuck him right out of the *Seiat*.'

He grinned at Jack. 'There's not much harm in it, but it is a bit of a bother. I'd much rather not go to *Seiat* tonight, but I must, or there'll be a mighty row at home,' he said.

I may have been younger than Wil but I thought *Seiat* more important than this. Wil looked lightly upon everything, and that would one day prove to be his ruin. Jack Beck's final comments made a great impression upon me.

'Well boys,' he said. 'I like the way of the Church better than the way of the chapel. All who belong to Church can do just as they like, without anyone to call them to account. Each minds his own business, which is the best way, I think.'

Wil Bryan was usually a zealous advocate of chapel, but this time he agreed with Jack. 'That's how it is, Jack. It's more comfortable in the Church, but safer in the chapel.'

I had never heard anyone discuss church government before and this conversation left a deep impression on me. It impressed me more than many a debate I heard later between persons of greater importance and assertiveness. However, I couldn't look on church discipline in the way Wil Bryan did. I was scared of going to *Seiat* that night.

Evening came and seeing Bob getting ready to go, Mam didn't think she needed to speak to him about the matter. However, as she and I got ready to go to the chapel, she turned and said to my brother. 'Bob, don't be stiff tonight, I beg of you.'

Bob said nothing, so we went on our way.

As I think of that *Seiat*, I remember all the old characters, who have, by this time, to use Mrs Tibbet's phrase, gone to their reckoning.

There was Abel Hughes, of whom I have already said something. He was a God-fearing man, firm in his faith, and strong-minded. His one fault was his severity.

There was harmless Hugh Bellis, a gentle, tender-hearted man, who always wept during the sermon. He was eager to offer forgiveness to all, no matter what sin they committed. Hugh was an exceedingly pious man.

There was Edward Peters, precise, and careful about the books, but crabbed, and unpopular with the children. He wouldn't allow them to leave in the middle of the service. He never spoke a word in public, unless it was about the collections and the seat-money. He was a good man at bottom, and he had the confidence of the congregation.

There was the preacher Thomas Bowen. He was lively, zealous, impulsive, constantly making mistakes and apologizing for them.

There was Mr Richards the Draper. He was a proud, showy man. He was always pushing to the front, but everybody would have preferred to keep him back.

There was William the Coal. He was a poor man, small of body and of mind. He was soft and easily persuaded. He got his name, William the Coal, because some or other member of his family had for time out of mind, sold coal by the penn'orth. Every summer, when work was slack, William was a regular at the *Seiat*. Then, when winter came, and trade picked up, he would take to drinking over-much, and in consequence, be excommunicated. The elders of the *Seiat* forgave him many a transgression because he was not quite like other people.

Mam would say, 'William has the root of the matter in him, but the trunk and branches are too weak to withstand the cross-wind.' I held the same opinion of William because every time he prayed he, would shed tears. To my boyish mind, everyone who wept while praying was only doing it for show.

There was John Llwyd, too. He was an unpleasant man: tall, thin, sharp-featured, coarse-skinned and fidgety. He was always finding fault with something or somebody. Wil Bryan called him the Old Scraper.

He was a shocking miser, which saved him from chapel censure. His love of money stopped him from getting drunk, or frequenting forbidden places. He set a rigid face against tea meetings, concerts, and every gathering to which a coin with either the King or Queen's head was a passport. He was great on economy, and the need to make provision for the future. His concern for spirituality in religion was tremendous, and he complained there was too much asking for money for preach-ing. Mam tried to believe that he, too, had the root of the matter, but she feared that root was worm-eaten somewhere, because his leaves were soured.

There is also Seth. Seth was a simple lad whose friendship marked an epoch in my life. There were many others but they do not figure in my story so I will not dwell on them.

The *Seiat* was packed that night. When someone is to be disciplined, the town turns out to watch. It is something of a similar nature that prompts those who go and see a man being hanged.

Wil Bryan and I sat next to each other in the midst of the children. I was surprised to see him so unconcerned. Thomas Bowen began the meeting, and I listened carefully for any reference to myself. He made none.

Whilst Thomas was praying, Wil whispered in my ear, 'If they ask us anything, say like William the Coal, that we'll never do it again, and they're sure to forgive us.'

Wil said a great many other things, but I was much too worried to heed what he said. Abel Hughes listened to the verse-recitals of the children. When it came to Wil's and my turn he ignored us, evidently the storm had begun. I held my head down for I knew that everyone was looking at me. I felt their eyes burning right through my velvet jacket so I looked at the floor. Glancing sideways I saw Wil held his head high. He looked quite unabashed.

Once Abel had finished hearing the children's verses, Thomas Bowen said a few words and then invited Hugh Bellis to speak. Hugh made some comments about last Sunday's sermons, pointedly explaining that he had received a great blessing from listening to them. He seemed to be struggling to find things to say. When he finished Thomas Bowen asked if anyone else had anything to say about the sermons. Nobody did. After a long silence Edward Peters stood up to remind everyone that next quarter's seat money was due to be paid and he would be happy to receive any money the brethren wished to pay that evening. An even longer silence followed his statement. After what seemed like hours of nobody saying anything Abel Hughes whispered to Thomas Bowen. 'You do it, Thomas.'

'No, you do it, Abel,' Thomas said.

Abel seated his velvet cap firmly on his head and got to his feet. He looked serious and agitated. I wish I could remember exactly what that true and honest man said but I cannot. I was too frightened of what was about to happen to me to listen carefully. I vaguely remember him saying something about unpleasant circumstances, and children of the *Seiat* behaving like the children of the world, of scandal brought upon the cause of religion, of the necessity of enforcing church discipline. He spoke for a long time and then in a serve tone of voice named Bob, Wil Bryan, and me as the offenders. With that, he sat down.

John Llwyd immediately jumped to his feet and said. 'Will the officers of the chapel please explain to the members what exactly the nature of the transgression was?'

'Hark at the old scraper,' said Wil in my ear.

'John Llwyd,' Abel said. 'You well know the nature of the offences, as does everyone else present and I see no need repeat the circumstances.'

Thomas Bowen stood up. 'My brethren, children will be children,' he said. 'And we should all remember that we were once children ourselves. I am very sorry for this business. Abel Hughes has done quite right in calling attention to it, but what can we do except give these poor lads a word of advice? I am not speaking of Robert Lewis now for he is of age and sense. But William Bryan and Rhys Lewis are young and unreflective. They are usually well-behaved, decent lads.'

He looked at us. 'Who recites his verses better than William or Rhys? It is a great pity the boys have done wrong. Have you anything to say William, my son?' he said.

'I'll never do it again,' Wil said.

'Good boy,' said Thomas. 'Are you sorry for what you did?'

'Yes,' said Wil, 'very sorry.' At the same time, he gave me a hard pinch in the leg, which made me cry.

'And what do you say Rhys?' asked Thomas. I burst into tears when Wil pinched me, so couldn't reply.

'We have no need to ask Rhys anything,' Thomas said. 'We can see his face is bathed in tears already.'

He turned to Abel.

'Abel Hughes, do you hear what the boys say? They are sorry and they'll never do it again,' he said. 'Could we ourselves do better than repent our fault, and resolve not to commit another? What are we to do with the boys?'

'Do what you like with them,' said Abel, his voice sounding harsh.

'Well, brethren,' said Thomas, 'We cannot do better with these boys than give them a word of advice and send them away, as we have another and weightier matter to attend to.'

Thomas Bowen gave us that kindly word of advice, told us to behave well in future and go home like good children. No sooner had he spoken than all the youngsters rushed out as fast as they could. I had just passed the doorway when Wil Bryan caught me by the arm, and turned me down the side of the chapel. I was annoyed with him.

'Why did you pinch me so hard in the chapel?' I said.

'To make you cry, you silly,' he said. 'I knew you hadn't a word to say for yourself, so crying did the job. Didn't I tell you they'd let us off? But we must find out what they are going to do with Bob.'

Down the side of the chapel, a door gave access to the steps that led to the gallery. Margaret from the chapel-house, who cleaned the place, used it to open and shut the building. It was unlocked that night and Wil pushed me inside. I was not happy about what he meant to do, but I felt I had to follow him, for he had an influence over me that I have never been able to resist.

We crept inside. In the darkness Wil whispered, 'Take off your clogs, and put them there on that side. I'll place mine here, so that we shan't make any mistake when we come down.' I did as I was told.

'Now up we go as quiet as mice,' Wil said.

Wil led the way up. We crept on all fours, until we reached the clock seat. There we could hear them discussing Bob's case. So deep are those words burned into my memory, I could repeat the pleadings word for word. But what purpose would it serve? That occasion is too painful for me to dwell on.

John Llwyd used cruel words as sharp as sword thrusts. I was furious. Whatever Bob's actions, I knew he was a hundred thousand times a better man than John Llwyd. Bob may have been wrong to set upon the old Soldier, but he did it to stop a greater wrong to me. Bob would sacrifice his life, for any one he saw being wronged, and I was his own brother. How could he not help me in my distress?

John Llwyd loved only money and had a heart no bigger than a spider's. Yet this man slavered his dirtiest insults over Bob. I have never forgiven him. His abusive words made Bob stiff-necked. My brother would have borne a sharp, stern reproof from Abel Hughes. A loving expostulation from Thomas Bowen would have soothed his wounded heart. However, the poison darts of this narrow-minded hypocrite made him obstinate.

'Will you repent of your evil ways before this *Seiat*?' John Llwyd demanded.

'I have nothing to repent,' Bob said before all the *Seiat*. We sat in the clock seat and waited to see what would happen next.

I was annoyed with Wil Bryan for his behaviour while the *Seiat* argued Bob's case. He was cutting his name on the seat with his pocketknife. Occasionally he paused to pass remarks about the various speakers. He spoke so loudly that I found myself begging him to be quiet, for fear we were heard. I couldn't help crying, I felt so bad for Bob.

'Have you got the toothache?' Wil said in a sarcastic tone of voice.

I formed impressions of several people in that *Seiat*, which I have retained all my life, as I sat in the clock seat. By now, I could see what the end of the business was going to be and I was worried what a dreadful blow it would be to my mother. She would never have dreamt that Bob might be excommunicated. But that sentence was inevitable, once Bob said he would do the same thing again under similar circumstances.

Wil Bryan, who was still carving his name on the seat, had to comment.

'Your Bob's not got it,' he said. 'If he'd only do like William the Coal, and put the blame on Satan and say he'll never do it again, it would be all right. But if he keeps on like this he's sure to get booted out.'

For all his light-headedness, Wil proved himself a true prophet. Thomas Bowen did his best to get Bob to admit that he had been to blame, but he couldn't. Abel Hughes also tried and failed.

The officers of the church were bound to do their duty. Abel Hughes got up to take the vote of excommunication. The old man's voice trembled, and the words stuck in his throat as he did so. The congregation gave a vote of assent, and Bob ceased to be a member of the Calvinistic Methodists.

Abel sank to his knees, and prayed for Bob to repent and return to the Cause, as strongly as any man ever prayed in his life. Bob turned on his heel and walked out.

I have wondered hundreds of times why Abel's supplication on Bob's behalf wasn't answered. Would the Church have excommunicated Bob had it known the consequences of the act? I like to think it wouldn't.

CHAPTER 12

Discussions by the Hearth

As I am being truthful, I must say that I am not blessed with many natural talents. However, I'm thankful I have a good memory. I don't think I would have even started this private autobiography if hadn't recognized the great pleasure I find in writing. As I review the events of my life, I find my family and relatives come alive in my mind. When I look over old letters, every word has unwritten associations. Some letters make me think of those who are now ashes, but who cannot be burnt out of my memory. Some I read with a sense of satisfaction whilst others recall painful events. Some stir up my whole nature and awaken feelings and ideas I had thought lost forever. The act of writing allows my much-loved dead to return from the caverns of my mind and the crannies of my memory to live again on the page.

The night of Bob's excommunication was one of the darkest nights of my life, but even this sad incident had a bright side. It made me think seriously about the nature of religion. What is it that constitutes the sacredness of church membership and makes it important? Mam had taught me that there was a great difference between religious people and people of the world. But as a child I understood this to mean that religious folk partook of the Lord's Supper once a month and didn't get drunk, or curse and swear. People of the world didn't belong to the Communion and could commit any sin they fancied.

The night Bob was expelled from the *Seiat* I began to question this view. I needed to understand why Bob, who I knew to be a good man, was forced out by the religious group our mother loved so dearly. I couldn't imagine that he would now take to drink, or that he'd curse and swear all the time. And I didn't expect him to stop reading the Bible and other good books, or kick up rows in the house like Peter the potman. Also I couldn't believe that Bob, now he was out of Communion, was a worse man than John Llwyd who remained in it. This was impossible. If being excommunicated didn't change Bob, what made a man religious?

I formed a high opinion of my mother's piety on that sad night. I have tried to reproduce the conversation she had with Bob when they both returned home, as accurately as I can recall.

Mam didn't know I'd heard the whole discussion of Bob's case, and it wouldn't have gone well with me if she'd found out that Wil Bryan and I had spied on the proceedings from the chapel-loft.

When we all went out to chapel, the last to leave the house would hide the door key under the water-tub. The first back could then get into the house. This was our family secret. As I was supposed to be first home I hurried along and just managed to get seated by the fire a couple of minutes before Mam came in. I was out of breath but pretended that I'd been waiting for some time.

'You've been a long time, tonight.' I said.

'Every wait is a long one,' she said, not mentioning Bob. She hung her blue cloak and great bonnet on the nail behind the door.

Bob was a while after her coming home. Mam had his supper waiting long before he appeared. He looked sad and dispirited. He sat by the fire without a word and took up a book to read. He told me later that he'd been talking to his friends after leaving the *Seiat*.

Mam had to coax him a lot before he'd come to the table. Neither he nor Mam seemed in the mood to eat, but I was relieved after my disciplining by the chapel and was hungry. It would have been a shame to let good food go to waste so I did my best to stuff as much down as I could.

When supper was over Bob took up his book again, and Mam drew her chair nearer the fire. I could see from her manner that she wanted to discuss something with Bob. When she was gathering her thoughts together, she had a habit of pleating her apron.

'Well, my son,' she said at last. 'This has been rather a bad night in our history. Poor as I am, I would give a hundred pounds if I could change what has taken place.'

'I don't see why you should look at it in that light. Mam,' Bob said. 'It won't make any difference to how I behave. Being a member of chapel doesn't guarantee a man's salvation, nor being cast out of it ensure his perdition.'

'Rhys,' said Mam, turning to me, 'You should go to bed.'

'I'll go just now,' I said and laid my head on the table. I pretended to drop off to asleep. I even gave a little snore. I was a sly young fox. They both thought me asleep and ignored me.

'Bob,' Mam said. 'I hope you didn't mean what you just said. You've been saying so many things since you've taken to coddling those old English books. I can't believe that's what you really think.'

I heard Bob put his book down. I didn't dare look up as I was supposed to be fast asleep.

'Mam,' Bob said. 'You know well there's no deceit in me, and I hate hypocrisy. I'd rather be expelled from the chapel for telling the truth, than stay in and be mealy-mouthed. I won't say things I neither believe nor feel. I know my excommunication is a sad blow to you, Mam. I'm sorry for that for that, but the chapel has chosen and I have accepted their verdict.'

'Do you set no value on your chapel membership, my son?' Mam said.

'Not if I have to buy that membership by double-dealing,' Bob said. 'I never complain, but you well know that neither my father nor you ever thought of giving me a day's schooling. You let me grow up ignorant of everything except the Bible. You sent me down the mine when I should have gone to school. I was an experienced collier before I was sixteen. I have had to educate myself. I have used all my spare time and what little energy I have left after work, to learn English. And I've had no help from any living soul. All you have done is complain that I waste the candles. I've been as faithful in attending chapel as any other lad of my age. I was a teacher in the Sunday School when I was seventeen. I'm not praising myself, but since that bother with my father, I've worked hard and done my best to keep a home for you and Rhys. What little I have to spare is used to buy books or subscribe to the chapel.'

Bob took a deep breath and paused for a moment. Mam stayed silent. Eventually Bob regained control of his emotions and continued.

'I've tried for years to pass on to my brother any knowledge I possess, so he might become something better than the poor collier I am,' he said. 'Then, when I saw Rhys oppressed and beaten unmercifully, I did what anyone with a grain of humanity would have done. I faced down the oppressor and rescued the oppressed. Like David when he was charged with guarding King Saul's sheep, I rescued a lamb from the lion's jaws.'

Bob's face was tense and his voice harsh with suppressed anger as he went on. 'But the *Seiat* decided this act of brotherly love is a great sin. Some of the members must be very happy that they have got rid of such a depraved creature as me.'

Mam looked annoyed. 'You have a tone of self-righteousness,' she said. 'You remind me of the Pharisee who began the prayer meeting in the temple of old. You have his tinkle down to a tee. And you're brought home that publican ring to your voice that you used in the *Seiat*.' She sighed and her face took on a look of sadness.

'What's come over you, Bob?' she said. 'You've become so stiff-backed lately. Pray for grace, my son. Pray to feel the rope, and see your filthy rags. If you are brought before your betters at the Quarter Sessions, it would be alright to talk of your virtues. But in the *Seiat*, before the Great Judge, the less you say of them the better. Use only the names that St Paul used for them, dung and loss. I've thought for some time notions were forming in your heart that you never found in the Bible. It has cost me many a sleepless night.'

'Mam, you know me better than anyone,' said Bob his hurt showing in his voice. 'But I must be extremely bad if my own mother holds such a poor opinion of me. If there is no doubt that I'm the biggest scoundrel in the neighbourhood, well, be it so.'

'No, not so, my son,' Mam said quickly. 'As a good son to his mother there is none better in the six counties. I'm thankful to you and the Good Lord for your kindness in working so hard to keep a home for me and your brother. But I speak of your soul. It doesn't matter whether or not I have a crust. But, my darling boy, it matters that your soul and mine should be under the dispensation of the Spirit of God. Blessed be His name. He gives me no rest, and I believe He means to make something of me. My only hope is that He will speak to you also.'

Mother was breathing hard with the strength of her feelings, and she stopped to take a deep breath before continuing.

'It breaks my heart, my poor boy to see you so little affected by your excommunication. You have been cast out among the dogs, the tempest and the storm. You have been ejected from the circle of the covenant and the intercession. You are without shelter, my dear son,' she said.

'It was the *Seiat* that decided I should be put out,' Bob said. 'The chapel repudiated me, not I the chapel.'

'No, my son,' Mam said, her voice taking on a stern tone. 'It was entirely your own doing, and you should be ashamed. You refused to repent and admit your sin. That's why the *Seiat* expelled you. Think back, how often did Thomas Bowen beg you own up to your fault and ask forgiveness?' She sighed a deep and bitter sigh.

'Your excommunication was painful for the *Seiat*,' she said. 'But what else can you expect if you will not repent? How can you expect God or man to forgive you if you do not repent?'

'I can't accept the opinions of old-fashioned people, when I do not agree with them,' Bob said. 'When I spoke of the matter to the Reverend Brown he laughed at it. He said he hoped I'd given the old soldier a good licking, as it would do him good.'

'Bob,' Mam said, her voice deeply angry, 'Don't call the great doctrines of the Gospel old-fashioned, in front of me.'

'I didn't do any such thing.'

'It sounded very much like it to me, Bob.' Mam said. 'Repentance is a fashion you'll have to fall in with, or you'll never enter Heaven. It's a fashion that's made thousands the conquerors of eternity. I'll tell you when it will become an old fashion. It will be when the summer has ended, and the harvest of the souls has been and gone. Then the sinners will turn to the old fashion, when it's too late. Pray, my son, you are not one of them. As to the Reverend Brown, I don't think much of him. He's nice one to guide our youth. If I wanted something for my soul's good, I'd not go to him. I'd have to go and look for him out in the fields, rabbit shooting. Mr Brown is a good neighbour, but remember what Twm o' Nant, said of him and his sort. Although Thomas was not all that he should be, he still hit it off at times fairly well.

She then quoted from memory this verse by the bard Twm o' Nant:

> Praised and reverenced, worthily, o'er all men the priest we see.
> But none is more accursed than he, if God-guided he not be.

'And,' Mam went on, 'If only that Mr Brown had half the spirit of the old Vicar of Llandovery. This is what the Vicar would have said to you, if I remember rightly.' Then she quoted from the Rev. Rhys Prichard's book *The Light of a Welshman's Candle*:

> Sinner repent, while you may. Do not harden with delay,
> Lest thy heart should hardened be. Here and now, I repent for thee.
> To the faithful and repentant, God is gracious, fair and constant;
> To the stubborn and perverse, God is cruel and God is fierce.

Bob sat quietly and listened to mother reciting. 'Your conscience knows whether Mr Brown or the old Vicar is right,' she finished

'I respect your words and those of the old Vicar,' Bob said. 'But I don't believe that God is cruel and fierce at any time. And I do not think he will make me burn in Hell for what I did to the old Soldier. My Bible tells me that God is Love.'

'What?' Mam said, clearly agitated by Bob's reasoning. 'You're not going to contradict the good old Vicar, who knew his Bible a thousand times better than you do hundreds of years before you were born? You're right to say God is Love. But for His Grace and Love none of us would be allowed to enter life. Let me tell you what I heard Mr Elias, blessed be his memory, say on the green at Bala. He said what I feel so much better than I can say it.'

Once again mother recited the words of John Elias, who was a member of the Bala Association of the Presbyterian Church of Wales:

> The love we see today. All other love outweigh.

'If you had but heard him tell of God's justice and wrath towards the wicked, it would have made your hair stand on end,' Mam said. 'If you are going to think notions of that kind, Bob, I'd as soon have John Wesley as you, every bit. Listen my son, the Old Vicar is quite right. God is always displeased by the ungodly, and that you know, better than I can tell you.'

Now it was Bob's turn to sigh. 'I haven't the spirit nor the desire to discuss this Mam,' he said.

'More's the pity,' she said. 'It's too much spirit you have as a rule. I'd hoped that it was a just a fit of obstinacy that came over you in the *Seiat*, and that your heart would be better than your tongue after all. But now I see I'm mistaken.' I could hear her pleating her apron, a sure sign she was upset.

'Now I see I'm to blame for not remonstrating with you about your condition. I can only pray, my son, that God's Spirit will return to your soul.' She sighed. 'There is greater need now, than at any time I can think of, for a revival of religion that will quell the false pride of the people and return them to their religious duty.'

'When God comes,' said Bob, 'He will have much more to do than that. He will have a great heap of miserliness and niggardliness to clean out of the churches. He will have to rout out the hypocrisy, narrow-mindedness and want of Christian charity which pass as sanctity, exactitude and zeal for church discipline. We saw plenty of that tonight. But when that day arrives we will see that some of those folk who clamoured loudest for my expulsion, will be cankered and rotten with worldliness and filthy lucre. They sell Jesus Christ for thirty pieces of silver every day they get out of bed. When that Great Visitation comes I will expect to find myself amongst a numerous company which I shall be ashamed to recognize.'

'You forget one thing,' said Mam. 'On that day everybody will have to face their own heart-plague. They will not have any spare to time to pick out the motes in other people's eyes, and indulge in their own self-justification. Did St Peter think of pointing to Judas's betrayal as a reason why he should not repent for his denial? No, he wept bitterly for his own faults.'

Mam stood up and faced Bob, who was still hunkered down, collier fashion, by the fireside. 'I would like to see a little of the same spirit in you, my son,' she said. Then she began to cry. This put an end on Bob's part to any desire to argue.

Now she had given full vent to her feelings, my mother caught me by the collar and shook me sharply. She didn't know I had been wide awake the whole time, and I am glad she never found out. She sent me up to bed, where I lay and mused over what I had heard, especially what they had said about my father.

Mam's pleadings didn't have much effect on Bob. Afterwards he seldom spoke about religious matters, and didn't mention the chapel. He did, however, continue to attend. In the house he kept quiet, almost always reading, to avoid arguing with Mam. But he didn't stop passing on his knowledge to me. How I wish I had nothing more unpleasant to write about him.

CHAPTER 13

Seth

I want to write something about Seth. He was a simple boy, whose friendship marked an epoch in my story, and a remarkable character I seem to have known all my life. I have milked my memory without success for any image of Seth looking any different from when I first met him.

If you asked me when I first saw the crab-apple tree near our house, and if I could describe to you the changes in the form of its branches, I wouldn't know. I remember when the owner of the Hall ordered it cut down. I can still see the hard-hearted woodman taking his axe to its roots and making the chips fly as the tree came tumbling down. That was when I lost a dear old friend that had often fed me crab-apples. They may have set my teeth on edge, but any eating was sweet when I had nothing else. This is all I remember of the size and history of that crab-apple tree up to the day the woodman cut it down.

My memory of Seth is much the same.

I think of Seth as a fresh-complexioned youth, inclined to be tall, thin and bony, with a slight stoop of the shoulders. He had a bit of a chin that lost itself in his jowls and a mouth always half open. His eyes were small, blue and empty except for a merry twinkle. He had an irregular nose and a forehead that retreated into his crown, which was high, narrow, and jutted out over the long nape of his neck.

His parents were simple, harmless folk who lived in a trim little cottage a little out of the town. His father Thomas Bartley was a cobbler by trade. He repaired footwear, but did not make it. In my mother's opinion Thomas and his wife, Barbara were not among the knowledgeable folk. They didn't know a single letter of the alphabet between them, and the only time they went to church or chapel was at harvest thanksgiving.

Thomas Bartley claimed that in his younger days he'd attended Sunday School regularly for four or five years. 'If I'd stuck at it a few years longer,' he would say, 'I would have mastered the ABC.'

He boasted that he had been to listen to John Elias, William Williams of Wern and Christmas Evans, the three giants of the Welsh pulpit, several times. However, if I asked him what sort of preachers they were, he would only say. 'Save us. They were rough 'uns, awful rough.'

Thomas and Barbara Bartley were two old fogies, but they were wondrously innocent and happy. If Thomas indulged in any sin it was a tendency to take God's name in vain. But this was from simplicity, not from lack of reverence. He wouldn't work on the Sabbath and would have felt guilty had he done so. But he saw no harm in spending Sunday with his pipe in mouth, watching the pig feed. He would laboriously calculate how long before it would be ready for the knife, what it would weigh, how much black puddings and brawn it would yield, whether it would make much offal to sell, to which of his neighbours he was obliged to send a bit of spare rib, and so forth. Thomas saw no harm when Barbara and he spent the Sabbath talking of such worldly things. But he wouldn't think of putting on his leather cobbling apron that day.

My brother Bob used to take his boots for Thomas Bartley to mend. He liked to draw the old man out, and I've heard him laugh till he cried as he told Mam about the queer notions he heard during these visits. Mam suffered from rheumatism. She had a bad attack once, just as Bob came back from visiting Thomas. Bob told the old shoemaker's latest story, and Mam couldn't hide a smile as he mimicked old Bartley's way of speaking.

This is the conversation Bob repeated to her.

'How's your mother, Bob?' said Thomas.

'Very bad, Thomas Bartley,' Bob said. 'She suffers much from the rheumatism, you know. She gets little sleep with the pain.'

'Save us. Save us.' said Thomas. 'D'ye know, Bob, I don't und'stand that Great Lord, look you. Don't und'stand Him, at all. A woman like your mother, who never did anything in the world agenst Him, to be plagued like that always, always. Don't und'stand Him, 'deed I don't.'

'You think too highly of my mother, Thomas Bartley,' Bob said. 'She finds fault with herself often, and fears every day she won't be saved at the end.'

'Not saved at the end. What's wrong with the woman? I never in my life heard anything bad of her, did you, Barbara? '

'Not I, in the name of goodness,' said Barbara.

'Of course not,' said Thomas, 'and nobody else, either. But look here. Bob, you're a scholar, and Barbara and I have often thought of asking you, only we always forget. Doesn't the Good Book say there'll be a lot saved at the last?'

'It speaks of a great multitude of the saved, which no man can number,' said Bob.

'To be shuar. Didn't I tell you, Barbara? The talk these ignorant people make. It's my belief, look you, Bob, if we are honest and pay our way and live somewhere near the mark, we shall all be saved.'

Then as his practical business sense took over from his vague theological concerns, he looked down at the shoes. 'Do you want soles as well as heels for these?' he said. 'They're beginning to go, you know. Better have them vamped now.'

Bob told many similar tales of Thomas's simple common sense, but it's Seth I want to discuss.

I have often heard of people who have been unfortunate enough to come into the world lacking sense but have some cunning beyond other people in compensation. Seth had none of this.

He was perfectly harmless and had a heart of wondrous love and tenderness. Whatever he was asked to do, he would if he could. What little he had, he'd share with others. His heart was always in the right place, but his poor head never was. He was a child in the body of a man. Whatever he might have thought, he couldn't express it. So he rarely spoke.

Everybody in the town and the surrounding countryside knew Seth. They accepted him and his affliction. So did every dog in town and country. They wagged their tails when they saw him coming, and he would pat their heads, and fuss them in greeting. He seemed happier wandering about than staying at home with his father and mother, and spent most of his time walking around, rain or shine, day or night. Perhaps Seth did have a special gift. He knew the name of every dog, horse and domestic animal in the district.

If I got up early, I would see him. If I happened to be out late, then I would bump into Seth. If I went to anything that was going on in town, I would see Seth. If a house or a haystack caught fire, there he'd be, trying to help with the buckets. He attended every preaching meeting, concert and lecture, but no one ever asked him to pay. They all made him freely welcome.

Seth came to every service at our chapel. He would listen intently to the sermon, but nobody thought he understood a word. I remember watching his face while the minister was speaking and sometimes seeing a gleam of sensible enjoyment steal across it. The look was brief and afterwards his face was as vacant and expressionless as ever. Nevertheless, in these fleeting moments he showed enough awareness to attract my attention.

Sometimes I would ask him what he remembered of the sermon.

'It was about Jesus Christ,' he would say. He only ever remembered Jesus Christ and no other details.

Seth held all preachers in high regard, and nothing gave him greater pleasure than to hold a preacher's horse, or show him the way to the chapel. Seth told all the children about his helpful actions with a prodigious passion. He may have had the body of a man, but his mind never grew beyond that of a child.

Seth came to the Children's *Seiat*, every week. He loved to stand in line with all the other children to recite a verse. However, he only ever knew one verse and that was 'Jesus Christ the same yesterday and today, and forever.'

We all wondered where he learned that verse but none of us, neither I, my Mam nor any of the deacons, ever found out. It seemed as if the words just grew within him and filled his mind, leaving no space for any others.

Once Abel Hughes passed him over and didn't bother to ask Seth to recite his only verse. Seth immediately broke down in tears and couldn't be comforted. As we children were all fond of him, we joined in his crying.

I have never seen Abel in such a sticky situation. He was normally determined and self-possessed but that evening he struggled to speak and pulled many strange faces. Desperately he tried to comfort Seth but failed. Seth and we children wailed on.

Abel felt so bad about what he had so thoughtlessly done that the following day, he presented Seth with a hymn book. He did this to make up for the hurt he knew he had done Seth. This worked. From that day on Seth wouldn't let go of his hymn book. He carried it to every service, opened it during the singing, and usually held it upside down.

Seth must have noticed that if someone hadn't caught the number of the hymn then their neighbours would show them their page. He would copy this and if anyone showed the slightest sign of hesitation, he would go to them and show his inverted open book, as if he knew the place. Nobody minded that he never did.

Sometimes Seth would behave oddly in chapel. The congregation were used to him and didn't bother, but it must have been disturbing for a strange preacher. He would stand up suddenly, put his foot on the bench, rest his right elbow upon his knee, place his chin in hand, and stare intently into the preacher's eyes. He'd noticed Wil Bryan, and me take notes during the sermon, and he copied us. Someone gave him a large square of paper and a stick of pencil. Seth would take the paper in his right hand and the pencil in his left and look anxious while he waited for the preacher to give out the text for the sermon. Then he'd scribble on his sheet the strangest shapes ever seen. When he got fed up he'd go back to staring intently into the preacher's eyes. As I write about this and remember that he always sat exactly opposite the minister, I'm surprised how well our visiting preachers managed to cope with him.

Seth enjoyed the ritual of worship. Margaret, the caretaker who lived in the chapel-house, said that she often found him waiting for her to open the door. Once inside he'd go to the Big Seat, take up the Bible, and mumble with a low peculiar sound.

'It was as if he was reading real words, but they were just noises.' she said. 'And then he'd go down upon his knees, and say prayers all of a gabble. He'd make up words that didn't make sense. But if anyone else came in, he'd stop and sit down quietly.'

Seth and I were great friends. If I'd been naughty and Mam stopped me going out to play, Seth would hang about outside. He'd wait for hours for me to be set free. I don't know why he took to me so strongly, but he'd always protect me if any of the others picked on me. I'm ashamed, now that I know how delicate his health was, how often I let him carry me on his back. He carried me scores of miles and never complained.

Sometimes folk would give him a penny or halfpenny. When they did, he'd consult me as to what to do with it. My advice inevitably was to spend it. However, I must move on. I have more important things to write about my friend Seth.

One day I noticed that Seth was coughing badly. He didn't want to play out but he didn't complain. I should have realized that Seth never complained. For the next two days, he didn't leave the house. This was unusual so I went round to see what was wrong with him.

'He's taken to his bed,' his mother Barbara said. 'Go you up the stairs and see him.'

I went into his room and he looked up in surprise. He seemed confused, and then he recognized me. His face broke into a smile.

'Rhys,' he said, and held out his hand to me.

All went well for the first few minutes but then his mind seemed to drift away. He called me strange names. He talked incessantly, but I couldn't understand the words he made up. When his mother came in and tried to calm him, he didn't respond but gabbled on. Then he sat bolt upright in his bed, and pointed to the corner of the room. He seemed to be seeing someone. We looked but there was nothing there. The expression on his face frightened me. I felt so sorry for him. Barbara nudged me to go, and I slipped away down the stairs quietly.

In the kitchen Thomas Bartley was pacing back and forth. He was clearly upset. 'Did Seth recognize you Rhys?' he said.

'He did,' I said.

'The doctor says he's got the fever, Rhys,' he said. Then he started to wail. 'Save us, save us. Ask your mother to pray for him my lad. Save us. What if I should lose him?'

Had Seth been the greatest genius in the world, his parents could not have been more concerned about him. I visited him daily, sometimes twice a day, but he didn't get any better. Only Wil Bryan and I were allowed up to his room to visit. He seldom recognized us.

On the ninth day of his illness, Wil Bryan came to our house late at night. 'Seth has taken a bad turn,' he said. 'He's calling out for you Rhys.'

It was nearly bedtime but Mam gave me permission to go with Wil and see him. As we walked towards Seth's house Wil said. 'I don't think Seth's long for this world, Rhys. I think he's going to clear out.'

Wil was perfectly serious but when we reached the house Thomas Bartley gave us a cheerful greeting.

'Seth's much better,' he said.

My heart leapt with joy when I heard this. Wil and I went softly up the stairs. Old Barbara and a woman neighbour were sitting by the bedside. They looked secretly pleased. 'He's been asking for you for some time,' the neighbour said.

Seth lay perfectly still. There was a look of strange beauty on his face. He gave us a smile. If I'd not known him well I would have said that he looked normally intelligent. He seemed so unlike his ordinary self that Wil and I didn't know what to say.

Perhaps I should make clear at this point in the tale that Seth always spoke of himself in the third person. For example, if he was going somewhere, he wouldn't say 'I am going,' but rather, 'Seth is going.' He'd always speak of himself as if he were someone else. Wil and I were in the habit of answering him in the same style.

Seth held out his thin white hand to us.

'Hello Rhys, hello Wil,' he said.

'Seth wants to speak to Rhys and Wil alone,' he said looking at his mother and the neighbour. They went down into the kitchen at once leaving us with him.

When we had the bedroom to ourselves, I bent over him and said, 'Seth is better?'

'Yes, Seth is better,' he said.

'Does Seth want to say anything to Rhys?' I said.

He flashed a cheerful, bright, intelligent look, which reminded me of one of those gleams I had seen steal across his face in chapel. Then he repeated the verse I had heard so many times during the Children's *Seiat*.

'Jesus Christ the same yesterday, today, and forever,' he said.

There was something in the way he said it which made me feel the words came not from his tongue, but from his heart. He kept staring at me, as if he expected me to ask him something further. I didn't know what to say.

'Seth'll get better soon.' I said, desperate to comfort him.

'No,' he said. 'Seth won't get better. Seth will never play with Rhys again. Seth won't go to Abel's chapel any more. Seth's going away, far away, to …' He pointed upwards with his finger, as if he couldn't find the proper word.

'Heaven,' I offered, but that wasn't the word he was looking for. Finally, he finished the sentence.

'Seth's going away, far, far, to live in the Big Chapel of Jesus Christ and wear a white shirt.'

That was poor Seth's idea of Heaven, the Big Chapel of Jesus Christ where he'd wear the white gown of an angel.

Wil Bryan, stood behind me. I could hear him breathing in short gasps, as though he had caught a cold. In school I had watched the old Soldier break his cane on Wil's back without as much as a tear or a cry from him. Now as he listened to our innocent old friend talk of dying, and of wearing the white shirt, Will was crying. He choked back his sobs and went downstairs to leave me alone with Seth.

Once Wil had gone Seth looked about him, and seeing that no one else was there, he said. 'Rhys'll pray.'

I understood what he wanted, but didn't know what to do. At that time, I thought only a preacher should pray for the sick. I hesitated.

Seth looked into my eyes with great earnestness. 'Rhys'll pray,' he repeated.

I couldn't refuse him. I was glad that Wil had gone, as I was afraid he would taunt at me later. I fell on my knees by the bedside, and prayed as best I could. I cannot remember just what I said, but I began by asking Jesus Christ to make Seth well again, after which I ran out of words. I fell back upon the Lord's Prayer. 'Our Father which art in Heaven …', I began.

In asking God to restore my friend to health, the words of the Lord's Prayer came sincerely from my heart. As I prayed, I felt Seth lay his thin light hand upon my head. He kept it there until I finished. 'But deliver us from evil, for Thine is the kingdom, the power, and the glory for ever and ever. Amen'

I waited to see if Seth would take his hand away, but he didn't. It weighed more and more heavily upon me, and grew cold, cold. It sent a strange indescribable shiver through my soul. I gently removed his hand, and, trembling in every limb, stood up.

Seth's eyes were wide open, with a distant faraway look. I spoke to him, but he stayed silent as the grave he would soon lie in.

'Seth, Seth,' I said. 'Speak to Rhys.' But Seth was too far gone on his journey to hear me.

Before me, I saw an empty house. The windows were clean and bright but his harmless, sinless soul had left. It had travelled far away, to the Big Chapel of Jesus Christ and would soon be wearing the white shirt of an angel. What had moments before been my living friend was now a dead and empty husk. At that moment I knew he was dead.

I let out a great cry of anguish, and his mother and the neighbour rushed to my side.

Although I cannot forget it, I won't try to describe the scene. It would be cruel to write of the wild uncontrollable grief of his parents. They had neither the strength of mind nor belief in religion to sustain them in such heart-breaking circumstances.

I set off home with a heavy heart. It was a fair distance from Seth's house to ours, and I had to walk it alone. Wil Bryan, overcome with grief, had left some time before me.

It was a bright moonlight night. The sky was cloudless, and the shining stars were piled at immense distances. I felt the moon gazing steadfastly at me, and the stars beckoning me upwards. The more I looked at them, the harder they seemed to stare back.

Had Seth gone past them yet, or was he only on his way thither? I wondered. How long would it take him to get to heaven? Would he arrive at that Big Chapel before I got home?

During my silent walk under the eternal stars something got into my head that made me think that I would become a preacher. Where the thought came from, or who sent it, I don't know. Perhaps the hand of poor simple Seth placed on my head at the moment he was hanging between both worlds first consecrated me for the work. Whatever it was, I knew from that night on that I would become a preacher.

However, there is more to the tale of this night. I had two or three fields to cross on my way home, and my path skirted the Hall Park. I must confess I was afraid as I hurried along that night. I was using all my strength to keep my spirits up.

As I got to the wood, I saw a human shape sitting by the hedge, right by the side of the path I was to take. My heart began to beat so violently that I not only felt, but could hear its violent throbbing. The hour was late, I was alone in the moonlit darkness and I had to summon up my nerve to walk on, rather than turn and run.

Summoning up all my courage, I went on quickly. As I got nearer to the man I saw he had a shotgun in his hand. It must be the gamekeeper at the Hall, I thought. I knew him well so all my fears instantly vanished.

The moon was behind the gamekeeper and I could see him only as a black shape. As I got close to him, I said, in a loud voice, 'Good night, Mr Jones.'

The harsh, unpleasant tone that answered was not that of my friend Mr Jones.

'Just you wait a bit, Rhys Lewis!' it said. 'Don't walk quite so fast, for fear you might come across one of your relations.'

I stood stock still, and saw not Mr Jones, but someone else, carrying an old-fashioned double-barrelled gun.

'Don't be afraid,' the stranger said, 'I won't shoot you ... if you do as I tell you. Take a seat by the hedge here, so that I can talk to you.'

I tremblingly obeyed. I felt I should know that voice, but I didn't recognize the harsh-spoken man. I sat down, as he told me, and he laid his gun against the hedge. He was so close to me that I could see the glitter of moonlight on it barrels. The man didn't speak. He filled his pipe and struck a match.

In the sudden flare of the match striking, I recognized him and nearly fainted with terror. I saw the ugly, villainous features of the dirty, bad fellow, who had come to our house late at night those years before. I knew him as the Irishman.

He'd changed. He looked a good deal sturdier. He began to question me, closely and authoritatively. He asked about mother and Bob, and about the owner of the Hall and his gamekeepers. I kept back nothing. I was so afraid of him that my clothes stuck to my skin with cold sweat. He seemed to enjoy my fear.

He kept me by that hedge for a long time. The Irishman, for that was the only name by which I knew him, was busy questioning me, when he suddenly went quiet. He snatched up his gun, and, taking his pipe from his mouth, listened attentively. The silence was oppressive. He gave a vigorous pull at his pipe, as if he feared the flame would die, while he listened attentively.

I could hear the distance sound of footsteps hurrying along the path I had walked. The Irishman pulled his hat down on his head. I heard a low signal whistle from behind the hedge. Without another word, he stood up, jumped the hedge at a bound, and disappeared into the wood.

Like a frightened stag, I ran towards home. I ran so fast a bullet could not have caught me. When I reached the road I stopped to take breath. In the distance, I heard a gunshot. Some shouting, another gunshot and a lot of commotion followed it. I set off quickly along the road and almost at once met my brother Bob. I told him quickly what had happened.

'Rhys, don't say anything about this to anyone, particularly not to Mam,' he said.

'I promise,' I said.

'It's time you were told some of the things that Mam has kept from you,' he said. 'But not now, and not here. Wait until Mam is asleep and we are in bed.'

He kept his promise. From that day to this I have never mentioned a word to any living soul of what took place on that night near the Hall Park.

Seth's friendship marked an important epoch in my history and by the day after his death, I knew much more about my family .

CHAPTER 14

Wil Bryan

I had never been to a funeral before I went to Seth's. The ceremonies we now use to bury our dead have changed so much in the last thirty years that I have decided to write a description of what went on. Seth passed away at a time the Flintshire Methodists were trying to encourage people to stop drinking beer at burials. They were trying to discourage the common practice of getting drunk at the Wake.

I went to Thomas Bartley's house the night before Seth's funeral and when Abel Hughes called. He came to console the grieving family and tried his best to derive some comforting moral from the sad event. Abel's sincerity and concern greatly moved Thomas and Barbara Bartley until the moment he raised the question of excessive drinking at funerals.

'I hope you will not encourage such a practice,' he said to Thomas, who looked upset at his remark.

'Abel Hughes, don't think you that I am going to bury my son as if he were but a dog,' Thomas said. He stood up and started to shout. 'No, No. As long as I am alive I'll put bread, cheese, baccy and beer out for anyone with enough respect to come.'

He stared hard at Abel. 'It's called hospitality,' he said

Abel tried to argue, but it was no use, Thomas was determined.

'No, no, no Abel Hughes,' he said, 'Seth may not have been like other children, but I ain't going to bury him with only a cup of tea.' He wiped his eyes with his coat sleeve. 'It ain't proper.'

Thomas Bartley was as good as his word. I arrived at the house with Wil Bryan, early the following afternoon. As we went in, we saw a table set with half a cheese, a loaf of white bread, a good-sized jug, full of beer, a number of new pipes, and a small plate containing tobacco

Thomas Bartley stepped forward to meet us. 'William,' he said, 'put something to your mouth.' He looked at me. 'Rhys, you put something to your mouth too.'

I was confused. What did I need to put into my mouth? Wil looked as puzzled as I was. He stared at Thomas. Thomas realized we didn't understand what he wanted. He went to the table, cut chunks of bread and cheese, and filled two small glasses with beer and gave them to us.

I put the glass to my lips. The beer tasted bitter and sour. Wil managed to drink his without pulling a face. I struggled to swallow my share but I noticed its effect at once.

I felt as if my hands were enormous, but I was on wonderfully good terms with everybody. I had a great urge to either sleep or laugh, and wasn't sure which I most wanted to do. All the same, I realized that neither would have been proper at Seth's funeral.

If this was how the demon drink affected people, I wasn't going to drink any more. No matter how much Thomas urged me I refused to put anything more 'to my mouth'.

Many of our neighbours were already there, puffing away at their pipes. More followed us in, and Thomas Bartley greeted each one in the same way.

'Put something to your mouth,' he said.

Each newly arrived man went to the beer jug, poured out a glass, and cut himself some bread and cheese. They all kept their hats on and stood about speaking of this and that. Nobody mentioned Seth's death. Most of them were smoking and spitting on the floor; it had been thickly scattered with white sand to absorb the spittle. Thomas kept the jug full. As each man refilled his glass, he turned the handle of the jug towards next man, who would then top up his glass.

If someone didn't turn the handle quickly enough, the more impatient would cry, 'Who does the handle point at?' This was a hint that the dawdler should either use the jug or turn the handle towards his neighbour.

The drinking went on for the best part of two hours. I could tell when any man had taken more than he could comfortably hold because the colour of his face reddened. James Pwllfford, the tailor was a little, talkative fellow, with a face normally as pale as death. As the afternoon wore on it became as rosy as any farm labourer's. And he was not the only mourner with flushed cheeks.

As the time to set off for the churchyard drew nearer two men came in from the next room. They were carrying pewter vessels, which looked like larger versions of the chalice used to administer the sacrament. Cuttings of lemon peel decorated the handles of these jugs.

'This is mulled ale,' Thomas said pointing to one jug that was steaming, 'and this holds cold ale. Now you make sure you all take some into your mouth.'

The first jug was steaming and bubbling. I thought the term boiling ale would better describe it. Both jugs smelt strongly of spice.

The men who were crushed into the front room, solemnly removed their hats and stood in silence while the cupbearers went around, offering each kind of drink with the seriousness of a minister in the chapel administering the Lord's Supper. Never to this day have I understood what all this was supposed to mean.

Once this ceremony was over the men replaced their hats and began to talk. Dafydd the Carpenter took a plate round, and the men each put down a shilling, while Wil and I put sixpence apiece, as he told us this was the 'customary share'.

Abel Hughes came in a few minutes before the time for raising the body. Thomas Bartley greeted him by asking 'Will you put something to your mouth?'

Abel said, 'No, I will not.'

This greatly offended Thomas. Only Abel Hughes was used to praying in public, but when the time came to carry Seth to the churchyard his refusal to put anything to his mouth had so annoyed Thomas Bartley that he wouldn't let him to pray over Seth.

I saw Thomas whisper in the ear of Dafydd the Carpenter. As the men laid Seth's body upon the bier, they dropped their hats over their ear, as if listening for the corpse to speak. The women stayed in the back room. They hurried to the window, and looked out, holding their handkerchiefs to their mouths. Dafydd, was a worldly man unused to public praying, but he fell on his knees beside the bier. He rattled off the Lord's Prayer at express speed, as if counting a herd of sheep.

The solemnities duly observed, the procession set off for the cemetery. Wil Bryan and I walked either side of Thomas Bartley. I carried a bunch of evergreens and Wil a bag of gravel, to place on Seth's grave. We followed the coffin to Top Church and took our places in the pews.

Mr Brown rushed through the burial service, but, even so, several of the congregation fell asleep. James Pwllfford settled into a deep doze, with his snoring muffled only by his nose being buried neatly in his waistcoat. We had to wake all the slumberers to follow Seth's coffin out to the churchyard.

When Rev. Brown finished the service at the graveside, Dafydd the Carpenter climbed up on a tombstone, and, thanked the neighbours on behalf of the family, for their kindness in coming to the funeral.

'Thomas and Barbara Bartley express the hope that, at someday not far distant, they will have the opportunity to attend your funerals in return,' he said. 'And the father of the departed hopes you will all join him at the Crown to continue the Wake, once the funeral is over.'

Once the grave had been filled in, the gravel scattered on top and the bunch of evergreens laid down, most of those present made straight for the Crown. Abel Hughes, Wil Bryan and I didn't follow them. Wil might have wanted to go, but he feared a row at home if he got caught.

While the menfolk were in church Barbara's women friends sat with her, comforted her and drank tea. My mother went, along with many other neighbours.

I don't know exactly what went on in the Crown, but some hours later, I saw Thomas Bartley being brought home. Two neighbours were carrying him whilst loudly disagreeing about which side of the road to walk. Thomas was quiet and seemed too tired to take part in their discussion. He didn't seem to care where, or even if, he walked. Soon after I heard James Pwllfford pass by our house.

'On Conwy's banks, once on a time,' he warbled in manner I thought most unseemly for a funeral guest.

If I intended to publish this account of the Seth's burial, some people would doubtless disbelieve that a funeral should be the excuse for such drunkenness. But others would admit my depiction is accurate, and even say I have glossed over many excesses and not told the whole truth. I admit I haven't recorded all the unseemly things that took place at Seth's wake. It is a great mercy that the old ways have been greatly reformed, but much more could still be done. True, the beer has been banished and tea and coffee, beef and ham, have taken its place. When people from a distance attend a funeral, it can only be proper to feed them. But why should excessive junketing take place among the neighbours on such occasions?

Poor families arrange a costly feast, simply for the sake of people who live close by. Such a foolish custom is a cruel hardship on the poor, and I think it both unnecessary and unseemly.

With Seth buried, I had only one bosom friend left, Wil Bryan. Yet I felt we were drifting apart. Wil had a lively, daring spirit that sprang from an open and kindly heart. But I knew in my soul that he was not a good boy. He spoke scornfully of the strict rules of the *Seiat* and he used impolite nicknames for nearly everyone he knew.

John Llwyd he called 'old Scraper'. Hugh Bellis, the deacon who often wept during the sermon he called 'old Waterworks'. Thomas Bowen, who was popular with us children, he called 'old Trump'. Abel Hughes, who wore knee breeches and had thin legs was called, 'old Onion.' He had an 'old'-type nickname for most of the chapel folk.

He called his parents 'the gaffer yonder,' and the 'old peahen yonder'.

My mother told me, 'Mark my words Rhys, there is a serious defect in a lad's character if he is in the habit of calling his father gaffer or governor'.

Wil had a special talent for finding descriptive names for people, and some of his satirical labels have stayed with their recipients to this day. However, I will not repeat them here, or encourage anyone else to specify them.

I didn't really think much about Wil's habit until he referred to my mother as 'the old Ten Commandments.' I was greatly upset at this and told Wil so, and, to give him his due, he never used it again. But thinking the matter over as I write, I cannot help seeing the appropriateness of the title, for my mother was always giving us commandments, and charging us to do this thing or that. Knowing that my mother was a woman of some insight, I wonder why she let me associate so much with Wil Bryan, until I remember his good points.

Wil had a knack of getting on good terms with everyone. He had a handsome, cheery face and a bold, brave manner. He would use his musical voice and smooth, witty tongue as weapons to win permission to be amusingly impudent. He knew my mother well. When she was low-spirited I often heard her say that a visit from Wil would cheer her up. She would smile and struggle not to laugh aloud at some of Wil's comments, though had I said the same words she would have boxed my ears. But her conscience, about condoning Wil's tongue must have pricked her, because she kept trying to give him good advice.

I recall a typical conversation she had with him.

'Wil, my son,' she said. 'You are capable doing much good or much of harm in this world. And I sincerely hope you'll get a little grace.'

'There's plenty of grace to be had Mair Lewis, isn't there?' Wil said. 'But I'm not greedy. I don't want to take more than my share, you know.'

'Don't you talk lightly of God's grace, Wil,' she said. 'You can never get too much.'

'So the gaffer yonder tells me,' Wil agreed. 'But, Mair Lewis, it doesn't do to be too greedy.'

'And pray who is the gaffer?' Mother said.

'The old hand,' said Wil, then seeing her frown, added. 'You know. My father.'

'Wil,' said mother, her voice taking on a hard edge. 'I exhort you never to call your father 'gaffer' or 'old hand' again. No good ever comes to children who call their father and mother 'him yonder' and 'her yonder,' or 'the old hand yonder' or 'the old woman yonder.''

She looked him sternly in the eye. 'Now mind you well. Don't you ever let me hear you call your parents such stupid names again?'

Wil pretended to look crestfallen and bowed his head.

'All right,' he said, and I saw the twinkle in his eye. 'In future I will call him Hugh Bryan, Esquire, General Grocer and Provision Dealer, Baker to his Royal Highness the Old Scraper, and... .'

Before he could finish listing the scurrilous nicknames he would use for his father's customers he had to make a run for the door. Mother, even though fighting to suppress her laughter, clearly intended to box his ears.

'He's a rough 'un, that boy,' she said, watching him run down the lane. 'But if he got grace, he'd make a capital preacher.'

Her assessment made me a little jealous. She'd never said I'd make a preacher. I knew Wil Bryan didn't intend to be one, and I also knew it was my chief desire.

I don't think mother thought of Wil as anything other than a mischief-loving lad until he began brushing his hair up from his forehead. When he took to making a quiff, by parting and oiling his hair, and combing it back from his forehead, his fate was sealed.

I thought Wil looked splendid with his quiff, and I hoped mother would give me permission to copy him. I was tired of mother's way of cutting my hair. She'd clap a large butter-basin on my crown, and shear around the edges until my head looked like a newly thatched haycock. But mother took innovation in hairdressing very seriously.

When she first saw Wil's quiff she took him to task.

'Wil, my son,' she said. 'I used to think you were a good lad, for all your foolishness. But the devil has found a weak spot in you.'

'What's the matter now, Mair Lewis?' Wil said. 'I don't think I have killed anybody of late, have I?'

'No, I hope not,' mother said. 'But you should kill The Old Man.'

'Which Old Man do you mean, Mair Lewis?' Wil said. 'Do you mean the gaffer yonder? No, in the name of goodness I won't kill the old hand.' He grinned at her from under his quiff. 'What would become of me?' he said. 'I should starve.'

'No, Wil,' mother said. 'You well know it isn't your father I mean, but the Old Man in your heart.'

'Old man in my heart?' Wil said. 'There's no old man in my heart, I'll take an oath to it.'

'Yes, there is, Wil,' she said. 'And one day you'll come to know it.'

'But how did he get in there, Mair Lewis?' said Wil. 'He must be very small, less than Tom Thumb.'

'He was in your heart before you were born,' mother said, her voice rising in anger. 'And he's bigger than Goliath.' Her eyes were burning with passion as she went on. 'Unless you take a smooth stone from the river of salvation, and sink it deep in his forehead, he will cut your head off with his sword.'

Wil grinned back at her, uncowed by her preaching.

'How, Mair Lewis, am I to drive a stone into his forehead, if he is in my heart?' he said, adding with a cheeky grin, 'And if he's in my heart how can he reach to cut my head off with a sword?'

'You well know who I talk of, Wil,' mother said. 'I mean the Old Man of Sin.'

'Oh. Now I see.' Wil said, 'Why don't say what you mean, Mair Lewis? Isn't there sin in the hearts of all of us, according to the old father up yonder?'

'There is indeed, my son,' mother said. 'And the sin in your heart is breaking out of your head, in the shape of that silly quiff.'

Mother went on a great length to attack the evil habit of brushing the hair off the forehead. I could see Wil losing patience with her then he turned and walked haughtily away.

As he left my mother turned to me. I could see a deep sadness in her eyes.

'Rhys,' she said, 'I don't want you to have any further truck with Wil Bryan. He has the sin of pride in his heart. I'm surprised Hugh Bryan permits such a thing.' She glanced up at the butter-basin on the shelf before she went on. 'If Wil were a son of mine, I'd cut his hair in a jiffy, that I would.'

'But why does the way he cuts his hair matter so?' I said.

'Because it feeds his vanity,' mother said. 'There he is looking at himself in the glass, every day. Thank Heaven we never had a looking glass in our family, not till your brother Bob brought one here, and I wish in my heart it had never crossed my doorstep.'

She glared at the small mirror Bob had bought for her. 'Your Nain used to say that people who look in the glass too often will see the Evil One, and I can believe her. I don't know what'll become of this ungodly generation.'

She sighed from the bottom of her heart. 'What religion needs is a speedy revival,' she said.

CHAPTER 15

The Beginning of Our Troubles

I knew it had to happen, but it still came as a shock when one day mother said, 'You're getting to be a big boy Rhys, and I can't afford to keep you playing about doing nothing all day.'

I shouldn't really have been surprised because I knew more of mother's affairs and troubles than she suspected, and I wanted to help her. I knew in my heart that all three of us depended on Bob's earnings, but, hard as he worked, they were barely enough to keep him in proper food and clothing. My brother had started to work in the mine long before he was the age I was then, and many boys I knew, younger than I, were already out earning.

'I don't know what you're fit for,' Mam said. 'But you can't go carrying your head in the wind at your age when I'm no better than a widow.' She looked me up and down. 'You're not strong enough to go to the colliery and you're not scholar enough to be a shopkeeper.'

She shook her head. 'And even if you were, I've no money to give you a start. I couldn't raise ten pounds to apprentice you. Not even if ten shillings were to get you into the best shop in the town, I wouldn't know where to begin to look for it.'

'I do want to help, Mam,' I said. 'There must be something I can do for a living.' I didn't dare say what I really wanted, and before I could even hint at it Mam went on.

'Look at you,' she said. 'Your shoes are worn to nothing. You wear the same suit Sundays and weekdays. If only you could earn enough to keep yourself in clothes it would be something.'

She glanced towards the kitchen cupboard. 'Food's so dear, and your brother's wages are so small that it's as much as I can do to make both ends meet, and I really struggle to afford an occasional penny for The Cause. Small wonder that I'm always moithering and scheming to keep things going ... and if the mine goes on strike I really don't know what'll become of us.'

She forced a smile. 'But, as Twm o' Nant says, It's a deal of skill gets Wil to bed.'

'But you keep saying that the Good Lord has helped our family to live honestly and pay our way, even if we have been hard up.' I said.

'Indeed I have, Rhys,' she said. 'But I've never seen any good come of keeping children too long without setting them to work; it only brings them up to mischief. I might be able to persuade Mr Pwllfford, the tailor, to take you on. But he's an unmannerly, good-for-nothing who often gets drunk. I fear your soul would not receive fair play, which is the main thing. I'd rather see you a godly chimney sweep, than an ungodly clerk of the peace.'

'But I'd have the children be calling after me "Tailor, tailor tit. Clogs on your stockingless feet",' I said.

'Well, that would break no bones in you,' Mam replied. 'You'd have a dry back and a trade at hand always. I'd rather you a tailor than a farm servant. The weather stiffens and freezes the souls as well as the bodies of such people. Always being in the company of animals makes them much like animals themselves. I never in my life saw so listless a set, with less of the man in them, as these farm servants. They were like slaves, too shy to raise their heads, save in the stable. How I pitied them when I was in service at Faenol. On wet days, when the poor things came in to supper, there wasn't a dry rag about them.'

Mother looked lost in her girlhood memories as she went on. 'They went to the long table, near the window, far from the fire. There were half a dozen of them. They came into the house softly and sat on the benches each side of the table with their heads hung down and their eyes looking up under their brows, just as if they had been thieving all day instead of toiling in muck and damp. Not one of them spoke a word. All I could hear was the sound of them chewing their pottage. As soon as they finished eating they watched the eye of the husbandman, for him to give a signal. Then came the noise of moving feet and benches, as the poor wretches went out in a row.' I could see a tear rising in her eye.

'I pitied them from my heart,' she went on. 'They somehow didn't look like men. Two of them were members of the same church as their master Mr Williams. Aaron Parri was an extraordinary man in prayer. I was so sorry to see such a distance kept between master and man. I'll never accept that our Saviour approves that kind of thing.'

Mother shook her head to clear the memories 'This is what I was going to say, 'she went on. 'I wouldn't for the world want to see you a farm servant. Perhaps your brother's right, a little learning always comes in handy. If you'd had a bit more schooling, I could have asked old Abel to take you into his shop. Surely, after all our acquaintance he wouldn't refuse. But I can't hope for that.'

She looked firmly in the eye. 'We were coming back from the *Seiat*, and Thomas Bowen told me it was high time you were taken into full membership.' She looked stern, 'I'd like to see you come forward, if you've properly considered the matter. You've already mastered the chapter from the *Preceptor* and have long since learned the parts of the Gospels which describe the Lord's Supper. But you must pray that your mind is inclined in the right direction, lest you be found unworthy.'

She sighed, 'I wish from my heart to see you apprenticed to the heavenly calling before you are apprenticed to a worldly one.'

'"Tis better youth the yoke should wear, than worlds of empty pleasure share",' she quoted. Mother was quite capable of going on in this fashion all day long, but it was plain that I had to think about how to earn my bread.

Should I go down the mine? The coal market was brisk, but then a swarm of officials and overseers – greedy, rapacious strangers to a man – were pocketing all the profits of Caeau Cochion Colliery. The poor workmen and their families were half-starved. My brother Bob had for some time been annoyed at the behaviour of the bosses, and I feared his pent-up righteous indignation would burst out one day.

I'd been told by some colliers' children that Bob had considerable influence with his fellow workmen. He'd taken the chair at a meeting to work out how to ask for an advance of wages, and he'd made a capital speech. I was proud of him, and not without cause, for he always took great pains with me.

He was always ready to guide my studies, and I am more indebted to him than to any man living for the direction my life has taken. After he was expelled from the *Seiat*, he never spoke to me of religious subjects, unless I first asked him. But whatever knowledge he could impart to me, to the best of his ability, he did. More than once, he made me promise solemnly that I would never become a collier.

'I'd sooner you went on the streets to beg, Rhys, rather than see you suffer the tyranny and arrogance I've known.'

But he need not have worried. I had no intention to go down the mine. Bob's daily reports of the hard labour and oppression created in me an unconquerable disgust towards working in the pit. I already knew what I wanted to do.

For some time, I had been secretly nourishing a wish to become a preacher. It's a long way from the pit bottom to the pulpit. I might have been foolish, but I thought it would be easier to climb to the pulpit from anywhere else than from the coal-face.

I hadn't told a living soul about my hopes. I have never fully understood what made me want to preach. I confess that my motive was not a desire to do good, or to convert sinners from the error of their ways. That hadn't entered my mind. It was admiration of the office that impressed me, or perhaps it was proud ambition. I would picture myself as a great, portly, pulpit-filling personage, preaching with zest. I imagined people listening for their very life, talking about me, and praising me, when my sermon was over. I would be doing this history an injustice if I were to say I knew nothing of religious impressions. After all the trouble mother had taken with me, it would have been a miracle if I had remained unimpressed.

I was aware of a fear of sinning against God, and dying the death of the wicked. But I couldn't account for the irrepressible desire I felt to become a preacher whilst still a mere lad. I regret to this day that I didn't tell mother what was in my heart. I'm sure she would have given me every encouragement. I feel that by not telling her I deprived her of the greatest joy and pleasure I could have offered her during her bitter troubles. I could not have better filled her cup of happiness than by revealing my resolve to one day become a preacher.

Be that as it may, I kept it all locked up in my heart. I was, at that time, more thoughtful than my associates. However, I was touched to the quick when Wil Bryan called me 'the holy one'. I felt a hidden purpose which he neither understood nor sympathized with.

I took a great interest in every preacher, and never tired of talking preaching to anyone who would discuss it with me.

By working hard, and with Bob's help, I was a better scholar than mother took me to be. I could read and write both Welsh and English tolerably well. Encouraged by John Joseph, at the Children's *Seiat* I had for some time been taking down the text on Sundays, with as many as I could of the heads of sermon. I remember being very angry with some preachers because they did not divide their texts, and very pleased with William Hughes of Abercwmnant, because his heads of sermon were pretty much alike, whatever text he took. They were usually three in number, and ran thus:

i. The object noted.
ii. The act attributed.
iii. The duty enjoined.

I often foresaw and wrote out these divisions during his introduction, and before he had named them. The old preacher had one habit for which I often wondered why he had not been called to account. Towards the end of his sermon he always said, 'One other word before I finish,' and then would speak a hundred words or more. He would next say, 'One word again, before I leave you,' and go on for another five or ten minutes. A third time he would say, 'One other word before I take my departure,' and we were sure of a long speech after that.

I thought it strange that he, a preacher, should not be called to account for telling fibs.

Wil Bryan would often cite such conduct as a preacher's excuse for saying that which wasn't true. John Joseph used to praise me for being able to repeat the heads of sermon. That pleased me greatly. About this time John set up a class to teach young men the elements of music and grammar. It quickly grew into a class for competitive recitations, essay writing, and religious controversy. It had many members, but I'm afraid to name them, lest I should be obliged to go into their histories. Wil Bryan was a member, but he didn't often take part in our public gatherings. His favourite business was to poke fun at our mistakes and shortcomings. He pushed this habit so much he became odious to the majority of the young men who resolved to get rid of him. As Wil was the only member who brushed his hair away from his forehead they convened a meeting to pass a resolution that no one should be a member of that Society who was found guilty of 'making a quiff.'

Wil was expelled. But he didn't care. To avenge his disgrace, he nicknamed us 'The Society of Flathairs'. Like the rest of his nicknames, this one stuck to us as long as we existed. Our minds absorbed impressions that have never been obliterated. The meetings created in us a taste for things religious, for which we could never be too thankful.

Shortly after Wil's expulsion from the society his name and mine were brought before the *Seiat* as candidates for full membership. Our applications were submitted by Thomas Bowen, the preacher, who was always zealous on behalf of the youth of the church. He was particularly careful we should not be left too long out of full membership. He was constantly urging parents to press home the matter to their children's minds and duly to prepare them for such an event. On the other hand, Abel Hughes would speak of circumspection and of the dangers of receiving into full membership those who were not yet ready.

Preacher and deacon being at opposite extremes, occasionally squabbled over the point. Thomas Bowen had long been talking of us coming forward, while Abel Hughes advised they should take time and go slow. In the end Thomas Bowen won, and so one night we were called up to the bench in the centre of the chapel for examination. I and others of the same age were anxious to be admitted, but Wil Bryan would have preferred to be left alone. Doubtless he feared the examination, for he had taken little interest in religious questions, although in natural ability he was far above the rest of us. There were six of us, and I sat at one end of the bench, while Wil Bryan, unconcerned as usual, sat at the other.

Abel Hughes got up and began the examination with me. He was rather hard on me, but I pulled through better than I expected. I knew from Thomas Bowen's voice and manner that I was answering satisfactorily, for he smiled, threw his legs about, one over the other, nodded to Hugh Bellis, and muttered, 'Ho' or 'Hmm' after each reply, as if to say, 'Not so bad, really'. Abel proceeded with the two lads next to me, with the same satisfactory result. He then sat down, and invited Thomas Bowen to examine the remaining three. Thomas Bowen got up, thrust both hands into his trouser pockets, assumed a satisfied look, and, addressed the deacon.

'Well, Abel Hughes, have you been pleased?' he said. 'Tell me, was I not right, in thinking the boys were quite fit to be received? Have I not said so for months? But we will proceed.'

And he did proceed, with the fourth youth and the fifth. He did not, I thought, put such difficult questions as Abel Hughes had done, and the answers came quite easily. After an answer he considered rather a good one, he would turn to Abel with a significant look, as much as to say, 'What do you think of that, Abel? Will it do?'

Presently it came to Wil Bryan's turn.

'William, my son,' Thomas said, 'you're a little older than the rest of the boys and ought, in my opinion, to have been admitted long ago. But there are people here who believe in taking time. I won't make my questions hard for you, although I know, were I to do so, you could answer them well enough. Will you tell me, William, my boy, how many offices appertain unto the Lord Jesus in his character as a Mediator? '

'Three,' replied Wil.

'Hah!' Thomas said. "Three!' Do you hear, Abel Hughes? Three! Had Dr Owen himself been here, he couldn't have answered better. These boys know a great deal more than you think, Abel Hughes. The Children's *Seiat*, and the Sunday School, have not been held in vain, you see. The boys have listened and observed more than we imagine, I assure you. I have always said this. Yes sure, three. Well, William, my son, will you name them?'

'Father, Son, and Holy Ghost,' said Wil.

A titter went through the chapel. Thomas Bowen looked as if someone had hit him with a hammer over the back of the neck. He sat down, in shame and chagrin, and fixed his gaze upon his boot-tips, uttering not a word save 'Hmm!'

'Go on, go on, Thomas Bowen,' said Abel eagerly.

Thomas pretended not to hear him. I don't know whether it was mischief or ignorance that prompted Wil to answer as he did, because he was wag enough and careless enough for either. Abel Hughes evidently thought it was not possible Wil could be as ignorant as his answer implied. By way of punishment he proposed that we five should be received into full membership, leaving Wil out until his knowledge and experience had matured. It was unanimously carried.

Wil didn't care a jot what had happened. Directly we left the meeting he laughed heartily, and declared he didn't want to become a full member, adding, 'It was a good job the old hand and the old peahen weren't in the *Seiat* tonight.'

More than ever I felt there was a serious defect in Wil's character, but I still loved him greatly. We were hardly out of chapel before he took hold of my arm.

'Let's go to the Colliers' Meeting,' he said.

I didn't know that such a meeting was to be held, but Wil knew about every public gathering that took place. I saw no harm in going with him. It was an open-air meeting. It was a lovely summer night and as we got near the field I heard a great noise. There were shouts of 'Hear, hear,' and 'Hooray'

There were hundreds there. My heart gave a jump when I recognized Bob speaking to the crowd. Wil and I pushed to the front. Wil shouting 'Hear, hear' before he could catch a word of what was spoken. Never shall I forget my brother's appearance. He stood upon a high mound, with a number of the principal colliers at the Caeau Cochion pit about him, and a tremendous crowd below. He held his hat in his left hand, and had his right extended. His eyes glowed like lamps in water, his lips trembled, his face was deathly white and formed as strong a contrast to his beard and hair as a snowball set in soot.

I remember wondering why Bob's face was so pale, while preachers' aces were so red when speaking. I knew from his appearance that every joint, bone and sinew of him was agitated right through, and I thought to myself what a splendid preacher he would have made, if he had not been expelled from the *Seiat* for his trifling fault. I had never heard him speak in public previously, and I wondered where he got all those words which dropped so fluently from his lips. His audience laughed, groaned, shouted agreement. They were entirely in his hand. I believed everything he said to be the perfect truth and it never entered my head that he could be mistaken.

I could repeat everything he said, but what purpose would it serve? It would have been better for him if he had not spoken a single word that night. He spoke of the injustice and hardship suffered by the workmen, which he attributed to the arrogance and incapacity of the officials. He proved, to the satisfaction of his audience that the 'Lankies' knew nothing of Welsh mining operations, that they oppressed the men, and ruined the masters by their behaviour. As he finished his speech there were loud cheers. I ran home to tell my mother what I had seen, and tell her what a capital speaker Bob was.

Mother sat before the fire, pleating her apron. As I came in she looked up with a pleased expression.

'You did well in your examination at *Seiat*,' she said.

I told her all about Bob. I said what a splendid orator he was. I said how the people shouted their applause, and so forth. She did not rejoice the news, as I had expected. She looked serious look. I couldn't understand her reaction.

'Well, well,' she said, with a heavy sigh, 'the sweet is never without the bitter. Trouble will come of this. A day of trial is at hand. Oh if he only had the grace not to say anything rash.'

She fell into a deep study and kept pleating her apron as she looked steadfastly into the fire.

I was sorry I'd told her the story, although I couldn't see why it should vex her so. I went to bed thoroughly dispirited, because I didn't understand the reason for my mother's sadness. The night was far advanced when Bob returned, and, although from my bed I couldn't hear exactly what he said, I heard hot words between him and mother. I fell asleep to the sound of their argument.

How true were my mother's fears? While the most extravagant sinners slept peacefully in the midst of plenty and luxury, and whilst I was sleeping heedlessly on my bed of straw, the trouble my mother had prophesied was already approaching our cottage door. Soon it would demand admission. The fact that Mam feared God above all and never spent six hours of her waking life without sending Him a prayer would not protect her.

CHAPTER 16

The Day of Bereavement

It is with melancholy memories that I write this chapter. If I could give a faithful history of my life, leaving out all mention of what it contains, I would do so, but I cannot. Now, in cold blood, and at an age more competent to form an opinion, I do not view the events in the same way I did at the time. But I will describe them as they happened.

Caeau Cochion was a major workplace of the neighbourhood where I grew up. It employed some hundreds of men and boys. The owners were English to a man. At one time a simple, honest Welshman named Abraham Jones managed all the works underground. Abraham was a deacon with the Congregationalists. He was a cool, strong-minded man, possessing great influence with those under him. Whatever disputes arose among them, it only wanted Abraham Jones to arbitrate, and he settled everything, at once. The secret of his authority lay in his special aptitude for spotting the source of the mischief, and the entire confidence everybody had in his honesty and his religious character. At all times he kept his eyes open for the welfare of the employers who paid him his salary, but he also looked out for the comfort and the safety of the men whom he saw every day toiling and sweating in the midst of danger. He was one of the most expert practical colliers in the country, and under his management everything went on smoothly.

The bosses however felt he had one great disadvantage. His English was so poor that, when reporting to them, he sometimes did not tell a clear story. He was greatly vexed at himself for that weakness. One or two of the directors enjoyed subjecting him to detailed interrogation about the work. He had nothing to fear about his conduct, but he struggled to explain himself when interrogated in an unpleasant manner. The cross-examinations so upset him that he felt relieved when a meeting of directors told him they had found an Englishman to replace him. They said the Englishman would be more able to give a clear account of the state of the colliery, and it would be better if he left.

This news removed a great burden from Abraham's mind. His chest swelled with pride as he addressed the meeting in his jerky English.

'Gentlemen,' he said. 'I am very pleased indeed to hear what you say. If he whom you speak of can keep the work going as smoothly and peaceably in the interests of both masters and men for six months, as I have done for six years, then indeed he must be a very clever man.'

He picked up his hat, made a polite bow, and left. He often used to say afterwards that he believed he got help from above to speak clear English as he took leave of his employers. When he went back to the pit and told the men, they were upset. Many a collier would have liked to vent their feelings in vulgar language, but in Abraham Jones's presence they gulped back their harsh words, and their eyes filled with tears as they mourned his dismissal. The tears trickling down their cheeks left clean white streaks on each black face.

The men were convinced it was not Abraham Jones's lack of ability or faithful service that prompted the directors to sack him. They whispered that some board members wanted to create a job for a hard-up friend. Whether it was right or wrong, this belief prejudiced the men against the new manager long before they met him. And when Mr Strangle did take over the job his appearance and manner deepened their dislike.

Mr Strangle was middle-aged, fat-bellied and blustering. He embodied in his person all the roughness, slovenliness and ignorance of a typical native of Wigan. His speech was coarse and uncouth. Even the uneducated colliers smiled to hear him say 'ay' for 'yes' and 'mun' for 'must.' But his speech was a trifling drawback compared to his insufferable self-regard and inconsiderate behaviour. The men called him 'Bulldog,' on the day he first came to work. Recalling his squashed nose and jowly jaw, I fancy no one would have denied his relationship with that species. If he were taken at his own word, he knew everything knowable, and never ever made a mistake. Mr Strangle had been a whole colliery in himself. He claimed to know the main coal, be a haulier, byeman, cutter, shelterer and cage brake man, and declared he knew all there was to know about chimney-stacks, engine-houses, boilers and all.

Bob said that Abraham Jones's old flannel jacket knew more about managing the Caeau Cochion works than Mr Strangle did. The antagonism of the men matched Strangle's own hatred of Wales and the Welsh; he delighted in snubbing people. He did everything connected with the colliery in a way directly opposite to Abraham Jones. The result was that the work speedily fell about his ears. Some hundreds of pounds worth of fresh timber had to be used to keep the place together. The state of things got so bad that the tradesmen of the town, and the neighbourhood generally, were in fear of a strike at the Caeau Cochion Colliery.

This was the state of affairs when the colliers held their meeting, and my brother Bob made what I thought was a capital speech. Next day, whilst mother and a neighbour were talking about the meeting, I got to know why my report of Bob's public statements upset her so. I overheard her speaking to our neighbour, Mrs Peters.

'It's worth suffering a little hardship,' she said to Mrs Peters. 'To keep the peace.'

'But it's high time someone spoke up,' Mrs Peters said. 'The men's earnings are so small it's impossible to maintain a family on them.'

'So why doesn't Mr Peters speak up?' Mam said.

'I've told him not to say a word, or draw attention to himself,' Mrs Peters said.

'So, Margad Peters,' Mam said. 'You're anxious our Bob and others should do all the fighting, while your husband and everybody belonging to you wait offshore, like Dan of old. You remain in ships, until you can come ashore for a share of the spoils once the battle is over. There is many a Dan in our days, as Mr Davies of Nerquis used to say.'

Margad didn't know enough Scripture to understand the comparison but could see it was aimed at her, so quickly changed the subject.

Mam was afraid that Bob would get himself into trouble, and she was quickly proved right.

When Bob got home from work that night he was unusually serious and thoughtful. After he had washed and eaten, my mother said, 'Bob, I know by your look you have bad news. Have you got notice?'

'Yes,' Bob said. 'Morris Hughes, James Williams, John Powel and me, are to finish next Saturday.'

'Well, and what are we to do then?' Mam said.

'We will do our duty, mother, and trust in Providence,' Bob said.

'Yes, my boy; but do you consider that you have done your duty? I gave you many warnings not to take a lead in this business. The men have cause to complain, and it's a shame for a heathen Saxon to come and take the place of a pious man like Abraham Jones. But you are young and have responsibilities. Why didn't you let someone like Edward Morgan lead the talking and messing in this matter? He has a house of his own, and a pig.'

Mam began to pleat her apron vigorously.

'It wouldn't have made much odds to Edward if he got notice,' she went on. 'But it's too late to lock the stable door now the horse has bolted. What'll become of us?'

'Mother,' Bob said, his voice serious. 'You taught me to do my duty, and leave the consequences to God. It was one of your first lessons, and I intend to act upon it as long as I have breath. I believe it is a good way to live. I expected the notice. A few must suffer before benefit can come to the many. I and my friends are the scapegoats for the three hundred or so who work at Caeau Cochion. If we can bring liberty and benefit to them, all well and good. I have only said what everybody in the works thinks. Others have shrunk from saying it in public. That some must suffer for the many is a great principle of God's government. Either the comfort or the life of one animal is sacrificed to keep other animals alive. As Caiaphas said, "It is expedient that one man should die for the people, so that the whole nation perishes not." The principle of the Sacrifice on the Cross is practised daily on a small scale, and ... '

'Stop your nonsense,' Mam broke in sharply. 'I won't hear you talk like this. Are you wrong in the head? Do you compare the Death on the Cross with your notice to leave the work? Do you mean to tell me there is anything in that to resemble the sufferings of the Saviour? If you do, you'd better get off to the Asylum as soon as you can.'

'Gently, mother,' Bob said. 'I needn't tell you, who are well acquainted with the Acts of the Apostles, that I am not the first who has been accused of madness on account of his ardour. I don't mean to compare my notice to the Sacrifice on the Cross, either for magnitude or intent, but solely on principle. If there is no comparison between the finite and the infinite, there is an analogy, and it is a metaphor I am using.'

'Come, come,' Mam said. 'Don't you throw your big words at me. Keep within the Scripture, and I'll follow you wherever you like; but none of your fine words, if you please. I'm sure "analogy" and "metaphor" are not Bible words, and, as far as I remember, they are not in Mr Charles's *Preceptor* either.'

'I know, mother,' Bob said, 'that you set great store by Mr Charles's writings, but if you would just read Butler's *Analogy* ...'

'Butler?' Mam interrupted. 'Don't talk of your butler to me. He's a pagan who never goes to any place of worship but Top Church, and who doesn't know anything but how to carry wine to his master. What do you mean by reading the butler?"

This was too much for Bob, who burst out laughing. This annoyed my mother so much that he had to rush to explain.

'I'm not talking about the Hall butler,' he said, 'I was thinking of Bishop Butler, who is a great and good man. And this is what I was about to say, had you let me. As sacrifice is a covenant of life, a blessing, and a profit. Before it was possible for sinners to find life, it was necessary that the Son of God should sacrifice himself.'

'Now you're talking sense,' Mother said quietly.

'Before that life could be brought to men it was necessary that the apostles and a host of other of the world's best men should suffer much, even to the laying down of their lives,' said Bob. 'And something of the same kind still takes place every day, only with this difference: the least are sacrificed for the sake of the greatest. The cow, the sheep, the pig and a host of other creatures, lose their lives so that you and I may preserve ours. And so it is in every state of being of which we have any knowledge.

'That rule prevails in society, in fighting for the right and against oppression. Some are sure to be trampled underfoot and hurt by the tyrant, even when he is in retreat. Someone must fight the battle of the Caeau Cochion workmen, so they can be rid of their tyranny. If my associates and I fall while sounding the battle-trumpet, so be it. The call to arms has gone out. We have justice on our side, and others will reap the fruits of the victory. With a little wisdom and determination, I don't doubt that things will change at Caeau Cochion before long. I only fear that the men will resort to unlawful means to attain their object. Many of them are devoid of judgment, and governed by hasty tempers. Unless they have a wise man to lead them, they will do more harm to the cause than can be imagined. But perhaps they will behave better than I anticipate,' Bob finished.

Either my mother did not understand what he had said, or she couldn't answer him.

'Pray more, and talk less, my son,' was all she said.

The notice given to my brother and the other men provoked much adverse comment at the colliery and neighbourhood. The town looked ahead to the following Saturday with serious concern. Some feared disorder amongst the workmen if the notice was enforced. Others thought the masters had merely adopted a ruse to frighten the men into silence. They thought that Mr Strangle would be getting himself into hot water if he were to turn away the best and steadiest hands in the colliery.

Saturday came. Wil Bryan, I and other youths, went to the pit's bank about the time the men were to come up, to see what would happen. Presently a pair of English police officers arrived on the same errand.

The workmen began to come up, a cage-load at a time, each group making straight towards the office for their pay. Instead of going off home after receiving their money, they settled down upon their heels, in scattered groups, all over the bank.

Whether it was by accident or design, Bob and his associates under notice were on the last load. They appeared at the pit's mouth with their picks tied up together. It was a clear sign they were to be dismissed. The men on the bank sprang to their feet. There were many warm and honest hearts in the crowd, despite their black faces and ugly dress. They were murmuring quietly as Bob and his companions went to the office. Then silence fell as the crowd waited for them to come out.

They had not long to wait. The activists hoisted their picks upon their shoulders in a show of unconcern at their dismissal. The crowd surrounded them and their fellow-workmen asked them if they had been paid off. Morris Hughes asked Bob to speak. He did so.

'My dear fellow-workmen,' Bob said. 'I and my associates have been paid off. We bid a last farewell to Caeau Cochion, and turn our faces elsewhere to look for employment.'

Before he could say more some of the men began shouting insults at the management. The two police officers stepped in and asked them to go home quietly.

Morris and Bob were thrust aside but the crowd called out for Bob to finish his speech. He did so.

'We leave you with an easy conscience.' He said. 'We have done nothing wrong, and we trust no one will condemn us for publicly repeating the conviction we held in private, that we were unfairly and unjustly treated. You must now fight for your rights without help from us. But, wherever we go, your welfare and your success will always be in our hearts. I know there are before me scores of men older, wiser and more experienced than I, but permit me to give you a word of advice. Take care not to do anything that you may be ashamed of later. Be led by the wisest of among you. As you battle for your rights, do so as men endowed with reason, who will be called to account for your actions. I think, and my friends here agree with me, that your best plan will be to lay your complaints before the directors in person. In Abraham Jones's time, if there was anything for which we wanted a remedy, all we had to do was to place the matter before him, and it would be sure of careful consideration. I fear it would be useless for you to appeal to Mr Strangle, because ... '

As Bob spoke Mr Strangle's name the man himself came out of the office, and glared at the crowd. Scores of throats roared like a pack of hounds in full cry. The colliers rushed towards him, and carried him off like a straw in a whirlwind along the road to the railway station. The two officers showed incredible bravery. They tried to rescue him from the clutches of the infuriated colliers, as did Bob and the others. But as Mr Strangle was freed from one swarm another fell upon him. One of the police officers, mistaking Bob for a ringleader, drew his staff and struck him over the temple. Bob fell to the ground. The next moment both officers were knocked senseless by the roadside and Mr Strangle was rushed away with a speed that must have been extremely uncomfortable for such a fat man.

I thought Bob was dead, for he lay to all appearance quite still upon the ground. There were only Morris Hughes and myself to look after him. I cannot describe my grief when I thought him to be dead nor my subsequent joy when he came to himself a few minutes later and struggled to his feet.

'Morris,' he said. 'It's all been in vain. These madmen have ruined the cause. We must stop this if we can.'

They went after the crowd and I followed them. Bob was having difficulty in keeping up the pace, as he was still dizzy from the effect of the blow. He took hold of Morris Hughes's arm as his legs gave way

The Day of Bereavement

under him. As we got near the station we found that the crowd had doubled in size.

'Thank Heaven!' Bob said. 'The train's not here yet. We might yet stop the fools from sending Mr Strangle away.'

We were within three hundred yards of the platform when we heard the workmen give a loud cheer.

'We're too late,' Morris Hughes said.

'Too late indeed,' said Bob, slackening his pace. 'We will lose the sympathy of the country and be seen as savages. Some of these lunatics will go to prison, and be punished for their folly. Everything is spoiled. I'm sorry I ever meddled in this business.' He burst out crying like a child.

The steam-engine whistled, loud and shrill, and demoniac shouts rang out from the platform. As the train left, the disorderly rabble made a rush for the town. When they came to the spot where Morris Hughes and Bob were, they wanted to take my brother up on their shoulders and exhibit him as their hero. Morris stopped them.

'My friend can't stand it,' he said. 'But if you choose to listen, he may have a word to say to you.'

The mob fell quiet to listen. Bob climbed to the top of a hedge, and, leaning upon Morris Hughes's broad back for support, spoke to them.

'My friends,' he said. 'Ever since the beginning of this agitation for the increase of your wages and the better governance of the Caeau Cochion pit, I have taken a public part in it and done my best to improve your circumstances. You know as well as I do that two or three of us, had we chosen to submit to the masters, might have made ourselves a comfortable nest here. Then you would not have been any better off. After what has just taken place, I must tell you, even at the risk of being treated as you have treated Mr Strangle, that I am ashamed of ever having had anything to do with you.'

Bob was too overcome to say any more, and the crowd dispersed. Some were swearing, others grumbling, others silent and thoughtful. But it is fair to say that amongst that unruly multitude who whisked Mr Strangle off to the station and bought him a ticket, were many who disapproved of the deed. They were, however, powerless to prevent it.

Before my brother and I could get home, passers-by had told mother about the affair. We found her waiting in deep agitation. She was somewhat mollified when Bob told her that he had done his best to stop Mr Strangle's compulsory departure. At the same time, I couldn't miss the signs of fear and uneasiness on their faces. Bob, didn't leave the house that night, but three of the friends who had been paid off like him came round to talk. They spent hours discussing the likely consequence of the day's foolhardiness. Mother said nothing, but I could see that she feared coming evil.

After Bob's companions left there was little talk in our house. My brother pretended to read, but I noticed he didn't turn the pages of his book, and I knew he wasn't thinking about its contents.

Later that night, as we were about to go to bed, we heard footsteps approaching the house. Next minute a knock came to the door. Before we had time to open it Sergeant Williams and another police officer came in. Mother's face grew pale, and I began to cry my loudest.

Bob told me to stop, and with difficulty, I controlled my feelings. Bob was perfectly self-possessed and invited the officers to take a seat. They sat down. I must admit that they were two civil men, and both considered their duty that night an unpleasant one. I was glad they were Welsh, because mother could understand all they said.

'I think,' Bob said quietly, 'that I know your errand,'

'Well,' said Sergeant Williams, looking towards my mother, 'it is a disagreeable enough errand, Robert Lewis, I must say. But I hope all will come off right on Monday, Mrs Lewis.'

He handed Bob the warrant to read, in order to spare my mother's feelings.

'Don't be frightened, Mrs Lewis, 'Sergeant Williams said. 'It's only a matter of form. We must do our duty, you know, and, as I have said, I hope everything will turn out right on Monday.'

Mother said nothing, but the twitching of her mouth and the lump in her throat, showed clearly the depth of her feelings.

Bob drew on his boots, making a show of being leisurely, then spoke to Mam.

'Mother,' he said. 'You know where to turn for support. My conscience is clear.'

He walked away with the officers. But they had hardly gone twenty yards from the house, when I heard high words and the sounds of a struggle. My mother's tried to restrain me, but I ran out, and saw a desperate fight going on between the officers and two strange men.

A tall powerful fellow was knocking the constables about unmercifully. The other was of middling size, but a perfect master of the work he was doing. I recognized him as the man I called the Irishman, who had stopped me on my way home the night Seth died. The other looked like Bob in build and gait, but he was older and stronger. Their intention seemed to be to give Bob a chance of escape. They ran away when they saw he didn't run but helped the officers to fight them off.

When I went back into the house and told Mam what I had seen she got up and locked the door.

Neither of us went to bed. I tried to hide my feelings, for mother's sake, and she tried to hide her trouble from me, but we both kept being seized by fits of crying. When the lovely Sabbath morning broke I saw people, as they went by to their different places of worship, look askance at our cottage.

Mam and I didn't cross the threshold. She kept murmuring about the day of Tribulation. We ate little. That day seemed as long as a week. Mother opened her big old Bible dozens of times, but as soon as she began to read, her eyes overflowed. She kept them fixed on the same spot.

People passed, going home from morning service, but no one called. They went to Sunday School and back, but none called at our house.

I felt sure some of the chapel folk would come to see us after evening service. None did. As Mam said, 'Nobody darkened my door throughout the whole of the day.'

We were anxious for someone to call to find out how many had been taken to the lock-up. Mother feared that Bob was the only one. The clock struck nine.

'We'd best go to bed,' Mam said. 'We should try and get some sleep.'

At that moment a knock came on the door. I jumped up to open it. There stood Thomas and Barbara Bartley.

'We couldn't go bed without coming to see how you are coping with your trouble.' Thomas said.

It was impossible to imagine two visitors more unlike my mother in character and disposition. Yet we were heartily glad to see them. They gave us a chance to pour out the grief that we had stored up within us during the erstwhile four and twenty hours.

Thomas and Barbara had been to the Crown, where they heard all about the business. They stayed with us for several hours. Recalling the conversation, I think it was one of the strangest and most amusing I ever heard, although I didn't think so at the time.

But this chapter is already too long, and what I am going to relate in the next chapter weighs heavily on my mind. All I will say is that the visit was a great relief to us, and mother and I were able to sleep that night without knowing that still more bitter things were yet to come.

CHAPTER 17

Further Sufferings

I can hardly believe that I am recording facts. What I have to write feels more like a nightmare from my imagination. It was Monday morning, and mother had been sitting before the fire for hours, in deep thought. She was pleating her apron. I easily persuaded her to let me go down town to see what was happening to my brother and the five other men taken along with him.

The streets were full of people, anxiously waiting for the police court to open. The town folk recognized me as the brother of the most important of the prisoners. I met some friends of Bob, who asked how my mother was, and gave me each a penny. I hadn't been in town long before Wil Bryan found me. He could always find me.

Wil said, 'Take care of those pence. They'll come in right handy just now.'

I didn't know what he meant, and was too distracted to ask him what he intended. I gave him the credit of seeing farther than me. Almost immediately afterwards, I chanced on other friends of Bob, and got more pennies. Now I had five in all. I had never before been so rich.

Wil had a penny of his own, and he suggested we should pool our funds. I handed him over my five pennies, not caring about them in my grief. I had boundless faith in Wil's honesty. No sooner was the money in his hand than he slipped into a shop where they sold pork pies. I thought he was going to buy an example of that particular delicacy, and had no objection. When he came out, I was disappointed when he showed me a silver sixpence in the palm of his hand. He'd changed the coppers, and with a knowing wink, he deposited the coin carefully in his waistcoat pocket.

I didn't know why he wanted a sixpence. I wondered if he was planning to hire an attorney with it, to defend my brother. I knew little about the charges of the legal section of the human race. I put myself completely in Wil Bryan's hands, to do as he pleased.

As we stood in the street, the owner of the Hall drove by and the crowd stirred. His carriage went rapidly towards the Court House where he was the principal justice of the peace. Before Wil and I could get there, the spacious court was tightly packed, and hundreds besides us were left outside.

There was a police officer each side of the door. These representatives of authority kept telling everyone that every inch of room inside was crammed full.

FURTHER SUFFERINGS

'I'll get us in.' Wil said in my ear.

I didn't see how he would manage that.

After a while the crowd shifted a little. Wil Bryan and I edged closer to the officer's blue coat-tails. Wil had to tug at the flap more than once to attract its owner's attention. The officer bent his head and Wil spoke a few words in his ear. The officer's eyes opened wide. It was as if he'd heard an astounding piece of news. He shook hands with Wil, and then let us into the Court House, leaving hundreds of great strong men struggling outside.

Our joint property had changed hands. The Americans talk of the 'Almighty Dollar!' But a book might be written upon the miraculous powers of a sixpence. Wil knew, while still a boy, that the password, the 'open sesame', to all places was a sixpence. In the present circumstances, I felt that my friend had employed our money to excellent effect. Had it been six shillings, instead of six pence, I wouldn't have grumbled.

The officer had told the truth when he said the court was full to bursting. Wil, however, didn't find much difficulty in finding us a place where we could see and hear all that was going on. He pushed me in front of him, like a wedge, into the heart of the crowd, and if he found a stoppage, he'd say importantly, 'Robert Lewis's brother. Robert Lewis's brother. Make way.'

These words speedily opened a path for us. The crowd must have thought I was going up to give evidence in the case. There was no end to Wil's scheming.

I'd heard that Mr Strangle had returned to Mold a few hours after he'd been packed off. Now I saw him in court looking surly and defiant. The magistrates on the bench were Mr Brown, the clergyman, and the Owner of the Hall. Mr Brown was a genial, kindly man, but the owner of the Hall was quite a different sort: huge, unwieldy, pompous, overbearing and merciless. He presumed that everybody and everything was created for his service. If the law had allowed him he would have unhesitatingly hanged any man caught killing a pheasant. He had indulged his natural taste for wine too often so his nose had taken on the colour of parboiled American beef. This monstrous lump of a nose sprouted up from his face and exhibited a perpetual shiver. It would snort like a warhorse when its owner was roused.

Nobody ever discovered what other qualifications the gentleman from the Hall possessed for the magisterial bench, except that he was a rank Tory, a zealous Churchman, was very wealthy and always wore spurs, except in bed. Mr Brown dreaded him, and I had noticed that when speaking to him on the road the parson always kept a wary eye upon those spurs. It was as if he feared their wearer might suddenly jump on his back and drive him to that place the wearer himself was eventually going to end up.

As senior magistrate, the Hall owner seemed to be in his element, as Wil Bryan put it. To try a batch of colliers was a congenial task for him. He believed they were poachers. Those who wished to know were aware that only three of the six prisoners before the bench had taken any part in the attack on Mr Strangle. The others, Morris Hughes, John Powel and my brother had done all they could to prevent the assault. But Mr Strangle and the two police officers swore that these three were ring-leaders in the scandalous business. Neither the overseer nor constables understood a word of Welsh, but they declared on oath that Bob had instigated the attack. They claimed they had heard him name Mr Strangle just before the rush was made upon him by the workmen. The prisoners had no one to defend them, due mainly to my brother's obstinacy. He wouldn't have any one to defend him, he declared, and his example was followed by the rest. The owner of the Hall accepted the evidence of the officials without question. Nothing could be said about the accused that was too bad for him to believe without hesitation.

Having heard the witnesses, he asked whether the prisoners had any defence to make. Of course, three of them had nothing to say, for they were clearly guilty of the offence with which they were charged. Morris Hughes and John Powel were not that ready of speech, particularly in English. After a second or two's silence Bob spoke.

'I am perfectly innocent of the charge of attacking Mr Strangle,' he said. 'I did my best to defend the gentleman, and whilst doing so I was struck down by the police officer.'

'Do you expect the Bench to believe a story of that sort, after all the evidence we have heard?' asked the owner of the Hall with a contemptuous smile.

'I hardly expect the Bench to believe anything I say,' Bob replied. 'But it is true. If you wish I can call several eyewitnesses to attest the facts.'

'Several who were doubtless mixed up in the business, like yourself?' said the magistrate with a sneer. 'If we listened to you, you never did anything wrong; you never in your life told a lie. But we happen to know something of your history. You are one of those who want to make the masters workmen, and the workmen masters. But just you wait. We'll see directly how all your speech-making pays off. We've heard of you already, and we know your family young man.'

'My family has nothing to do with the charge now laid against me.'

'We think it has everything to do with it,' the magistrate replied.

'If so, you had better fetch my mother here,' said Bob.

'No,' said the magistrate. 'We've heard quite enough from you. We don't need any old women here.'

'As far as I know,' Bob said, 'you already have one on the bench.'

'I'll have none of your impertinence, young man, or you'll pay for it,' the magistrate said, sounding furious.

Mother had often advised Bob to hold his tongue, but he always found it too hard to do. His excuse was that it was a family failing. The owner of the Hall spoke briefly to Mr Brown, who listened in trembling deference. Then the Hall Owner spoke.

'The Bench does not see any necessity for a remand to a higher court in this case. The evidence is, to their minds, conclusive. It very much regrets that more of the scoundrels have not been brought before it to receive their deserts, but it is determined to make an example of those whom the police have laid hands on. The Bench is resolved to show that the master is to be master, and that a workman is to remain a workman. It wishes to show that the colliers must not take the law into their own hands, and that proper people have been appointed to administer the law. The Bench is determined to demonstrate that the law is stronger than the colliers, however numerous they may be. And so the Bench sentences five of you – namely, Morris Hughes, John Powel, Simon Edwards, Griffith Roberts, and John Peters – to one month's imprisonment with hard labour, and Robert Lewis, whom it believes to have been the chief agitator, to two months' imprisonment with hard labour. The Bench trusts this will be a warning, not only to the prisoners but to others who ought to be with them, who are equally guilty, not only of creating a disturbance and breaking the law in this fashion, but also of poaching on gentlemen's estates.'

As soon as sentence was handed down there was a general movement in court. The noise of people's feet and the talk were so loud, I could hardly hear my own sobbing. Wil sympathized with me and did his best to comfort me. So poignant was my sorrow that he was at a loss to know how to ease it. But suddenly a thought struck him. He handed over all he possessed to me, namely, his pocket knife.

'I give you this to keep forever,' Wil said.

I have that knife to this day, and, although it is not worth sixpence, I rank it as the sacrifice of a heart full of compassion. I wouldn't part with it for a hundred pounds.

A vast crowd had now gathered outside the Court House. They wanted a last look at the prisoners as they were taken to the county jail. The majority of the Caeau Cochion workmen were sober, industrious and moral. But, as commonly happens in large works, there were a number of worthless characters among them, and when these indulged in excessive drunkenness the better class of colliers got blamed for their misdeeds. Several of these drunks had been soaking themselves in the public houses that morning, and they were not in the best of tempers.

But I am constantly slipping into detail, despite promising myself not to do so. So, how some of the colliers set fiercely upon the police conveying my brother and his associates to prison; how the assailants were arrested, tried and found guilty; how the military were called out, were attacked and beaten; and how, under the crudest provocation, the soldiers opened fire upon the rioters, killing several, and so on – that I choose not to narrate in detail.

I will say that when the disturbance was at its highest, the feeling of the majority, which included some men of reason and intelligence, was in favour of the colliers. When things had cooled down, and there was a chance to look calmly at the circumstances, those people acknowledged the iniquity of the whole proceeding. On reflection they understood the frightful lengths that even sensible and religious men may go to if they are governed by their passions, instead of reason and grace.

I was afraid to go home, because I knew what a shock this shame would be for my mother. Someone had already told her about my brother's fate, and I feared the additional shame would be her death. Fortunately, I was wrong. That day proved to me that true religion can bring consolation to its owner in time of tribulation.

When I went into the house I met two women neighbours coming out. They had been consoling my mother, who had been weeping. When she saw me she smiled. That was like a rainbow in the clouds after a heavy shower, and proved clearly that God had not forgotten his covenant with her.

'Well, my son,' she said. 'It's getting worse and worse with us. But I believe the light will come soon. The darker the night the nearer the dawn, the tighter the cord the sooner 'twill break. The Lord, I believe, has a hand in this. The furnace must be seven times heated before relief will come to sight. I never dreamt it would go so hard with your brother, but I think none the less of him for what has taken place. I know he is innocent, for he never told me a lie in his life. There are a hundred times worse than he now at large. From a child he was too ready with his tongue, and all the bother I had with him was from him telling too much of the truth. He was always too decided of purpose. That was why he left the *Seiat*. But he has led a better life than many of us who are members. Who knows but that the Great King's design has been to bring him back, and to show him how he has lost the shelter and the defence.'

I have noticed since, that every mother, if her son is overtaken by disgrace or death, forgets all his faults and speaks only of his virtues.

'It would be impossible for me to believe that Bob is not a Christian,' said Mam. 'Even if he is not in the house, he still belongs to the family. I am certain that whilst in that far-off country of the prison a yearning will arise in him for his Father. How did he look, tell me?'

'He was as well as could be expected.' I said.

'Middling well? Yes?' Mam said. 'It's wonderful how he can stay so composed. I know what is uppermost in his mind, and that is what'll become of us two. How will we live? There was never was a lad who thought more of his mother, my poor darling.'

She burst out crying, and I joined in with her. Once we were both cried out, she spoke again.

'Do they have a Bible in jail?'

I nodded to reassure her, although I did not know.

'They have? I'm glad to hear it. But Bob knows enough of the Bible to chew the cud upon, for two months anyhow. What vexes me most is that I never got to see him. I could not bear to go to the Court. Do you think he'd get a letter if we were to write?'

I nodded again.

'You do? Well then, I'll not sleep tonight until you've sent him a word. I'm glad you're a bit of a scholar, because I don't want the entire world to know our affairs.'

I was obliged to set to at once and write a letter. Mam suggested I wrote it first on the unused leaf of a copy book.

'We might want to change it before we send it,' she said.

I still have original draft. The best way to finish this chapter is with a transcript of it. There is nothing special about it, but it is precious to me as proof of my mother's acquaintance with the Bible. I quote it exactly as she dictated it, except for a few changes in the colloquialisms where her meaning was not quite clear.

> Dear Son,
>
> I write you these few lines hoping you are quite well as it leaves us at present. I feel mixed and moithered very much, and I know you're the same. 'My complaint today is bitter', Job twenty-third and second. 'But who is he that saith, And it cometh to pass when the Lord commandeth it not?', Lamentations, third and thirty-seventh. I know very well you'll be troubling your mind about us as we are about you. But I hope you know where to turn, as you said I did, when you were leaving the house on Saturday night. 'And call upon me in the day of trouble. I will deliver thee, and thou shalt glorify me', Psalms, fiftieth and fifteenth. If I'm not deceiving myself too much, I think I've had a fulfilment of that promise today. Dear son, I fear greatly you will let your spirits go down and lose your health because you've been wrongfully put in prison. Perhaps it'll be some comfort to you to call to mind those spoken of in Scripture who were wrongly put in prison like yourself, and the Lord showed afterwards that they did not deserve to be there. If you have leisure turn to the following chapters: Genesis thirty-ninth, Acts fifth, eighth and sixteenth. 'Remember also it was from prison and from

judgment that He was taken,' Isaiah, fifty-third and eighth. You know the trouble I got with your father. The trouble today is very different. I'm pretty sure that even if you were a little amiss you were quite honest, and that your conscience is easy, as you said. If that is anything for you to think of, though you are in jail you're not a jot the worse in your mother's eyes, and I hope you're no worse in your Redeemer's eyes either. Some time, I much hope you'll come to see you have offended the Great Lord by leaving the *Seiat* and, though I believe you're not at any time strange to the great things of the Gospel, I trust I shall see you, when all this is over, turning your face towards the shelter. Dear son, the wind is high and the waves are rising, but if through that we are brought to call on the Master to save us, all will be well. Read Luke eighth and the eighth of Romans. If Morris Hughes and yourself are put with each other, it'll be no harm in the world if you gave a tune now and then, as Paul and Silas did of old, and I know of no better verse for you than Ann Griffith's 'Living still, how great the wonder. When the furnace is so hot.'

You know how it finishes, and who can tell but that you'd get inspiration by singing of the One whose fan is in his hand. I have a lot of things I would like to tell you, but I must come to an end. Keep your spirits up. Two months is not much. It'll be over very soon. Pray night and day. If they stop you from reading, nobody can stop you from praying. In my mind you were a good enough boy before, but for one thing. But something tells me you'll be a better man than ever after the present trouble. We wish to be remembered to you very warmly. This in short from your loving mother and brother,

Mair and Rhys Lewis

After I had copied out the foregoing and read it to mother many times over, I put it carefully into an envelope and addressed it. Mother made me write 'Haste' on one corner. She hadn't much faith in gum, so she insisted I used red wax, which she sealed with her thimble.

When all was done, she seemed calm and resigned to the decree of Providence. My brother's imprisonment affected our worldly circumstances, and marked an epoch in my history which I will reveal in the next chapter.

CHAPTER 18

Thomas and Barbara Bartley

Looking back to my early years, I notice that I had little of the carefree childhood that most lads have. Even before I learned of our poverty or the troubles of my family, my mother's puritanical austerity restrained my play, reduced my companions, and restricted my enjoyment. Knowledge of the Fall of Man, and the Two Covenants, was instilled in me when I should have been playing marbles. Other youngsters were hunting the hare, while I learned psalms at home. I was the worst at games in Soldier Robin's school. Even the town girls made fun of me.

I would not want to be disrespectful to my mother, for I know her intentions were as pure as a sunbeam. But it was her ignorance that contributed to my bodily weakness, my sadness and the depression of spirit that still afflicts me. I never knew the innocence of boyhood. Instead she instructed me in the sins of my father Adam, the details of my depraved heart, and the tricks and wiles of the Devil. My mother's religious gifts revealed the dark side of human nature in all its deformity, and her teaching had its effect. No wonder my pals called me 'the old man'.

I was thirteen when Bob went to prison. My religious training made me take it hard. I felt such sorrow that even my faithful and merry friend Wil Bryan couldn't cheer me up. My sympathy for my brother was genuine but I suffered a burning conviction that he was innocent. My admiration of his character grew accordingly.

My family pride was wounded, and I wanted to challenge Providence. When I heard that the Hall owner's game was almost wiped out the day after Bob and his associates had been sent down, I confess I was delighted. I was pleased that someone had taken revenge on him, even though I dared not say this to my mother.

I missed my brother. Our home was like a body without a soul. I felt as if I had been living in a working mill, and all its wheels had suddenly stopped.

I missed his male aura, his resonant voice and his ready wit. Home was no longer home for me. Mam said nothing, but I knew she felt the same. Her face lost its youthful bloom for ever. She would go to the door and look towards the station, hoping for her boy's return. She was convinced of his innocence and the injustice of his imprisonment. I'm sure she expected God to intervene and force Bob's release. She kept making meals for three and would lay three cups on the table at tea time; then she would quietly put one of them away, thinking I hadn't noticed.

She spent her days in a state of dreamy absent-mindedness. She carefully tended his books and turned the pages of the English volumes she had previously criticized, even though she couldn't read a word of English. I find it hard to describe her feelings in words. Her distress reached deep into the depths of her soul and stirred a whole host of the painful memories. But her sorrow was not hopeless. She reached up from the abyss of affliction to grasp the firm faith of Him who rules all. She read her Bible a lot and tried to speak cheerfully to me, but I could see she was making a great effort.

Thomas and Barbara Bartley were the first to visit us after Bob's arrest. I am still thankful for their kindness at that time. They were simple, harmless old souls and seemed wonderfully happy to me. They were alike in both looks and ways of thinking. Whatever Thomas might say, Barbara would confirm with a nod, and whatever Barbara said, Thomas endorsed, saying, 'To be shuar.'

They were always looking in the same direction. The circle of their lives was small, and they were not educated. How to plant a potato patch and kill a pig of ten-score weight were the two poles around which their world made its annual revolution. Providence, when drafting Its scheme of life, had forgotten to set trouble or trial against the names of Thomas and Barbara Bartley. The only exception was the death of their son Seth, and even that led eventually to perfecting their happiness.

Thomas was a well-known mender of shoes and an excellent neighbour. He was never short of work. He was not a teetotaller, but he only got drunk on special occasions, such as Whit Monday after his sick-benefit club walked in the town parade. Barbara would never admit he was drunk; all she would say was that he had 'taken a drop'. They had good hearts and thought that it was enough to live honestly. And they lived up to this ideal, for no one ever accused Thomas and Barbara of subverting a man from his cause, or ever said that Thomas put bad work into a shoe.

They thought they didn't need religion, as they had more than a formal honesty; they were always ready to do a kindness, and their willingness often took them well beyond the call of neighbourly duty. In my life I have met people of higher spiritual pretensions but whose religion failed to match up to the basic goodness of Thomas and Barbara Bartley.

These two old folk came to visit us in our trouble, and we had a long talk: too long for me to repeat in full, but the few words below are a sample of what they said.

They sat down and Thomas said. 'Well, Mair Lewis, you're in a bit of a bother, ain't you? I'm sorry in my heart for you.' Barbara nodded her head in agreement.

'I am so, Tomos *bach*,' Mam said. 'And I'm much obliged to you for your sympathy. "His way is in the sea, and His path in the great waters. Clouds and darkness encompass Him" but He knows.'

'Hold on a bit, Mair *fach*,' said Thomas, 'You're wrong there. Poor Bob's gone to jail not over the sea to be transported. You've got your head in the ash-pit over this, and you're imagining things to be worse than they are. Save us. The boy hasn't gone near the sea.'

'I know that, well enough, Tomos. It's of the Great King's love I'm speaking,' Mam said.

'Ho. I see, Mair,' Thomas said. 'Barbara an' I can't read, you see, and so we don't know much about the Great King. To tell the truth we never speak of Him, except when somebody dies or gets killed. We wouldn't want to make a mistake and offend Him though.' Barbara nodded her agreement.

'I'm sorry to hear that, Tomos. We ought all to think and speak a deal about the Great King, inasmuch as it is in Him we live, move and have our being. The Psalmist says, "My meditation of Him shall be sweet," Tomos. And in another place he says, "Evening and morning and at noon will I pray and cry aloud, and he shall hear my voice." If we were more like the Psalmist, we'd be nearer the mark, Tomos *bach*.'

'Well indeed, Mair, Barbara and I try to live as near the mark as we can,' he said, 'Don't we, Barbara?' Barbara nodded.

'As far as living honestly goes, you are quite right,' Mam said. 'But religion teaches us that something more is needed before we can enter into the life eternal, Tomos *bach*.'

'But how can we do more than live honestly, Mair? I'll swear I have a good heart, and I'd rather do a kindness than refuse. Wouldn't I, Barbara?' Barbara nodded in agreement. 'And I never bear anyone a grudge, do I, Barbara?' Again Barbara nodded.

'And as to religion,' he went on, 'you religious ones seem worse off nor anybody. Here's you, Mair Lewis, you have been professing as long as I can remember. You're always talking about religion, the Great King, the world to come. But who has met with more trouble than you? You'd think you'd had enough trouble with your husband, and here you go again with Bob sent to prison. He's one of the tidiest boys that ever wore a boot. He was always talking about religion when he came over to have his boots mended and there he is, worse off than anybody. I told Bob that if that's what religion is about I can't und'stand the Great King at all. You religionists do seem to be always in trouble, with your heads in your feathers.'

'Religion doesn't promise to protect a man from his trials, Tomos. There is some truth in what you say, that religious people are more often afflicted than others. "Thou who hast shown me great and sore troubles," says the Psalmist. "In the world ye shall have tribulation," says the Saviour. And Paul, in the Acts, says that "we must, through much tribulation, enter into the kingdom of God". The great thing for you and me, Tomos, is that these misfortunes sanctify us, that we are able to see the hand of the Lord in them all. We do not let our spirits sink into sorrow.'

'They tell me, Mair,' said Thomas, 'there's nothin' better to raise the spirits than ... 'He turned to Barbara, 'What do they call it? The thing they sell in the druggist's shop, What's its name, Barbara?'

'Assiffeta,' Barbara said.

'To be shuar,' Thomas said. 'If you take a penn'orth of asiffeta, a penn'orth of yellow janders drops, and a penn'orth of sour rhubarb, there's nothing better for lifting your spirits, they do say. I never tried it myself, I prefer a drop of beer to help. After Seth the beer did me a power of good. I could cry much better after a few pints. I shouldn't wonder if asiffeta would do you good, too, Mair. Barbara wanted to put a drop in her pocket for you, but I told her you wouldn't take it. You religious folk being so odd about things of that sort.'

'I hope, Tomos,' Mam said, 'that I have a better receipt for raising spirits than anything sold in the druggist's shop or the public house. To my mind, Tomos, nothing but Gilead balm and Calvary ointment can raise the afflicted spirit.'

'Very true but I hope it isn't too expensive.' Thomas said. 'The same thing won't cure everybody, and I always say so, as Barbara knows.' Barbara nodded yet again.

'You misunderstand me, Tomos,' said Mam. 'What I mean is the only thing that can raise an afflicted spirit is the sweet and precious promise of the Bible, knowledge of God in Christ, confessing their sins, and a trust in the dear death on Calvary. I hoped that your son's passing would lead you and Barbara to hear the Gospel, and help you seek consolation in its truths instead of trying to drown your sorrows in intoxicating and worthless drink, Tomos *bach*.'

'Do you know what, Mair?' said Thomas. 'If you only belonged to the Ranters, you'd make a champion preacher. But I don't agree with you about the drink. I know you understand more than me, but doesn't the Bible call it strong drink?'

'It does, sure enough, Tomos'.

'So James Pwllfford the tailor says. And the Bible would not have called it strong drink if it didn't strengthen a man.'.

'It's so strong that it'll knock you down, Tomos, if you don't take care,' Mam said. 'Seriously, Tomos *bach*,' she added, 'isn't it time that

Barbara and you began to think about your souls? You're getting old now. Don't you ever feel the need to come and hear the Gospel? Don't you think it high time you both sought out that Friend whom you and I will stand in need of before long? I'm making bold with you, but you know it's for your own good. My dear, good old neighbours, I've thought a deal about you, and prayed for you. The Great King has been good to you. What a comfort you have been to each other over the years. It would be a great pity, Tomos *bach*, if you were both left behind at the last. You'd like to see Seth once again, and be with him evermore?'

Thomas and Barbara nodded in unison.

'I've no doubt that Seth is safe in Heaven,' Mam said. 'The wayfaring men, though fools, shall not err. Don't you remember what Seth told the boy here when dying, that he was going far, far away to the great chapel of Jesus Christ? That is where he's gone for sure. But remember, Seth came to chapel, Tomos. The poor dear never missed a service. We took no notice of him and thought he didn't know what was going on, but Seth was building up a fortune. He found a pearl of great price, and it was worth his life eternal to him. There are more pearls in that field, Tomos. And you, my dear neighbour, must pay heed to the means of grace, or you'll not go to the same place as Seth.'

These last words had a striking effect upon Thomas and Barbara. Thomas stared straight into the fire place, so overcome with feeling that great tears rolled down his cheeks and dropped onto his cord trousers. Barbara rubbed her nose and eyes with her apron, and it was with difficulty she restrained a sob as mother spoke of Seth dying.

Mam saw the iron of conversion was hot and set about beating it into shape using the sledge-hammer of the Scripture that she knew so well. She turned their hearts to and fro upon her anvil, until she had struck a living spark from every side. My mother never let slip a chance to give advice or offer a verse from the Bible to anyone she thought in need of religion. She forgot her own troubles in her eagerness to help these good folk, who she saw as careless about the welfare of their souls. I haven't her focus, and it shames me that I am not more my mother's son in this.

Thomas was growing uneasy and anxious to get away. Mother took the hint. She stopped evangelizing when Thomas gave a heavy sigh and rose to his feet. 'Barbara, we must go home, look you,' he said in a half choked voice. 'What have you got in the basket there?'

He handed the contents of Barbara's basket to Mam. 'Champion stuff, Mair. We fed that pig on taters and oatmeal, it never had a single grain.'

Mother started to thank him but he cut her off. 'Don't mention it. You're warmly welcome. Have you any taters in the house?' Mam shook her head. 'If you send Rhys over tomorrow, I'll give you a few of the best pink eyes you ever tasted. They eat like flour.'

'Tomos *bach*,' said Mam, taking hold of his coat, 'you've always been wonderfully kind to me. Now, I urge you, be as kind to your own soul. Promise me you'll come to chapel next Sunday? You'll never regret it.'

Thomas cast his eyes upon the ground and, after a second or two's silence, said: 'Mair, if all the preachers spoke as plain as you, I'd come to chapel every Sunday. But, to tell the truth to you, I can't understand them. They always talk of things we don't know nothing about.'

'Will you promise, Tomos *bach*, and bring Barbara to chapel with you?' Mam said, holding more tightly to his lapel. 'The light will come, if you will only seek it.'

'What do you say, Barbara?' Thomas said. Barbara nodded.

'Well, name of goodness,' Thomas said. 'We'll come. Goodnight, and God be with you.'

After they left Mam wasn't as excited by the bacon, as I was. She found something else to delight her.

'Now I see it, Rhys,' she said her voice joyful. 'The Great Lord sent Bob to prison so that Thomas and Barbara Bartley might be saved.'

I didn't intend to write so much about Thomas and Barbara Bartley when I started this chapter, but, as the good book says 'it is not in a man that walketh to know how to direct his steps'. How right it is.

CHAPTER 19

Abel Hughes

Over my lifetime, I've paid attention to men and their habits, and I've noticed three main types.

First, there are those who come entirely under the sway of the Devil and their own evil dispositions, but who, through good fortune, then come under the divine influence of the Gospel, and find mercy. As the good book says 'the former things have passed away, and behold all things are made new.' Their passions are held in control, their hearts and course of life change, and even their consciences, are forever saying of the Evil One, 'he hath nothing in me.' A heavenly beauty distinguishes this section of my fellow men.

Then there is another class, in whose hearts religion has something to do, and who themselves have something to do with religion, but the Prince of this World has little to do with them, and on occasions a cloven hoof comes into view. It seems that both heaven and hell lay claim to them. And yet, on hearing them pray and tell of their experiences, I feel like a jury trying a man for his life. I'm ready to give them the benefit of the doubt. What it is important for them and for me to remember is that God will have no doubt as to our characters in the great Day of Revelation to come.

Then there is a third class. They profess no interest in religion, but their mode of life does show many virtues. They are honest, straightforward, amiable, and obliging, kind towards both man and beast, and would sooner wrong themselves than wrong anyone else. Their innocence reminds us of our first parents before the Fall. They are not religious in the accepted sense of the word, and yet many of religion's fruit grow within them. They don't trouble their conscience with impious acts, nor read or think enough to give rise to unease and doubt. They are often pretty happy. I am greatly attracted to this class of people and sometimes envy their lot.

Thomas and Barbara Bartley are in this last category. It was their kindness towards Mother and me in our trouble which made me look upon their like with interest and emulation. While Mam and I suffered such family distress, I wondered about the coldness shown by the officers of the church of which my mother was such keen member. I saw a strong contrast in the ready kindness and sympathy of Thomas and Barbara Bartley.

When I mentioned this to mother, she didn't support my poor opinion of our leaders.

'This is quite in the order of things, my son,' she said. 'There is something which causes the brethren to behave a little coolly towards us. Perhaps the Great Ruler is keeping the best wine until the last. If we are fit objects of succour, the Head of the Church will take care of us in His own good time.'

I didn't have to wait long to find my mother had it pretty right. Early the following morning, our revered old deacon Abel Hughes visited us. If I were writing his biography, rather than my own, I would have many interesting things to say about him.

I like to think I have changed and grown, despite my disadvantages. But some old-fashioned notions, formed when I was a boy, still cling to me. I'm ashamed to admit to them, but I can't get them out of my mind. Were I asked by some young man from an English town for my views on the subject, I would give them, easily and honestly, but underneath I would know I harboured thoughts of a different kind, moulded long ago, and a deep part of me.

One of these is my notion of what makes a good church deacon. It is not Theophilus Watkin, Esq., of Plas Uchaf, who made his fortune by management of the world in a very short time. He lives and dresses in a style in keeping with his newly exalted station. He keeps a liveried servant and takes his wife and daughters in full dress to all the principal concerts. He is called an ornament to the big seat of the Methodist Chapel at Highways. He is liberal with his money for the cause, generous to the poor of the church and seems to respect and hospitably entertain ministers of the Word. Yet he never goes to the Monthly *Seiat*, and rarely to Sunday School. That is not compatible with his position and the society in which he moves. He is always zealous in support of the pastorate and humble and self-denying at Church Meetings. He always lets the minister do all the speaking.

Surely he is a worthy official, and a great acquisition to the cause? Yes, exceptionally so, and I feel proud of him. But, then again, there is Alexander Phillips, known by his bardic name Eos Prydain. He is a hard-working young choir-leader, an expert in looking after the church books, always ready to plan, and perform, a concert. He is always trim in appearance. He is an admirable man, even if he is a little reserved in the *Seiat*. It would be almost impossible for the brethren to hold a tea party, or get up a competition meeting without his invaluable services. He is fond of a joke, but always observes proper behaviour. He is of admirable use to the cause, and thought a good deacon. Even so, my antiquated notions will whisper to me that Theophilus Watkin and Eos Prydain do not quite come up to the diaconal standard.

Abel Hughes, however, fits my notion of a traditional deacon. He is somewhat advanced in years and wears knee-breeches, dark coat and vest, with a black kerchief, tied several times about the neck. He sports a broad-brimmed, low-crowned beaver hat, with his face clean shaved up to within half an inch of each ear, where it shows a tiny lock. His hair is kept cut parallel with his heavy brows which overhang a thoughtful face. This is his physical aspect, but he also has a spiritual personality.

His grasp of the Scriptures is strong, and he is an earnest enforcer of the teachings of the Gospel. He is always at the Monthly *Seiat* and attends every service. He holds, and expresses, original, inspiring and tear-compelling views, whether at prayer meeting or when introducing the service for a preacher. He is precise to the point of harshness in matters of church discipline, but is also tender hearted and pious. He leads a blameless life and is never frivolous. He expects all who belong to church, even the children, to behave seriously and with decorum.

This is Abel Hughes. He first gave me the standard of what a deacon should be. This notion, however erroneous, is embedded in the depths of my consciousness.

A model deacon would be somewhere between Abel Hughes and the sort of people who are called deacons in these days, who are often little more than ministers' lodging house keepers or clerks of the church. Mam saw in Abel Hughes a man almost without fault. This was because both deacon and member ate the same spiritual food, drank the same spiritual wine, and exchanged ideas on the subject of practical religion. In chapel and at home. Mam and Abel were unassuming and homely; and, after the manner of old people, they never addressed each other as Mr and Mrs.

Abel Hughes was the person that Mam most wanted to see in her trouble. And nothing would please me better than to be able to write down in full the talk which took place during his visit. But I cannot. Although I have an excellent memory, the conversation was so different from that with Thomas Bartley that I failed to understand most of it. But I feel I should try to record some of the talk, for mother said some things about the value of personal religion which stuck in my mind.

Abel entered the house without knocking as was usual for him, and mother gave him a look that was almost hauteur. I could see traces of moisture in her eyes, and the movements at the corners of her mouth and throat showed that she struggling to stop herself from bursting into tears.

Abel held out his hand.

'Well, Mair,' he said 'and how are you?'

'Wonderfully well, considering. I'm troubled on every side, yet not distressed; perplexed, but not in despair. I am cast down, but not destroyed.'

'I was certain, Mair, that you knew where to look for help, whatever your troubles were. Otherwise I would have come sooner.'

'Well,' Mam said. 'I hope I don't need much nursing. I'm not like the woman from London House, who stayed weeks away from chapel because the deacons didn't call on her when she had a bit of a toothache. Do you think that, at my age, I haven't learned to walk?'

She gave him a hard stare. 'But it would have done you no harm, Abel,' she said, 'If you'd come to inquire for me a little sooner, especially after our long acquaintance.'

She shook her head as if to clear her thoughts. 'Although, if you didn't come here for a month I shouldn't think any the less of you,' she said. 'Indeed, Abel, I feel almost thankful you didn't come, because if you had, I wouldn't have caught the sight I did of the One (Here she began to quote a poem) "Who above every other,/ through the whole creation wide,/ deserves the name of friend and brother,/ and who'll e'er the same abide/ against man's hard lot forlorn./ Our Protector was he born".'

'You know, Abel,' she said. 'Joseph sent every man to go out from him before he made himself known to his brethren. I hope my present trouble is but a cup placed in the sack's mouth, so that I may be brought to know the Ruler of the country.'

'I am glad to find you in the green pastures, Mair,' Abel said.

'Where did you expect to find me, Abel? Not out on the common, surely? After all our religious efforts, it would be hard if we found ourselves without a shelter on the day of storm. If I'm not deceiving myself I have nothing worth talking of but the fair pastures. As you know, Abel, I'm wholly without help, and worse off than if I were a widow. My son who was my sole support has been sent to gaol ...'

She stopped speaking and buried her face in her apron, quite overcome.

'There is truth in those words, Mair,' Abel said. 'I've been young, and now am old. Yet I haven't seen the righteous forsaken, nor his seed begging bread. The Lord trieth the righteous, but the wicked and him that loveth violence His soul hateth. Many are the afflictions of the righteous, but the Lord delivereth him out of them all. Light is sown for the righteous, and gladness for the upright in heart. I am certain, Mair, that light has been sown for you, though it might seem like night with you now. You will see it budding and sprouting in this world, even if you are not allowed to see it in full growth. Be of good comfort, trust in the Lord, and He will deliver you from your tribulations.'

'I try to be so, Abel, as well as I can,' Mam said. 'But hearing you speak, I can't help thinking of Twm o' Nant's words. He wasn't religious, but he said a great many good things, and he said this.'

She began to quote again. '"Easy 'tis for the hale and well/ The sick man to take comfort tell." Yet I feel very thankful to you for your cheering words, and I've been wondering and wondering why you didn't come here sooner, Abel?'

'I didn't give much thought to you, Mair,' said Abel. 'I was sorry to miss you from chapel on the Sunday, although I didn't expect you, given the circumstances. Bob wasn't a member with us, although he was more what a member should be than many of us. No one said a word against his character, and he was one of the best teachers in Sunday School. But these strikes are queer things Mair.'

Abel clasped his hand to together as if trying to hold back his feelings. 'They've come to us from the English. They're not our way. I fear they'll do much harm to the country and to our religion. We brethren though ought to listen. Bob became a leader because he had understanding and the gift of speech. Nobody doubts his honesty of purpose. Indeed, many sympathize with the colliers in their campaign for an increase in wages and against the tyranny of their employers. But no one can justify their attacking the overseer, and driving him out of the country. According to first accounts Bob was guilty of this act. Had I run straight to sympathize with you, people would say the chapel was no better than the agitators. The Cause would suffer, and our good name would be soiled.'

He paused and looked a Mam straight in her eyes, his full of sincerity.

'Now I am happy to tell you, Mair,' he said, 'that no one believes Bob is guilty even though he is imprisoned. Good men, who saw the whole thing, testify that he and John Powel tried to stop the others. And I have other good news for you. The men refused to work under Mr Strangle so the masters paid him off. They have sent for Abraham Jones, the former manager, and reinstated him. The works will restart tomorrow. Mr Walters, the attorney, got the employers and workmen to talk by acting as interpreter and arbitrator between them. If this had been done at first, the whole trouble might have been spared. The masters now know that Bob and his associates had good cause to complain against Mr Strangle. So you see Mair, things are not so bad after all.'

'So, they'll surely let Bob out of prison now that they find he's innocent and that what he said was right,' Mam said.

'No, I fear not, Mair,' Abel said. 'When magistrates make a mistake, they never try to put it right. They're like a man who, having told a lie, thinks the best thing he can do is to stick to it.'

'But is it possible,' Mam said, 'that Mr Brown, the clergyman, can go up into the pulpit to preach of justice and mercy, after he has sat upon the bench and allowed the owner of the Hall to administer injustice?'

'He'll preach just the same, Mair,' Abel said.

'I'll defy him to preach any worse, Abel,' Mam said. 'But where people's consciences are, I don't know. I'm very thankful I'm not in the Church of England.'

The two went on to talk about religion and its consolations for some time. Abel's visit was a great blessing to Mam. She seemed happier, not least because Abel said no one believed in Bob's guilt. But we couldn't live on happy feelings. It was a long wait for my brother's release. Wages had been reduced under Mr Strangle's management, so mother had nothing to fall back on. For the first three weeks our friends were kind to us, but time soon wore away the sharp edge of sympathy.

Bob still had five weeks to serve, and never shall I forget those weeks. At the time I wouldn't tell even by my greatest friend that I was hungry. I confess it now. But it is impossible for any man to realize our situation unless he has experienced it. To be in perfect health while your stomach is filled with voracious lions with nothing to appease them, is something I cannot describe. But I know from experience just how it feels.

Mother was not given to complaining and had a spirit of foolish independence, otherwise we would never have been in want. I inherited her weakness. I wouldn't admit, even to Wil Bryan, that I suffered great pangs of hunger. But Wil guessed, because I often saw him go into his house and bring out a great piece of bread and butter, or bread and meat. He would take a bite or two and then pull a wry face.

'I don't have any appetite today,' he'd say, 'and if you won't eat it, Rhys, then I will have to chuck it away.'

How my inner lions raged, so, rather than allow him to waste good food, I would accept it from him. Ah, Wil, how well didst thou understand my proud heart, as well as knowing my empty stomach!

Mother sold many small things, taking care to sell them only to strangers. She would not admit to the chapel people that we were in such straits. It can only have been because of her spirit of independence and false pride.

Once, after a long fast when we had nothing in the house, we went over to Thomas and Barbara Bartley's. Mam pretended we'd gone to congratulate them on coming to the service. I don't doubt that she rejoiced to find the two old folk had started to attend chapel. But there was also a secret understanding between us that we shouldn't be allowed to leave Thomas Bartley's house without a good meal. We went there three times, on one excuse and another, and not once did we come away empty-handed or empty-bellied.

This time is a painful one to write about so I will gloss over many incidents of misery which come vividly before me as I write. One, though, I cannot pass over.

It was between breakfast and dinner times – that is, other people's, breakfast time and dinner time having no special significance for us. We hadn't tasted anything since the middle of the previous day. Weak and dispirited, I tried to pass the time reading. Mother sat still and meditative. Presently she got up, put on her bonnet, and then sat down again for a brief while. She got up a second time, put her cloak about her, and, after a little musing, sat down once more. Evidently, she was feeling some deep conflict of mind. I heard her mutter something, but all I could make out was 'meal' and 'bread.'

After a minute or two she rose resolutely to her feet, fetched the basket which she used to carry things from the shop when Bob was at work, from the back room.

'Where are you going?' I said.

'Well, my boy,' she said. 'It's no use moping about here. We can't hold out much longer, look you. They say it's the dog who goes who shall get. I'll go far enough so that no one'll know me.'

I realized she meant to go out begging. I was heart-sick at the thought. I stood against the door.

'I cannot let you do that,' I shouted. 'We can hold out until tomorrow at least,' I pleaded in a quieter voice.

It didn't take much to persuade her. She put her basket aside, and took off her cloak and bonnet. Having given way a little to our feelings, I fancied my hunger had entirely left me and that I could now go for many days without food. If there is one act of my life that gives me satisfaction, it that I stopped Mam going out to beg on the streets to feed me.

Had I let her go, my faith in God's promises would be less than it is today. I cannot describe the pleasure which the memory brings me, despite the hard pass we came to: I was able to lay her to rest without her ever having gone out to beg. We didn't cross the threshold for the rest of that day.

The hours dragged slowly on. Then, as night came, we heard a loud sharp rap at the back door of the house. We both got up to answer it. We opened the door but there was no one there. As we were about to shut it I saw something on the door-step. It was a small brown-paper bundle, neatly packed.

I took it into the house and read my mother's name written clumsily upon it. I recognized the handwriting as that of my best friend. The package, like the heart of the sender, contained a great many good things that brightened the face of my mother. Yet the mystery surrounding them made her pause before eating them. She thought for a moment.

'David, when in want, did eat of the shew-bread,' she said. 'And the Saviour afterwards defended him for so doing. And although we do not know where these good things have come from, I don't think we shall do doing wrong by using them.'

She did not ask me if I could guess where the package had come from, and I didn't give her the slightest hint. Had I done so, I don't think she would have touched the contents, for I strongly suspected that the sender had not acquired them, honestly.

My noble friend, Wil. I know very well thou wouldst have shared thy last bit with me, and that, although thou didst not afterwards mention that parcel to me, nor I to thee, I am as certain thou wert the sender as I am that it was from thy hand that I received the bread and cheese the previous day.

CHAPTER 20

The Vicar of the Parish

I have already said that Mam had a sort of foolish pride and independence of mind. If she had been more pliable and easy-going, we need not have suffered quite so much destitution. But I only once remember her being rude to a gentleman of position as if she were his equal, at a time when she didn't have any of the daily necessaries of life. I trust any friends into whose hands this autobiography might fall once I rest below the earth will forgive me for believing my Mam was the best mother in the world. But I should be unfaithful to my promise to tell the truth and the whole truth, if I overlooked her weaknesses.

She was a woman with a hot temper and strong feelings. She gloried in being a plain speaker. My experience of plain speakers is that while they excel in straightforwardness, they sometimes forget the feelings of others, and can show a lack of that suavity and good taste that should adorn the character of every true Christian.

In a small, quiet town the Vicar of the parish is an important person. The townsfolk are often over-ready to acknowledge the importance of the fortunate occupant of the Vicarage. On his side, the fact he cannot be removed from office gives him a tendency to accept as his due whatever of importance might be laid upon him. Mr Brown was no exception to this rule.

If any man in Mold was less respected than he deserved to be, that man was not Mr Brown. He was a portly, double-chinned, genial gentleman and, although I would on no account suggest that he walked as other men, he was in a literal sense of the word carnal. His bulk showed that his living, worth seven hundred a year, was not without its material blessings.

I must pay tribute to his memory by saying that his ear heard the cry of the needy, and his pocket was opened to the poor and afflicted. Widows and orphans found a kindly friend in him, especially if they attended Top Church. Although Mr Brown was more interested in the welfare of his own flock than of poor Dissenters, he did not forget them. If Dissenters appealed to him for help and he did not wish to contribute from his own purse, or from those legacies left to him 'as long as water ran,' by the departed whose names appeared on the walls of the church, he would always put in a good word for the applicants to some guardian or other, to secure them a few pence from the parish.

If anybody wanted a letter of recommendation, they went to Mr Brown for it. No town voluntary organization of any consequence was complete unless Mr Brown's name was connected to it. However severe their rheumatism, the shaking old man and the bent old woman would doff their hat or curtsey to Mr Brown when they met him. Those idlers and loafers who hang around street corners, whose means of living no man knows, when they saw Mr Brown they ceased their funning, hid their cutty-pipes in their palms and touched their hats to him as he went by. There was a kind of winsomeness, distinction, charm – I hardly know what to call it – about Mr Brown's manner at all times. I fancy everyone at the time was as incapable of describing the thing as I am now. It was something in the air which influenced all – aye, even the Dissenters.

I remember Mr Brown once honouring a Bible Society meeting with his presence. When he came in, never was there such a clapping of hands and stamping of feet heard. Some people, forgetting where they were in the joy of the moment, excited themselves until they were fairly out of breath. Several Dissenters, to say nothing of Church folk, shed tears of joy on the occasion, the reason for such an extraordinary manifestation of feeling, doubtless, being a sincere respect for the good old Book, coupled with the knowledge that a gentleman of Mr Brown's rank and position was a patron for that Society whose object it is to give 'a Bible to all the people of the world.'

Mr Brown said little at the meeting (he never could without a service book), but he was there, and that spoke volumes. It made some people, who thought they could read the signs of the times, rather fancy that the millennium was not far off.

For all this, Mr Brown was an unassuming man. The deference paid to him would have made many another lose his head. But even his warmest admirers admitted he had one drawback: he could not preach. His delivery was slow and painful, but, like a wise man, he took care never at any time to tire his hearers with over-long verbosity. He had a habit, when in the pulpit, of turning up the whites of his eyes, which was to some people 'as good as a sermon.' Besides, he made up for his shortcomings in the pulpit by the fact he was a justice of the peace. This character gave him an influence over some whom he could never have reached within the walls of his church.

'Ned the Poacher,' seeing him on the street, would 'make sly eyes' at Mr Brown, and it was easy to read in his face the consciousness of an unusual width of pocket in the skirts of his velvet coat.

'Drunken Tom,' too blind to see anyone else, would spot Mr Brown from afar and, after a stagger and a glance through his half-open eyes, as through a mist, would make a desperate attempt to walk straight until Mr Brown had passed.

If he had not, in his magisterial character, come into contact with these gentry on Monday mornings in the County Hall, Mr Brown's influence with them would have been nil. Mr Brown was a man of considerable importance amongst all classes, and he feared no one but the owner of the Hall. Mr Brown was pretty much what he ought to be, or mother would never have esteemed him so highly. As I have said more than once, her prejudice against Church of England people was something awful. As to Mr Brown, I heard her praise him many times, but always taking care to qualify her eulogy by saying 'as a neighbour.' It was 'as a neighbour' alone she gave him a good word.

In speaking of religion, she unhesitatingly expressed her fear that Mr Brown had not 'proved the great things.' One observation of hers about him I shall never forget. She happened to be talking to Margad Peters, who was a Churchwoman, in praise of a Methodist preacher, when Margad said, 'Our Mr Brown is a very good man, only he is not much of a hand at preaching.'

My mother replied 'That's exactly the same, Margad, as if you were to say James Pwllfford is a very good tailor, only he can't stitch.'

Margad must have felt the force of the observation; as they sometimes say in the House of Commons, 'the subject was then dropped.'

As might have been expected, the conviction and sentence of my brother Bob by Mr Brown and the owner of the Hall, did not increase my mother's respect for the Vicar. She considered the magistrates had shown lack of judgment and unpardonable haste. Whether it was concern for us as his parishioners or a consciousness of shame for the part he had taken in the trial that brought the reverend gentleman to visit us, I cannot say for certain. But I am willing to put the best construction on his conduct and believe his motive was pure and praiseworthy.

When I recall that visit I am ashamed of the reception mother gave our visitor, especially when I consider the respect paid to Mr Brown by the most of the town people. Perhaps I ought to say that, although Mr Brown was Welsh on his mother's side, he spoke our old Cymric tongue imperfectly.

'Good morning, Mrs. Lewis,' said our vicar, panting for breath and wiping the perspiration from his red face and sleek, fat neck.

'Good morning,' said mother stiffly, and without the least attempt at a curtsey, or as much as asking him to take a seat. But Mr Brown sat, unasked, upon an old chair by her side, which, like all the rest in our house, was so terribly rickety that I dreaded every minute it would give way beneath the unusual load laid upon it. It was horribly uncomfortable, and creaked like an old basket.

There was a brief, painful silence. Then Mr Brown remarked, 'Very fine day, Mrs Lewis.'

'The day is right enough, Mr Brown. Were everything like the day, no one would have cause to complain,' replied mother drily. She gave way to her old habit of pleating her apron, which showed she had something on her mind that she wanted to say.

'How do you get on, as things are now, Mrs Lewis? Do you have enough food?' Mr Brown asked, kindly.

'I get on better than I deserve, and have had enough food to keep body and soul together. I have no one to thank for it but the One who feeds the young of the raven, who maketh his sun to rise on the evil and on the good, and sendeth rain on the just and on the unjust.'

'You say very good; you 'cognise the hand of the Great King,' said Mr Brown.

'I hope I do,' said mother, tartly. 'But while recognizing the Great King's hand, I can't shut my eyes to somebody else's hand also. Those wretched people of old who saw the hand of the God of Israel, knew something of Pharaoh's too.'

'Yes, very bad man, Pharaoh, Mrs Lewis.'

'Bad enough,' returned mother; 'and though he was drowned in the Red Sea, his children were not, more's the pity. There is reason to fear that some of his offspring, and of Og, the king of Bashan, live on to persecute God's people to this day, even though the Bible says that Og was utterly destroyed.'

'You know a deal of Scripture, Mrs Lewis,' said Mr Brown, approvingly.

'I'm afraid, Mr Brown,' said mother, 'that many know a deal more than I do. "Blessed are they that do his commandments, that they may have right to the tree of life, and may enter in through the gates into the city."'

'We must all try to keep the commandments, Mrs Lewis, or we will never enter into the life.'

'We must, as a rule of conduct,' Mam said. 'But we'll never enter into the life unless we do something more. I know this much of divinity, that we were shut out forever on Sinai and that, if we wish to enter into the life, we must turn elsewhere for the foundation of our hope. That's what the Bible and Mr Charles's *Preceptor* teach us. And I believe them, whatever the Common Prayer may say. I pronounce nothing about that.'

'You chapel people know nothing 'bout Common Prayer. Common Prayer very good book, Mrs Lewis; same as the Bible,' said Mr Brown.

'I say nothing about your Common Prayer, Mr Brown, but I'll say this, that God's Book is the Bible, and I have no fear in saying, further, that the next book to that is Charles's *Preceptor*, and, if I were to live to a hundred, no one will change my opinion upon the point,' my mother said, vehemently.

Mr Brown, smiled at her simplicity. 'Well, we'll let it be so, Mrs Lewis. I do like to see people zealous. But what I was wondering was, how you were getting along, now Bob's in jail', he said. 'Do you have enough to eat, you and the boy here? Though you don't come to Church, I was thinking, Mrs Lewis, to give a bit of ... of assistance to you ... or to get a little from the parish, till Bob comes back.'

Mr Brown spoke in a kindly tone, and I have no doubt that he sympathized greatly with mother and me in our distress. However, his words, touched a chord in mother's self-reliant nature which evoked a response that I considered rude and unbecoming towards a gentleman occupying a position and enjoying a respect like Mr Brown. I can remember, word for word, what she told him in reply.

'Mr Brown,' she said, 'I know only of One who can give a bruise and heal it, who is able to cast down and raise up. So, if you came here thinking to put a plaster upon the hurt you gave, your errand has been in vain. A kick and a kiss I call a thing of that sort, Mr Brown. After you had put my innocent boy in prison, it would be very difficult for me to take any help from you, let my distress be what it may. Perhaps you will say I am making bold, and so I am; but I must speak what is on my mind. I'll feel easier then. I am surprised at you, Mr Brown! I used to think well of you, as a neighbour. But, if it makes any difference to you, you have gone down ten degrees in my sight. I think I know with whom I am speaking; because, as Twm o' Nant said,

> Praised and revered worthily,
> O'er all men, the priest we see;
> But none more accurs'd than he
> If God-guided he not be.

And I don't much fancy, Mr Brown, that God guides you when you associate and co-operate with a man like the owner of the Hall, who cares for nothing on this earth but his racehorses, foxhounds and furniture.'

'Mrs Lewis! Mrs Lewis!' Mr Brown said.

'My name is Mair, Mr Brown. I'm but a poor woman, and I don't want to be 'mistressed' if you please. But I tell you again. Your place is not on the bench, hearing every cause, clean and dirty. A priest has quite enough to do to look after the souls of his congregation, if he has that work at heart, without meddling with other matters. If I were Queen, I would say to every priest, and preacher too, for that matter, as the Lord said in another case — and one which it would be well for you and I to think more of — "What hast thou to do to declare my statutes?" That I would. Paul, before his conversion, was on the way to Damascus with his pockets stuffed with summonses for putting good men in prison, but after that great event I warrant you he tossed them all over the hedge, and nobody ever heard of his sending anyone to gaol again. He had better work to do by a great deal. Another thing, Mr Brown, I don't know how you can expect a blessing, or give sleep to your eyes, or slumber unto your eyelids when your heart knows, by this time, that you have hurried an innocent lad to gaol. And it is not because I'm his mother I say so. He is one with a good deal more in his head than many who think themselves somebodies. One who, although, more's the pity, he does not now profess religion, has led a life against which no one can say a word. I have no wish to hurt anybody's feelings, but my son never, in his life touched a drop of intoxicating drink, nor was he ever in the Cross Foxes playing bagatelle, or whatever you call it. And although he was but a common collier, I think as much of him as other people do of their children who have been brought up in boardin' schools, and taught to frivol, and to feed their pride and fulfil the desires of the flesh. That I do. No one need have spoken to me of help from the parish, if you, Mr Brown, and the owner of the Hall had not wrongfully imprisoned my son. I hope, still to avoid going on the parish, although there are many to whom it is useful. But as to going to Church, I never will. As you know, I've been there several times at thanksgiving services; but I am bound to tell you I never found anything for my soul there. Methodist have I always been, and, by the help of God, Methodist I shall always remain. I'll try and rough it, somehow, till my son comes back, without help of either parish or parson.'

Mother delivered this address fluently, and with a withering scorn on her face which I never seen it wear before or since. Constant fear that the chair would give way under Mr Brown and deep shame for my mother's audacity threw me into a great sweat. I was glad from the bottom of my heart to hear her put an end to her lecture.

Mr Brown looked thunderstruck and wounded. And not without cause. But he was not the man to defend an act, though it were his own, if he thought it to be unjust. Mother knew him well enough to make bold with him in this. She knew also that if the belief were common in the town that Bob and his companion had been wrongfully imprisoned, no one could be more fully aware of the fact than Mr Brown. He was never a stranger to public opinion.

Mr Brown didn't attempt to defend himself. When he got up to go I felt mightily relieved, because I was convinced, now, that the chair would not break. Before leaving, he said, morosely almost, 'No one ever spoke like that to me before, Mrs Lewis; and p'raps you'll want assistance from me yet.'

'I don't deny the first, Mr Brown,' mother said, 'because I hope you never before put an innocent lad in gaol. It is no harm in the world for you to hear a bit of the truth sometimes, and I feel very much what-d'ye-call-it after telling you what I have. But as to the other thing, namely that I'll come to ask you next time, I have nothing to do but trust in Providence. If I ever throw myself upon your good mercy, you may be sure that I shall have first tried everybody else in vain.'

Mr Brown left, fuming.

'I said nothing too harsh to him, did I?' Mam asked after he'd gone.

I said I feared she went a little too far, and had hurt his feelings.

'Don't talk rubbish,' she rejoined. 'His skin is much thicker than you imagine. The Saviour and his Apostles spoke a good deal plainer truth to the High Priest than I did to Mr Brown. I knew very well where I stood, and I'll defy him to send me a summons, big a man as he is.'

That night, Abraham Jones, the overseer at the Caeau Cochion Pit, came to our house to notify mother that good and constant work was being kept for Bob when he came home, and to offer whatever money she might need in the meantime.

"Bob can repay it from his wages when he returns," Abraham said.

Mother, having cried a little and expressed her thanks over and over again. She gave Abraham, a zealous Congregationalist, particulars of the parson's visit, which diverted him greatly. He handed mother a sovereign by way of loan. She looked at the coin on every side and from every angle, as at an old friend whose face she had almost forgotten.

'A good man showeth favour and lendeth,' she said. 'He will guide his affairs with discretion. Do you know what? I had nearly forgotten the sort of person our Queen was. I remember a time when I was right well acquainted with her. I hope we'll see each other oftener in the future. Long life and grace, both to her and her children, is the sincere wish of my heart.'

CHAPTER 21

The Conversion of the Bartleys

Time passed, as it always does, bringing with it, as it always does, not only its troubles, but its consolations. Through the kindness of overseer Abraham, our cupboard was no longer empty, the lions no longer raged within my stomach. The nearer the prospect of Bob's release, the brighter mother's face became. Yet I knew from what she said that she was not without her fears about the effect an unjust imprisonment might have had on his spirit, and a thousand other things that a careful mother troubles herself about under such circumstances.

John Powel had already come home, and, although he couldn't tell her much about Bob, the two not having been confined together, Mam had been able to draw enough out of him to make her look forward with fear and anxiety to my brother's return. Before that happened two things cheered her greatly. Not to enlarge (as I sometimes say in my sermon, although I then deliver myself of every word I originally intended), I will merely touch upon them.

The visits which Abel Hughes, our revered old deacon, paid to our house became so frequent that I took them for granted, except on some special occasion like the one I have already described. But I do remember one visit about a fortnight before Bob came out of prison. Mother and he had been talking for some time. I wasn't taking much notice of them, as I was sitting at the table near the window, practicing writing; I had not forgotten Bob's advice to work hard and try to improve myself, so that I wouldn't end up as a collier like him. Then I heard Abel mention me to mother.

'It's high time, Mair, for that boy to think of doing something, especially with the way things are with you now.'

'I'm of the same mind as you, Abel,' Mam said. 'But what can he do? I don't know. He isn't strong, nor much of a scholar.'

'But he's a big lump of a boy to be doing nothing, Mair.'

'Exactly,' Mam said.

'I could do with a lad in the shop there, now, if I were sure Rhys could earn his keep.'

'I've been thinking the very same thing a dozen times, Abel,' Mam said 'only I feared Rhys wasn't scholar enough. I know you'll give him fair play for his soul, and I don't think he'll be any trouble for you. He's a pretty good lad, considering. It's odd, Abel, but the older I get the more I start to agree with Bob that a little learning comes in wonderful handy. Only not too much of it, I'll stick to that.'

'What're you doing there, Rhys?' Abel said, coming towards me. 'Do you know what, Mair? He writes a very decent hand. Tell me, who taught you?'

'Bob,' I said, timidly.

'How are your sums? Can you do simple addition? '

I smiled, almost sarcastically, before answering. 'I can do addition, subtraction, multiplication and division of money.' I said.

'What's that he's saying, Abel?' Mam said.

'Oh! Only that he knows how to reckon money,' Abel said.

'Rhys!' Mam said, giving me a hard look; 'I never caught you out in an untruth before. Do you want to break your mother's heart? Haven't I had enough trouble already, without you telling a lie to my very face? The old saying is a true one, Abel. No one knows what it is to rear children. I tell you, honestly, I don't want to mislead you; but he has never had any money to handle. I'm surprised at you, Rhys, for saying such a thing to Abel Hughes.'

Many of the old Methodists believed that laughter was not becoming to the Gospel, and I never remember hearing Abel Hughes give vent to his feelings by laughing before. He was so unused to the business that his laugh sounded like a cross between a screech and a groan – but laugh out loud, he did.

'Don't worry yourself, Mair *fach*,' he said. 'Rhys and I are only talking of the tutor's rules for calculating money.'

'Ho, say you so? I never knew Mr Tudor had any such rules,' Mam said, 'although I've heard he's got plenty of money, and that he takes good care of it. If he were to come here to reckon my money, he could leave his rules at home, goodness knows. The children of these days know more than their parents, or they think they do. But, as you understand each other, go on.'

On we went, Abel asking and me answering. Abel was astonished to find how much I knew, for I had but little schooling. He clearly admired Bob for the trouble he had taken to teach me.

'I hope Bob has taught him nothing wrong, Abel,' Mam said. 'They talk so much in English these days that I can't tell what's happening in my own house.'

'Bob has been doing only good in teaching Rhys these things,' Abel said. This was a sweet morsel to my mother's ears, coming from him.

'I've often quarrelled with Bob,' Mam said, 'because there was too much book and slate going on, and too little of the Bible. But I'm glad to hear you say that he taught the boy no harm. Although I'll stick to it, in today's youth there's too great a tendency to neglect the Bible.'

The upshot of Abel's visit was an agreement between mother and him that I should go for a month's trial to his shop, eating at his table but coming home to sleep. This is one of two things which brought comfort to my mother. I had a job in a post where I would get fair play for my soul, as she put it.

The other was that Thomas and Barbara Bartley continued to attend service, and there was every reason to believe the Truth was, to some extent, working upon their minds. Mam and I often used to visit Thomas and Barbara, and during our time of need there was a kind of understanding that we should never leave our neighbours' house fasting.

I would be doing mother a great wrong if I suggested that this was her only or her chief object. She felt as much interest in their salvation as Paul did in that of his 'kinsmen according to the flesh.' She watched the couple carefully as they listened to the Sunday's sermons, and on Monday morning she would visit them to test how much of the truth they had understood and the effect it had had upon their minds. I am tempted to record a few of the conversations during these visits, but I might seem to exaggerate my mother's zeal and devotion to the cause of explaining things in the simple language of truth.

Thomas would often say, 'It's a great pity you don't belong to the Ranters, Mair. You'd make an uncommon good preacher.'

Our chapel friends understood my mother was instrumental in bringing Thomas and Barbara to the means of grace. Their wonder and joy knew no bounds to see the two old folk who had spent their lives wholly heedless of religion now attending every public meeting.

'If your brother's imprisonment has been the means of bringing Thomas and Barbara Bartley within the sound of the Gospel,' Mam would say, 'and especially if it will be the means of bringing them to Christ, I shall never regret the bargain. I think that the truth has laid hold of my old neighbours' minds, and I shouldn't be a bit surprised to see Thomas and Barbara come to the Lord's Table before Bob returns home. I fancy I am as good a Calvinist as anybody I have met, but the devil's work has failed with Thomas and Barbara. They are both good soil for Gospel seed. They have not the thorns and briars of envy and deceit, nor the reeds and fens of fleshly lust. The spirit will have less work therein making a new heart. Bob was always talking of Thomas and Barbara's ignorance and harmlessness, and he made much fun of them. Nothing would please me better, when he comes home, than to be able to tell him that both are saved. You may think I'm talking nonsense, with Bob himself not being in Communion, but I can't help thinking that Bob is one of us and he'll return to the *Seiat* directly. What do you think, Rhys?'

Thomas and Barbara Bartley's history taught me a lesson I have never forgotten. Those preachers who some people think small are a much greater blessing to a particular section of their hearers than those who are considered great. Thomas and Barbara received little good from the ministration of the preachers whom my brother Bob favoured. But both would praise highly those whom he held almost in contempt.

This pleased my mother. She took it as proof of her oft-repeated comments to my brother that 'Not everybody is a Paul or a Peter, many have been saved under Thaddeus, or the Master would not have called him to the work'.

A few days afterwards, as we were at breakfast, mother said. 'This is the last Sabbath for Bob, poor fellow, in the house of bondage; thanks for it. And yet I'm almost afraid to see him come home lest his spirit has hardened under trial. Who is to preach next Sunday? Were Bob home today, I know he wouldn't care much for the minister. He was always disposed to underrate William Hughes of Abercwmnant. But I think William is one of the chosen, and I get a blessing from hearing him. Although we shall no doubt have today, as usual 'the object noted,' 'the act attributed' and 'the duty enjoined,' as Bob used to put it, it doesn't matter a bit. William Hughes is sure to say something worth hearing. Let us hope his Master will be with him, and that he will achieve a conversion.'

William Hughes kept his appointment. It is rarely a little preacher does not, except he be little enough to imitate the failings of a great one. I remember well the text that morning – 'Turn ye to the stronghold, ye prisoners of hope.'

I fancied everybody was thinking of my brother Bob when William Hughes was speaking of prisoners. The old preacher appeared unusually spirited, and was listened to with the most marked attention. I have my notes of his sermon before me as I write. On looking them over, I find they contain the soundest doctrine, but, marvellous to relate, the ordinary divisions are not preserved. Possibly I was careless in my note-taking. They run thus:—

    i. The objects noted: Prisoners.
    ii. The provision made by grace on their behalf: A stronghold.
    iii. The duty enjoined: Turning to the stronghold.

Mother helped the service to such an extent that I almost expected to hear her rejoice out loud. She did once under Cadwaladr Owen's ministration, and Bob was so offended he wouldn't speak to her for two whole days after. Towards the middle of the sermon Abel Hughes rose from his usual place under the pulpit, and stood in front of the Big Seat: a sure sign that the preacher was saying something especially beneficial.

I took such particular notice of our deacon's actions because I had heard my mother say to him, more than once, after a rousing sermon. 'Well, Abel, you too were forced to come out of your kennel today.'

To me, a sufficient proof that William Hughes excelled himself on that morning is afforded by the imperfection of my notes; my experience being that when a preacher speaks sluggishly I can take down nearly the whole sermon, but, if he has a swing and go about him, I forget my book and pencil and lose myself in what he says.

When we came out of chapel Thomas and Barbara Bartley were waiting for mother. All three, held an earnest conversation as they walked home together. Wil Bryan and I followed them a little to the rear. I couldn't resist telling Wil that I was going apprentice to old Abel.

I was surprised at the look of commiseration which passed over his face. 'Goodbye, my hearty. This child,' he said, striking his chest, 'would sooner go apprentice to a weaver or barber. You'll never more have any liking for play or laughter. From this time out you'll get nothing in the world but *Seiat* and a verse. Before this day month, I'll take an oath, you'll be obliged to learn to groan like an Irishman with the toothache, and to pull a face as long as a fiddle. You'll certainly be fit for heaven any day then. I'd rather go footman to the King of the Cannibal Islands than go 'prentice to the old onion. I'm sorry for you Rhys, but since the thing is settled you must fire away. I'd sooner go oyster-fishing on the top of Moel Fammau than go 'prentice to old Ab.'

I knew Wil was speaking his mind honestly, but I told him I didn't look on my future in the way he did. His reply surprised me.

'Listen here, old hundredth. I'll swear it's about time we made a preacher or a deacon of you.'

Wil didn't realize that I could have not asked for anything more than to be made a preacher if it were possible. However, to avoid his teasing I kept the thought to myself.

When I got home mother was humming a tune. She didn't say much, but I could see many signs of her inward happiness. I imagined it was that stronghold of which the preacher spoke that made her heart rejoice. I don't remember her saying anything about the sermon except that William Hughes 'had felt his feet under him'. That was her way of saying that she felt that a preacher had found Divine Inspiration.

At six o'clock that evening, William Hughes addressed a successful meeting, at which I took down the following notes.

> Text: 'Come unto me, all ye that labour and are heavy laden, and I will give you rest.'
>
> Heads:
> i. The objects noted: Those who labour and are heavy laden
> ii. The duty enjoined: 'Come unto me.'
> iii. The precious promise to those who obey: 'I will give you rest.'

I don't remember anything particularly sparkling about that sermon, but after service, in the *Seiat*, Abel Hughes put his usual question. 'Is there anyone who has remained afresh?'

I wondered what made him ask so formally, as he was looking straight at two who had 'remained afresh.'

John Llwyd, who Wil Bryan called 'the Old Scraper', said, 'Thomas and Barbara Bartley have remained.' Although everybody knew it already.

'Will you have a word with them, William Hughes?' Abel said to the preacher, adding, 'But don't expect much from them, they have not been hearers for long.'

Abel sat down beside the preacher and whispered in his ear, telling him about the converts. After a few moments thought, the preacher got to his feet. He crossed his hands upon his back, under his coat-tails and walked, somewhat reluctantly, towards Thomas and Barbara.

The conversation which followed went somewhat after this fashion.

'Well, Thomas Bartley,' the preacher said, 'I know nothing about you, so perhaps you wouldn't mind telling us, freely, a little of your history.'

'I will, name of goodness,' Thomas said. 'Father and mother were poor people, and I was the youngest of three. There's none left except me, and I don't know of anybody belonging to us but one cousin down in England, if he's alive. We're a dying-out sort of family. '

'I didn't mean you to give the history of your family,' the preacher said, looking a little irritated. 'What I wanted to know was about your own experience. Why did you and your wife decide to remain behind tonight?'

'Oh, beg pardon,' Thomas said. 'Well, I'll tell you. Barbara and I, for weeks past, have been thinking a lot about coming to the *Seiat*. Mair Lewis told us it was high time, and that we could never do anything better. So, hearin' you a-begging us so earnestly this morning to turn to the stronghold, we both made up our minds to stay tonight; because we knew very well it was to us you was talking.'

Barbara nodded in agreement.

'You did well,' William Hughes said. 'And I don't doubt that the friends here are very glad to see you. Very likely you look upon yourself as a great sinner, Thomas Bartley.'

'Well, I'll say this much,' Thomas said, 'I never nursed a spite towards anybody, as Barbara knows and I always try to live honest.'

'I am glad to hear it; it isn't everybody can say that much,' Mr Hughes said. 'But we are all sinners, you know, Thomas Bartley.'

'Yes, yes,' Thomas said. 'Bad is the best of us; but I'm thinking some are worse'n others.'

'Can you read, Thomas Bartley?' the minister said.

'I've a grip of the letters, nothing more. But I'm awful fond of hearing others read,' Thomas said.

'It's a great loss not to be able to read, and it's got somewhat late in the day for you to think of learning,' Mr Hughes said.

'I know I'll never learn, 'cos there's nothing quick about me, more's the pity,' Thomas said.

'You not having heard very much of the Gospel, Thomas Bartley, and not being able to read, you should be doubly diligent, in attendance on the means of grace from this time out,' Mr Hughes said.

'If we live,' Thomas said, 'Barbara and I have made up our minds to come regular to the means, because the time passes better by half here than if we stayed moping at home. To tell you the truth, Mr Hughes, we find great pleasure in chapel, and if we'd a-known it sooner, we'd have been here these years since, but no one ever asked us till Mair Lewis almost forced us to come.'

'What gives you such pleasure in chapel, Thomas Bartley?' asked the preacher.

'Indeed, I can't tell you exactly, but Barbara and I feel much more what-d'ye-call-it, since we've been coming to chapel.'

'Very good, 'the preacher said. 'But what do you think of the stronghold I tried to say something about this morning?'

'Well,' Thomas said, 'I thought you spoke up nicely about it, only I couldn't catch exactly all you said. But Mair Lewis explained to us on the way home that Jesus Christ dying for us was the stronghold, and that trusting Him for salvation was turning to the stronghold. I thought so too, only I couldn't put it into words.'

'Whoever this Mair Lewis is,' the preacher said, 'she is pretty near the mark on that.'

'Yes, I warrant her. Mair is a real good 'un, of that you can be sure, Mr Hughes,' Thomas said.

I heard mother whisper to Abel. 'It's obvious, that Mr William Hughes does not understand his customer,' she said.

William Hughes tried once more to get Thomas to come to the point.

'Thomas Bartley,' he said, 'will you tell me why it was necessary that Jesus Christ should die for us?'

'Well, so far as I can make out,' Thomas said, 'it was nothing in the blessed world, only he himself wanted to.'

'But wasn't there anything in us which obliged his dying, Thomas Bartley?' the preacher asked.

'Nothing at all, to my mind,' Thomas replied. 'Perhaps I'm wrong, though. I only fancy no one told him to do it, and that he took everybody by surprise, as they say.'

Mr Hughes looked as if he had been pitched from his saddle. Turning to Barbara he said, 'Well, Barbara Bartley, can you read?'

'Just a grip of the letters, same as Thomas,' she said.

'Will you tell us a word about your feeling?' Mr Hughes said.

'Same as Thomas, exactly,' Barbara said.

William Hughes went back to the Big Seat.

'Abel Hughes,' he said, 'you know our friends here better than I do, will you speak to them?'

Abel got to his feet. I knew that if anyone could find out whether a spark of the divine fire had descended upon the souls of Thomas and Barbara, it was Abel. I never saw his like at probing the soul of a man.

'My dear old neighbours,' our senior deacon said, his voice trembling with emotion. 'I need not tell you that my heart rejoices to see you making the effort to turn to that stronghold we heard so sweetly spoken of this morning. I hope, and for that matter believe, that your intention was perfectly good in staying with us tonight.'

He turned towards the congregation. 'My friends and I feel,' he said. 'That we have been severely reproved here tonight, and I trust we all felt the same. Thomas Bartley told us that no one except Mair Lewis ever asked him and his wife to come to the means of grace. Let us be ashamed and repent.'

He turned back to face Thomas and Barbara. 'Well, Thomas Bartley,' he said. 'I'll try and talk so that you can understand me. Do you find any change in your outlook and mind, these days, different to what you used to, we'll say three months ago?'

'A great change, thanks to you, Abel Hughes,' said Thomas Bartley.

'Well, tell us, in your own way, what it is.'

'You never met my worse at speaking, Abel Hughes; but before I began coming to chapel, Barbara nor me never thought anything on the blessed earth about our end. But now there isn't a day goes by that we don't talk about it. I think a good deal of what'll happen to us when we go from here. Will Barbara and I be together, and shall we be comfortable?'

'That's right, Thomas,' Abel said. 'What do you think you must get from here, so you may be made comfortable after going from here?'

'Well, I can't tell you, exactly. But I'm thinking its trust in Christ, as Mair Lewis says.'

'Don't change your mind on that, Tomos *bach*,' Abel said. 'You and I, and all of us, will be quite safe if we only trust in Him. You had a son, Thomas, who has gone to Him, without doubt. Seth, innocent as he was, got to know the Man. I cannot wish you both better than to be able to tell, as clearly as Seth did, where he was going.'

When Abel mentioned Seth tears fell down Thomas's cheek. He was so choked up that he was unable to say anything more. Barbara was also weeping into her checked apron.

Abel Hughes was a stern man, but he had a large heart. When he wept, his tears affected everything round about, save the rocks. He too was quite overcome by the response of Thomas and Barbara.

When he regained his composure he asked the church to show its assent to the reception of Thomas and Barbara Bartley into membership by show of hands.

Before any hand could be raised, John Llwyd stood up. 'Is Thomas Bartley an abstainer?' he said.

'Hark at the old Scraper,' Wil Bryan whispered in my ear.

Abel, seemed not hear John Llwyd's question. 'I declare that the Bartleys have been duly admitted.' he said.

I was sitting near the Big Seat, and after the preacher had brought the *Seiat* to a close I saw Thomas Bartley go up to Abel. He put his hand in his pocket. 'Abel Hughes, is there any entrance to pay tonight?' he asked.

'No, Thomas,' Abel's face broke into a smile. 'You'll have a chance to put something on the church book by and bye.'

'To be shuar,' Thomas said, and away he went.

CHAPTER 22

A Visit from More Than One Relative

Had I known, before I started to write this autobiography, that it would grow to such a length, I probably wouldn't have begun it. Here I am with twenty-one chapters set down, some of them long and some of them lean, yet only just, as it were, sharpening my pencil for a start. I have said so many things, of all sorts, that I do not remember if I have already described what I feel when writing almost every chapter: namely that there is too great a profusion here of 'I,' 'my mother' and 'my brother,' of 'she said,' 'I said' and 'he said'– which, if the work were published, would probably bore the reader.

But what else can I do? I have begun the work, I'm not willing to leave it unfinished, especially since I have not touched upon some of the most important events of my life. The truth is, my brother Bob was a hero in the eyes of the Caeau Cochion workmen. He differed from most of them in language, manners and habits, yet I am sure, if they had had to choose a king from their midst, Bob would have been made their monarch.

Superior intelligence and purity of speech and conduct will, sooner or later, win the admiration of even the most reckless and ungodly. Bob had worked in the Caeau Cochion colliery since he was thirteen years old, yet I never heard him swear. When meal times came round down the pit, and the miners working the seam gathered in their *caban*, he would be asked to explain the events in the news. He had an excellent memory and a fluent tongue, and his explanations cheered the heart of many colliers older than he, as they crouched down to eat by the light of the Geordie lamp deep in the bowels of the earth.

When he grew to manhood he became a leader among his fellow workmen. Although he couldn't control a fierce crowd of colliers, he was always looked upon as their adviser. When Abraham Jones had been manager he put Bob in charge of the work if he was away. So it was not a surprise that when Abraham was reappointed my brother's former companions awaited to his release from prison with happiness.

Although it was only a few days since I had begun to work for Abel Hughes in his shop, the old man kindly gave me a holiday to greet my brother on his return home. Bob was expected by the midday train, and from early morning mother busied herself cleaning the house and preparing a hearty reception for him. She was nervous and agitated.

'I have been a good while trying to decide what we shall give the boy to eat when he comes,' she said. 'They tell me that too heavy a meal for one who has just left jail will make him ill. Now I think of it, Bob used to be wonderful fond of currant cake. He might like a delicacy which won't weigh too heavy on his stomach. Perhaps a cup of tea and some cake would be just the thing. If you'll run to the shop for three penn'orth of the best flour, a ha'porth of carbonate of soda, and a quarter of a pound of currants, I'll be no time making it.'

I was very ready to do my share of the work. Like Bob, I was partial to currant cake.

Long before the train was due the tea things were on the table, the cake had been baked, and the kettle had boiled and got cold many times over. I was at the railway station at least half an hour too soon, Wil Bryan, to give him credit, was there before me. Scores of stalwart colliers lined the platform, all in high spirits and good voice. Some chucked me familiarly under the chin, others pulled my hair and ears, meaning well, of course. Yet others gave me pennies; I preferred that.

Wil Bryan looked almost enviously upon my store, but did not ask me for any of it, as he had before, when I'd thought he meant to hire a lawyer to defend Bob. Now he seemed puzzled to know what he should advise me to do with the money.

'It's a great pity Bob doesn't smoke,' he said. 'That brass of yours would have done nicely to buy him a tobacco box.'

He made one comment I remember well.

'A collier who's taken to jail,' he said, 'has the advantage, that they can't give him the county crop. I'll defy 'em to cut his hair any shorter than it is already.'

And he let drop a great many other observations, which I thought at the time to be the essence of wisdom.

The crowd of colliers who had come to meet Bob grew ever larger. I was surprised not to see John Powel there, as he was Bob's greatest friend. I kept thinking what a disappointment it would be to Bob not to find his old companion there to welcome him.

The distant puffing of the train sounded down the track. My heart began to beat rapidly. Wil Bryan made his mouth into a circle and began to imitate the engine. The station bell rang, and the train came into sight at a speed which I thought would make it impossible for it to stop.

Pull up it did, though. There was a great rush of steam from the engine, a clatter as the fireman threw coal on the fire. There was the opening and slamming of doors, a thunderous banging of boxes upon the platform and the rushing hither and thither of passengers and other folk, all talking and chattering. The station was a wild scene of noise and confusion. I looked in every direction for Bob.

'All right,' the station master shouted, and the train went on its way once more.

The colliers stared at each other with disappointment.

Wil Bryan ran up to me. 'It's a right mare's nest,' He said. 'Bob hasn't come.'

My spirit sank within me, and I could hardly hold back my tears. The colliers tried to console me, saying that Bob would arrive by the next train some three hours later. I went home crestfallen. Long before I got to the house, I saw mother in the doorway expecting us. When she saw me alone, she fled inside. Her disappointment was painful.

I told her the colliers were certain he would come on the next train. The cake was left uncut, and the kettle, which had boiled dry, was refilled. I went to meet the train a second time and found a greater crowd of workmen than before. I had a foreboding that Bob wouldn't come by that train either. It turned out to be true. But this time my own disappointment lost its smart when I thought about the blow it would be to mother. Her heartstrings had been strained to such a pitch of tension that I fancied they might break with this fresh news.

Nearing the house, I saw that she wasn't standing in the doorway. I went in but found she was not so much cast down as I had anticipated.

'I knew he wouldn't come. Something told me so,' she said, before I had time to speak a word. 'The furnace is not yet seven times heated, it would seem. Something has happened to him.'

She buried her face in her apron and burst into tears. I followed her example until we were both cried out but felt little better.

We didn't eat a single morsel. Mother didn't care whether I went to meet the last train or not. I went anyway. There were a number of the Caeau Cochion workmen on the platform who had been working the pit during the day. They appeared fresh washed with their faces clean, except for a little shading about the corners and lids of the eyes. I noticed also that great numbers of those who had not been to work that day were half-drunk. The train came, but without Bob. Those who had drink taken began cursing almost everything but especially the two justices, Mr Brown and the owner of the Hall.

Wil Bryan tried to persuade me to wait a while before returning home, there being signs, he said, of a row worth the seeing brewing among the colliers. But I took no notice and at a great personal sacrifice, he came back with me.

Wil was always in his element in a row. Wherever there was trouble, there was Wil. At Soldier Robin's school it was his whole delight to set the boys a-fighting. At chapel, he preferred accounts of a wrangling teachers' meeting to listening to a good sermon. Ever since he began to part his hair and make a quiff, mother had been prejudiced against him. She began putting me on my guard in case he tried to corrupt me.

Wil understood this well, and whenever he visited our house he took care to pull his hair down over his forehead before coming in. This had a good effect on mother, and I think would have overcome her prejudices had she not accidentally caught Wil going through this preliminary. She severely reproved him for his hypocrisy. But Wil understood my mother perfectly and managed her with remarkable skill. When it served his purpose he could, in his own way, talk almost as religiously as she did. I don't think she was displeased to see Wil coming home with me that night.

She'd had a neighbour or two in to cheer her, and believed that Wil was a support to me. When we entered, we were both struck with her calmness.

'The old woman keeps up like a brick,' said Wil in my ear.

'I see,' Mam said, 'it's bad news you have again. But it's only what I expected. Something has happened to him or he would have been home by now.'

'Don't be down-hearted, Mair Lewis,' said Wil. 'I believe Bob will turn up from somewhere, just directly.'

'You've no foundation for that belief, William,' Mam said. 'Tonight, look you, I'm made to feel the words of the wise man coming home to me: "Hope deferred maketh the heart sick". And then Job, when he was in trouble, said, "Thou washest away the things which grow out of the dust of the earth, and thou destroyest the hope of man. Where is now my hope?" As for my hope, who shall see it?'

'Well, but didn't the preacher say the other Sunday, Mair Lewis, that it came right for Job in the end, after all the messing about he got, didn't it?'

'It did, William,' Mam said, 'and were I as trustful in my Redeemer as Job was, it would have come all right with me too, look you.'

'It's sure to come all right with you, Mair Lewis. You're as pious as Job was, I'll take my oath of it.'

'Don't presume and blaspheme, William, 'my mother said, her voice stern.

'I'm telling the truth, from my heart,' Wil said. 'You're as pious as Job was, any day he got out of bed. And, according to the way the preacher gave his history, I see you both very much like each other. Job had a bad wife and you've had a bad husband, and you've both stuck to your colours, first class. So I'm sure the Lord'll not be shabby in your case, in the end either, you see if He will.'

'I beg of you not to say any more. Wil,' Mam said. 'You ought to know I'm in no humour tonight to listen to nonsense from you.'

'Nonsense?' Wil said, honestly indignant. 'It's no nonsense at all. I'll bet you, that is I'll take my oath, it'll be all right with you in the end. Didn't the preacher tell us about Job that the Lord was only trying him? That's what He is doing with you. He only just wants to show the kind of stuff that's in you.'

'William,' Mam said, seeking to turn the conversation, 'were there many colliers at the railway?'

'Thousands and thousands,' Wil said.

'There you are again,' Mam said. 'There's only three hundred altogether in the Caeau Cochion pit.'

'Well, yes, in a manner of speaking, you know, Mair Lewis,' Wil said. 'I'm sure there was near a hundred there.'

'Didn't one of you happen to speak to John Powel? What did he think about Bob's not coming?' mother said.

'John Powel wasn't there,' we both replied.

'Not there! John Powel not there!' Mam said, in surprise.

'He was working the day shift,' Wil said.

'Who told you that, William?' Mam said.

'No one. I only thought it,' Wil said.

Mother fell to pleating her apron and musing. Presently she said, 'William, you wouldn't be long running as far as John Powel's house and telling him, if he is in, I'd like to see him.'

'No sooner said than done,' Wil said, jumping to his feet.

'It's very dark, William,' my mother said, following him to the door; 'and it is almost too much to ask you to return. Rhys'll come with you to learn something from John Powel, so as to let you go home.'

'Stand at ease, as you were,' Wil said in English. 'If the darkness is very thick, I'll cut through it with my knife.' And off he went.

'There is something very lovable and decent about that boy,' mother said. 'I can't, for the life of me, help liking him. But I'd like him better if he was a little more serious and spoke a little less English. I don't think there is any guile in his heart but I fear he'll make you like himself. Why didn't you tell me John Powel wasn't at the railway?'

Wil seemed to be gone a long time but he had gone straight there and come straight back to tell Mam that John Powel was not at home and had not been home all day. When she heard his news Mam fell into a deep study.

She took no notice of what Wil told me, almost in a whisper.

'I called to tell the gaffer yonder I'm going to stay with you tonight. We missed some splendid sport. The colliers burnt straw effigies of Mr Brown and the owner of the Hall, and capital ones they were too. There's been three battles, and One-eyed Ned has been taken to the round house, even though he fought like a lion with the policemen.'

Wil rattled along with his story, but I wasn't really listening, so I can't record it. Seeing I wasn't interested he stopped talking, and within a minute he was fast asleep. His heavy breathing seemed to fill the house and roused mother from her reverie.

'William,' she said, 'it's time you should go home, my son.'

'Not going home tonight. I told the gaffer so,' Wil mumbled and fell asleep directly. Mother went back to her apron-pleating, and stared into the fire.

I simply enjoyed the silence. I love quiet. I don't know if others do the same, but I spend hours at a time in the quiet of the night staring into the fire. I imagine thousands of things which never had an existence and will never come to pass. It's a legacy my mother left me that I've never managed to shake it off, it clings to me to this day; some nights I live an age in a few hours.

I have dreamed myself married to someone whose name I do not know. Our children fill the house with their clatter; they grow up and are sent to school. I try and train them as best I can; they give me all sorts of trouble; they leave home. At last their mother dies, and I, a white-headed old man, am bereft of all save my crutches. I am cold, and the clock is striking one. I spring to my feet, thinking all these events are my vain imaginations, and I remain a shivering old bachelor. I go to bed and, before closing my eyes, I resolve never again to give my fancy such free rein. It is not only unprofitable it is probably sinful as well.

The next night I read till I am tired and then say to myself, 'Rhys, you'd better think over one or two matters before you go to bed, just for five minutes.'

No sooner do I think this than I start building castles in the air once more. I imagine a great many things, and fancy myself in one situation or another for an hour, two hours, sometimes three. I should stop such a practice. And yet I love it. Like the man who is a slave to strong drink, I hate my failing from the bottom of my heart – yet I still take great pleasure in it, while always resolving someday to shake it off.

But to return to my story.

I loved the silence, which Wil's breathing and the fact that something often rose in his throat, as if it would choke him, just enhanced.

Mother and I said nothing. I have since thought that our fancies unconsciously travelled side by side, so completely were we absorbed by the same focus. I don't know how long we sat, but I remember fancying a score of times, that I heard someone walking up the courtyard towards the house, the footsteps dying away within a yard or two of the door. I felt certain they were Bob's, and held my breath in expectation.

However all ended in silence. So sweet were my fancies that as soon as I had finished with one I began another. If Wil had not suddenly awoken as Mam sprang to her feet, I would not have known whether it was my fancy or if I really had heard someone knocking at the door.

Before Wil was fully awake from his sleep and I from dreams, Mam had opened the door. What a disappointment. There stood the man I detested with all my soul: the man I called the Irishman, who had stopped me near the Hall Park on the night Seth died.

'Well, Mair, how do you do, this long time?' he said.

At every critical juncture of my early life this man was would appear. I would rather have seen the Devil on the threshold. Wil recognized him, for he knew as much about him as I did. I could never conceal much from my friend, and he, for his part, never betrayed my confidence.

Directly mother saw who our visitor was, she drew herself up. She had lost none of that pluck she drew on whenever there was a real need for it. Standing before the Irishman she stopped him entering the house.

'James,' she said. 'I have told you many times I never want to see your face again and that you are not to come near this house.'

Wil picked up the poker, and hearing him, the Irishman thrust his head forward to see who was there.

'Isn't that Hugh Bryan's son?' he said, looking at Wil.

'Yes,' Mam said.

'I thought so by his nose,' the Irishman said.

'What do you see about my nose, you kill-pheasant, you?' Wil said, his tone showing his hot temper.

'William, hold your tongue this minute. It's best for you,' said mother.

I could see from the Irishman's face that nothing would have given him greater pleasure than to wring Wil Bryan's neck, and my mother knew that too well.

Still toying with the poker and muttering his anger, Wil said to me, softly, 'Shall I give him a downer?'

If I'd said 'yes' Wil would have used the poker on the instant.

'Take care Wil,' I whispered. 'The Irishman is not one to trifle with.'

Wil kept a tight grip on the poker. He fixed his eye upon the visitor as the chick does on the hawk that is about to swoop upon it. But Wil was not afraid of the man; I saw from his look that, had the Irishman laid a hand on mother, or tried to force his way into the house, Wil would not have asked us what he should do with the poker.

Mother and the Irishman were, by this time, speaking so low that we could only catch a few words of what they said.

I heard her telling him, earnestly and threateningly, to go away. I saw him look towards Wil, and heard him say to mother. 'Can he hold his tongue about tonight?'

I couldn't make out my mother's answer, she spoke so softly. All of a sudden the two stopped speaking. The Irishman looked in the direction of the road and the blood drained from his face. He froze and didn't move from where he stood.

A moment later we heard footsteps approaching the house. In that moment I saw his guilty conscience.

'Hullo, gamekeeper. What do you want here?' a voice said from the darkness. The Irishman got to his feet and ran. I saw no more of him that night.

Bob and John Powel walked in, shutting the door after them. I won't attempt to describe my or my mother's joy. However paradoxical it might appear, we both showed our happiness by bursting into tears.

Thinking back, I fancy Wil's method of showing his feelings was more reasonable. He danced round the kitchen, whistling and singing 'When Johnny comes marching home, my boys.'

Running the poker up and down his left arm as if it were a fiddle bow, Wil waltzed several times around the kitchen before mother noticed the ungodliness taking place in her house. She soon put paid to his pranks.

I was comforted to see that imprisonment didn't seem to have changed Bob's appearance. His face showed the same calm thoughtfulness and determination it always did, and there was nothing in his gait to suggest that he had lost his independent spirit. Hard labour was not a new thing to him, and this probably accounted for his wellbeing.

When mother came to herself she inspected him from crown to sole, and vowed that, like the youths of the captivity, he looked all the better for his hard fare. She then began to question him. When she asked him how it was he did not come home by the mid-day train, John Powel answered.

'I am to blame for that,' he said. 'I found out that the workmen were determined to make a fuss and an exhibition of Bob, and, knowing he wouldn't like it, I went to meet him. I kept him back until everybody had gone away to bed. I am sure I shall catch it from you for what I've done.'

Mother forgave him there and then.

When Bob's turn came to ask about Mam's news, I expected one of the first things she would tell him was that I was apprenticed to Abel Hughes. But I was disappointed.

Now as I recall her words they are a great comfort to me, for they clearly show where her thoughts were and what brought her heart its greatest joy.

'The best news on earth I have to give you, Bob,' she said, 'is that Thomas and Barbara Bartley have joined our church, and there is every reason to believe them both to have been really converted.'

'And fine fun there was with them,' Wil said.

'It's best for you if you don't you talk of fun in *Seiat*,' said mother. 'The two were a trifle comical, as you might expect, Bob. But to my mind, the ring of a call was there, plain enough.'

'And,' she said, glancing around at us four, 'I have been thinking a good deal of those words, my dear boys: The last shall be first. It would be a hard thing, wouldn't it, if Thomas and Barbara, for all their ignorance and drollery, were saved in the end, while we children of the kingdom, were cast into outer darkness?'

Mother spoke far more in the same strain and Bob paid close attention to what she said. I fancy his eyes filled with tears more than once. Mother was so absorbed in her theme that she forgot to offer my brother and his friend something to eat. But it turned out that both had been feasting before coming home, and mother was at last considerate enough to place the currant cake before Wil and me.

I set about it with a clear conscience. If Wil and I did our duty as well and thoroughly as we did when the currant cake was brought face to face with us on that midnight, Wil would not be where he now is, and I would be a much better minister of the Gospel than I am.

Mother ordered Wil and me off to bed. I felt perfectly happy, and from what Wil said the moment before he began to snore, the only trouble on his mind was my refusing to let him to give the Irishman a downer with the poker.

CHAPTER 23

Bob

Months went by, and the work at Caeau Cochion prospered under the management of Abraham Jones. He had by this time brought the place to order. Expenses were now lower and profits greater than when the 'Lankie,' as he was called, was overseer. The workmen received a wage they could not complain about. Those unpleasant words oppression and injustice were no longer heard in our house, and Bob was satisfied with his earnings. Within a few weeks he had paid off every farthing of the debt Mam had run up during his imprisonment. Poverty and want were banished from our cottage.

But was my mother happy? Bob's wages were more than enough to meet the family needs, and mother no longer struggled to pay her way. To me it appeared that Providence smiled upon us and our troubles were over. But one bitter thing still had a permanent place in our thoughts, though none of us ever mentioned it. Bob's exclusion had become an old story we took no more account of than we did of original sin it was something that we could not shake off.

As far as I could see, prison had had little effect on Bob's spirit. He spent all his spare time reading. Mam kept telling him he'd be sure to ruin his eyesight. He came to chapel just as regularly as before, but he would not take up his class in the Sunday School again. There was one other change in him. We never saw him read the Bible in our presence. This greatly troubled Mam; she was afraid he might not read it at all.

He usually stayed up after mother and I had gone to bed. Mam came up with an idea to quiet her fears. She took care to place the Bible in a particular position upon the table near the window every night. This enabled her to check next morning if Bob had moved it. She was reassured to find that the Bible had been moved every night so she concluded Bob was reading it. Despite his reserve about being seen to consult the Good Book, Bob showed more and more tenderness towards our mother. He became more respectful in his conversations with her and more tolerant of her prejudices.

But I was sure that mother was not happy. The bloom did not return to her cheek, nor did the black marks fade from beneath her eyes. She seemed to have aged ten years over the three months since Bob was arrested. I think, though, that bloom would have come back, and the shadows retreated from her eyes, if Bob had said, 'Mam, I am troubled, and intend to offer myself to rejoin the *Seiat* next Sunday.' But he never did.

Mam often spoke about the danger of tribulations not leaving us where we were but driving us farther from God. Bob understood the point of her comments, but he did not take this idea to apply to him personally. One night Mam stopped speaking in parables and asked him directly how he felt about his duty to return to his religious professions. Bob was just as forthright in his answer.

'You know that it is not my fault that I do not profess,' he said. 'It was not I who threw away my profession but the church who took it from me. As far as I'm aware, there is nothing different in me now from what there was when I professed, except that I have been to prison. I should not think that adds to my fitness to profess. If I did offer myself to the church, the first question they would ask is have I repented the fault for which I was excommunicated? I should have to answer that I have not repented and never can repent. Either the church or I would have to behave like a hypocrite should I return on those terms. The church alone is responsible for my non-profession, if profession means writing my name in the Communion book.

'But I think there is a far superior confession of faith,' he continued. There are men to be found (and I do not claim I am one, lest you should tell me that I am self-righteous), but there are men whose chief object it is to find out the truth, from whatever direction it may come. They constantly seek the God of Truth, and know what it is to lose many a night's sleep in painful expectation of the light. They know what it is to be wounded by doubt and unbelief, and yet they do not stop searching for the balm to heal them. I call them God's sons, even though they may not have their names in any book of Communion.

'I have a deep respect for some members of the church as true-principled, piously disposed men. They are after their own fashion, strict disciplinarians. But they only see one kind of sin. Are Robert Lewis and William the Coal the only transgressors? Can you explain to me why William is often censured and John Llwyd never? No one doubts William's innocence. His besetting sin is to forget that his head is not strong enough to resist the effects of more than two glasses of beer. He has a tendency to fall upon his back, or lurch on one side, which no one wants to justify. But where is the regulation that calls a man to account for avarice and parsimony?

'Are some to be allowed to sow the seeds of discord, persecute their fellows, and blacken their characters, by living on envy and bitterness of spirit? Should they be encouraged to criticize preachers and deacons just because they are preachers and deacons? "What thou hast to do, do it quickly," said Christ to Judas, and Judas obeyed the command. But some people can't come up even to Judas's standard. They sell their Master every day for thirty pieces of silver, but they do it slowly and with no sign of speedily hanging themselves afterwards either. It would seems there is no discipline for folk like them. Has the church only punishment for William the Coal and me? When William takes too much drink, every expulsion notwithstanding, he puts all the fault on Satan. And when I knocked the Old Soldier on his back after seeing him cruelly beating my brother, the spirit and letter of the rules demanded my expulsion. In the great day to come when all the secrets of our hearts will be revealed, if I were compelled to stand in either William the Coal's shoes or John Llwyd's, I know which I'd choose.

'I'm as strict an abstainer as anyone in church, and I grieve as much as any man over the evils of intemperance. But our God is not the God of temperance alone. He is also the God of justice, love, magnanimity and meekness. The New Testament teaches me He is so. But when did you see Abel Hughes (and all respect to Abel, who I believe is a sincere Christian), when did you see him stand up and move the excommunication of anyone for avarice, hard-heartedness and hard-facedness? Who have you seen expelled for persecuting his betters, for foul-mouthedness? No one, I'm sure, but not because none are guilty of such sins. Would that Paul had lent me his authority and the mantle he left behind him at Troas. Then you would see that others besides William the Coal and myself were delivered over unto Satan.'

Mother heard him right through, sitting quiet and self-possessed. I was surprised, for I remembered times when she would not have let him go on in that way for half a minute without setting upon him fluently and unsparingly. Indeed, had Bob dared speak like this some six months previously I'm quite sure she would have boxed his ears. Now, though, she listened attentively to every word he said, and, were they the last words he spoke from his deathbed, her face could not have been more serious and sorrowful. She looked as if she had let go of every hope, and was trying to keep calm and resigned in the face of doom.

From childhood my mother had filled me with religious ideas and the terms of divinity, and she had prepared me well to grasp the bitterness of her disappointment and sorrow. I could understand her feelings as she answered Bob.

'Well, my son,' she said. 'I never expected to live to hear you talk like that; although I feared it would come to this. I have listened to you carefully, in case I misunderstand and misjudge you. I can never express my feelings when you were taken to jail. I now know you were, wrongfully imprisoned and I give thanks for that. Many a sleepless night I lay thinking of you. I feared my heart would burst before the morning; if I'd not believed your imprisonment was something in the Lord's hand to bring you back to the fold, then my heart would have broken. Your words tonight have disappointed and hurt me. Your soul has gone into a far country, and I fear you will be left to yourself. I do not believe that God's Spirit does not wrestle with your mind. But remember, my son, you may vex Him, and there's an end to patience, even of the Almighty. You can not imagine the state you'd be in if He were to say, "Let him alone." You spoke of people whose chief aim was to find the truth. I understood from what you said that you put yourself among them. But what truth do you mean? If it is the truth about God, about sinners and about eternity, I know you'll never find that outside God's own Word. And here is what it says, "If ye continue in my word, then ye are my disciples indeed, and ye shall know the truth. The secret of the Lord is with them that fear him." And the same Word says, "He that is not with me is against me; and he that gathereth not with me scattereth abroad. Whosoever shall be ashamed of me and of my words in this adulterous and sinful generation; of him also shall the Son of Man be ashamed when he cometh in the glory of his Father with the holy angels."

'Who are these people you talk about,' she went on, 'who lose sleep in searching for truth, but whose names are not on any book of Communion? I'd like to know them, because I never saw anyone with the least grain of understanding about him who did not belong to a Communion. I can't understand you, even if you do yourself. To speak plain, I think you've got some notions from those old English books that have addled your head. I was saddened to hear you speak the language of a backslider when you pointed out the failings of those who profess. I thought you were above taking shelter behind malice of that sort, and though I admit there is a deal of truth in what you say, your conscience must tell you a story of that kind won't hold water when you stand before the judgment seat. Beware, my son, beware. I've no wish to hurt your feelings, and I wouldn't for the world say anything to drive you further away, but really I'd like to hear less of the publican ring about you.'

She paused and look at him as if studying his condition.

'I try to believe there is no difference in you since you have ceased to profess, and I can't tell you how glad I am that you still come to service regularly, and you haven't given way to sin. But please remember, my son, that when a shower comes the rain is always heaviest under the eaves. There is no veranda to God's house; so that if you're not inside you would be better be out in the open. It's your own business, my boy. Something tells me I will not be long with you. Between one thing and another I feel that I'm drawing near to the far country. With each sounding I find the fathoms getting fewer and fewer every day. But my ship would ride more lightly if I could cast into the sea my worries for you. As with the wrecked ship of St Paul, I have been rather sorely tossed of late, but the Great Lord has seen fit to show me a creek with a shore to it, and I have taken the hint that my soul shall not be lost. I have no desire to grow old, because I know I shall only become a drag upon you both. "Although my house be not so with God," you know who I'm referring to, and I hope God will visit the soul of him, "yet He hath made with me an everlasting covenant."'

She turned and looked at me.

'Rhys,' she said. 'I really think you are in a place where you will be granted divine justice. And if I could only see you, Bob, like you used to be, I wouldn't care how soon I was called away. The eternal world is quite new to me, and I don't know what change I must go through before entering it. But at present I can't see how I'm going to be happy, even in Heaven, without knowing that I have left my two sons zealous in the cause of our dear Methodists.'

Mother wiped her eyes with her apron and began to pleat it, as she always did when upset. Bob and I had never heard her speak so bluntly about her departure from this life. Her words sounded to me not like the complaint of the hypochondriac, but like the voice of a prophet of God who was speaking an awful truth. My heart jumped to my throat, and when I looked at Bob I saw his eyes were wet.

Bob was difficult to move, once he formed an opinion, but he had a tender heart. His love for mother was intense. He would have died for her, should it have been asked of him. His whole soul was stirred, and it was only by a great effort he was controlling his reactions. He and I felt like those disciples of old when Paul told them they should no longer look upon his face. We were both silence for a minute or two, then Bob spoke.

'I can't understand, mother,' he said. 'Why you should grieve so much on my account, and especially why you should talk of dying and leaving us. You're not a drag on me at all and as long as I have health and strength it will be my pleasure to make you happy and comfortable. Why are you so disheartened? Do you see a falling off in my character? What difference would it make to me if the church showed their hands, and Abel Hughes wrote my name in the book? I know you would not wish me to quibble, and I will never do so. I find it painful we cannot agree. But I say again that I hate hypocrisy. I cannot pretend that I feel this way and that, if I do not. It is a privilege for a man to be a religious professor, but the church has deprived me of it, and what can I do? You may say I have transgressed, but I disagree. I will never believe that religion is antagonistic to the best feelings of human nature. If tomorrow I saw the strong chastise the weak, and knew myself to be stronger I would put him on the ground at once with a calm conscience. I would have done nothing but my duty. You must admit that Heaven will have a scanty population if only those who have their names on the books of the Methodist *Seiat* are to enter. I don't believe you are so narrow-minded as to think that.'

'Will you answer me one question? 'Mam said.

'A hundred if I can,' Bob replied.

'Good,' Mam said. 'If you answer two or three to my satisfaction, I shall feel easy. Do you see yourself a miserable sinner eternally and hopelessly lost, and do you confess it? Do you see in the Lord Jesus Christ a perfect and sufficient Saviour? Do you feel that you must rely entirely upon his deservedness for your salvation? And is your conscience perfectly easy that you are upon the path of duty?'

I saw from Bob's face that he had been squeezed into a corner. For some time he said nothing. Mam fixed him with her eye as if she reading his very soul.

'There are but few, even of the professors, who can answer questions like those, clearly and unequivocally,' he said.

'What am I to understand by unequivocally?' Mam said. 'Don't hide your meaning in words which are beyond me.'

'Well,' said Bob, 'we'll put unequivocally on one side. I say again, few even of the really religious could answer your questions clearly and without hesitation or doubt. You can't expect me to answer them with authority. I shall be thankful if I am able to do so after reaching your age. I don't want to conceal my meaning from you. I am in darkness now, and am feeling my way. I can honestly say I continue to seek, but spiritual truths escape me. I assure you that my soul's cry is, "Light, light, more light." At times I think I glimpse it from on high; but it is only as a lightning flash that leaves me in greater darkness than before. At other times I get a different kind of light from below. If I follow it I find myself among bogs and marshes, and realize it is just the glimmer of a corpse-candle.

'What am I to do? I'm not willing to shut my eyes and despair in the dark. If I did that I should be like Satan, who loves to lurk in the great abyss. I do not love darkness. I rub my eyes, stand a-tiptoe and crane my neck for some sign of morning's glow. But all I see is the billowing black clouds of night rolling across the uncertain bed of truth. I had decided not to say anything to you about the state of my mind, for I know it will pain you. I am already sorry that I have not kept it to myself, yet I could not, now you have asked me. I know you do not understand me. You live in the midst of the light, so my words seem mad. But I assure you my words are true and sober. I feel that you believe me to be careless of religious matters, but the Omniscient knows that I am not so. If the future is utterly dark, I am sure there is light beyond. The enjoyment I see you taking in it at all times convinces me. Why it is withheld from me, I do not know.

'Every day I go down into the darkness of the pit, but there I have my lamp. When I venture into the world of mind and spirit the darkness is great, and my lamp goes out. What have I done to prevent the dawn from breaking upon my soul? Perhaps you can tell me. I feel I am not as other people. I smile and laugh for appearances sake, but my heart is sad and my spirit weeps and moans. How can I laugh when I do not know when a mass of coal may crush me into yet deeper darkness than the one I already inhabit? You bid me pray, but the aspirations of my soul are a constant prayer. And when I put my desires into words, they come back to me, saying, "O, wretched man that you are."'

Mother, tried hard to put on a cheerful face.

'Well, my dear boy,' she said. 'I'm afraid you're in the melancholy. I used to think no one was troubled with that but the preachers of old, and I haven't heard of it troubling any of them since the time of Michael Roberts of Pwllheli. You are low-spirited, my son. You must take a little physic and a change of air. There's nothing in the world like it, they say. Sing a bit, my boy I'll help you.'

Mam began, as best she could, to sing the hymn,

> O Unbelief, how great thy power.
> A wound to me thou'st given.
> Spite which I'll trust, to my last hour,
> The greater grace of Heaven.

From then on Mam changed her tone and manner towards Bob. She spoke consolingly and encouragingly to him. But he only shook his head, as much as to say she did not understand him.

I think it must have been a fortnight or so after that conversation that I was returning from the country where I had taken a shop parcel; my first months with Abel Hughes mostly involved running errands. It was a lovely night, and I knew every house, hedgerow, wall, gate and mile-stone along the way. I fancied the trees gave me each a Good Night as I passed, as if to show that they remembered me from the time Wil Bryan and I came birds'-nesting and a-nutting that way. Even then I was a bit of a dreamer and enjoyed the romantic scenery and the profound calm.

I have always preferred the country to the town. The noise and bustle of the town impede me hearing the voice of God speak through nature. The night, because of its silence, has a great charm for me. People would laugh at the notion if they were to read it, but I have often wondered why police officers are not more refined and spiritual than other men. They have the time for reflection, in God's air during the deep silence of the night. Overhead they have the blue glittering firmament, as John Jones of Talsarn describes it, "when all about the land is wrapped in slumber." What a glorious opportunity to commune with nature and God. They experience a deep silence, broken by nothing but the occasional dog barking from some farm house in the far distance.

But for the other duties connected with that office, I should like to be a policeman, to enjoy being out at night. But I stray from my story.

I was returning from the country, fanciful and happy, not thinking that anything unpleasant awaited me. As I got near home I saw many people running towards the town. I hurried after them and overtook a lame old collier. I asked him what the people were running for. 'An explosion, my son, at Colliery Caeau Cochion,' he said.

His words seemed to give me wings. My feet did not touch the ground. I was lifted and carried along by the whirlwind of fears which rushed into my heart. I abandoned the high road and took a straight line for home, leaping walls, hedges, stiles, totally unconscious of any obstacle in my way. I thought of no one but Bob. Was he amongst the injured? Going by the time of day, he should have been home long before this, for his turn finished at seven o'clock. Yet it was only a few minutes past seven. If Bob were burnt to death, what should I do? I prayed that the fire had not touched him. But if it had reached his face, what a pity. How ugly he would look if he lost an eye. Such were the dreadful thoughts that ran through my mind as I overcame the distance between me and the knowledge of what had happened.

I quickly got within sight of the house, and found Bob had indeed come home.

He had come in a trolley filled with straw, supported by two men, one on either side. I rushed to his side. I listened to him groan, as the men carried him upstairs. Mother was deathly pale, but perfectly calm. Bob, black as the coal and charred to a cinder, lay quite still. His bright and intelligent eyes had been burnt clean out of his head, yet he still lived. I would not have known him from any other person in the world.

Dr Bennett, the works surgeon, was in the house, and he examined Bob. He shook his head to indicate there was no hope. I envied him the great tear stealing down his cheek. For once, I couldn't cry. Sometimes trouble is so severe that our usual tokens refuse their services out of diffidence. So was it with mother and me. We could not weep.

Someone, I forget who, gave Bob a draught of water and he seemed to revive. We heard him say 'Mother?'.

'Can you see a little, my son?' Mam said going to him. She did not know that he had lost both his eyes.

'Yes, Mam,' he said. 'I see the light at last.'

A moment later he spoke, in English. 'Doctor,' he said. 'I can see broad daylight.'

With those last words Bob left all doubt behind him. And the darkness fell upon Mam and me.

CHAPTER 24

Comforting and Sombre Memories

A precious privilege of living in a rural district is that few catastrophes happen, so it is rarely plunged into grief and sorrow. Not so with towns that include large works or pits. Sometimes the day opens its tender eyelids upon a town already awake and bustling. The rising sun smiles upon it sweetly, as the mother smiles upon a happy child when he wakes in his cradle.

Droves of colliers turn out of their houses, with their Geordie lamps hanging from their belts. The clatter of their clogs along the hard road and uneven pavements is music to the ears of many Welshwomen I know. In others it awakens the sorrow of a widow, who comes to the door with a child in her arms and another clinging to her apron while she vainly looks upon the crowd hoping that her man will return whilst knowing he never will.

You may see a well-built powerful man rushing out of his house. His bearing showing the pride he takes in the thought that he is going out to labour for wife and children. Before he has gone far a tiny, bare-foot, bare-legged, half-dressed boy with the remnants of last night's supper on his round, fat face runs after him. Father forgot to kiss him before setting out. Shamed by his remissness, he lifts the child up on his strong, broad breast and, ignoring the mixture, on the cheek, gives him a resounding kiss. The mother, following the child out of the cottage door, laughs merrily at them both.

Who dreams that that kiss might be the last? The pit engine, the rhythmic heart of the district, pulsates rapidly and regularly. The smoke of the great chimney rises in a thick black column, straight to heaven. As a boy I used to think that God needed the smoke to make clouds, which is why it rose straight upwards on a fair morning.

Tram after tram, wagon after wagon, can be seen coming from the pit's head, laden with the best coal. The wagoner, knee-breeched and whip on shoulder, walks as if he has one foot in a furrow, and shoots furtive glances at all he meets, to see whether they have noticed his well-fed horses and If they notice the tails he took such trouble to plait the night before and tie with blue and yellow ribbon.

Children play about the streets and make fun of the wagoner's thin shanks. They mimic his fashion of putting a 'y' after his horses' names. Boxer-y, Blaze-y, and the like. He takes no notice of them. The townsfolk all seem happy and contented, apart from Mr Roberts, the pudgy old butcher, who is half asleep in his shop chair. In the intervals between his customers' visits he seems to be wondering how, had he been a beast, he became fat enough to be ready for the knife. He watches as the lean, sallow-faced cobbler passes him at a jog trot with an apron full of mending jobs.

Although it is still early, the more organized among the colliers' wives are already in Mr Roberts's shop, looking for something nice for their husbands' dinners. 'How can a man work hard if he has nothing to his taste to eat?' they say. 'The men earn good money, so why shouldn't they have a few delicacies now and then?'

When the pit does well the business establishments have a thriving look about them. Their owners employ the morning's lull to dust the premises and put things in order. The ancient dame who keeps the toy shop is said to have a 'full old stocking' where she keeps her money. And why should that be a wonder? Boys of every age and size, going to school, slates scored with the previous night's homework slung over shoulder, flatten their noses against her window pane. Each vows to have his chosen toy with his next pocket money. Happy creatures, I say.

Then, within the hour, news can run like wild-fire that there has been a fall underground, and so many men have been killed. Or perhaps that water has broken in, and so many have been drowned or trapped in the upper portions of the work.

Lamentations, loud and deep, are heard all over the neighbourhood.

The lad who, on his way to school in the morning, had hoped for his father's help in buying a cricket bat, finds himself an orphan. The stalwart father, in the flower of health, who lifted his child like a feather for his morning kiss is brought home on a trolley, dead.

Oh ye simple farmer folk of Anglesey, who have no collieries. What know ye of sudden heart-rending visitations such as these? In the long nights of winter when ye sit warming yourselves by your roaring coal fires, instead of piles of smouldering peat, remember that what ye enjoy is bought with blood.

There was no warning of the explosion that caused the death of my brother Bob. A few minutes earlier the neighbourhood had been all peace and happiness. Now it plunged into raw, indescribable sorrow.

Every workman had his Geordie lamp, so no one knew how the accident happened, and we never did find out. It was not, however, the why and the wherefore of the accident that troubled my mother and myself but its results.

Mother lost a son who had stood her in a husband's stead since he was but a youth. She was wholly dependent upon him for her livelihood, and loved him more than her own life. She had never concerned herself much about me but never a day passed that her soul was not entwined with Bob's.

I lost a brother, outstanding among brothers, to whom I owed all I had by the way of learning. Even now I would be something quite different to what I am but for him. If I attempt to describe the extent of my grief at his loss I will make myself an object of contempt in these reminiscences.

I envied mother, who held up so bravely, whilst I became a worthless, inert mass. How precious now is my memory of her conduct! If all the works of the Puritan fathers, and everything ever written about Christianity, were placed in a great pile before me, and if I could comprehend the whole of their reasoning, my mother's calmness and self-restraint in the face of this terrible affliction would present an infinitely stronger argument of the truth of the Gospel.

Was it that she did not feel as deeply as other women bereaved by this catastrophe, those who scream and become hysterical? She did – and more so, I am sure. But she had a hidden spiritual support to fall back upon that enabled her to view the direst calamity as an indispensable verse in the chapter of her life, without which the context could not become clear. It was not physical strength that sustained her, for that had been declining for some time. It was her spirit and the support of the Great Lord.

She had thought Bob the smartest, handsomest fellow in the neighbourhood and suspected every girl who came to the house of having designs on him. When he was so dreadfully disfigured by the fire she resolved, the moment his spirit fled, she would never look upon his face again. When his coffin was brought home (a fearful object in a cottage with no room in which to escape the sight) Mam gave the carpenter strict orders to screw the lid down at once. She was afraid grim curiosity might lead someone to stare at his unsightly features. It is a fact that, when those we love are overtaken by sudden death, the failings and faults that were theirs when living, withdraw into the distance and grow smaller to the view.

Memory does not care to view our departed ones save in their Sunday best. Mam had prayed a deal for Bob, and had been greatly troubled by his condition. There had been nothing in his conduct to concern her except his reticence and the fact that he was not a member of her church. But now his burnt body lay at rest between four boards, she did not concern herself in the slightest about the safety of his soul, now far removed from all human aid.

I was sitting in silence with her before the hearth. Pleating her apron for an hour, she stared abstractedly into the fire. Suddenly she asked,

'What did he say in English to Dr Bennett? Tell me Rhys.'

'That he could see broad daylight,' I said.

'And what did the doctor say?'

'That he was beginning to ramble,' I said.

'I thought that was what he said. Just as Festus told Paul, "Thou art beside thyself." The natural man receiveth not the things of the Spirit of God, neither can he know them, for they are spiritually discerned.'

Then she added, as if to herself. 'Rambling indeed. No fear of Bob's rambling. It was the spiritual light he spoke of, that light after which he had been groping for so long. And there shall be light in the evening. Wonderful! Wonderful! He was obliged to lose both eyes before he could see. For judgment Jesus came into this world, that they which see not might see Him.

'I would rather that he had been professing; but I never thought him irreligious. Abel Hughes always said Bob had a better grain about him than the half of us. But it made my mind easier when he said a fortnight ago that he wasn't careless about the things of religion. He said that the cry of his soul was for light. God has said, "Ye shall seek me and find me, when ye shall search for me with all your heart." "I said not unto the seed of Jacob, seek me in vain." "Ask and it shall be given unto you; seek, and ye shall find," is what the Saviour said on the Mount. I do not believe Bob to be lost. I hope I'm not sinning, but I am certain he is in heaven. And if I go there myself, as I expect I might, and find him not there, it will destroy all my happiness.'

There was nothing else for me to do but to trust that Mam's faith was true. Some learned man, reading what I am about to say, might laugh at me. Let him laugh. For I believe that pious people, however ignorant they may be, possess a sort of spiritual perception. They receive, perhaps unconsciously, some kind of communications from the eternal world which are not given to the Godless. I am perfectly well aware that this idea is incompatible with the knowledge of some able men in this enlightened age, when religious people are looked on as old-fashioned, and the Bible is considered a harmless little book. Their promise is that the discoveries of science will soon enable the boy at school to write upon his slate all the hidden mysteries of nature, the secrets of being, and the aspirations of the immortal soul.

My recollection of Bob's death is still fresh, but I do not intend to linger over the period when his mortal remains lay waiting to be taken from our sight for ever. If I were to attempt to describe my feelings at the time, it might be regarded as a want of taste on my part. Although every family knows Death, he always comes as a stranger. He visits us unasked and is never welcome. But the less welcome, the more likely he is to speedily to return.

It is a strange and wonderful occasion when the body of a beloved one lies in the same house with us, and we await the hour appointed by the custom of the country and what is considered propriety, before taking it to its last resting place. How difficult it is to grasp that he who the day before, looked at us, spoke to us, ate, drank and walked about as we did, now lies still, cold, dumb and deaf.

How cruel it seems to leave him in a room all by himself. The season is inclement, but we have not lit a fire. Does he think us unkind? Would he leave us so? We know him to be far away from us, and yet we are conscious that he is in the next room. Why else would we speak so softly, as if we were afraid to wake him?

How slowly the hours drag. How unfeeling is the practice of drawing the curtains to shut out the light of day. We make a night of the occasion, as if we had not enough darkness already in our souls. The gloom becomes oppressive, and the desire to get everything over and done with grows strong. Are we really in a hurry to bury him? Oh no. But the time is long and cheerless. We try to read. Our eye looks at the book, but the mind wanders off to some strange place.

The slightest movement makes us listen, and listen eagerly. Our ear is strained in the direction of the next room. Was that the sound of his well-known cough? Did he move? It is all just fancy, for the house is as quiet as the grave.

We drop into a short sleep and awake thinking that we have been dreaming. We go over the circumstances once more. Everything appears different. Life, wealth and fame have lost their charm for us. The things of this world are vain in our sight, and we wonder how anyone can devote themselves to matters earthly. How can anyone laugh? We forget that a few days previously we ourselves were guilty of just such conduct, and that soon we will again be exactly as we were.

We form many good resolutions, but all will be sadly qualified, if not entirely forgotten, in two months' time. Death is a black and hideous monster but, though it throws some gleams of light on things for the living, how much more so for him it takes away?

When death ploughs the heart, and trouble softens it, the evangelist has an excellent opportunity to sow the good seed, which can find deepness with ease. And though the earth will harden again, the seed may someday sprout and break forth through its crusted covering to bear fruit a hundredfold.

The visits of our chapel friends to mother and me in our trouble brought us such blessing and comfort as I cannot properly describe nor value. Mam said that next to the priceless promises of Scripture and her faith in God as Over-ruler of all, she valued most the cheering words of the religious brethren and sistren. Many came to comfort us, and not least among them were Thomas and Barbara Bartley. They were both so childish, so simple, but showed a sympathy so real and so genuine that it was impossible not to prize it.

Mother could hardly help smiling at some of Thomas's artless questions, such as, 'Mair, do you think Bob has told Seth yet that Barbara

Comforting and Sombre Memories

and I have come to *Seiat*? That is, if they have happened across one another, for there's such a crowd of them up there, isn't there?'

'For all I know, it may be he has, Thomas,' mother said.

'They'll light on each other someday, surely,' Thomas said. 'Two men will meet before two mountains, so they say.'

He sat silent for a moment as pondering what to say next.

'Barbara and I thought a deal about you last night, Mair,' he said. 'And we couldn't in no way see what you are to do now, except come to live with us. We have as much room as you want, and a hundred thousand welcomes.' He turned to his wife. 'Isn't it so, Barbara? We've made the place ready for you, and you two must come over tonight. You don't bury Bob till the day after tomorrow, and why should you stay here breaking your heart?'

Barbara gave a nod.

'You're very kind and very neighbourly, Thomas,' mother said. 'But I can't think of leaving Bob by himself here, though it is all a fancy.'

'To be shuar,' said Thomas. 'I never thought of that. No, no, honour bright. Come to think of it, it would look a bit cold for you to leave him, specially since you've no fear. But we'll talk of that some other time.'

'What have I to fear, Thomas? There is nothing here but the poor body, the empty house.' Mam said.

'It wasn't that I was referring to,' Thomas said.

Mother knew what he meant. Thomas knew more of our history than I did. Mother nodded her thanks for his thoughtfulness, and said, 'The door has a lock and a bar to it, Thomas.'

'To be shuar. But you must come over the day after tomorrow. We'll no more miss the bit of food you'll eat than that of a chicken.'

The day after tomorrow came, but my memories are dark and confused. I felt as if I were in a dream. Two impressions remain in my mind, which I recall today. First, there were a great many people at the funeral, and, second, Wil Bryan walked beside me, with a good-sized box-plant under his left arm and a bag filled with sand in his right hand. I have a faint recollection of hearing Mr Brown's deep voice hurrying through the burial service, and a vivid one of Wil Bryan on his knees by the grave-side sanding it, and planting it with box.

Little did I think then how soon he would be at the same task again. Wil was usually a very talkative fellow but, when feeling deeply for another, he was always silent. He spoke not a word till we were halfway home from the churchyard.

Then I remember well his words.

'Rhys, do you know what Bob would say if he knew Mr Brown was going to bury him? He'd have used Robbie Burns's last words, "Don't let that awkward squad shoot over my grave." That's what he'd have said, I'll take oath.'

Wil was clearly thinking of Bob's wrongful committal to prison by Mr Brown in his capacity as a Justice of the Peace, and he voiced my brother's feelings to the letter.

Thomas Bartley was but a young convert to the Cause, and old habits and notions not strictly compatible with his religious profession still showed in him. Although ready and willing to renounce them, he couldn't do so without a bit of a wrench. On the day of Bob's burial, Thomas asked my mother whether she meant to provide a little bread and cheese and beer for the people at the Brown Cow. He added that he thought they kept the best beer and offered to take all the expense upon himself.

Whilst thanking him for his kindness, mother took pains to explain the unseemliness of the custom of feasting at funerals, and of bringing intoxicating drink to the funeral table.

'To be shuar, Mair,' Thomas said. 'You're the best judge. You know more of the Bible than I do, and I always defer to you. But I thought it might look a little cold not to offer a bit or a drop for anybody.'

Mother met our good friends halfway by letting Barbara provide tea and invite a few of her nearest neighbours to partake of it on returning from the funeral. They sat and talked about the dead, which eased Thomas's conscience a little.

After the guests had gone and mother, I, Thomas and Barbara were left to ourselves. Thomas sat musing for a while.

'Now, Mair,' he said. 'You must get out of this. You shouldn't stay in this house breaking your heart. People never do any good, living by themselves. You've no notion how comfortable we'll all be together. It'll save Barbara and I coming over to hear you expounding. D'ye know what? It'll be as good as a sermon for us to have you over yonder, and we shan't miss your bit of food any more than if you were a chick.'

'I don't know how to thank you enough for your kindness,' Mother said. 'And after your mention of a certain matter the other night, I have made up my mind to accept your warm-hearted invitation, on condition that I pay for my place as long as my money holds out. I have a little put by, and I shall have a little more from the sale of the things here. Possibly that may be enough to last me as long as I am with you.'

'We'll settle all that another time,' Thomas said, filling his pipe.

I was bewildered. I had never dreamt my mother would deign to receive such a kindness, even from Thomas Bartley. Circumstances must have absolutely compelled her to do so. I knew that independence of mind and a dread of being a burden to anybody were deep traits of her character.

Barbara was helping Mam on with her cloak and bonnet when the real reason suddenly occurred to me. Now I knew why mother had readily accepted Thomas Bartley's invitation. It was her fear of our old visitor, the Irishman.

A few minutes later we were all four wending our way to Y Twmpath, for that was the name of Thomas Bartley's house. We travelled like a sort of railway train. Thomas was in the lead, like the locomotive, the smoke from his pipe puffing into the night air. I was behind him, with mother after me, like passenger carriages. Barbara, was like a stout luggage van that wobbled along at the tail end of our train.

We were all silent, except Barbara, who was troubled with rheumatism. She would groan, like a luggage van that needed its wheels greasing. Thomas, like the locomotive, would give a sort of whistle saying 'Are you coming, you women there?'

I am describing the journey as I see it now, not as I saw it then. The thought of leaving the old house where I was born and which held all my memories, filled me with great sadness. This would be my first ever night away from home.

I had always thought of Y Twmpath as a model of cosiness and comfort. And our welcome there was real, but as I went to bed, the bed in which Seth died, I felt a great wave of regret for the old house, for Bob and for the old days. I hid my head under the bedclothes and stuffed the sheets into my mouth to stop myself crying out loud.

In the morning Mam saw my swollen eyes, and she choked back a sob. Thomas Bartley made a great effort to divert our minds from our trouble and keep us cheerful. He took us down the yard to see the pigs and fowl. He didn't stop talking the whole time. Mam listened carefully to everything he said, but she knew he was talking for the sake of it. He went on at some length.

'Mair, here's the best pigs I ever had to thrive,' he said. 'I wouldn't give a fig for one as wasn't mischievous. These would eat the trough if they didn't get their food in time. That one without a tail is master of the place. I always rear two; they thrive so much better; kill one and sell the other. I never feed them India meal, because the bacon when you put it in the pan will melt to nothing before it's cooked. If you want good bacon, tatties and oatmeal is the best for fattening them. You can boil a little nettles now and then for a change. And for a pig who's lost his appetite I put red raddle in his food. There's nothing in grain to fatten a pig. Nothing at all. D'ye know what, Mair *fach*, I'd never eat bacon if I had to buy that American stuff. How do you tell what they fatten their animals on out there? They say American pigs eat those runaway Black slaves who die out in the woods '

He waved towards the cockerel.

'Hullo, Cobbin!' he shouted. 'There you are. Now there's a bird for you, Mair! But for that white feather in his tail he'd be pure game. Look at his breast; it's as black as a bilberry. Before I came to religion,

I'd have cut that cock's comb for him, but now I know it isn't right. I shouldn't try to improve on the work of the Almighty. These game hens aren't great layers but their eggs are richer.'

'Barbara,' he yelled, turning towards the house, 'is breakfast ready?' Hearing her say it was, he answered. 'Right, we'll come directly.'

He turned back to mother.

'Fowls pay very well, Mair, if they're well fed. Look, you're getting fond of them already. When they hold their heads to one side they're well settled. Let's go back to the house and see what the old woman's got for us. I don't know about you, but I could eat a horse's head.'

After a fine breakfast I set out for the shop, and mother came a part of the way. It was clear she wanted to have a word with me in private.

'I see you're fretting,' she said, placing a hand upon my shoulder. 'But you must buckle to, my son. We must both submit to God's will and not give way. You are only beginning life, while I am drawing towards its end. If you're a good boy, God will take care of you. Work to please your master, and you'll please God too. I'll ask Abel Hughes to let you sleep at his house, because we can't impose too much upon our friends' kindness. If you like, you can run over each evening, after shutting shop, to see how we are getting on. I hope I don't have to ask for parish relief, but I have a little money saved, and it may last as long as I do.'

I tried to say what was on my mind, but the words stuck in my throat. All I could do was to cry. Mam pressed my head to her breast and, when I was cried out, she dried my eyes with her apron and said. 'There! Off you go now, and don't you forget what I told you.'

So I went, but on the road I couldn't help thinking of my mother's fear of going on the parish. I felt that I had neither age nor position to support her. It was only a few months earlier that she had spoken so loftily to Mr Brown, the clergyman. She had said that she would never be obliged to seek help from either parish or parson. That must have been a bitter memory for her.

I am quite sure that she would rather have thrown herself upon the mercy of the relieving officer general for all in adversity, Death himself, than submit to Parson Brown. And I heard in her voice that morning which something that suggested that was her secret prayer.

CHAPTER 25

An Elegy in Prose

Before I close this second epoch of my history and start to tell of the time I found myself alone to fight the battle of life, I must first deal with two or three characters. My mother, in particular, deserves rather more attention than I have yet devoted to her.

During the whole of her stay with Thomas and Barbara Bartley my mother received great care and attention at their hands. As long as she lived at Y Twmpath she made it her work to prepare the two old folk for admission into full church membership. It was not a simple task. She spent weeks coaching them before she felt confident enough to ask Abel Hughes to call them forward for reception.

The occasion caused much amusement in the *Seiat*. Their answers were simple and original. Some laughed, others cried, and some did both at once. I won't dwell too long on the events of that *Seiat*, but I'll outline what went on.

Thomas would look at mother when answering questions. He referred to Mam as an authority in doctrine, and he was like a lad watching his father for approval whilst reciting his verse at a church meeting, his expression showing a mixture of doubt and fear. On the whole he satisfied his questioners with his knowledge and readiness for admission. Barbara didn't do quite so well during her examination. Most of the time she would say that she felt exactly the same as Thomas. She clearly saw herself as a duplicate of her husband, and if Thomas had answered correctly she didn't see any need to repeat his answer. I have always thought that the two of them thought in unison and acted exactly alike. Indeed, I am tempted to go a step further and say that they seemed to share the same consciousness. They were like a clock with two faces, always showing the exact same time of day. Eventually Barbara was unanimously received into church membership on the strength of Thomas's answers. That night the old couple went home arm in arm, close joined as a double-kernelled nut. They were both excessively happy and magnified the importance of what they had done.

Mother looked forward to the occasion with both interest and anxiety. Thomas and Barbara were her special disciples, and she took pleasure in seeing that her instruction and prayers were not wasted.

That night was the last time Mam went to chapel. Her health had been failing for some time, and Bob's death hit her hard. 'Between one storm and the other,' she said, 'I have been tossed quite badly of late.'

Bob, the staff on which she had leaned, was broken. She had neither the health nor the strength to earn her own living, she hated being dependent on the kindness of friends, and she dreaded being thrown onto parish charity. Instead she raised her finger to the King of Terrors, and beckoned him to her. Death had no sting for her. Her heart and her contemplation had long since secured her a home on the other side. She was not a money-lover. What little she had saved when Bob was getting good wages, when added to what she got from the sale of the furniture of the old house, was to her the sand in an hour glass. It was the measure of her life.

Now I am a minster, I find that some kind woman – and all women are kind to a visiting preacher – will on a Monday morning boil me an egg for breakfast before I return from an engagement. As I watch the sand trickle down the glass to time the egg, it reminds me of Mam. As my host watches the sand, so did Mam watch the little money she had. It gradually dawned on me that when she reached the last penny in her purse she would take her leave.

She did not suffer much pain in her latter days. She went to bed to die, much as a woman might leave the cold wind upon a railway platform to take shelter in the waiting room while waiting for a train. She kept watching the line, as if tired of the delay. She remained calm and collected; her well-thumbed Bible was always open by her side on the bed. To pursue the railway metaphor, she kept checking her ticket. She died wearing her spectacles.

I grieve in my soul that I am not a poet, dear mother of mine. If I had the divine inspiration, I would sing thee a sublime elegy. Whatever my shortcomings, I would try to share my sorrow from the workshop of my heart. I may not be an elect of the bardic order, but I will not let this moment pass without making an effort to pay tribute to thy memory, even if I must do it in plain prose.

Is it womanish, a sign of weakness, for a man to be over-fond of his mother? If so then am I womanish and weak. For I have come to know thee as the fairest, dearest and best of womankind.

I believe that my notion of thee was born into the world with me. It has no beginning in my memory, and it is not the fruit of observation and reason, for my reason says different. I felt nearer to thee than thou wast to thyself. But I do not think that thou didst feel thus towards me. I knew thy face years before I knew my own. If I were to see both our faces in a glass at this moment I should recognize thine first. It was thy face I knew and none other. I was a child in thine arms upon the lake bank, and thou didst direct my eyes to the shadow in the water. What care and trouble thou didst take over me.

Before I could speak thou knewest my wants and desires. When I was ill there was no sleep or rest for thee. When I was well and active thy soul was filled with delight. Thou didst teach me our language, without thyself knowing its grammar. And for thy years of labour thou didst not receive a single penny in payment.

We spoke the dear old Cymric, as thou knewest none other. Thou didst not believe there was any tongue to match it. Thou hast imprinted its letters upon my memory while my heart was young and malleable. I could not, even if I wanted to, erase them from my mind. How sweet is the recollection of the first lessons in syllabification thou gavest me. Thyself, thou wert uninstructed, and thy prejudices were many and strong. Thou wouldst not believe there was anything worth mention outside the Welsh language, nor any real religion except amongst the Calvinistic Methodists. Thou wert one of the best-read women I knew, although thou couldst easily count all thy books upon thy fingers. They consisted of the Bible, Bishop Charles's *Dictionary of Religious Quotations*, his *Preceptor*, the Hymn book, Bishop Gurnal's *Works*, the *Pilgrim's Progress*, and the *Welshman's Candle*. And there were two others, Roberts of Holyhead's *Almanacks*, and the works of Twm o' Nant. This was the entire extent of thy library, but every book was black with thy thumb-marks, and hung down at the corners like the ears of Moll o' Glasdwr's old dog.

Thy volumes were not left on their shelves to gather dust. Thou didst make the time to read and study them. In this way thou didst furnish thy mind with their contents so that thou couldst at all times quote them from memory to suit the occasion. And thou wert as familiar with, and just as at home in, the exalted speeches of the books of Job, Isaiah and Revelations as thou wert in the fairs and fixed feasts of the *Almanack*, with its doggerel prophecies, such as 'snow for all, towards the fall.'

When I think of thy piety, I wondered what pleasure thou didst find in the Bard of Nant, who was not a man with a Methodist's heart. With relish thou wouldst read those severe buffetings the old satirist gave to irreligious parsons and unjust stewards. Was it Twm o' Nant who created in thee such prejudice against the Church of England? Thou saidst that thou believed the bard was converted before his death. For I heard thee, dozens of times, repeat these lines of his.

> My conscience, that captive maid of wondrous grace, before me laid the startling story:
> Greatest prophet thou they say, that sojourns in Samaria. Come, I implore thee,
> Recover my leprosy clean. No more do I prefer Abana and Pharpar,
> They're rivers impure, I ween. Give me of Jordan water — the Son of Man's, 'tis seen.
> Nought e'er can flood my soul's dark dross. Save Jesu's blood, who on the Cross

Died, and was so sacrificed that, through His loss, we life might win,
Lord, though we sin.
Thy Son's pierced side poured out its crimson tide; O precious blood!
shed not for woeful world in vain.

But the book thou wert most at home with was the Bible. Thou didst never tire of reading it, or of proclaiming its truths. Never didst thou doubt its inspiration, or that it was the Word of God. If Bob happened to suggest the merest hint of a mistake in the translation of some verse, thy anger would be fanned to a white heat. And, partial though thou wert to the Rev. Charles, thou wert offended with him when he said, in his sermon that a few words in a certain place should be altered a little. Afterwards thou didst complain of him to Abel Hughes, saying thou didst fear too much learning had made him mad. One of thy chief reasons for not being over fond of student preachers was that one of them once declared his text to read better in English than Welsh. Thou saidst with great passion that thou hadst no patience to listen to apprentice preachers trying to improve the Word of God.

Thy ignorance made thee speak thus, but perhaps thou gained credit in Heaven even for that. Twas thy zeal for the Bible, thy love for every verse and word, made thee jealous of any effort to meddle with it.

And what wonder is that? The Bible was the foundation of all thy consolation. Its promises sustained thee in every case of trouble and affliction. If anyone had succeeded in shaking a grain of thy faith in its divine inspiration, all would have been over for thee. Thou hadst put thy trust entirely in its Truth and loved it so absorbedly, that I believe Thomas Bartley when he said that, at thy death, he found thee gazing through thy spectacles at thy well-worn Bible. Thou wert unwilling to leave it, and would have taken it with thee if only thou couldst.

The circle of thy life was a constricted. Thou knewest nothing of the world. Thou hadst no notion of its size, its bustle and its wickedness. Thy path was narrow and its hedges high. Yet thou didst succeed in keeping to the middle of it, without ever falling into the ditch. That path led thee into life as a little tributary flows into the great broad river leading into the sea. Thy way was narrow but just. Thou knewest that the Saviour was born a Jew, but thou didst believe that He was more of a Welshman than anything else. In this thou wert right, for are not the faithful, of whatsoever nation, conscious that the man Christ Jesus is nearer related to their own race than to any other? This is clear proof of His fitness as a Saviour, wherever found.

What I write about thee will not be read until I, like thyself, have gone over. I can tell the truth about thee, without diffidence or false modesty. Thou wert endowed with strong instincts and an excellent memory. Hadst thou received a good education, I do not doubt but thou wouldst have become a woman of note.

Uninstructed though thou wert, thou wert seldom imposed upon. Yet thou wert deceived once, and deceived grossly. But for this fact my hand would not now be writing a summary of thy life history. For I would not have been born. Thou wert deceived by one who ought to have been thy guide and protector. He won thy heart and affections when thou wert but a fair young girl.

He who should have been most faithful unto thee, thy husband and my father, deceived thee. He was, I have heard, a sturdy, handsome man but irreligious. He wished to speak with thee but thou wouldst have nothing to do with one who had no religion. He came to the chapel, but with what intent? He became a member of thy church so he could converse with thee, tenderly and religiously. He was a detestable hypocrite. He was ready of speech like thyself, and in this respect you were both well matched. But he lied to thee about how he envied the preacher and the pleasure he found in chapel.

He seemed a new man but there was a legion of devils in his heart. Thou didst listen to him, as ninety-nine out of a hundred girls would have done. Ye were married one lovely May morning, amid a shower of presents and good wishes from thy friends. But, once wed, God and thou alone knew what thou didst suffer, what trials thou didst undergo. And the wretch inflicting this suffering on thee was my own father.

When thou died I rejoiced that I had neither seen his face nor heard his voice. I only caught one faint glimpse of his form in the darkness that notable night in my history when Bob was arrested. He was in the company of the Irishman whom I hated with all my heart.

My dear old mother, what a mercy thou shouldst have found, while yet a girl, such a strong religion. Thy husband's vile ways and devilish disposition left thy faith in God untarnished. The thought of the bruises thou didst suffer from his cruelty still makes my heart bleed. Yet still thou couldst pray for him. Many a time thou couldst not go to chapel because of a black eye the inhuman scoundrel inflicted on thee.

My flesh creeps, and my sinews tighten, when I think how thou didst suffer. How fortunate for thee, Mair Lewis, that his wickedness grew, so that he was obliged to flee the country. He nearly made an end of thy life, many times, without thought of escape, and without giving the authorities any idea for his arrest. But when he came near taking the life of another, one infinitely less worthy than thee, all the country demanded his arrest, and every police officer burned with the desire to capture him. Thanks be to Heaven.

Thou heardst no more of him and no more didst mention his name. Thou wentest through poverty and want after Bob's imprisonment and death. But there was neither shame nor dishonour entailed in these.

What vexation, what sorrow and what hardship thou didst suffer before I was born. Thy house was a den of hard-hearted, reckless poachers. They neither feared God nor respected man. No living creature knows what thou suffered for thou didst not speak of it. From aught thou saidst to me, I did not know the hundredth part of thy troubles. I had grown to a biggish boy before I learned anything of thy history, save what I had heard in the hints and taunts of my enemies. All I knew was that that in thy cupboard was a skeleton of some kind. Bob was the first to tell me, in bed on the night of Seth's death. And that was only after I had told him about the man who had stopped me near the Hall Park, and what he had said to me.

I have many times asked myself if thou couldst have had a spark of affection left for the man who brought so much misery and shame upon thee. Perhaps thou didst harbour a spark of love for him. The last thing thou saidst to me before dying was,

'If ever you and your father meet face to face, try and forget his wickedness, and if you have any good to do him, do it. He has a soul to be saved, like you and me, and it does not much matter now how he behaved towards me; but it matters everything that he should be saved. If you should ever see him – and who knows but you might – try and remember he is your father. I have forgiven him all and pray that He whose forgiveness is life everlasting will do the same.'

Wil Bryan said of thee that, like Job, thou didst 'stick to thy colours, first class.'

I have not come anywhere near to relating all the counsel and advice thou gavest me in thy last days. Perhaps someone reading this will fancy I have over-coloured thy virtues. The fact that thou wert my mother may make this so. But I will chronicle thy last words to me, which were so helpful to me in later life. Thou saidst:

'If you are called upon to suffer in this world, do not complain, for it will make you think of a world in which there is no suffering. Do not make your home in the world, or dying will turn out to be a harder job than you think it is. Test all things against the word of God, yourself especially. Take the Bible as a weather-glass for your soul. If you lose your relish for reading it, you may be sure there will be no fair weather waiting for you. Pray for a godly life, but do not expect to live old, for fear you may die young. Try and find a religion of which no one can have any doubt, and which you yourself trust.

'One of the poorest things on earth is a sickly religion. It stops you from enjoying the things of this world, and does not help you to enjoy the things of the next. Take hold of a religion whose sheets will encompass others beside yourself. If you can be the means of saving but one soul, you will gain your way farther into heaven after death than if you were worth a hundred thousand pounds and had done nothing for others. You cannot expect a penny piece from any of your relations; but you can become rich in the country in grace, if you try.

Abraham would never have been heard of if he had no better property than camels. You will have three enemies to fight, the world, the devil and yourself. And you will find yourself the hardest to conquer. In that battle, remember you have a whole armour of prayer, watchfulness and the Word of God about you. You're sure to lose if you do not take unto yourself all three. If you vanquish your enemies during life, you will see only their backs when you come to die.

'I am going to leave you, and I trust in the Lord that I am a vessel of mercy. You will find in the purse in the pocket of my black gown enough money to pay for burying me. If it should ever rest with you to do a good turn for Thomas and Barbara, don't forget their kindness towards your mother. I wish you had had a talent for preaching, and were inclined that way. But it can't be helped. Try and be religiously useful in whatsoever you do, and you'll never repent it. If I am to see you from the other world, I should like to find you a deacon.'

At the time I never imagined these directions would be thy last. When next I saw thee, Barbara Bartley had done all that death had left undone for thy face and closed thine eyes. Barbara said that thy departure was like the 'outing of a candle'.

Death was not unkind to thee. He left a cheerful smile upon thy face, a smile like that of a child dreaming in its cradle. The more I looked at thee, the more didst thou seem to smile. It was as if thou wert trying to tell me thou wert happy. Thy unwrinkled cheeks were white as snow, but across thy nose ran a streak of blue, the last trace of thy spectacles as thy blood grew cold.

Three hearts beat rapidly and regretfully by thy bedside knowing that never again would they hear thy voice. Three consciences testified that thou hadst done all in thy power to purify and guide them to the path of life. Thy lips didst not move, but I fancied I heard thee say:

'I have fought a good fight. I have finished my course. I have kept the faith. Henceforth a crown of righteousness is laid up for me, which the Lord, the righteous judge, shall give me at this day – and not to me alone, but unto all them that love Him.'

Troublous was thy life. At many junctures thou wert poor. But the great crowd that came to pay a last tribute of respect to thy memory showed that others beside myself saw something in thy character worth emulating. Never was Wil Bryan so often and so severely reproved as by thee, yet on the day of thy funeral he testified that thou wert 'a stunner of a woman.'

As I write this Thomas and Barbara Bartley have grown old, but they still speak of thee. Barbara yet has only a grip of the letters, same as Thomas, but on Sunday afternoons she puts on thy spectacles and turns over the leaves of thy old Bible, as she seeks to imitate thee.

CHAPTER 26

The Sinner and the Spectre

Time is a rare old physician, excelling all his rivals with a twofold qualification, indispensable to his profession. He has the power of healing and of deadening. In the latter he has a helper, older and more experienced than he, the Devil by name. When I found myself without a home, without a mother and worse than fatherless, I fancied there was no earthly comfort left to me, and that none of the things of this world had any charm. I also thought that nothing would be easier than to follow my mother's advice to the letter. I felt not the slightest inclination to do anything else. My course lay clear before me: a thoughtful, studious and religious one. All my leisure hours would be spent in reading good books, particularly the Bible.

No resort would have any attraction for me but our church. I would faithfully attend that old chapel where Mam and Bob had spent their happiest hours. Looking back, I realize that under mother's care I had been kept in closer repression than any other boy in the neighbourhood. But I felt that mother had been right, and I decided to stay within my old bounds. I felt this gave me greater freedom, whilst suiting my tastes and desires. I wanted to become useful to religion. I revisited my boyish ambitions to be a minister. I didn't see too many obstacles in my path towards that goal. All I needed to do to fulfil the dying wishes of my mother was follow the natural bent of my mind. My character was untarnished, and I resolved to keep it so. I did not intend to turn aside from the straight path.

But how my heart deceived me. I imagine Time ruffling his forehead, and his devilish assistant, laughing up his sleeve at my good resolutions. I was soon to find that my nature contained a foul dirt-heap of depravity which had never before been stirred.

The Corner Shop where I was an apprentice was one of the oldest establishments in the town. My master Abel Hughes was a careful, just and sharp-eyed man. Our merchandise included general drapery, but we mainly sold cloth and flannel, and our stock was always top quality.

The shop was often quiet, we were rarely busy except on fair days. I believe Abel Hughes did not care that fairs were only held four times a year. Ours was a good, steady trade with customers and their families who had done business with the same shop from time out of mind.

For the most part they were country people, the majority of them Methodists. The verse 'Do good unto all men, especially unto them who are of the household of faith' was still in fashion.

Abel Hughes kept the very best material, and he earned a reasonable profit on it. He would not overpraise his goods, nor reduce his price by as much as a halfpenny. Should a customer not like what he offered him, Abel would advise him to leave it alone; I never heard Abel swear that his stuff was worth more than he asked for it. In those days lies were not so common in business. Abel never spent a penny on posters, his only use for the printing press was for bill-heads.

The shop window was small, and the glass in panes of about a square foot each. Large plate glass windows had not yet come into use. The window dressing could easily be done in an hour, and that only once a fortnight.

Even in broad daylight the shop was dark. It had an atmosphere of moleskin, cotton-cord and velveteen so thick that I felt I could cut it into lengths with my scissors. When a customer came in, the first thing Abel did was to offer him a chair and start a conversation. The man would sit for at least half an hour, sometimes even longer. Eventually he would buy an expensive parcel, before being asked into the house for a cup of tea or a bit of dinner. Abel did little business after sunset. The shop had a gas supply but only one jet was ever lit, just to show that we were open for trade.

There was not much book-keeping work to do. A single long, narrow account book served as both day book and ledger. When a customer paid his account, we would let him see us cross it out; we didn't need to give out receipts. It was the same sort of way of doing business that Noah might have used before the Flood, if he had kept a shop. And Abel Hughes did well and saved money.

How would such a simple and honest business fare in these days? Today people beat about for customers in every possible direction. It does not matter how they obtain a buyer. Making money is to some folk as important as earning immortality, and immortality of no more consequence than a yard of grey calico.

In those innocent days a chain of honesty still restrained the neck of greed. Traders stuck to their own business and lived amicably, without trying to undersell or cut each other's throats. They did not make a spectacle to put their neighbours in the shade. If they held a position free from care, achieved comfortable circumstances or had a bit put by in an old stocking, they were satisfied. There was nothing in the outward appearance of these happy people to distinguish them from those who had less. That such a person was rich was a matter of belief, not of proof. Few people made a parade of opulence only to come down with a crash, leaving creditors to regret their folly in trusting them. It was even less common for anyone caught deceiving or cheating his neighbours to later fill a public office or swagger in the Big Seat or the pulpit. Such things happen more often today, I am sorry to say.

What would become of Abel Hughes if he kept shop today and remained uncorrupted by the times? I think he would starve. I also believe that he would have starved willingly, rather than conform to the avarice, deceit and trickery of this present age. He would not lie or pretend to sell his goods for less than he had given for them. He would not take a customer by the scruff of the neck and drag him into his shop. He would not induce any man to buy something he did not want. He wouldn't wear a perpetual smirk on his face. In other words he wouldn't act the monkey. By the very nature of things he would die of want, or be forced into the workhouse.

The Corner Shop employed an assistant named Jones – all draper's shops seem to have an assistant named Jones. I have a vivid memories of the particular Jones who worked for Abel Hughes. If I close my eyes I can see him standing behind the counter. The tip of his bright scissors show above the edge of his waistcoat pocket, and he has a swarm of pins stuck into the left lapel of his coat. They look like a horde of mountebank's children, all trying to see how far they can cross their centre of gravity without falling over.

Jones was a little, limp fellow. He looked as if Providence had intended him for either a tailor or an umbrella-mender. He had a great shock of hair, all cut the same length and lying flat upon his pate like a pound of candles. His head had evidently pillaged his cheeks, which were utterly hairless, bar a meagre tuft on his chin and a slight fur sprinkle on his upper lip. He looked a bit like a stricken, grizzly old woman.

Jones couldn't grow a moustache, as his lip-hair was not worth the trouble of cutting; a penny spent on a shave would have been a waste of money. His nose was not well-kept. It was a blue-red standing libel to its owner's sobriety. He had a way of holding his arms as if he thought them to be in his way and would rather be without them. His feet were wide, flat and jointless. When he walked they turned out at such an angle it seemed they wanted to go off in different directions. They looked as if they had once had a dreadful quarrel and would never make up, despite all Jones's coaxing.

Jones was never offended, no matter what was said to him, but he heartily hated a busy day. He would not sleep a wink the night before a fair, and he would stay out of everybody's sight, behind a pile of cloth. Be it summer or winter he was always the same. He looked as if he were nearly frozen and needed to run to the fire to warm; he was a monument to winter. His feet turned out like those of a round table, his arms hung like a doll's, his eyes opened and shut like a cat's on the hearth. When thinking nothing and doing nothing, he was in heaven.

Jones was a creature whom nature favoured by concealing his age; He had nothing like the horns of the cow or the teeth of the horse to give away his maturity. A new customer coming into the shop and seeing only his back, would swear that Jones was an apprentice in his second year. If he saw Jones's profile, behind a heap of cloth, he might have thought him Abel Hughes's sister. If he saw only Jones's feet alone, he might assume him to be an old man of eighty. But if he got a full view he would be desperately puzzled whether to hail him with 'My son' or 'Well, father'.

I said that Jones always seemed the same, but I should withdraw my words. As I observed him more closely I saw that the weather affected him greatly. Even though he was already small, the cold and wet shrunk him up like a piece of Welsh flannel. But, unlike the flannel, he did not thicken in the shrinking. I think his intention in retreating into himself was to evade the fall of temperature. In this task he was very successful. When the weather grew warmer Jones would occasionally take a stroll, and begin to thaw. His mouth was always half open so the wind entered it and plumped out his flesh a little.

The weather influenced Jones, and Jones had an influence upon the weather. In winter his frozen look, with his nose and hands blue with cold, could make a customer's teeth chatter. This would plant the idea of procuring a warm top coat. Abel Hughes often said that Jones could sell more lengths of overcoat cloth than anyone he ever saw.

The fellow was a perfect ice-box. For all that, people wondered why Abel Hughes kept a man like Jones in his shop. The wages he paid Jones were small. Abel was a just man with his honour above question, but he only paid Jones about a third of what assistants get in these days. And yet Jones had had the impudence to marry. But Abel was also a merciful man; he knew Jones and his wife must have their daily bread somehow.

The pair lived happily, and were wise enough not to add to the population. Abel Hughes often said that one Jones was enough in the world, and Jones believed him in this as in so many things.

Mrs Jones was a buxom, red-cheeked woman. When she walked out with her husband they looked like a cow with her calf, or perhaps a lion with its next meal. To labour the point, Jones's size relative to his wife, was like a cockle-boat beside a ship.

Why have I written so much about Jones? Because, sadly, he was the means of stirring up and drawing forth my wickedness.

Parents are often advised not to let their children mix with mischief-making, irreverent companions. To my mind it is just as important not let them associate with anyone who is too simple and unsuspecting. With such folk the temptation to wickedness is greater. If Adam and Eve had not been quite so innocent, perhaps the Devil would not have paid them so much attention. When you see the guilelessness of a child in a grown-up man, the temptation to offer him an apple becomes exceedingly strong.

I had not been long in Abel Hughes's shop before I realized that I could poke Jones in the eye and convince him every word I said was gospel truth whenever I chose. I began 'accidentally' treading on his corns, for the fun of hearing him squeak. I would persuade him to use vile-smelling stuff to help his whiskers grow. My tricks were endless, but I would never have thought of such behaviour if not for his simplicity. As this went on, time wore away my regret, and the Devil put a wet blanket over my good resolutions.

Jones couldn't read, and except at Sunday School I never saw a book in his hand. His head was as empty of knowledge as a potato. He was credulous to a remarkable degree; he would believe almost anything. When Abel Hughes's back was turned, I would tell Jones the most fearful and wonderful things. I made up the stories from a mix of what I had read and what I invented. He swallowed every word. It didn't strike me at the time that I was to blame for what I did. If Jones had been less gullible I shouldn't have dreamt of stuffing him with so much fiction as if it were fact. The credulous attention he paid to every word I said gave me a grand opportunity to exercise my gift.

I am too ashamed to relate all the tricks I played upon him, and it would serve no useful purpose if I did. But I will admit that Jones was the means of arousing something within me. I didn't know then what to call it, but now I would call it sin. This behaviour was nothing anyone had ever taught me, and my mother would never have permitted it. It was something that had always been within me, but it had not been awakened before. I used to think of it as a kind of talent and waited to hear someone say, 'Bravo, Rhys.'

It was not my conscience that encouraged me, nor my mother's spirit, because, as I lay in bed and shut my eyes, I fancied seeing her frown at me. But even had I realized that it was the devil who was encouraging me, I might still have been seduced by him. I went from bad to worse. But what purpose would it serve to chronicle my evil deeds?

I feel quite unequal to the task of describing this period of my life. I meekly trust my misdeeds have been erased from the book of record. In one sense I was not the master of myself. When I first went to Abel Hughes I was a troubled, serious boy who was naturally sad and had no inclination for frivolous play. Abel knew this and held a good opinion of me. He must have thought that it was not necessary to keep a close eye on me.

Miss Hughes, his sister kept house for him. She was a kindly, religious old maid, who thought nothing bad of anybody. She opened her heart to my orphaned condition. When alone with her I would tell her of the hardships I had undergone, and her eyes would fill with tears. Often she would go to the cupboard, and give me an extra slice of pudding or some other delicacy. I quickly saw the importance of making a fast friend of her. Abel Hughes spoke no more than was necessary either for business or instruction, but his sister was fond of a chat, and I, made sure to appear to take special pleasure in her small talk. Yet something inside me kept softly saying 'fiddlesticks'.

She loved to hear everything I knew of everybody and everything. My store of knowledge may have been scanty, but as it ran out I simply drew on my imagination, which was always lively. With my tales I won Miss Hughes's favour, and found it paid well.

If Abel accused me of any wrongdoing Miss Hughes came forward to argue it was due to my ignorance that I did so. If I showed something in my character that was not quite in keeping with Abel's views, Miss Hughes would make it bright as burnished gold. I also used Jones to show up my virtues, because Miss Hughes had no patience with Jones, except as a way to prove my superiority to him.

How did I feel? What did I think of myself?

I felt myself a different lad from what I had been when Mam was alive. Miss Hughes didn't know everything about me and I couldn't help being aware of the difference between Miss Hughes and Mam. Mam could see more through an oaken board than Miss Hughes could through her spectacles.

Was I a bad boy? Perhaps, but who would dare to say so?

Abel and his sister didn't know half of my history. Why should they? Mam knew all my affairs, even my thoughts. Abel Hughes and his sister didn't need to know, that in my mind someone said 'Bravo Rhys'. I believed I was my own master and could twist Miss Hughes round my little finger.

I am ashamed to remember, how free I made with her. I flattered her shamelessly.

'How old do you think I am?' she once asked me.

I had seen the date of her birth in the family Bible, kept in the cupboard and knew she was in her sixtieth year.

'Well,' I said. 'Though you look young. Miss Hughes, I shouldn't wonder if you were somewhere about forty.'

She laughed.

Mam had once told me that Miss Hughes had never had an offer of marriage and, knowing that, I flattered her.

'I know the reason you never married, Miss Hughes,' I said,

'Well, tell me why,' she said.

'You didn't want to leave the master,' I said.

'That's a very fair guess,' she said and gave me tuppence. 'Now you be sure you don't tell Abel about this,' she said as she handed it over.

I also noticed that either I, or Wil Bryan had changed.

'D'ye know what,' said Wil to me one day. 'You're like any other boy now. I'll never call you Old Hundredth again. I nearly gave you up at one time. When you went to old Abe I thought your hair would begin to whiten before you were seventeen, and you would be crying 'Amen' and 'Hallelujah' in chapel every Sunday, as your mother used to do.'

He looked serious for a moment. 'I don't want to speak lightly of your mother,' he said, 'far from it. Amen and things like that suited her well, but that's no reason why Abel should make an old man of you before you even wear a hat. That isn't true to nature, you know. Just you watch the big cat and the little one. The big cat is quiet and sad-looking. The little cat frisks and tumbles and tries to catch her tail, just as if she wasn't in her senses.'

'I'm not a kitten,' I said.

'Well look at the mare and her colt then. When she's not working you'll see the old mare, stand in the middle of the field without budging a step or moving, except a little of the head when the flies are about her ears. She looks as miserable as if she were thinking of her end in the tan-yard, and you might swear she was almost sleeping on her legs. But watch the colt; see how he prances around, nose in air, tail erect, and kicks at nothing. If somebody comes along the road, he'll run after him on the other side the hedge, neighing madly as if he wanted to see all that was going on. The world is new to the colt and the kitten. It's the same, exactly, with old and young people. But to keep you shut up in a clock-case, there was no sense or reason in that; it isn't true to nature. She might as well have made you wear an old man's night cap, or dressed you in breeches, leggings and a beaver hat, and sent you every Saturday to William the barber to be shaved, as waste the whole week starching and smoothing you up for Sunday.'

'It's not true to nature, Rhys,' he said in English. 'Or that's what I think.'

I am sad to admit that I agreed with Wil. From then on we became faster friends than ever. His people became my people, his affairs mine. Wil was no stranger to the Corner Shop. Abel Hughes went to Session or Monthly Meetings, and that took him from home for a day or two. When he was away Jones had to sleep on the premises, as a protection from thieves. On such occasions I found it easy to get Miss Hughes to allow Wil to spend the night with me. Wil could also creep up Miss Hughes's sleeve with the greatest ease. He would delight her by telling her stories or singing her songs, in both English and Welsh.

Wil was always pleased to get an invitation to the Corner Shop.

'I really enjoy the chance to have a little fun with The Genius while old Abe is away.' He always called Jones the Genius.

I only had a small, narrow bed, and I remember Miss Hughes commenting on it to my companions.

'Do you really want to sleep here tonight, William?' she said. 'I don't know how the three of you manage to get into that bit of a bed.'

'We're splendid, Miss Hughes,' Wil said. 'Rhys one side, me on the other and Jones in the middle. It's like a tongue sandwich.'

'If you want it to be like a tongue sandwich you should be in the middle, William,' Miss Hughes said.

'That's one up for you, Miss Hughes,' Wil said. 'But, if we follow your plan, there'll be more tongue than bread.'

Miss Hughes couldn't stop herself chuckling at Wil. She wondered why her brother was not fonder of him. She obviously thought him a clever, witty fellow. She never let Abel know that Wil visited the shop when he was away from home.

Once, when Abel was at a Methodist Session in Bala, Wil and I went too far and nearly put ourselves into the hands of the law. I wish I did not have to tell this story, but it had an important impact on me. I will keep my account of the foolish incident as short as possible.

Wil and I wished Miss Hughes good night and retired to our room. In a spirit of mischief, Wil suggested we place Jones on his trial for the murder of a creature which I need not bother to name. Wil acted as counsel for the prosecution and judge. I was the jury and I found the prisoner guilty. Wil duly sentenced him to be hanged. Jones enjoyed the joke immensely.

In the top of the door was a large nail for hanging clothes on. Wil tied a cord with a noose at the end of it. We stood Jones upon a foot-stool, placed the noose about his neck, with a laugh. Then as we stood back the stool overturned. It was a pure accident.

Jones made some realistic choking noises. At first we thought he was only pretending to hang, just to keep up the fun. Then I noticed that the stool lay on its side and Jones's feet were suspended a couple of inches off the floor. I have never been so frightened in my life. I quickly cut the cord and Jones came tumbling down, in a faint. Wil, who was just as frightened trembled like a leaf. We lifted Jones onto the bed. For a moment or two he lay still. Then he spluttered and noisily sucked in air. I can hardly describe our joy when he started to breathe again. My conscience blazed with the thought that I had been within an inch of taking the life of one of the most harmless people in the world.

At last Jones came to himself. He saw how distressed I was and looked at me compassionately.

'I forgive you for everything,' he said. 'It was a joke that went wrong. No serious harm done. We can forget it.'

As soon as Wil had Jones's agreement not to mention the matter again he jumped into bed and within five minutes was fast asleep. My conscience and fear were not so easily allayed. I couldn't sleep. Jones fell into an uneasy sort of slumber for a few hours and then woke with a cry of terror. A hundred different thoughts crossed my mind, and I decided I needed to change my ways.

The room was dark, and the night was long. Shortly before dawn I suddenly noticed I couldn't hear my bedfellows' breathing. Both lay as if dead. The silence was oppressive. The room became bright, but not with the light of dawn. The growth of the glow was swifter and, to my mind, looked like the approach of the shining face of an angel. The light grew brighter, but it was not coming through the window. It seemed so sweet to my eyes that I began to enjoy the sight. I might have been dreaming, but I believe I was wide awake. The light reached a beautiful climax that I cannot properly put into words.

I never saw anything I can properly compare it to. Before me in the midst of that brilliant but subdued glory I saw a chair: not a chair that furnished my room but the old oak armchair from my family home. In it sat my mother. I cannot remember what dress she wore, for I looked only at her face. It showed all its old peculiarities but was a thousand times lovelier than I had ever known it.

I wasn't afraid, but I could feel my guilty consciousness. Mother looked neither angry nor happy.

'Come to me,' she said.

I jumped out of bed and fell upon my knees before her. I held my cheeks between my hands and rested my head upon her knees, like I did as a child as I said my prayers before going to bed.

'My son,' she said. 'I warned you to beware three enemies, and told you of the armour you should gird about you. But, after all the trouble I took, I fear you have no religion, and know nothing of the great things.'

Before I could answer her, the vision faded. I felt my forehead grow cold where it rested on one of Abel Hughes's chairs. I jumped to my feet and saw the grey light of dawn at the window. Had I been dreaming? I don't know, but I thank God for sending me that vision, and I never forgot those words of my mother's.

CHAPTER 27

My Days of Darkness

Any of my friends who have bothered to read to the end of the previous chapter will no doubt think I am far too superstitious and will probably be laughing at me now. But if I am to tell the whole truth, I must accept that I might seem delusional. This I cannot help, for I have yet touched only lightly on the time I left the straight path and lost touch with the religious knowledge and instruction I received from that most pious woman who was my mother.

Have I skipped over the details of my conduct because it was not as bad as I thought at the time? No, for, even with hindsight, I feel my thoughts and actions were too vile and hideous to share. I want to forget them. But that is as difficult as forgiving them. God alone can do both, but even He must find it harder to forget than to forgive. If He had said He would forget, I would have thought that impossible.

I try to believe the word of the God of Truth, but in a spirit of thankful humility I find it beyond my comprehension to accept that He in His omniscience will extend His pardon to me. If this thought is madness then I must trust to the Great Forgetter to forget this also.

During this wanton period I was a church member. Once a month I went up to the Lord's table. None of the pious old brethren expressed any worry on my account. No one spoke to me about the state of my soul or my religious faith.

This memory of my own situation makes me shudder at the thought of the spiritual condition of hundreds of the young in our towns. Like myself they might be religiously brought up from childhood. They attend service pretty regularly to please their good old mother at home, or to avoid the chastisement of a strict employer. Having reached the necessary age they partake of the sacrament but what else do we know of them? They may go for weeks without opening the Bible. They may live a life completely without prayer. They may patronize forbidden, wanton places and enjoy vicious and rotten thoughts. They may read such books as are printed in hell by the light of the never-dying flame. They may be systematically damning their souls, but how would we know, for they attend chapel?

We are thankful that they still come within sound of the eternal tidings of salvation to satisfy their mother. But will God be merciful to them for this lip service? Why are the means of grace such a burden to them? Why do they not show more interest in Biblical subjects? Why do they consider them dry and boring?

If only we could know they lose at least one hour's sleep thinking of the things that will determine their everlasting welfare. If the heart of the shapely, attractive, tender girl who is the best of all workers for a bazaar would but flutter and palpitate as fast over God's great matter as it does over the trash in that penny dreadful we saw her buy the other day. Why is there such distance between the officers of the church and the young men and maidens under their charge? We do not know the answers to these questions, and in many cases all we know is that they come to chapel.

I well know how difficult it is to bridge that distance without scaring their souls and driving them farther away. How can we help them without meddling or setting up a kind of confessional? I know I have been guilty of the things I speak of while keeping up my church membership. I have every reason to suspect others are as guilty as I was.

But who were my companions in depravity? They were church members too, like me – though I am pleased to say their numbers were small. If I were to publish this history, I would ask a few simple questions about the consciences of our church youth. Let me give you an example.

> You boy, John Jones? If we leave God out of the question, would you want your mother to know how many chapters of the Bible you read from one Sunday to the next?
>
> How often do you pray, and what sort of prayers do you use?
>
> Would you like your mother to know the places you go to after shutting shop or leaving the office?
>
> When you're with your friends, how do you think you mother would know you? Would it be by your voice or your words? From what she heard you saying, would she recognize her son?
>
> Would you care to tell your father what you spend your money on, and would you like him to know were each penny comes from?
>
> Would you show him the book you locked up in your box the other night?
>
> If he knew as much about your goings-on as you do, what do you think he would call you? Would it be hypocrite?
>
> Does your opinion of yourself match how the old people of the chapel see you, or what your parents think of you?
>
> When you have acted in ways you know neither your parents nor the church will approve, have you said to yourself 'It'll be alright when I go home, for I'll get a deacon's ticket with the inscription:

> To the Calvinistic Methodists.
>
> Dear Brethren,
>
> This is to inform you that the bearer, John Jones, is a member of our church of Take-everything-for-Granted.
>
> Grace be with you. Amen.'

To the pure all things are pure; and it may be that I, who have been guilty of much impurity am prone to believe that impurity is more common than it really is.

But I know one boy who regularly attended service because he dared not do otherwise, for fear of upsetting his employer. He was never absent from the Lord's Table, but if his master and the deacons had known his real character, they would have expelled him from the church at once. I was that boy.

My mind was depraved, my heart was hard and cold, and my conversation, when the brethren were out of earshot was unbecoming, to say the least. I knew the words of the Bible, but I used them in jest, to create laughter and seem witty.

I now believe the main cause was because my heart was hardened. A saying my mother used warned how the light use of Bible words blunted the edge of their proper purpose.

'Same as that hatchet there, over there,' she said. 'We've used it to break coal, for hammering, and everything else. Now when we want to chop a bit of a stick there's no getting it to catch.'

She was proved right, in my case. I was, at that time, quick of apprehension and had the skill to put my thoughts forcibly into words. This gave me a liking for controversy, and I was so ready for such work that Wil Bryan called me Stir-the-Fire-Poker.

I always took the doubtful side of a question. I did not want get to the truth, but to beat my opponent in debate, and relished starting from a point of disadvantage. I got to think there was no fundamental difference between the true and the false, that evil and good were of no consequence. When debating with chums of no great ability I could lend a more favourable colour to the false than they could to the truth. I began to over-value my argumentative skills and think myself somebody.

I regularly went to chapel but seldom found a preacher who could please me. I told myself this was because there were so few who could tell me anything new. I picked holes in their reasoning and mocked the errors in their speech.

I no longer bothered to write out the sermons. It seemed to be not worth the trouble. I liked the chance to show my talents at Sunday School. I have many times thought that it would have been a kindness if Evan the butcher, who towered over me, had taken me to the back of the chapel and given me a good thrashing with his stout ash stick. Even better if he had then ducked me in the rain-tub. It would have done me, and those who encouraged me, all the good in the world.

I am only sketching out my period of folly with little detail because I am ashamed to admit, even to myself, just how bad I became. From my upbringing I was conversant with the facts of the Gospel, but I was as ignorant of its spiritual blessings as any pagan.

That was my situation when I almost sent poor Jones to his death, and saw the apparition of my mother. That vision was a turning point of my life. I have blessed that phantom a hundred times over.

A swarm of thoughts passed through my mind that night. My mother's words, 'My son, I fear you have no religion, and that you know nothing of the great things,' pierced my heart like a red-hot iron. Her words were true to the letter, and as I took them in I became wretched. I had grown used to presenting myself as what I was not. I tried to do this after that dreadful visitation. I tried to look cheerful and happy; but I failed.

I lost my appetite. Miss Hughes implored me to see a doctor.

'Rhys,' she said, 'I don't know what to think of you. You don't eat more than a bird, and you won't take a little of the wormwood tea. What's the matter with you, tell me?'

But I said nothing. She didn't understand my problem. I tried to shake off my depression by joining with my old companions in their pastimes. But this only added fuel to the fire in my conscience. I made the excuse that I didn't feel well and I went back to the shop.

From then on I remained indoors after the shop shut.

To avoid Miss Hughes's conversation I pretended to be absorbed in reading, but I couldn't concentrate. My mind wandered about aimlessly before returning to my unhappiness.

Hitherto God, sin and the world to come had been mere words. Now they were living realities, and their terror touched every nerve of my soul. The *Seiat*, which had been simply a kind of club to which I belonged, now become in my mind a spiritual congregation of the elect. I was acutely aware that I knew practically nothing about its nature, constitution, sustenance and support. My name was entered in book of membership but I felt a wide gulf between the church's life and character, and my own. I would sit for hours worrying about my condition.

I tried to dissect my problem and put myself through an internal cross-examination.

> What is wrong with you?
> Are your wits falling into bad repair?
> What harm have you done that has not been done by others, and much worse?

Then I would remember my mother had said these were the Devil's questions. I could get no comfort from them, once I realized they were the Devil's work.

I tried to dwell upon something positive in my past, but my conscience rushed ahead and raised an army to defeat me. My memory lost heart and let my conscience have it all her own way.

Every instinct of my soul conspired against me. I read a great deal of the Bible in secret. But the good book did not speak to me, I felt its promises were not for me. There was no light for me, even though that was my aim in reading. I felt an unpleasant consciousness of God's presence closing around me, especially when I was alone. When I tried to pray the Presence seemed to take to flight.

One night in my bedroom a Catholic sentiment took me over. I'd lain sadly musing until the candle had nearly burnt out. A dreary, oppressive feeling of loneliness stole over me. I decided God had no compassion for me. He was angry with me. My friends didn't know what was wrong with me and couldn't help. Neither good nor bad Angels took any interest in me. I was alone in the great, wide world. My soul grew cold within me, and I could find no ray of warmth to cheer it.

Then I thought of my mother. She had loved me so well and couldn't have forgotten me. I fell on my knees and prayed to her. I clutched at this straw to save me from drowning. But it brought me no blessing.

I saw my folly. I knew the way of salvation; it had been made plain to me in my youth. Now I felt that path was intended for others, and I could not tread it.

My close acquaintance with the Gospel had stopped me from grasping its inner spiritual meaning. I was fated to remain in the outer court, a martyr hung between the world and the church. I pictured Christ, to understand His sympathy with fallen humanity, His love and pity for the sinner, but my heart grew cold, and I could hear only my mother's voice saying, 'My sheep hear my voice, but my effort proved vain'.

I was trapped like this for weeks, suffering feelings of unmitigated depravity combined with painful separation from things spiritual. I didn't stop trying to pray, but my appeals were brief and pointless. I had played the hypocrite and dissembled so often that I was unable to communicate through prayer.

My supplications were flawed. Here some examples:

> Great Jesus, Son of God, I have dissembled overmuch in Thy sight for too many years, and I do not wonder Thou hast deserted me. Thou knowest how bad I have been. Save Thou and I, none knows all my doings. If Thou wilt not forgive me, do not, I beg Thee, tell my history to mother or Bob, or anybody. Although I want to, Thou art aware I do not know Thee, and I fear Thou art offended with me forever. Let me live a little while yet. Amen.

Jesus Christ, lest thou be worse offended with me, I go upon my knees again tonight; but I have nothing to add that I have not said many times already, except that I have lost my health. But Thou knowest all, so I need not tell Thee. Amen.

I dared not go to bed without first falling on my knees, but at times a haughty, defiant spirit in my prayers made me say things like:

Oh, Saviour of sinners.

What more can I do? I have called upon Thee hundreds of times, but Thou dost not listen. I have read tonight Thy Sermon on the Mount, and it condemns me utterly. But why didst Thou say, 'Ask and it shall be given unto you; seek and ye shall find'? I have asked and sought! Were it not for fear of sinning further against Thee, I might almost think Thou wert not as good as Thy word. Thou knowest I am a bad boy. But Thou art called a friend of publicans and sinners? Were they not the same who called Thee 'a gluttonous man, and a wine-bibber'? I, too, am a great sinner; still Thou art no friend of mine. Dost Thou find any difference between sinners? Hast Thou favourites? What use is reading the Bible? It has nothing in it for me; and I find no pleasure in sinning. If Thou art resolved not to hearken unto me, leave me alone to sin. Thou permittest that much even unto the devil. If I err, why dost Thou not open my understanding? If Thou put me in hell, I will eternally proclaim it to all that Thou didst reject me, a youth of seventeen, notwithstanding Thy saying that 'him that cometh to me I will in not cast out'. If I have sinned an unpardonable sin against the Holy Ghost, Thou knowest I did so in ignorance. My heart is like a stone, and I cannot change it. Much as I would like to love Thee, I cannot. But Thou knowest I hate the Devil and his angels with a perfect hatred; and still Thou placest me in their midst. I will never speak a word with one of them ... never, never, even were he to put a red hot iron to my lips. Have my wits gone astray? I hope so, because Thou pitiest the insane. Do with me as Thou seest best.

Amen.

As I couldn't find a ray of light from either reading or prayer, I stopped reading the Bible or did not pray in the morning.

But I couldn't give up praying before going to bed. That was too difficult. I have always found it easier to forget God in the morning than at night. I believe I am not alone in this; even in irreligious company no one went to bed without first going upon their knees, although they never thought of doing so when they rose in the morning. Our sense of dependence and responsibility is stronger in the night than in the day. How foolish we are. We feel more able to take care of ourselves in the morning than we do just before we sleep.

I turned from the Bible to works of humour. But they gave me no fun. The jokes were like those offered by a clown to a man on his

My Days of Darkness

death-bed. Only a true-hearted man with a considerable degree of piety, can enjoy real humour. He can fill his mouth with laughter without pouching his cheek with poison.

I kept all my trouble to myself instead of looking outwards. With a single exception I don't think anybody knew I was in such distress. That friend I had not spoken to for some time, until one day I received the following note from him, in English.

> Dear Rhys,
>
> I rather think you are in want of a sackcloth. I can lend you one. The ashes, of course, you can have anywhere you like. Glad to tell you that this chap is up to the knocker.
>
> Yours truly,
>
> Wil Bryan

I saw he had realized why I was staying in at night and avoiding his company. I dreaded meeting him, for fear he would make fun of me. Yet I envied him, because his parents were lukewarm and unconcerned about religion. The pains Mam had taken with me and the deep religious instruction I had had, made me feel my responsibility was much greater than his. His note only compounded my unhappiness.

My master, Abel Hughes, took me to task for not being more attentive to the customers almost every day,

'Rhys,' he said, 'you're getting worse, not better.'

I began to hate the shop. I no longer despised Jones but began to envy him for having almost no soul. I sank into a state of melancholy indolence and dullness. The Devil whispered to me.

'Religion is folly,' he said. 'The Bible is a string of old wives' fables, and your wretchedness is nothing but a bout of indigestion.'

But as he spoke I thought of my mother's life, her probity, her faith and how she rejoiced in the Holy Spirit. I thought of her resignation and fortitude under the most severe suffering, her boundless confidence and glorious triumph in the Valley of the Shadow of Death. With her example, I felt the devil and all the infidels in the world could not move me. I felt a great qualm of regret for her come over me.

I was trying my master's patience a great deal. The only thing he could say for me was that I stayed in at nights. If I was sent on an errand, I would forget why I was going and have to come back to find out. I was confused and awkward behind the counter and kept making mistakes with prices.

I made Abel tired and testy, but Miss Hughes still spoke up on my behalf. Then one day Abel called me aside.

'Rhys,' he said, 'I am greatly disappointed with you. I used to think that you would turn out a good, active and capable lad but all I can see is that you are getting worse and worse every day.'

I just hung my head and wouldn't look him in the eye.

'As a matter of fact,' he said, 'you're just not worth your salt.'

I knew he was speaking the truth, and so didn't say anything. His words had a great effect on me. I decided that I would not eat any more of his bread since I did not deserve it. I summoned up what was left of my self-respect and decided I would leave the shop and run away. At that moment, I didn't care what happened to me. When supper time arrived, I refused to sit at the table.

Abel would not ask me twice. Miss Hughes, realized that her brother and I had had quarrelled. She couldn't enjoy her meal, for she loved me and did not want to see me suffer.

The prayers that Abel led that evening were dry and hard. Miss Hughes paid no attention to them, being worried about me. I felt that Abel was right when he said I was not worth my salt. I decided to clear my character and reveal my situation before I left.

Abel sat down in his arm chair, after prayers, and began to smoke. He kept silent. He was obstinate, firm and resolved. I waited for a chance to talk. He stayed silent for some time and then in a harsh crabbed voice he said. 'Are you not intending to go bed this night?'

'I'm not going until I have told you why I have been so awkward in the shop,' I said. 'I want to explain my unhappiness of spirit.'

As I told him of my troubles I began to weep freely. Through all my difficulties and despair no tear had come to my eye since the day my mother was buried. However, I had hardly opened my mouth to tell Abel my story when the dam burst. All my words were drowned in a deluge from my heart.

Oh what comfort there is in telling one's troubles! I have rarely met a kind-hearted woman who, seeing a strong youth in tears, did not join in with him. Miss Hughes was kind-hearted. Our shared tears were a great blessing to me. They showed that my heart was not as hard as I had thought but they also helped me regain sufficient composure to tell the whole story.

I concealed nothing, not even the one thing I conceal here. It was to do with him personally and I conceal it in obedience to his express wish.

'Do not mention that to anybody else,' he said. 'Because, if it gets to men's ears, although God will forgive you, it will be held against you as long as you live.'

I knew I was dealing with a master who was every inch a man. This knowledge helped to confidently share all my feelings without reserve.

I believed that, after hearing my story, he would show sympathy to me, forgive my failings, and direct me into the right path. I knew there were thick walls around his heart, but, once I gained an entrance, I did not expect him to cast me out.

He listened to me attentively but he did not condone my confession. Indeed, he seemed to be taking delight in my misery. When I had finished, ail he said was:

'Very good. If that's the case, go on. You'll run away better directly.'

'Abel,' said Miss Hughes. 'You're hard-hearted. Is that all you have to say to him?'

'Marged, I don't need you to tell me anything about my heart,' he said. 'I know more about it than you are ever likely to find out, in the name of goodness.'

What a blunt old Calvinist I thought, feeling even sorrier for myself.

'But I'll tell you this much, at any rate,' said Miss Hughes. 'You should help the boy, and give him some words of advice.'

'Do you know, Marged,' Abel said, 'that He who began in us the good work will also finish it? It doesn't do to raise one too speedily from the pit. It is He who has opened the wound, and He Himself will find a salve for it, in His own good time.'

'You should show the lad where the salve is to be found,' said Miss Hughes, 'or you may as well not be deacon, in my opinion.'

'I warrant you he knows already,' Abel said. 'He's not some half-heathen come to Communion for the first time, not like Thomas Bartley. We can't tell him anything he doesn't know already. When his complaint comes to a head he'll find the Doctor's address easy enough. The best thing for him tonight is to sup and go to bed.' With that the old man coolly refilled his pipe.

Although I had got only cold comfort from Abel, I felt he now saw me in a different light. And with Miss Hughes's promptings added to those of my own stomach, I took some supper. Then I went to bed, but not to sleep, rather to reflect on my situation.

My desire to leave had gone. All my thoughts ended in a sigh. How was I to deal with my present condition, and what would be my future?

How and whence the light came, I will tell in the next chapter.

CHAPTER 28

Master and Servant

I learned something from my impromptu confession. My complete admission of the truth had scoured out every dirty corner of my conscience. Even though I made it to a man rather than to God, it bestowed a peculiar strength on me. I resolved to try again to solve my problems.

I had unlocked the doors of my heart and by throwing them open had let pure fresh air enter to give my struggling soul relief. By inviting Abel to partake in my realisation I had shifted part of my burden on to his shoulders.

Is this why everyone is anxious to hear that a condemned murderer has admitted his guilt? Is it that we instinctively know it will strengthen him to face his dreadful fate? Or is there a deeper motive which we do not often acknowledge: a secret desire to share the burden of his conscience. If you hear the complete confession of a sin, be it black as hell, you take on part of the strength of the one who tells the truth. Truth strikes the devil in the forehead and stops you acting the hypocrite.

A father may apply the rod with some degree of relish across the back of a boy who is a sneak. But a mischievous lad who openly confesses his guilt often induces a rheumatism of the paternal shoulder-blade which postpones the beating, most times for ever.

Why should God want to hear us confess our sins?

If God knows everything he already knows the full extent of them. It must be because He wants to hear that we are finally telling the truth. Even if that truth is one of ugly rebellion against Himself.

In this world there are two types of sneaks. There are natural sneaks and spiritual ones. Both are equally repulsive in the sight of God. God told His Son to tell the truth, even though He be crucified for it. Truth, even if it is hard and hideous, is more acceptable to God than any feigned lie, even one masked with groans and tears. God says to the hypocrite and the sanctimonious, 'If thou lovest darkness, if thou wantest to live in thine own cave I will provide a dwelling place where never gleam of light shall enter, save that of the upended lamp of thy conscience.'

I had turned myself inside out before my master. My condition was no more hopeful, nor was my future any clearer. But I felt strengthened, because I was no longer a hypocrite and had told the naked truth about myself. Perhaps I might be sent to perdition, but I wouldn't pretend to go there under the banner of heaven.

The previous evening Abel Hughes and his sister had known nothing of my inner wickedness. I hadn't slept when I came down the stairs the following morning. Now those good people knew almost as much of my wicked history as I did myself. Now I could look them in the face with honesty. But where had this confidence come from?

For one thing, I was no longer skulking in darkness. I had admitted my sins. For another, I believed them both to be truly religious. They loved God, and so they also loved man, even though he might be in the gutter. If I had not been so sure they were religious, I couldn't have made the full confession I had.

Had I mistaken Abel Hughes's real character? Heaven knows his name is enshrined in my heart and memory. But had I been mistaken to trust him? If so, it was too late. I had admitted all my faults to him. I knew that his rectitude could be as severe as that of Moses in Sinai. But I also knew that his heart brimmed with the forgiving and appeasing principle of the blood of Calvary. I trusted him, although I also feared him.

Abel and his sister were courtesy and kindness during breakfast. I was abashed and felt I did not deserve such caring treatment. My feelings welled up in my throat, and the food nearly choked me. I couldn't help feeling that there was something God-like in the forgiveness and the courtesy of these two pious people. When Abel conducted the family prayers at the shop's morning service his delivery showed unusual ardour. To speak truly I enjoyed Abel's morning prayers far more than I usually did.

However I was still unhappy and felt disgraced. I'd decided to ask the master to have me expelled from the church. I already believed that he would do so no matter what I said, but I wanted to punish myself.

Abel came into the shop a few minutes after me. He looked over an invoice and then passed it to Jones to check.

'Should someone inquire for me Jones,' he said. 'Say that I'll be here directly. But don't come to fetch me, because I have other business on hand.' He turned to me. 'Rhys, you'd better come and help me.'

He walked into the parlour and I followed him. As soon as we were inside he locked the door.

'Sit down, Rhys,' he said waving me to a chair.

I sat down, and he sat directly opposite me. My heart beat against my chest like the wings of a newly caught bird stuffed into a cage. Had I mistaken my master's real character after all? Had I been foolish? My mind raced as I waited for Abel to speak. He looked me straight in the eye for a moment or two in silence. I made an honest effort to return his gaze.

As I looked into his eyes I caught a glimpse of mercy and forgiveness hiding behind the seriousness of his expression. I have often thought that most good men, and some bad ones, have two faces. Along with the rough, frowning exterior you can sometimes glimpse a tender, merciful one, just as behind the hypocrite's smile you can sometimes catch sight of the Devil on his shoulders. As he began to speak I fancied I saw a merciful man beneath the clouded brow of Abel Hughes.

'Your mother, who is this day in heaven, and I were great friends,' Abel said. 'I promised her, before she died that I would take care of you and do my best for you. She had a high opinion of you.'

He slowly looked me up and down. 'Too high, I fear. But then she was judging you would turn out as she intended, with all the care she took of you, all the religious instruction she gave you, and all the prayers she offered on your behalf.'

He looked down with a sad expression in his eyes. 'When you were telling me your story last night, I was thankful that your mother was in her grave. She could hold on to her faith through the bitterest of trials but if she had lived to see your debasement it would have been too much for even her to bear. You would have broken her heart.' He shook his head slowly.

'She used to tell me what help she got in forgetting all her trouble with your father, all her poverty and hardship, from seeing you grow up,' he said. He clasped his hands together almost in a posture of prayer. 'She liked the way you would learn chapters from the Bible unasked and could repeat parts of sermons while you were but a child. She might not have told you, but to others she would talk about you by the hour. She would often ask me if I thought you would make a preacher. If she were alive today I'm sure she would have rather heard you had died of starvation by the roadside than that you had fallen away as you have done. Thankfully she was spared this, and went to her grave believing her youngest son would not disgrace her teaching.'

He sighed before continuing. 'Well, I must say,' he said. 'I've been sadly deceived by you. But I believe you've made an honest confession. And I believe what you have told me is true. But have you told me the whole truth?'

'Yes, I think I have told you everything,' I said, wondering where the conversation was going. He was stern, but not as angry as I expected.

'Very well,' he said. 'Have you told anyone but my sister and me?'

'Not a word to any living soul,' I said.

'Good,' he said, his expression lightening a little. 'You've made a clean breast of it, but I don't see any good coming of your telling anybody else. These things have a way of being thrown in your face for the rest of your life. It often happens a man's neighbours reproach him his old faults for years after God has forgiven him.'

I nodded to show I understood, and my heart lightened a little to hear him speak of God forgiving me.

'If I had not known from experience something of the depravity of fallen humanity,' he said, 'I might have reacted differently to your confession. But I know how hard the struggle against temptation is. Of how it feels to be overcome again and again. I also know something of coming out of the fight victorious.'

For a moment his expression looked distant as through he was thinking of times long gone. Then he came back to himself and his expression hardened.

'Some will say it's my duty to turn you out of doors, make known your faults to the world and expel you from the church,' Abel said. 'And they will call me merciful for not doing more.' He paused.

Once more my heart fluttered madly within my chest. Had I mistaken that look of mercy? For what seemed an age Abel simply looked at me. I held his gaze and waited my fate, I could not guess what he was thinking.

'I shall neither the expel you or denounce you.' He said. 'Why should I? I also am a great sinner. Last night after you had gone to bed I sat and prayed. If we were each to make full and complete confession of our faults, what strangers we should become to each other. The real differences between the best and the worst of us is so small.'

I took a deep breath and for a moment I felt the beginnings of hope stir in my heart.

'Tell me now, and honestly,' Abel said, 'have you declared war against the devil and the depravity of your own heart? Are you resolved, with the help of God, either to conquer or die in the fight?'

'I have,' I said. 'I hate myself. I hate my actions. I hate my evil habits. But I find no pleasure in any others. I have no love for myself or for anything outside myself. So I can only say I hate everything.'

'So it would be vain for me to offer you the counsels which are given every day to all men. You have heard them hundreds of times from the pulpit and in *Seiat*. They have become meaningless from mindless repetition by those who give and those who hear them. But did you ever before feel as you have felt for the last few weeks?'

'No,' I said. 'Of that I am quite sure.'

'Good,' Abel said, nodding his head solemnly. 'Do you remember when you were contented in spirit, when you enjoyed the service in chapel, and were able to go to bed at night unmoved by fears and the reproaches of your conscience?'

'I do, so well,' I said. 'It was quite normal for me for many years.'

'Can you tell me what made you happy at that time?' Abel said. 'Was it your own innocence, or was it because you had never thought about the matter? Was it because you knew God? Was it because you understood His infinite love to give His Son to die for us? Was that what made you happy?'

'I don't know,' I said.

'Try and think,' Abel said. 'I will wait a minute or two, while you think about it.'

I sat for a few minutes in silent thought pondering his question.

'I think my contentment lay in my complete lack of knowledge of myself, and of the real nature of God and his ordinances,' I said. 'Now I think of it, I believe my ignorance of myself and of God caused my happiness.'

'Just so,' said Abel, nodding his head sagely. 'But a further question if I may?' He looked at me and waited. I nodded my head.

'You recollect a time, do you not, before you committed the sins which you confessed last night? 'I nodded again.

'Good,' he said. 'When you committed the first sin, how did you feel? Was it as if you were starting a new road, or that your old path had just deteriorated? Did you feel you had changed direction in your life?'

'No, I don't think so,' I said. 'I was always in the same road, but it became worse the further I walked.'

'I guessed so,' Abel said. 'There is greater hope of your salvation today than ever there was before.'

'I don't understand,' I said. 'Please explain.'

'Even during your best period you never knew you were a sinner, nor did you have any idea about the God you seemingly worshipped.' Abel said. 'Your ignorance was a castle of false bliss. You were on the path to destruction from your birth. Now God in His mercy has raised a storm about you and blocked your way onwards. You must return to the crossroads and take a new turning. And this is what happens in the life of every man who is saved.'

'How can I do that?' I said. 'God will not listen to my prayers.'

'Have you asked Him?' Abel enquired. 'Have you told Him the whole story of your sinful way, and asked Him to guide you towards the new?'

'I have asked hundreds of times for His guidance,' I said 'But I have never told Him the extent of my sins. What purpose would it serve? God already knows them better than I do myself.'

'That is where you are quite wrong,' Abel said. 'If you were right there would be no need for prayer at all, because God knows your heart's deepest and most secret thoughts and desires.'

'So what is the point of prayer?' I said.

'God will not listen to your prayer, or mine either, if we keep back anything we know to be at fault in us. You don't have to tell Him publicly, you can do it in the privacy of your own room. Remember your bible Rhys. You can be sure that the publican had gone over all the particulars of his sins before entering the temple. I do not believe Christ would have answered the prayer of the thief so briefly unless He was pinched for time. There never was any good of doing things by halves. Open out your heart before God and make a full, detailed confession of your faults. You will not bore Him. To Him a thousand years are as a single day. Sins are an abomination unto Him, but He is never displeased to hear a truly repentant sinner confess them. All you need do is tell Him of your sincere desire for forgiveness and to escape their influence.'

Abel paused and sat silently for a minute or so. He seemed anxious to see if his words had any effect upon me. I felt deeply moved by what he had said, but struggled to find words to answer him.

'I thank you from my heart, master,' I said. 'But I despair that my sins are great and manifold.'

'They are greater and more numerous than you have yet imagined,' Abel said, 'But so are mine. We are both in the same unlucky boat.'

'You are a deacon and a good man,' I said. 'How can you liken yourself to me?'

'I have never told this experience in *Seiat*,' Abel said. 'But if you live to my age, you too will have experiences that you will not speak of either to the church, or even your greatest friend. You will know feelings that you cannot put into words, even to yourself.

'When I was just a little older than you are now, I thought the idea of incarnation of the Son of God to be unreasonable, improbable, in fact quite beyond belief. I didn't have your religious upbringing but went to day school. I was fond of reading and study. I sometimes wallowed in the vilest sins of the flesh but I would occasionally go and hear the Gospel. It took a vague interest in the preacher. Like Zacchaeus of old, I climbed to the top of a tree to get a good view of the preacher and congregation. But I did not find Salvation.

'Then there came the great religious revival which so impressed your mother. She was always talking about it as the time when she, I and hundreds of others became aware of our sins. In that frightful knowledge of my sinfulness I saw God's purpose in the Incarnation. You will never find anyone who has been awakened to the enormity of his sins who doubts the need for Christ to come down to earth in the flesh. It is those who do not know they are sinners who are the exceptions.

'Remember the old religionists of the great revival which your mother spoke of. Did you ever see their like for the intensity of their love towards Jesus? Their love annihilated every obstacle in its way. Ask yourself, Rhys, why this was so? They were people who had a vision of sin. Such visions are not common these days. Likewise, you have seen your condition in its true light. Do you not begin to see a reason for the incarnation? Do you not see something in your despair and wretchedness that shows His errand to the world was not in vain? If you remember Solomon, he recognized his insignificance and doubted whether God would dwell with man on earth, even though he built a great temple for the Lord.

'For my part, the only thing I can see which could have moved the bowels of God's infinite compassion is man's terrible wretchedness. I am an old man, and an old sinner, but am prouder of the name of Jesus than if I were an Angel, because it makes me feel I am part of that great scheme which God made to come forth from Himself. It is in the Incarnation, my son, that your salvation lies if you but seek it.

'To me the existence of man, of sin and of misery are inexplicable, save in the glow of that accursed death upon the Cross. In the darkness that prevailed from the sixth until the ninth hour I see light and the possibility that man in his sinful condition may find hope.

'It is the old story that I have to tell. But for this story, the country would not have asylums enough to hold its madmen. There is no other story worth repeating, no other name under heaven wherein it will help you to confide. Have you not wondered why God is silent? If you have not, you assuredly will someday. When I was a young man the idea oppressed me greatly. I often walked alone out into the night, especially if the skies were clear. The sight of moon and stars made me despondent. How far, how old and how silent they seemed. They were fixed in the firmament, just as they had been when my father, grandfather and great-grandfather had stared up at them. I was in awe of how many generations of men had looked at them. I could look at the same sky and see it as it was at the time of the Druids, at the time of St Paul, and at the time of Moses, Abraham, Noah and Adam. And yet the stars were forever silent. How vast a store of experience they must have gathered. But they would not tell me anything to calm my restless mind. I asked in vain to know what lay beyond them. They just twinkled, voicelessly, down upon me. They created within me an uneasiness, great doubt and unspeakable thoughts. I looked up many times expecting some extraordinary manifestation, but in vain. Things went on as usual. And if you and I go out tonight after dark we will find everything just the same as when Isaac sat and meditated in the field beneath the same heavens. These thoughts made me gloomy.

'There was something in the depth of my soul which wanted a sign from God. I thought of the pillar of cloud by day and the pillar of fire by night which guided Moses. Why did God not give me a sign? If He would, there would be some sense in it. It would be something that a man could see and be certain about. Joshua in the Valley of Gibeon commanded the sun to stand still in God's name. It did so. There was something noble in that sign. It brought hope to the uneasy mind of man. But why have we been deprived of any such signs for centuries? Why have ages passed in painful silence? I felt that God had gone and left everything empty and mute.

'I had an overwhelming desire to see God come back to the world from that far distance where He had retired. I would willingly have accepted another Deluge even if it drowned me. At least I would have the comfort of a clear sign, whatever my fate might be. My understanding of God's purpose and intent for man and his future was seriously disturbed. I never had a moment's peace and quiet for my mind until I came to believe in the great fact of the Lord's appearance as flesh. I knew the story of Jesus, but I did not believe it until I came to feel the depth of my depravity and realized my wretchedness. Without a belief in Christ's Incarnation as flesh, there was nothing but the silence of the grave for me to look forward to. This question haunted my perturbed soul, but the life, teaching, death, atonement and resurrection of our Saviour defies a soul to put a question which cannot be answered.'

He stopped for a moment and looked at me.

'Now, my son,' he said. 'You know the story of Jesus as well as I. But do you really believe it. I don't expect a decisive answer from you until you have thought about it. I don't give much weight to the sort of instant belief which some people claim. A man does not gain belief except by hard study, deep meditation, and unceasing prayer. My great wish is to set you on the way to seriously seeking the help of the Spirit, to set you on the right path. If you apply yourself diligently, the day will come when you will be thankful for your present misery, and the eye of your mind will be opened to His love. Now, Is there anything you want to ask me?'

'Sir,' I said. 'I feel there are many things I would like to ask you, but I cannot put them into words. I feel a great want, but I cannot explain it, and I don't really know its nature. I had thought no one else felt as I did. But you, sir, have given the history of my own heart. I feel a void which needs filling, but that which could fill it is out of reach for me. How can I satisfy my want and find the peace that you have found?'

'Your heart is by nature empty,' said Abel. 'But once it is roused, it constantly aspires. To one who has read and studied a little there is a danger of following the dreams of his heart and mistaking these for religion. Guard yourself carefully against this religion of the sceptic. You will not find sceptics amongst the illiterate, ignorant classes. They are found among the studious and well-read.'

'How is this?' I said.

'Reading and study awaken the heart to its wants,' he said. 'It then questions itself, and once that questioning begins it can become an endless quest. The sceptic will continue the process of self-inquiry without ever getting an answer to his great questions. At first the questions themselves are his great things, but as his questioning goes on his inability to answer becomes a greater thing. Question by question he satisfies himself with his lack of knowledge. He appeals to his heart and understanding and has to sum up his belief in the three words: "I don't know." I am no philosopher, but I have a restless heart that is always asking questions. But if I couldn't find a better creed than "I don't know," I would be the most wretched man alive. Better to be any sort of creature – an elephant, an ass, or a monkey – than a man. If the best I could achieve by investigation and study was "I don't know," I should raise my hat to every donkey I met, and call him blessed.

'But, thanks be to God, I had a revelation. Two facts are plain. The first is that my heart, once awakened, keeps questioning ceaselessly. The second is that my heart's only answer to its own questions is, "I don't know."

'The Bible answers the most abstruse questions of my heart. It explains my existence, my wretchedness and my future. It can direct me to One who can relieve the disquiet of my soul. I believe that Book emanated from God. If it were not so, then show me its equal, or its superior! I challenge any man or nation to produce anything like it that is not indebted to the Bible itself for both thought and matter.'

He stopped and shook his head as if to clear his thoughts.

'But I digress,' he said. I was warning you of the danger of living on the dreams of your heart and mistaking it for religion. Don't linger within yourself in melancholy or sentimental study, or the high points of your life will be groans and tears. That is not religion. Religion is more practical. It is a constant going out of yourself. Truly the kingdom of God is within you, but is only worthwhile when it goes out from you. You'll do your soul more good in one day of looking to Christ and striving to do his commandments, than you will from a hundred years spent looking at yourself.

'When you lose yourself in doing the ordinary duties of life as a service to God you become religious. Serving a customer conscientiously from behind the counter to the best of your ability as is pleasing to God as anything you do whilst on your knees in your own room. Amidst all the world's stupidity, ignorance and darkness, of some things we can be certain. If you know that it is right to tell the truth, then tell the truth all the time. If you are sure that to live honestly is the proper thing, then live so honestly that your conscience never troubles you. Whatever admits shabbiness and meanness is detestable to God. The more you act like a gentleman, the higher you will stand in His esteem. Try to keep your heart as pure as God's own. You can do nothing worthwhile without His help. Every attempt to lead a Godly life will awaken and set in motion conflicting tendencies in nature, but the struggle will bring you to the only One who can help you. Believe that God sympathizes deeply with your degradation, otherwise He would not have sent His Son to die for you. But know also that He has no sympathy with you if you give in to your weaknesses. Only when you are fighting sin will His strength and sympathy flow into you.

'This is the beginning of your religious career, and I impress upon you that religion is not a matter of ambiguity. There are several in church with us, such as William the Coal, who often fall into evil. Afterwards they are deeply affected by the sermon, they weep in *Seiat*, and blame Satan for their sins. Your mischievous friend Wil Bryan taunts William for doing this. William believes that feeling the import of the sermon and crying in *Seiat* are real religion. I do hope God has some bye-law for his salvation.

'Rhys, my son, it is not after a fall that religion's bitterest tears are shed, but in the struggle. Perhaps I have spoken too much. I know you have sinned against me, and I forgive you from the bottom of my heart. I believe you are sorry for your sin. If I, a poor weak sinner, can forgive you, then surely He who is infinite in pity can also forgive you if you are truly repentant.'

'Thank you sir,' I said. 'It is more than I deserve.'

'Now, go back to your work, like a man,' Abel said. 'And remember, that from now on I will expect you to conduct the family worship alternately with myself.'

With that Abel unlocked the door and walked out, leaving me as if in a dream, although it was no longer a dark dream. I trembled at Abel's last words which gave me responsibility for the family prayers. From then on I looked upon him no longer as a master, but as a father.

CHAPTER 29

Help from a Cleaner of Clocks

My heart-to-heart with Abel Hughes in the parlour remains a source of light and blessing in my memory. I realized that, even though I had been religiously brought up from childhood, had taken an interest in chapel matters, had enjoyed learning the ordinances of the Gospel and been well thought of in the *Seiat*, I had never understood the great questions of eternal life.

From Abel's words I now knew that there is a peculiar moment in the life of every believer, whether they have been religiously brought up or not, when a spiritual light flashes in their mind. This always makes the individual see themselves and all around them in an entirely new way. I now understood that the more I contemplated myself, and more I thought about the secrets of my own heart, the sadder and more despairing I became. My introspection made me less use either to myself or to anybody else. The depths of my soul contained only darkness and terror, and my way out was to fix my contemplation on the spotless life and atoning death of my Lord and Saviour Jesus Christ.

Some time after our talk Abel pointed out the moral of my worst moments.

'If you were suffering from biliousness,' he said, 'you wouldn't treat it by staying in your bedroom, looking at your tongue in the glass and despairing at its nasty fur coating. That wouldn't help you get better, would it?' I nodded agreement.

'I know you'd have sense enough to take to some exercise and perhaps call your companions together to climb to the top of Moel Fammau,' he said, 'Then you'd get the uplifting view of the Vale of Clwyd while the fresh air of the old Moel would banish the bile from your belly. You'd be good and ready for your dinner when you got back. The same ideas apply to religion. I tell you, you'll never do any good by thinking too much on yourself. Get out among the highways and fields of the Gospel. Take your friends for a climb to the top of the hill where the gentle Lamb suffered. You'll find yourself healthier, purer and more cheerful.

'There's a world of meaning in the words of old Dr Johnson when he said, "Gentlemen, let's take a walk down Fleet Street." He had many good memories of Fleet Street, and when he tired of his own company he would take a walk along the road he loved so well. The old Doctor's words have been good advice for me. For you the Gospel can be like Fleet Street was for Dr Johnson. It will be fascinating and full of bittersweet memories. Many a time when I have been tired of the shop, when I've been fed up with selling grey calico at a groat a yard, bored with brown holland at tenpence a yard and other stuff like that ... then I've left everything and gone to talk with your mother or someone with similar religious good sense. That was my walk down Fleet Street. Take old Johnson's advice, and when you feel depressed and bored take a stroll along a path which promotes good memories.'

I tried to act on my master's advice, and succeeded so well that I stopped acting like a roosting hen with my head under my wing. I worked hard at forgetting myself. I thought more about Christ and his words. I enjoyed the bright side of the Gospel. Now Abel explained it to me, I finally learned the secret of my mother's happiness.

'Remember your mother,' Abel said. 'Do you know anyone who met with so much trouble? And did you ever see anyone enjoy so much happiness? Where did that happiness come from? Did she mope and look inside herself? No she did not. She'd learned to look at something better, her Saviour. The greater her trouble the greater her happiness. Her poverty made her think of the riches in Christ. The abuse she had from the hands of your inhuman father made her love the Saviour's gentleness.'

He went quiet for a moment as if not sure whether he should tell me some secret.

'Don't be angry with me,' he said. 'But when I heard that your mother was in trouble, I'd laugh and say, "Well, that's another feast for Mair Lewis." You should be a brave lad, for you come from a noble mother. I never saw one like her for trusting the promises of her religion. And she had no business to die when she did. She wasn't old or diseased. Let me tell you what she told me when she went to live at Thomas Bartley's.

'"Abel," she said, "there's no reason why one who has everything should live on the parish? I swear I'll never take a penny from the parish," and she never did.

'I've thought a great deal about her. When she thought she might be forced upon parish relief I fancied hearing her say, "Hold on, relieving officer. That's an insult to my family. I'll get up and go to my Father."

'I think that she became insistent upon death. She saw it as a way to prove the truth of the gospel promise that the righteous shall not be forsaken. Thomas Bartley took the same view. He said to me that he "craved like a cripple" for her not to die, but die she would. I don't praise your mother for what she decided, but there's something in religion which makes you independent of this world and its things.'

During the first years I was apprenticed to him Abel had hardly spoken to me. He restricted his conversation to the absolute minimum that was needed between master and servant. But he changed after the evening of my dramatic revelation. He became much kinder and more caring and talked to me in a more affable manner. After we had shut up the shop he would bring up some interesting subject or other to draw to my attention. He would then give his view on the topic in an open and lucid manner. He would mention books he had read and share his critical analysis of their strengths and weaknesses. He told me tales of the old preachers, describing what they looked like, what they wore and their style of preaching. Sometimes he would recite bits of their sermons in such a lively manner that I almost regretted that I had not been born earlier to hear them for myself. He was determined to break down the barriers between us. I already held him in the greatest respect and thought him to be an exemplary deacon. Now the trouble he took to guide me in the knowledge of religion and his forthright generosity fostered my love for him. I felt completely happy to be part of his household.

Miss Hughes was pleased that her brother was so much more sociable.

'It's nice to see you without your nose in a book or your head up the chimney all day long,' she said. 'You've found a son, old man and grown the tongue and heart of a father.'

I was happy for the first time since my mother and brother had died. I took a new delight in the business of religion and the ordinances of the Gospel. But my happiness was not quite complete.

I knew I hadn't behaved well towards my old companion in mischief, Wil Bryan. I had never told him why I had avoided his company. This was not gentlemanly behaviour, and I knew his friendship deserved better.

To put my mind a rest I decided to speak to him and tell him how I'd changed. Now I hoped, that with the help of God, I was on track to become a good boy. Secretly I hoped I might also be able to win Wil over to a similar resolve. There was nothing on earth I wanted more than to get Wil to change his ways. He was still a church member, although considered by the others of the *Seiat* to be a rather ungodly lad. He was David to my Jonathan and the thought of losing his friendship was terribly painful. Wil Bryan had a large and generous heart. I couldn't forget the loyalty and kindness he'd shown me in our childhood.

There was a great disparity in station between us when we were lads. My family was poor and Wil's well off. But he never ever as much hinted that he recognised this difference. Many a time he kept the wolf from my door, but he never hurt my feelings or upset my proud spirit as he helped me.

At school Wil was strong and resilient, while I was weak and delicate. He'd use his strength to help and support me. I couldn't just abandon my old pal. I knew that despite his friendship towards me he had not always been a good influence. If I spoke with him perhaps he would lead me astray again. But I didn't want Wil to think I was mean and unkind. I decided to talk at the first chance I got, even though I was afraid of meeting. He had always been stronger-minded than me and he was full of natural talent. I empathized with his waywardness but was afraid he might jeer at my change of heart. If he was going to laugh at me I would have to endure it in the name of our past friendship.

I wanted our reunion to appear accidental but found I didn't need to contrive it. I came across him unexpectedly on the High Street. His face wore its usual cheerful smile and my neglect of him had not spoiled his good nature.

'Hello there my old millennium,' he said and held out his hand to me. 'How have you been doing these past few centuries? I was starting to think you'd ascended to heaven, but I knew you wouldn't leave without saying goodbye to your old mate. Is it true that you've had a reformation? You know what? I am just as disposed to go to heaven or enlist as a soldier. I don't care which but I'm sick of living at home. We had a deuce of a row there this week. It was about nearly nothing. I'm not going to keep putting up with such humbug.'

I walked alongside him. 'What was the bother about, Wil?' I said, my pleasure at meeting him showing in my voice.

'You know that old eight-day clock in our kitchen?' he said.

'Yes, your father's very proud of it,' I said.

'Well, it's started to lose a bit lately,' Wil said. 'And I fancied I could mend it if I had some spare time. I've never tried my hand at clock cleaning, but I'm not stupid as you know.'

I nodded in agreement.

'Well, the old folk went off to Wrexham Fair,' Wil said. 'They left me strict instructions to weigh and wrap sugar. Well I thought that was unworthy of my abilities so I decided it would be more congenial to try clock-cleaning. It seemed a better use of my valuable time to put the old time-keeper to rights. But it turned out to be a bigger job than I'd expected. There I was Rhys, pulling the whole thing to bits. I made notes of where every piece came from and where it needed to go back. After I'd cleaned the lot, I rubbed a little butter into every wheel, screw and bar, we had no oil in the house, and all was going well except the timetable. It was getting late in the afternoon. I'd gone without my dinner, so as not to lose any time. It was time to put the pieces together if I was going to be finished before the gaffer came home. So far so good. I was ready to set old Eight-Day to rights. I consulted my notes and you've never seen such a mess. I couldn't make out a word of what I'd written. But I've learned something. A man who takes up cleaning clocks, just like a man who sets out to preach, needs be able to do the job without notes. Now I was in a right fix. To be fair I was labouring under many disadvantages. The only tools I had were a knife and a shoemaker's awl. I was sweating like a pig for fear the old gaffer would get back from the fair before I got his precious clock back together. I worked like a slave, and slapped the bits together as best I could. But when I'd finished I had a wheel to spare. I didn't know what on earth to do with it, so I put it in my pocket.'

He reached into his pocket and pulled out a small brass cogwheel which he showed me.

'I put old Eight-Day back in his place, and wound him up sure to goodness' Wil said. 'But the first thing his nabs did was to strike, and strike, and keep on striking until his weights hit the ground and he could strike no longer. That blessed bell struck thousands upon thousands of times. The sound got right into my head and I think it drove me a bit mental. It made such a din I was worried the neighbours'd think the Hall owner's daughter was getting married. After striking all it could, the next thing the old fellow did was stop stock still. If I shoved the pendulum he went pretty well, but as soon as I stopped shoving he stopped as well. I couldn't help laughing out loud. I couldn't have held back even if someone threatened to kill me. Here endeth the true account of my first attempt at clock cleaning. But there's more to the tale. Presently, Rhys my boy, the ancient pilgrims came home, and the first thing they did was look at the time. I'd tried to guess it as near as I could, and had set the hands where I thought they should be. But the old woman spotted the clock was stopped.'

'What's the matter with this here clock, William?' she said.

'Has it stopped?' said I as innocent as I could.

'Looks like it's been stopped for some two hours,' she said, jogging the pendulum while I was struggling to contain my laughter.

'What's the matter with the old thing?' she said, her voice getting fierce. She gave it the sort of shake you see people give a drunk who's fallen asleep by the road side.

To cover up my chuckling I made a joke. 'Perhaps he's ruptured himself, Mam,' I said. 'Like the Hall owner's hunter did. We'll have to either open him up or shoot him.'

At this point the servant girl came in and told the old folk I'd spent the whole day cleaning Old Eight. Then what a commotion there was. Mother bust up and the Gaffer went mad. I reckon the old man would have liked to give me a licking, but he knew he wasn't strong enough. I fell about laughing which only made it worse. Anyway next day they sent for Mr Spruce, the watchmaker, to set old Eight-Day aright. But he couldn't because I had one of the wheels in my pocket. I had my retribution,' he said as he waved the brass wheel at me.

'After trying for an hour old Spruce the Mainspring said, "I give up." But once the old folk's backs are turned for six hours or so I'm going to work a miracle on the old Eight Day with this missing bit.

'There now Rhys. I've told you my troubles. So is it true that you've been born again?'

'Wil,' I said. 'I think it's time for us both turn over a new leaf. I don't know if I've been born again or not, but my mind has undergone a wonderful change. I've learned to look upon things in a new way. I've lost all pleasure in our old ways. Matters of religion have obsessed me for months past. I couldn't stop worrying. I'm resolved to become a good boy, if God will help me. There's nothing on earth that would please me more than if you would join me in my resolution. Wil, you've always been a great friend to me, and I don't want us to grow apart. You know as well as I do that things can't go on as they have. It can only end badly. Don't you also worry about our future, Wil?'

'You carry on with your sermon and I'll just listen,' Wil said.

'It's not a sermon, Wil,' I said. 'I'm just talking to my old friend.'

'Well, if it's not a sermon, it's better than many that were meant to be.' Wil said with a laugh. 'But I'll be serious. I've noticed for some time that you were going that way. I said as much, now didn't I? I don't much wonder about it, as religion comes natural to your family, apart from your father. No offence. If I'd been brought up like you there'd be a touch of religion about me too. But my folks aren't interested, except for making a bit of a show Sunday. I'm no example of morality but I think I know what religion is. Your mother and old Abel, have shown me that not everyone involved with the bag of tricks are hypocrites like my folks.'

'You shouldn't speak so lightly of your parents, Wil,' I said. 'It isn't proper.'

'I don't speak lightly of them. I'm speaking about their religion. A man and his religion are two quite different things. The gaffer is a top-notch business man, he's clever at a bargain and a good money-maker who supplies plenty of grub for his family. But he can't repeat two verses of Scripture accurately. No more can I. He only looks at the Good Book for a couple of minutes before going to *Seiat* on the Sunday. His Bible, which he got at his wedding, is as good as new. He never opens it. It's not like your mother's, worn and tattered. But if his daybook or ledger caught fire overnight he'd be able to copy them out perfectly the next morning.'

Wil stopped and turned to face me, looking straight into my eyes.

'It's a fact, Rhys,' he said. 'Do you think I don't know what religion is? The gaffer pays into the *Seiat* book regular as clockwork. He puts down four shillings a month each for Mam and himself and a shilling for me, regularly. He thinks he's building up credit in the great ledger in the sky. But it's all my eye, Rhys. I know right enough how things should be done even if I don't do them. Even if the gaffer imagines he can appease his conscience with subscriptions, I know you can't fool the Almighty. To do it right you have to live religiously three hundred and sixty-five days in the year, and not just on Sundays. Father and mother would love to be honorary members of the church if there were such a thing. But there isn't. I know that just paying lip service will do them no good at the end.'

'But Wil,' I said. 'You know what you ought to do and aren't doing it. That's not responsible.'

'I'm not telling you anything new,' said Wil. 'I learnt it all when I was a kid. I'm just telling you about the kind of upbringing I've had, and what I see at home. Isn't there a verse somewhere about it being enough for the disciple that he be as his father?'

'"It is enough for the disciple that he be as his master, and the servant as his lord,"' I said. 'Matthew, Chapter ten verse twenty-five.'

'Quite so,' he said. 'I can never repeat a verse without making some mistake.' He shook his head.

'I know hundreds of comic songs, to reel right off,' he went on. 'But when it comes to religion, father and master, it's all the same. The point at issue is that it's not enough to be a Sunday-only practitioner, you have to carry it through the week. I've seen so much humbug and hypocrisy I'm ashamed to stay in the *Seiat*. Everybody knows I'm not fit to be there. Even the Great Lord knows I'm only there because my father forces me to go. I've got pockets full of wild oats, and I'm going to go out and to sow them. As a family, the Bryans have no more religion in them than does a milestone. Perhaps they have less, for at least a milestone serves the purpose for which it was made. Rhys, you know I'm not by nature a bad sort. I've sometimes thought if I'd been born the son of someone like Abel Hughes, I might have been different. But I am who I am, and that's the end of it.'

'You're wrong there, Wil,' I said. 'You well know you can change. You've got brilliant talents, and you shouldn't put them at the service of the devil.'

'You stop just there,' Wil said. 'You can't tell me anything I don't already know. I'm not hypocrite enough to claim I'm turnip-headed. But where religion is concerned brains without grace are no use. And you can't buy grace in a shop. It's not like asking for a pound of sugar. You get grace straight from the head office or not at all.'

'Then why not go to head office for it?' I said.

'I knew you'd say that,' Wil said. 'But it's easy to say and dammed difficult to do. Something keeps telling me I've not yet had my innings.

Old Abel has bowled you out, and I'm very glad he has. But I'm still at the wicket. Perhaps one day I'll be caught out or spread-eagled. I hope so, because I don't want to have to carry my bat out of this world. I wish I could find religion, but I can't find the right sort. I can only see imitations. You never saw me cry, did you?'

I shook my head.

'Well it may surprise you.' Wil said. 'But many a night I've been unable to sleep. Something inside me keeps telling me I'm a wicked boy. I've had many a right good cry on my own at night. I think I've opened some private part of my heart and freed a little devil to become my master. But in the morning I get over it. I never get any help from my parents. Your mother, God bless her, used to try warn me. She called it the old man taking over my heart. The Bible tells of bad sorts of devil who have be driven out with fasting and prayer?'

I nodded, not wishing interrupt him.

'Well, I can't for the life of me pray,' Wil said. 'So I can't possibly get rid of them that way. That's the humour of it, and I won't sham. As to fasting, why, I give my devil a dozen meals a day sometimes. He must be as fat as a pig in mud by now. But to tell you the truth Rhys, I'd like to starve him. I knew you were afraid to meet me. You thought I'd make fun of you? But far from it. I'm really glad you've found your way. You want to become a preacher, don't you?'

I shook my head, not wishing to admit the secret ambition I felt unworthy of.

'You needn't shake your head,' Wil said. 'You will be a preacher. I've known it since you were a kid. It's what your mother wanted for you. Now she's up in heaven she's asked it of the Almighty, and He's bound to oblige her. You may not believe me, but I've often felt uncomfortable thinking I've done you harm. Since you've known a bad turn you'll make a better preacher than if you'd kept to the straight line. No one can play whist unless he knows how many cards of a particular suit are out. I never saw any milk-and-water fellow make much of a mark at preaching. They don't know the ins and outs of going wrong you see. They preach well, but with nothing extra. If you hear a man who preaches well, take a look at his history. You'll find he's been off the rails at some time. St Peter went off the rails. And, he smashed up his engine too. But he turned out a stunning preacher afterwards. He became boss of a whole Church. If you're set on it, you be a preacher.'

I shook my head again, knowing I wasn't worthy of the ambition.

'You needn't keep shaking your head, I tell you again,' Wil said. 'You're bound to be one. And I'm going to give you some words of advice. It may be the last chance I get, because if there isn't a change back home I'm soon going to be waving farewell to my native land. Rhys, you're much cleverer than I am in Scripture, but I might have noticed things you haven't. I'm going to give you a bit of advice that you won't get in the *Seiat*.'

We sat down together on the wall outside the Top Church and Wil began to lecture me

'Always remember to be true to nature,' he said. 'Once you start preaching don't change your face, your voice and your coat, all within the first fortnight. Preaching is God's work, but a change to your heart, your throat or your voice will be your work. And there's no need for it. You'll do very well as you are. Don't try to be somebody else, or you'll end up being nobody. Some preachers are like a ventriloquist. At home he stays himself, but once he gets into a pulpit you'd think he was another man. And that other man is the lesser of the two, because he's not true to nature.

'Don't go droning your words at the congregation like you haven't any sense. The fact you are in the pulpit doesn't allow you to be sillier than you are anywhere else. If you had a row in the street and chanted in a sing-song voice they'd cart you off to Denbigh asylum – and quite right, too. When you hear a preacher tuning his voice as if he were at a concert, before breaking off and talking like anybody else, it makes you think it's just affectation and all a dodge. I stop listening, and so do most of his congregation.

'Never open your eyes when you pray. It's not respectful to watch the time when you're talking to God in public. I've seen men do it and it's quite spoiled the pudding for me.

'And, Rhys, once you are a preacher don't pretend to be holier than you really are and keep shaking your head at folk. You'll make the children afraid of you. We had a preacher lodging at our house last Monthly Meeting, who made me afraid in my heart. He was in good health, and he ate heartily. But at meals he kept groaning like he had everlasting toothache. He might as well have worn a coffin plate upon his chest. I felt I was at a never-ending funeral all the while he stayed with us. I'd have found it much easier to talk with the Apostle Paul, or Christ himself, had they visited us. He just wasn't true to nature. If you give yourself airs of that sort, then keep them for when you get back to the house you rent.

'Always be honourable. Never forget to give the girl at your lodgings sixpence, even if you haven't another in your pocket. If you aren't a generous Christian in your behaviour she'll never believe a word of your sermon. If you smoke – and all great preachers smoke – then use your own tobacco. If you keep filling your pipe from your host's pouch there'll be grumbling after you've gone.

'Now Rhys, you know I quite enjoy a bit of nonsense, but if you preach seriously, don't tell funny stories when you get back to your host's house. It will make you look a humbug. A preacher should be true to nature in the pulpit and at home. If someone who has almost made me cry in chapel, then makes me laugh in the house, it spoils the sermon for me.

'Don't beat about the bush when you're preaching. Get to the point, hit the nail firmly on the head and have done. Don't ramble on about the law and technical things like that. I and my sort know nothing about the law. Make your point simply. By Jesus Christ, if you can't get everyone in chapel to listen to you, give it up as a bad job and stay selling calico.

'If you go to college, and you will, don't be like the rest of the students. Most students are as alike as postage stamps. Try and be the exception to the rule. Don't let the deacons introduce you as a young man from Bala. If you preach well it will be enough to say Rhys Lewis, without saying where you come from. Whatever else you learn in college make sure you study nature, literature and English. Those subjects will pay you back for your effort. And if you do well, don't act like you've swallowed the poker and forget your old chums. Don't wear spectacles just to impress people that you've ruined your sight with study, or to give yourself a chance to ignore old friends in the street. Everyone'll know it's fudge. When you're ordained, don't put on a white neckerchief the very next Sunday. It won't matter if you never wear one. Paul and his companions never did, for they'd no way to get them starched.

'Never break a preaching engagement if even if you're offered better pay elsewhere. If you do you'll make more infidels than Christians. And don't become stingy. I'd rather hear of you going on the spree than that you've turned into a miser. I've never known a miser change, but scores of drunken men turn sober. If you went on a spree just once they'd stop you from preaching. But if you were the biggest miser in the country you'd be allowed to go on just the same.'

He stopped and grinned at me.

'Now my old fellow,' he said. 'Isn't that pretty good advice, considering who I am? The *Seiat* will tell you all you want to know about prayer and so on, but it hasn't the courage to tell you the home truths I have.'

Wil reached out his hand to shake mine. 'Now give me your paw and let me wish you well, old boy. '

He shook my hand firmly, and before I could say a word he was gone.

CHAPTER 30

The Poacher

Before our meeting I had thought I knew Wil Bryan as well as I knew myself. I had assumed him to be frank, open-hearted and easy to read. Now I saw depths in his character I hadn't realized were there. To me he'd always been a model of vitality whose talents flourished even though he neglected them.

Wil didn't enjoy reading, but what he did read he absorbed completely and without effort. He was too lazy to take much trouble, but he did everything without effort. He remembered everything he saw and heard, with the exception of verses. His memory seemed to take down everything in shorthand. Wil was a shrewd and a keen observer. He was constantly spotting something or somebody interesting in the dullest of places. He was remarkably perceptive. On the way back from one of our various expeditions he would dumbfound me with the things that he had spotted but I had not noticed. He used to liken me to blind Bartimaeus of Jericho. How I envied his ability to see things as they were, not as they seemed.

He had a natural flair for detecting deceit and trickery. He called it his nose for humbug and fudge. His knack of painting things in their true colours always impressed me. Indeed, I tried to emulate him. With all his insight, I was surprised he thought that he'd done me harm. Then I recalled how, when I told him how much I had benefited from a sermon, he would destroy my good feeling by pointing out the humbug he had seen that I had missed. I believed I could trust his honour and rely on his generosity but assumed he was incapable of serious feeling, and indifferent to the state of his soul. When I told him of my decision to reform I expected him to mock me. I was surprised when he rejoiced in my turnabout and dumbfounded when he told me that he longed for a similar awakening.

He said he didn't want to leave the game still carrying his bat and was hoping someone would bowl him out. He'd admitted that in the deep silence of night his conscience tormented him, asking him, Wil, why art thou wicked? Poor old Wil. His parents didn't help him turn around the evil spirit in his heart. If he'd been taught more than worldliness and worship of the golden calf at home, he might well have become an ornament to his nation.

There is some duality even in the most reckless. Although, depravity may rise to the surface, in the depths of the heart there is something which doffs its hat to goodness and truth. In later life I knew a drunken, wholly irreligious man. He got a letter from his son who had left home. It told of the son's acceptance into full church membership. The old drunk was so overcome that he hid in another room, out of sight of his family, and wept out his joy. What a genuine homage to the power of religion.

Despite all his frivolity and mischief Wil Bryan had a serious side. In the quiet of the night his conscience made itself heard, and his soul cried for help. I never imagined him caring about such things. My friend had told me secrets of his heart that I'd never suspected.

I was surprised that he guessed I wanted to become a preacher because I hadn't told a living soul of my ambition. It's true that as a lad I day-dreamed about joining the ministry but for some years now my way of life had not favoured such a choice. I had thought I'd grown out of that boyish desire. When Wil insisted that I become a preacher nothing could have been further from my thoughts. I was far too worried about the condition of my soul to think of anything more. But Wil's words, 'You needn't shake your head. You will become a preacher,' haunted me.

He had said it with such certainty that I wondered if he was an unwilling prophet, like Saul of Tarsus? I couldn't stop thinking about his prediction. I kept thinking of the strange and wonderful feeling that came over me the night Seth died. During my attempt to pray by his bedside something had told me that I must become a preacher.

But I knew I had been wicked, sinful and flippant since my mother died. I could hear the devil mocking me: 'Who art thou to think of preaching? Thou who hast broken every commandment a thousand times?'

Dozens of lads in Mold knew about my old life. How they would jeer at me if I talked of being a preacher. How dare I mention such a thing? How could I preach to them knowing they would be thinking of my old tricks? Me a preacher? It was quite impossible.

But Wil had been so confident in saying I would have to become one. He knew more about me than anybody else alive. He knew all of my faults, yet he had said, 'You are bound to be a preacher.' Stop fooling yourself, I told myself. You're uncertain of both your salvation and your faith. A preacher should be sure of his own salvation. I was not.

I concluded that I had no chance of becoming a preacher; it was out of the question.

The weeks passed by, and I found myself losing interest in light-coloured clothes. Not, I told myself, because I thought of being a preacher, but simply because black clothes were more becoming. I had bright clothes that were almost new in my chest, but I didn't wear them. When I bought a new coat I had it made a little longer-bodied. I didn't want it as long as those worn by the preachers, as I didn't want anyone to think I might be imitating them. Nothing could have been further from my mind. I became interested in books of divinity, and was puzzled why the other lads of my age did not did not enjoy them as I did. Where once I had criticized the preachers and found fault with their sermons I came to be amazed at how well they managed to fulfil their duties.

For some time I had hated it when Abel put up the visiting preacher in his home. Now I valued the extra time I got to spend talking privately to the speakers. I would never ask to see Abel's diary, even though I longed to know who would visit to preach in the coming months. But when Abel happened to leave it on the mantelpiece, I could not resist the temptation to look quickly through. I felt guilty as I opened it, rather like a Jew not of the priesthood who was stealing a look at the contents of the Ark of the Covenant. Once I had seen inside it I had much less respect for that diary. I found it contained notes about who could not be depended on and many unfilled promises made by preachers who had found better paid places.

But I still loved to see a preacher come to Abel Hughes's house. If he was young, and especially if he was a student, I could be bolder. I could ask him how old he was when he began to preach. Did he find the work hard? Was it his own idea to take it up, or someone else's suggestion?

I had no thought of beginning to preach myself. Nothing could have been further from my mind, I kept reminding myself. If I secretly cherished the idea, the memory of the disgrace attached to my family was enough to erase all hope of it becoming a vocation for me. Then I was forcibly reminded of background.

A strange character known as Old Nicklas lived in Mold when I was a boy. He was more often called Old Nick after his evil namesake. As a boy I thought Nicklas had a strong family likeness with the devil. He was tall, muscular and strong but with a distinct stoop. He was an old man, but age hadn't softened his natural roughness. His bristly hair did not whiten, and his repulsive face was too firm to wrinkle. He had all his teeth, and he walked with his head down and his hands under his coat-tails resting in the small of his back. He did not look you in the eye, he would only look at you sideways, out of the corners of his cunning eyes.

He was a terror to the children. If any cried or wouldn't come home when called, its mother would be heard saying, 'You wait a bit, my boy. Here's old Nicklas coming for you.'

This threat would stop the crying or send the youngster running into the house scared for his life. My mother never threatened me with Nicklas, but I was still afraid of him. If I was with a crowd of boys at play and we saw Nicklas coming we'd hide. We'd keep as still as mice until he'd gone. Wil Bryan said that he wasn't human but was the offspring of a Gipsy woman and the Evil One.

Old Nicklas never spoke to his neighbours, and nobody seemed to regret it. He arrived as a stranger and kept his life and background a complete mystery. Many wild and fearful stories were told about him. The credulous and superstitious believed them. He was reputed to belong to a high-ranking family and be very rich. Mam said he had sold himself to the Evil One and now lived on his payment. Her views of the financial resources of the Evil One were broadly based. She often said, 'The love of money is the root of all evil, so I'm sure the Devil has an enormous old stocking stuffed full of cash stowed away.'

To be sure Nicklas wasn't poor. He owned his house and had paid a good sum for it.

His house, Garth Ddu, was well named as black promontory. It stood like a dark carbuncle in a secluded grove about half a mile from the town. It backed onto the grounds of the Hall. The house and garden were surrounded by a high wall that Nicklas built as soon as he moved in. What little of the structure could be seen looked antiquated. It was swathed in ivy, which covered the roof and windows. Any passing stranger could easily have thought the house unoccupied. The field in front of the house was overgrown and neglected. No one walked on it except Nicklas, who could sometimes be seen with his head down along the hedgerow with a gun under his arm. Perhaps he was hunting a badger or a bird. No one knew.

No one had been inside the walled garden since Nicklas took possession. The only human feet known to have entered that dark compound were those of Nicklas and a disreputable old woman called Magdalen Bennet; the town folk called her Modlen of the Garth. Not even the tax collector was invited past the door in the wall. Nicklas had nothing to do with his neighbours, the little business he was forced to do with the outside world was entrusted to Modlen. She bought his food, the few clothes he required and his weekly newspaper.

Many folk asked Modlen about Nicklas's way of life. But all the old woman would say was 'Is that a question you're after putting to me?'

The most she would say, even to her closest friends, was that he spent his time digging his garden and shooting sparrows. Modlen found any talk of her master distasteful and, because she was a good customer, the shopkeepers didn't pester her. Yet they all speculated about the capacity of Nicklas's stomach, which seemed too small to hold all the food she bought. Additionally, judging by the copious amounts of powder and shot supplied to him they wondered that there was a single sparrow was left in all the county.

It was Modlen's talk of digging which gave rise to the conviction that Nicklas had a splendid garden. If he spent so much of his time digging it must surely be well worth the seeing. Many people wanted to see what a lovely glade was hidden by the high walls. But with time his hermit's life and mysterious past became an old story. People were not much interested in the queer old man of Garth Ddu. Many people thought he had something wrong in his head. This widespread impression, when added to the fact that gunshots were often heard within the garden walls, protected Nicklas from the unwanted attentions of his neighbours.

I did not see much of Wil Bryan after our dramatic conversation. To his credit I believe this was due more to Wil's resolve to do me no more harm than anything. But the result was that I no longer had a close friend of my own age. I had Abel Hughes, but he was an old man.

As I avoided the other lads of the town and spent most of my spare time alone, I found that the more I read, the more the great questions of life weighed down my soul. If I shone some light upon one dilemma, then I would stumble into another. I hardly ever got on top of my gloom. I pined for a confidant of my own age to whom I could open my heart when I found myself in a logical difficulty or got a new insight on some subject.

I was in not good health, and my inclination to stay indoors didn't improve my fitness. During a spell of fine weather Abel insisted that I should take more regular walks.

One evening, towards the end of May, I went for a long ramble into the country. The air was clear and beautiful as I took the footpath by the side of the river Alun. I passed a few clerks amusing themselves fishing. Then, having walked a fair way, I decided to cut across the fields back to the town. I cut across the farmland away from the path and trespassed until I reached high road leading to the Hall. I have always enjoyed the isolated landscape around the Hall. I had no respect for its owner but I admired the god-like majesty of the avenue of tall trees shadowing the road. It brought the verse from Chronicles 'Then shall the trees of the wood sing out at the presence of the Lord, because he cometh to judge the earth' into my mind with a new and mystic meaning.

No wonder Wil Bryan talked about nature so much, I thought. A powerful feeling of reverence comes over me when I find myself in the shade of a great forest. Perhaps, as a Welshman, I've inherited a sense of awe from the Druids of old. The Bible speaks with admiration of the cedars of Lebanon, and I am closer to God in a wooded country than in a bare and exposed one.

The silence of the night was broken only by the distant baying of a hound from the Hall and the more immediate crunch of my footsteps on the roadway. I felt close to God as I walked down that avenue between the giant trees. They stood straight like grenadiers of God. The wood was getting thicker and gloomier. The night surrounded me as the trees masked the twilight. Then, I saw a big man with his head bent towards earth looming out of the darkness. I recognized him, it was Old Nicklas.

The sight of Old Nick made my flesh creep. I hadn't seen him for some time, but there was something in his look that night which fitted the black loneliness of the place. My feeling of reverent security evaporated instantly. The trees were no longer God's grenadiers, they had become grim witnesses to a ghastly murder.

My hand was trembling and my heart racing as I buttoned up my coat. I quickened my pace.

'Good night, Mr Nicklas,' I said, forcing my voice to sound bolder than I felt.

Old Nick didn't answer or even raise his head. I walked on a few yards before I looked back. I saw Old Nicklas ambling leisurely on his way. What a fool I felt at being so frightened. Poor Nicklas was just a harmless old man.

Leaving the main road, I followed the path leading alongside Garth Ddu. As I drew near I couldn't stop myself from standing to look at the old house.

How silly that local people believed such baseless myths about its lonely owner. I'd never heard Nicklas say an offensive word to anybody. But he did live an odd sort of life. However, looking at the facts I decided that he was inoffensive. If he chose to create a mystery around himself then he had a perfect right to do so. What wrong had he ever done anybody?

The more I thought about it the more I warmed to the idea that there was a certain charm about his secret, reclusive life. Nicklas must enjoy it. Then I felt a growing curiosity about his house, knowing its owner was away from home. What did his garden look like? Why was there so much talk of its secret beauty?

The wall was not too high for me to climb so I decide to try. I had just placed my hands on the top and was about to pull myself upwards when I felt a strong grip on my collar. I was pulled away from the wall and shaken as a terrier shakes a rat.

As I was slumped down I saw the figure of old Nicklas holding me.

'A thief is it? A thief in the house of Nicklas of Garth Ddu,' he said. 'You're being rather venturesome my lad.' He gave me another shake and almost shook my soul out of my body.

'Who are you?' he said. 'What are you? Where d'ye come from? Speak or I'll rip you into four quarters and a head. Say your prayers.'

If he hadn't had hold of my collar, gripping me as a cat holds a mouse in her paw, I would have fallen to the ground with fright. My mouth and tongue were dry as crumb cake, so I couldn't speak. I was sure he was going to murder me, but I couldn't even croak. A hundred thoughts flashed though my mind. Was I going to be tortured to death? Would I get into heaven while my soul was so tainted? I thought of my mother, of Bob, of Abel Hughes and all their associations, then I prayed to God to save me.

All this happened in an instant. I was terrified as I looked up at the fiendish face of old Nicklas. Still I was struck dumb. He loosened his hold on me, but didn't let me go. He seemed somewhat pleased with the scare he had given me. He spoke in a milder tone,

'Who are you, and what do you want?' he demanded.

Suddenly my tongue freed itself. I answered him with a tremble in my voice. 'I'm not a thief Mr Nicklas. I'm apprentice to Abel Hughes,' I said. 'I only wanted to see your garden. That's all I did.'

'You want to see my garden, eh?' he said. 'You've been listening to Modlen's nonsense. What's she been saying, a garden worth seeing. Yes indeed well worth the seeing. If the old hag doesn't learn to keep her mouth shut then I'll shoot her, dead as a door nail, I will. And I'll flay alive any boy I catch climbing my garden wall and feed his flesh to my dog. That'll save having to buy meat for him. So you want to see my garden, do you? Well, you shall see it, for it's worth seeing.'

He laughed an evil sounding chuckle. 'Ha, ha! Come you inside.'

Nicklas kept his grip of me with one hand while with the other he took out a latch key and unlocked the door in the wall. He dragged me through and locked the door behind him. Then he let me go and told me to follow him. I was astounded when I saw the famous garden.

It was a total wilderness. Old Nick couldn't have put a spade near it for years. Apart from the path it was overgrown with thorns and brambles. Some of the bushes were fresh, others dead and decayed, yet others shrivelled for lack of nourishment, all were a tangled mess. Still Nicklas took me round, pretending to point out all sorts of different fruits, flowers and plants which were not there. He used technical names, and went on a great length about the virtues of each variety. He sounded just like a professional gardener as he showed me his neglected wilderness.

He finished the tour with a harsh, jeering laugh. 'Well, was that a garden worth seeing or not?' he said.

I waited to be told to go, but instead he began to mumble disjointedly. His words could have been the ramblings of a maniac. This is what I can remember of what he said.

'Who's Nicklas of Garth Ddu? Where's he from? Who does he belong to? How does he live? You'd all like to know, wouldn't you? But you won't. You think Nicklas is a fool, but he is what he is. Who was his father? David Nicklas, Esquire, a great man, a wise man, a merchant, a miser and an idiot. And did he smother his wife and Nicklas's mother after Nicklas of Garth Ddu was born? Who saw her die? How much did David Nicklas, Esquire, merchant, miser and idiot, pay the doctor not to say?

'Where did David Nicklas, Esquire, merchant, miser and idiot, send Nicklas of Garth Ddu to a wet nurse? Did he pay two hundred pounds to have the child poisoned?

'When did David Nicklas, Esquire, merchant, miser and idiot, find out Nicklas of Garth Ddu had no brains? How much did he offer the schoolmaster to kill him with Latin? Was it a hundred pounds? Was it two hundred?

'Did David Nicklas, Esquire, merchant, miser and idiot, twice try to kill Nicklas of Garth Ddu? Did he try thrice? Did David Nicklas, Esquire, merchant, miser and idiot have a stroke once? Did he have a second stroke? Did he have a third stroke? When David Nicklas, Esquire, merchant, miser and idiot, had his last stroke, did Nicklas of Garth Ddu sit on his chest and squeeze his throat?

'Did he squeeze it once? Did he squeeze it twice? Why don't you answer me? Have you a tongue? Where did Nicklas of Garth Ddu get his money? How did he get his money?

'Would he have had any money if he hadn't sat on David Nicklas, Esquire, merchant, miser and idiot's breast? Would he have had any money if he had not squeezed David Nicklas, Esquire, merchant, miser and idiot's throat? How much money did he get? Did he get two thousand pounds? Did he get five? Did he get ten thousand pounds?

'Don't you hear? Why don't you answer?'

'I need time to think about it Mr Nicklas,' I said.

'Think about it,' he said, his voice rising to a shout. 'Never take time to think about it or your head'll go bad, and you won't be able to sleep for three weeks. You'll have to walk all night if you're going to think about it. Don't think or you 'll go soft in the head. Can't you speak? Are you deaf or dumb? I had a cousin who was deaf and dumb. He was always thinking and he died in the Asylum. They wanted Nicklas of Garth Ddu to go to the Asylum so that they could take his money. What do they do in the Asylum? Nothing but think about it. Do they think for a week? Do they think for a year? Why won't you answer? If you don't tell me I'll make you.'

With that he dived into an old summer-house overgrown with a thorns. Out he came waving a double-barrelled shot gun.

'Do you see this?' he said, waving the gun under my nose. 'What's it for? Will it kill once? Will it kill twice?'

He held the gun out to me. 'Here, take it and shoot me. One barrel at a time, mind,' he said and then quickly pulled it back. 'No, wait. I'll shoot you first in the head with one barrel, and you shoot me, after, in the breast with the other. We'll toss-up who gets to shoot first. Heads or Tails? Who's to shoot first? Let me think about it. But no, I mustn't think about it or my head'll go wrong. Why does Nicklas of Garth Ddu keep so many cats? To drive the Devil away, of course. Sometimes a mood of murder comes over me, and I want to kill somebody. Who shall I kill? If I kill Modlen, there'll be no one to fetch my things. Should I kill the cat? Should I kill her and hang her up, so the evil spirit goes away? But what if the cat won't come? What am I to do? I'll shoot the old tree over. See, like this.'

With that Nicklas fired both barrels towards the trunk of the old tree.

I couldn't decide if the strange old man was a fool or a knave. While he performed his bragging speech I thought he was a scoundrel of the first order. Someone that Wil Bryan would call a perfect humbug.

He was obviously making an effort to convince me he was insane. But I couldn't see any sign of madness in his face. He was continually scanning my face to see if his ranting was frightening me. The longer he went on the more I got control of my fear and became calm. He could see as he finished that I was no more afraid of him than of a sparrow.

As the sound of the gunshot died away a short man rushed out of the bushes and made his way towards us. He must have been alarmed by the shots. I recognized the newcomer immediately.

'Hullo, Rhys,' he said, holding out his hand which I refused to take. I saw at once the man I had hated most on earth ever since I had first seen him. I still thought of him as the Irishman.

'Nicklas,' he said. 'Do ye know who this is?' Nicklas shook his head.

'It's our old pal's kid,' said the newcomer, waving Nicklas towards the house.

Nicklas's eyes opened wide in bewilderment, but he obediently went into the house.

'So you won't shake my hand, Rhys?' the Irishman said. He waited until Nicklas had gone into the house. 'How did you get in here?'

'Uncle,' I said. 'If I shake hands with you my hand will rot and I will encourage it to do so. I detest you with all my heart. Now let me out of this accursed place.'

'What's wrong with you, boy?' he said. 'Why are you so angry? Why do you hate me so?'

'Why do I hate you?' I said. 'You well know. You're the cause of all my and my mother's misery. You ruined my father. You taught him to poach. You encouraged him to act so he had to quit the country. Why do I hate you? Apart from my father you caused my mother the most trouble. You kept coming to our house to disrupt our comfort. How many times did my mother give you the last shilling she had in the world just to get rid of you? And how much more would you have blackmailed us for, if you hadn't been afraid of Bob?'

'Bob was a fool,' he said. 'Your father and I gave him a chance to run on the night he was arrested. But he was a ninny and got taken to jail.'

'Don't you call my brother a fool. Bob would have been ashamed to take help from such scoundrels as you and my father. Tell me the truth, Uncle. Where is my father? Is he hiding here? Is he? Tell me.'

'He is not,' the Irishman said. 'He's in a much warmer place.'

'Where?' I shouted. 'Explain yourself and tell the truth for once. Where is he?'

'How can I tell you? I've never trod the grounds where your father has gone. He's kicked the bucket I tell you. And you as a good Methodist should have a band of black crepe around your hat.'

I'm not proud to admit it, but my heart leapt with joy at this news.

'Is my father really dead?" I said. 'Don't try to fool me. I want the truth for once.'

'I never spoke a truer word,' he said. 'Your father was fond of drink. Well, we had a bit of luck. He got his hands on much more brass than was good for him. He became too free with the whisky and had a stroke. I told him to take care, but there was no talking to him. He turned his toes up in Warwick. I just happened to be in Leamington so I called in at Warwick and met your father. I was with him when he died in a disreputable public house where he was lodging. I emptied his pockets once his last breath was gone. He didn't want to die; your mother had told him they are all teetotallers in the next world. But it was his own fault. I warned him against too much drink. The Union paid to bury him, them thinking I was only a sort of friend of his.'

'If you're telling the truth,' I said. 'Then this is the best bit of news I've ever had. If you had only died with him, then I couldn't have asked for more.'

He laughed.

'Well, when I die,' he said. 'You nephew, as my nearest relative, will inherit all my shooting grounds. They're extensive. They run from Warwick to Denbighshire? Twm o' Nant's ghost looks after one end of my estate and Shakespeare's minds the other. They're my two head keepers, so your father used to say. No wonder you want me to die, so that you can inherit your Uncle James's estate.'

'Stop fooling about and let me out of this horrible place,' I said, walking towards the door in the wall,

'Wait a while. What's your hurry?' he said. 'Tell me how the old roundhead is with you. Can I visit you on the sly, when I'm hard up? I can see you're a bit of a buck; that's a smart watch you're wearing. Perhaps you'd enjoy you UncleJames popping in to see you now and again. Have you got half a crown about you? I'm just a bit short at the moment. And, while I think about it, what'll you give for the pawn ticket your father left? Would you like to have it to remember him by?'

I felt a powerful improper spirit, take me over. I had a strong urge to hit the rascal. I prayed for strength to resist the impulse, and it was granted. No doubt it was the best for me.

'Open that door,' I said, 'and let me go on my away.'

'You haven't paid the gate,' he said, holding out his hand.

I am my mother's son so I gave him all the money I had: two shillings it was.

'Thank you,' Uncle James said, bowing formally to me. 'I'll see you again, when you are a bit more flush.' He took a latch-key from his pocket and opened the door.

As soon as I was safely through the doorway, I turned and faced him. I looked him straight in the eye.

'Uncle,' I said. 'You are under my thumb now I've found your hiding place. If ever you contact me again, or I hear that you're in the neighbourhood. I'll tell the police where you are.'

'What?' he said, his fear showing in his voice. 'You can't split on me, I'm your own flesh and blood. Do you want to soil your own clothes?'

'Trust me, I'll do exactly as I say,' I said.

'You'll never see me again,' my uncle said, 'so do your worst, my proud chicken.'

He tried to spit in my face but I dodged his drool as he slammed the door.

I went home filled with a feeling of joy. A great burden dropped from my mind. But had my uncle told the truth? I knew from hard experience he was an expert at the art of telling lies.

CHAPTER 31

Dafydd Davies

It's a happy man who can look back over his life and say that he has always behaved just as he should have done, and been true to himself. But do many such men exist today? If we all took heed of our consciences, then most of us would have to admit that we did not always fulfil our moral duties. Hardly any of the philosophers who have thought deeply about the nature of duty have managed to act in the way they think is right. Some pride themselves on taking a strong view, on always doing what is proper, but others point out that worldly situations are awkward. Sometimes events can encourage a man to deviate from his creed. I think it is one thing to hold firm views but quite another to always act in accordance with them. However there are men in this world who try to act according to their convictions no matter what the consequences.

I have promised to tell the truth about myself in this memoir, so I have to admit that I have not always done what I knew to be right. Immediately after my unexpected meeting with my uncle, the first question I faced was, what should I do?

My conscience said, 'Your path of duty is clear. Go at once to the police and tell them what you know.' But something inside me softly suggested, 'Circumstances alter cases.'

I needed some time to think before I decided what to do. I felt in need of advice. Should I take counsel from a wiser man than myself? Who would be better to ask than Abel Hughes? I wondered if I should tell him the whole story and then act upon his advice. Then I thought I should think the matter through myself before choosing a course of action.

These ideas ran through my head as I walked back to the town. By the time I got back to the shop I hadn't decided. I went to bed vowing to sleep on the dilemma.

Sleep didn't come. I kept worrying about what might happen. The more I thought about my choices, the more clear it seemed there was greater personal advantage in doing nothing. The more I deliberated the more I pushed pure, clear, unselfish duty into the background.

Who was this man I called the Irishman? Well, he was a full-blooded brother to my father. But what was the character of this uncle of mine? I had found he was one of the most cunning, lazy, degraded rogues that ever walked the land of Wales. Mother found him so despicable that she and Bob tried to completely suppress knowledge of his existence.

When I first met this depraved scoundrel, by the Hall park on the night Seth died, he told me that I was related to him. When I told Bob the man claimed to be my uncle he decided to tell me his history.

'Work was distasteful to him from his early youth,' Bob said. 'He lay in his bed while honest folk were doing their jobs. Then, when others rested during the night, he would go up and down the country up to no good. He managed to live, eat and drink to excess, even though he never worked. No one knew where his money came from. The folk of the town guessed that the game on the Hall estate made a big contribution to your Uncle James's upkeep. He was no stranger to the inside of a prison cell, but he was pretty good at tricking both police and gamekeepers. It was a wonder to those who knew him that he avoided their clutches for so many years.

'Our father,' Bob went on, 'began his life as a competent workman, but he began to take the occasional tipple. Then he took to sitting drinking for hours on end in the Cross Foxes. His drinking made him idle. His drinking and idleness made him short of money, and his poverty led him to harshness, bitterness, bad temper and cruelty. You have no idea of the life our poor mother led before you saw the light of day. What a trial it was for our mother to try to live religiously with such an irreligious scoundrel as our father.'

I was shocked when Bob told me some of the cruelties our father practiced on our beloved mother. But to describe them here is too painful for me.

'Our Uncle James,' Bob said, 'didn't have much trouble in ensnaring our father with his evil habits. The pair became professional poachers and were surprisingly good at avoiding the law. This was partly due to the fact our father, who was extremely strong, was the terror of the police. Uncle James was only a cunning weakling, but he was more daring than our father. The havoc the two of them inflicted on the game of the Hall owner made him dance with fury. But he couldn't stop them. He kept changing his game keepers, but they were no match for our father. Finally the Hall owner employed a couple of Scotsmen who had a reputation of being hard men. Within a couple weeks they were both wounded and laid up. One of them was so badly hurt he was not expected to live. About that time Uncle James and our father were nowhere to be found, though they were much sought for.'

All this had happened before I was born. To use her own words, Mother was worse than a widow. Bob thought the best thing that could happen to her would be to be rid of them both. She suffered great hardship before Bob was old enough to support the family. But her poverty was nothing beside the anguish my father's irreligion caused her. She lived in constant fear that he might come to visit us and be caught.

Her sorrow was increased by my uncle's furtive visits, which Mam saw as a warning that her husband might be about too. Uncle James's visits always took place on dark nights, and he always demanded all the money my mother had. She would give it to him to get rid of him. After every visit she would remain sad and silent for days. These visits continued until Bob grew big and strong enough to stop them. We never told anybody about my uncle's calls, except Thomas and Barbara Bartley. It was to protect her from those dreadful visits that the kind-hearted old neighbours persuaded her to move in with them at Y Twmpath. I can't think of any other reason she would have given up her home.

Over the past few years I had thought that the town folk had forgotten about my father and uncle. Nobody ever mentioned their names to me. But, as I reflected, I realized it was their respect for the memory of my religious mother that encouraged them to behave to me as if I had no dishonour in my family history. Meeting Uncle James showed me it was quite possible for the whole history to return. And if it did, then I would have to bow my head in shame.

Now that the idea of becoming a preacher possessed me, the thought that the characters of my father and uncle could be paraded in the light of day was horrendous. But if the news of my father's death, far from home, was true, I could fulfil my ambition. As I write this I am ashamed to admit that I was glad to hear of my father's death. Indeed I rejoiced. I felt as if I had been let out of a dark, dank dungeon into the fresh air.

But what was I to do about my uncle? My conscience kept telling me that I wasn't acting honestly. I'd discovered Nicklas was deceiving his neighbours and not leading the reclusive life he pretended. At best he was giving shelter to a fugitive from the country's laws.

I could strip Garth Ddu of its false seclusion. But should I? My conscience said, 'You should, without delay.'

And there was my uncle. He didn't deserve to be at liberty. His crime was an old one but that didn't lesson its evil. The law wanted him now as much as it did on the day he committed the crime. It would be easy to convict him. The two badly injured gamekeepers were still alive and still worked for the owner of the Hall. They would still be capable of identifying him.

Even though my uncle's criminal act was eighteen years old, if I whispered half a dozen words in the Hall owner's ear it would fan his vengeance into a flame at once. He would spare neither trouble nor expense to secure my uncle's arrest. That he was my father's brother didn't make me feel he deserved my mercy. I could credit most of my early troubles to him. He had destroyed my father's character and shortened my mother's life.

My sense of justice said it was my duty to disclose his location to the police, and the little devil of revenge lurking in my heart kept saying, 'What a splendid opportunity to repay the old fox for all the worry he has caused you and your family.'

But there was another side to the question. The man to gain most advantage if I turned informer would be the owner of the Hall. I didn't care at all about pleasing him. He had sentenced my brother to two months' imprisonment without any evidence of wrongdoing. He had taunted Bob about his father in a public court. I had not forgiven his meanness and injustice. Since the day they wrongfully took Bob to prison, I had harboured a deep hatred for the police. My sympathies were with my brother. Will Bryan had also contributed to my prejudice by calling them pettifogging Bobbies. Why should I offer up my uncle as a sacrifice to the police officers?

Besides, I reflected, in the town there was much fellow feeling with a poacher. They were not looked at in the same way as other lawbreakers. Some folk would admire my unselfishness in giving up my uncle to the authorities, but far more would think me a traitor. I would become one who, as my uncle said, had soiled his own clothing.

If I were to make public my discovery the whole business of my father would come down on my head. My father might have died, but the memory of his crimes would be a new talking point in the smithy, the Cross Foxes, the Crown and around every hearth. Older neighbours who knew the background would say that the man who did these crimes was the father of the youth who was apprenticed to Abel Hughes. The chapel children, whom I worked so hard to teach, would wonder that the man on trial was my uncle, and the dead man, who had been as bad as him, was my father. This was very hard for me to contemplate.

Even if I were to tell the police of my uncle's retreat, it was unlikely they would catch him. By now James Lewis would be far away. Old Nicklas would say my story was a lie. I would be reviving unpleasant memories to no real purpose except to make people think I was poking fun at the police.

Then I remembered my mother's words. 'If ever you meet with your father, try and forget his sins; and if you can do any good to him, do it.'

This must apply equally to my uncle. If my mother had been in my place she would not have given her brother-in-law over to the authorities. She was a good woman. Could I not also be good and keep this secret to myself?

Just before I finally fell asleep I resolved to keep quiet. I decided there was no danger of my uncle's confronting me again. Whether this was wise or not I would have to wait and see. If I succeed in finishing this autobiography it will be easy to keep a secret when the keeper happens to be the man who would be most hurt by its disclosure. Keeping it for another's sake is the rub. The Devil never tempts us to disclose a thing for our own shame, or that of our family.

After a few days I began to congratulate myself upon my shrewdness. But I must admit, I didn't feel the unalloyed contentment that a man enjoys if he does the right thing. I felt more like a worldling who had driven a good bargain. God knows I had the desire to do what was just but didn't have the moral courage to do it at the cost of placing myself in misery and disgrace.

I would like to able to say this was the only time I gave in to expediency. It is said that performing a single act to which conscience does not say Amen prepares you for more acts of a similar nature. Is this always true? It was not on his occasion. By valuing my self-interest and happiness above my clear duty, I forced my moral nature to stir. This was probably in an effort to atone for my sin. However, as I was inclined to believe my uncle about my father's death, I felt freer to do what I could in the cause of religion.

Here I had an excellent master in Abel Hughes, and he gave me time off work to attend every service held in the chapel. I made full use of his good will. Poor old Jones was never keen on going to chapel. He was at his happiest in the shop. Like a well-trained sheepdog, he knew only one thing. He knew how to measure cloth, fold it and pack it into customers' parcels.

If Abel Hughes had pointed to a pile of worsted and said to him, 'Jones, lie down there,' he would have obeyed and been happy never to move from the spot until Abel ordered him to. I fancy Abel thought it no use sending Jones to chapel. It would be like trying to make a black cat white by washing it in soap and water.

This made it easier for me to begin to attend services and meetings once more. But what changes had taken place in chapel since I had last been regular in my attendance?

Change always makes me mournful. It reminds me how short a man's life is and how quickly we have to give up our posts to other people. After I'd been away for a few years there was no place like the chapel to bring home this lesson. How struck I was with the changes that had taken place in the congregation. I saw many strange faces looking around me and noted how many of the old ones were no longer there. And some of my old acquaintances' heads had whitened, whilst others were completely bald.

The last time I mentioned the chapel and its affairs in this memoir was when I was between nine and twelve years of age. How different it looked when I was eighteen. All the faces in the Children's Meeting were new. John Joseph, our old leader, had gone to Australia. Abel Hughes was now getting too old to manage the children, as he did not cope well with the Solfa, so he left that work to others. And who were these others?

Since I had decided to sort myself out I had taken charge of teaching the youngsters. Alexander Phillips, whose bardic name was Eos Prydain, looked after the singing. The literary society, which Wil had called the Society of the Flat Hairs, was long since dead; the Solfa had seen it off. It did not kill it intentionally but it became almost impossible to get the boys to learn grammar, write essays or take part in doctrinal debate when they could be singing. The Solfa Society had several advantages over the old Literary Society. It was so much more fun to sound 'Doh' all together than to conjugate a verb on your own. And sight-singing was of greater use in the world of *eisteddfodau* than a proper understanding of the justification of faith, no matter how useful it might be in the world to come. What's more, the Solfa Society had been set up on sounder and more liberal principles than the Society of the Flat Hairs. It embraced everyone. Young folk, middle-aged folk, old folk, women and men, all were welcome. A singing society had unquestionable advantages and could give satisfaction to both sexes. If a meeting had been spent practicing in the mode of 'lah,' it was the easiest thing in the world to close it with a rousing song in some other, more uplifting, mode.

For singers, the Solfa Society had many advantages over the old Literary and Theological Society. The Flat Hairs grew shy and bashful as they struggled to define the meaning of religion. But the Solfa Society taught its members to hold up their heads and show the world they knew what's what. They learned how to show the vulgar rich that they could not have all the gloves and rings to themselves.

The formation of this Society marked an important epoch in the history of the town. The habit of carrying your Bible to chapel began to disappear; you carried a Tune Book instead. True, here and there some old woman would be annoyed to see this "Hymn Book" usurping the Good Book. Like all reforms, it met with opposition from the old-fashioned, but it was useless to kick against the progress of the age.

Abel Hughes, my master was sensible enough, but he didn't much like change. He refused to change the Sunday night *Seiat* into a Singing Meeting. He made a stand against rehearsing secular choral pieces on the Sabbath, even when there was an impending National *Eisteddfod*.

'Singing is not more important than preaching,' Abel said. 'And the Tune Book does not deserve greater attention than the Bible.'

He would never ask the preacher to cut his sermon short to make more time for hymn-singing.

For all Eos Prydain's glaring at him, Abel would still slur his words and miss the key with might and main even when singing 'He, led unto Calvary hill, was willingly nailed to the Cross.'

Had Abel lived a little longer he would doubtless have come round to the good things the Solfa Society did for religion. I threw my lot in with it heartily. I was a member for over a month before I learned that I had an unpromising voice and lacked both the patience and the brains to become proficient in the mysteries of the musical science.

If I follow my promise to tell the honest truth, I must admit I was taken aback to find that a boy of eight, whom I had great difficulty in teaching to spell in Sunday School, was the best sight-singer in the Society. When I saw that I would lose influence over him in the Sabbath class if he saw how unmusical I was, I made myself scarce.

To this day I regret that I did not master the Solfa. A knowledge of Solfa is becoming an indispensable skill for a minster. Perhaps the next generation, when going to a Sessional Ordination Meeting, will find the catechism of the Confession of Faith replaced by an examination in the Solfa. Soon a preacher will not be judged fit and proper according to New Testament standards unless he can also explain the difference between the major and the minor key.

I am sorry I neglected the opportunities for musical development that were once within my grasp; alas, I am now too old to learn. But I indulge too much in side issues, and there is a danger, should anyone ever read these lines, that I might be thought sarcastic.

The chapel had seen many other changes, not least was the death of several old brethren, whom I had held in great respect as a boy.

Edward Peters, the crabbed old man who had carefully kept the books of accounts, had for some time been confined to his house. But still he didn't go to bed on a Sabbath night without first establishing the total of the collections. His last words before dying were, 'Remember, the quarter's pew rents are due next Monday night.' He was like a coconut, hard on the outside but with the true milk of religion in his heart.

Hugh Bellis, whose tendency to weep during the sermon had encouraged Wil Bryan to call him Old Waterworks, left the weeping and groaning to the children when he entered into that joy which he could not speak of while on earth except with the sweetest of tears.

Of the old deacons only Abel Hughes was left, and of him my whole heart said, 'O king, live forever.' He was supported in the Big Seat by Dafydd Davis, who had come to us from another church. He was already a deacon, and we accepted him as such.

Thomas Bowen, the preacher and children's great friend, had also gone to that far country to which Hugh Bellis had previously voyaged.

John Llwyd, the perpetual fault-finder, who Wil Bryan had called the Old Scraper, was still with us; Wil had by that time changed his nickname to the Chapel Nuisance Inspector.

Thomas and Barbara Bartley were faithful attenders, and their religion was forever brightening. They were now thought of as two originals of the *Seiat*. If Abel Hughes found the conversation flagging, he would turn round and say, 'Thomas Bartley, what is your opinion upon the point?'

We then usually got something to liven us up. Thomas would relate an experience, which was always diverting. As Wil Bryan said, it was all the more so because it was true to nature.

I will give a few examples of this as I finish my history. I have mentioned several times that William the Coal was given both to drink and to laying the blame for his drinking on Satan. Now William was too old to earn extra money by labouring at the hay harvest, his lack of spare cash had made him tolerably religious. As Abel Hughes used to say of William, 'Poverty is indispensable to the godliness of some people.' (Although he as an ardent Calvinist, Abel held liberal views in some matters.) But I also heard him say, 'I do hope that when Death comes to William the Coal it finds him poor. Because William always stays very pious on an empty pocket.'

We now had three deacons at the Chapel. These were Abel Hughes, Alexander Phillips (also known as Eos Prydain), and Dafydd Davis.

They could not have been more different. Abel was a studious old man of deep convictions, who had read widely both in the Welsh and the English. His opinion was greatly appreciated at the Monthly Meeting. Our preachers paid him a deal of deference, as he was a man of undoubted piety. Like fate he was slow, but sure.

Eos Prydain was young and unmarried. He was an expert and assiduous singer with a gay-spirited attitude towards the younger folk and popular with them. He had given years to the study of music and had made himself a master of the art. Seldom have I seen his equal when organizing and conducting a concert. His contribution to the musical parts of the service was exemplary. His only fault was a tendency to turn the leaves of the tune book during the sermon, and look as though he was mentally rehearsing the next hymn instead of listening to the preacher.

Dafydd Davis was a middle-aged man who spoke only the Welsh. He had been brought up in the country to be religious, sensible and earnest. The only book he recognized was the Bible. His main purposes in life were his religion and his farm, and he knew no more about politics than his forefather Adam. He acknowledged two masters, God and his landlord. To the former he gave his whole heart, and to the latter the respect he deserved. He was an honest, upright and faithful servant to them both. He would have been better off had he devoted more time and thought to running his farm. He grieved more over a backsliding member of the church than for any sheep which strayed from his fields. When he lost three bullocks to the foot and mouth, he thanked God he had others left alive as good. But when a pious church sister died he stayed in mourning for weeks. The potato blight was a hardship for him, but he was more upset by the depressed state of religion. He would dutifully thank the Lord for an abundant harvest, but be far more pleased with a revival of religion. He would consult the weather-glass now and again to help him plan his farming, but not a day passed without his consulting the Bible to forecast the weather awaiting his soul in the next world.

The world and its bustle did not bother him much. He was like a man on board a ship in mid-ocean, who had a compass and knew the direction of the port where he heading. He was a serious man. I never saw him laugh, but his face always wore an unconscious smile. It was an outward symbol of his quiet mind. I'm sure that smile was a great source of annoyance to the Devil. Sometimes you meet men with a fluffy effeminacy about their religion that makes you think they would be less religious if they were more enlightened. Dafydd Davis was not that sort. The Bible was the primary study of his life. If I read out a portion of the life of Christ by one evangelist, I felt sure that every word the others had written was there in Dafydd's mind, and he would be able to quote it from memory. I greatly admired him but wondered how a man who spoke no English had mastered his Bible so well.

There is a risk that I might have a high opinion of Dafydd Davis because he supported me so well. He took me with him to hold prayer meetings in private houses, and first induced me to speak at them.

I was eighteen years old, the secretary of the Sunday School. I always led my students in prayer to start each session, but I didn't pray in public. Dafydd Davis often held prayer meetings in houses, but I stayed quiet at them.

As we were leaving one such meeting, Dafydd Davis caught my arm.

'Rhys,' he said, 'the next prayer meeting will be at Thomas Bartley's house. I'd like you to say something about a Bible chapter. The friends will be glad to hear you. You have a week to prepare, and I feel sure you would do so, will you not?'

His words hit me like an electric shock. I have already mentioned my diffidence, and I was quite taken aback at the idea of leading part of the meeting. How it went I will reveal in my next chapter.

CHAPTER 32

An Abundance of Advisers

We all have early recollections of an old house that holds a fond place in our memory. In my case that memory hovers lovingly around Thomas Bartley's old house, Y Twmpath. I see it in my mind's eye, with its cosy kitchen, its ancient black furniture, its great settle, pewter plates and the wide chimney seat, where I warmed myself hundreds of times. Everything about that kitchen is in my mind, even to the chunks of bacon, the ropes of onion, and stems of wormwood wrapped in an old newspaper hanging from the ceiling beams. An old parish constable's staff hangs from a leather lace on the wall: it's painted blue and red, and dates from well before the modern Bobby. Wil Bryan, used to look at it and say. 'I wonder how many poor fellows have been knocked over the head with that weapon.'

One of my favourite memories, dates from when I used to walk to Y Twmpath holding mother's hand. I would hold a taper to light Thomas Bartley's pipe. Since her spirit has flown on to the next world, such memories have crowded on me.

Seth's simple soul was the first to pass to glory from Y Twmpath, but I am sure it wasn't the last. When a member of the family leaves home, news about the place where he's gone becomes precious. If the country is a good one, the chances are this will create a desire for the whole family to follow. Would Jacob have gone to Egypt, had his son Joseph had not been there to greet him? Thomas and Barbara Bartley became more interested in the next world once Seth had gone before.

Holding prayer meetings in their house was one way to learn more about the affairs of that world to come. For some time I'd been taking part in their gatherings, to the great approval of Thomas Bartley.

'Rhys my lad, you are as well read as a parson,' he would say.

Old Thomas, who only had a grip of the letters, was secretly amazed that any young man should be able to read at all.

I was pleased when Dafydd Davies asked me to discuss a chapter at a prayer meeting in Thomas Bartley's house. I spent every spare minute of the next week thinking about the task. I struggled to decide which chapter of the Scriptures to take as my text. At first I thought one of the parables might be suitable. But, having chosen one, I quickly found I couldn't think of much to say about it. Perhaps an exposition on one of the miracles might be easier to draw lessons from. However, once I started to think it through I decided I'd made another mistake. It would be easier to deal with a single verse rather than a whole chapter. But if I did that it would make everyone think I wanted to become a preacher on my first outing.

If Dafydd Davis had chosen a chapter and asked me to discuss it I might have found it easier. It seemed simple to talk sense about a verse or chapter, when I heard the preacher doing so. Now that I had to do it myself, I realized how difficult it was.

How often have I heard brethren say, 'Why, I could have preached a better sermon than that myself!'

If you believe that, then try and do it. You will soon see you can't. If it were so easy, then why would so many folk find themselves in such a sweat over writing a few lines of a letter to their aunt? The words that read most simply and roll off the preacher's lips the easiest, are those that have cost the most sweat to write.

I spent days changing my texts, and being unable to choose a portion of the Bible to say something sensible about. As I became pressed for time I had to make a choice. I read all the commentaries I could find, and wrote out every word I meant to say. I then memorized my speech and timed how long it took to deliver; it wouldn't do to for it to be too long or too short. By the night of meeting I felt pretty well prepared and confident I could make a good impression. This was an important occasion for me, and I began to think of it as the beginning of my ministerial career.

I was daydreaming of what would happen after I had spoken a little about a chapter in the house of Thomas Bartley. Only Dafydd Davis and I realized it was going to happen. Nobody else knew that I had been given a week to prepare. I fancied it would take several people by surprise.

I imagined them talking after the meeting: one would say, 'Didn't the boy discourse well on that chapter tonight? He's got the makings of a preacher in him, to be sure. I was quite astonished.'

His companion would reply, 'I didn't much wonder, there was always something serious about him.'

I imagined these scenes and other such vain imaginings. The only person with deep knowledge of the bible at these home prayer meetings was Dafydd Davis, and he was always so kind to me that he didn't make me feel at all nervous.

Wednesday night came, and I went to the meeting a little late, so as to be more like a preacher. One of the brethren was reading, and the room looked full. I sat near the doorway. Thomas Bartley beckoned me to sit nearer to the candles. I tried to signal back that I was fine where I was. Such modesty made me out to be nobody, though I secretly thought myself somebody that night. I was enjoying acting out this mock humility. But Thomas kept beckoning. As I didn't want to attract attention I moved closer. When I sat down, closer to the candle light, I saw Wil Bryan in the far corner. As I caught his gaze, he gave me one of his special winks. He closed his eyelid only about a tenth of the width of his eye, but the gesture was full of meaning.

I felt a great lump fill my breast. The Evil One must have invited Wil to that meeting, for he hadn't been for many months. I felt timid in his presence. A brother prayed, but I didn't listen. I tried to collect my scattered thoughts. The lump in my chest got bigger and started to choke my throat. It wasn't that I was afraid of Wil, but I would rather he hadn't come that evening.

Dafydd Davis called another of the brethren to lead us in a hymn. As we were singing a stanza my legs began to tremble. I couldn't reason with them or get them to stop. Then I remembered that Dafydd Davis he said that he would call me forward to speak. I didn't want Wil to think I was doing it on my own initiative. Then I started to worry that Dafydd wouldn't remember, in which case I resolved to do nothing but lead a prayer.

My resolution steadied my legs, and somewhat reduced the lump in my breast. The second brother finished praying, and then Dafydd Davis stood up and beckoned to me.

'Rhys Lewis, come forward, my son,' he said. 'And continue the service and discourse a little upon a chapter.'

There was no escape. I had to go through with it. I went forward, determined to do the best I could. I couldn't look at Wil Bryan, yet I couldn't avoid seeing him. His expression spoke clearly to me, and what it said was, 'I told you that you were bound to be a preacher.'

I began by reading out the chapter I had chosen. I could hardly recognize my own voice, I sounded so hoarse. Then, as I started to discuss what I had read, every thought and prepared word took flight, never to be seen again. I felt as though the room was getting darker and the people farther away. The candle, like my breath, seemed on the point of going out. I could feel myself rambling and drying up. The next thing I remember was hearing Dafydd Davis begin to pray in a loud and rousing voice.

I was eaten up with shame. The castle I had built so carefully had collapsed and my heart lay buried in its ruins. I was an object of pity to all present and it was galling to my ambitious spirit. But I had a crumb of comfort, only Dafydd Davis knew I had been given a week to prepare. All the others thought it was unplanned. I slunk away as quickly as possible when the meeting was over. I didn't look at a soul. But I couldn't escape my old companion. Wil cornered me before I could get through the yard gate.

'Don't take so hard because it didn't go so well, old fellow,' Wil said. 'I'm sorry, but you weren't really ready for it. I felt so bad seeing you break down. But never say die. It wasn't all your fault. You shouldn't have tried to do an impromptu exposition. There aren't many university dons who could've done it, not on the spur of the moment. If Dafydd Davis had any sense he'd given you a few days to prepare. It's too much to drop on a man there and then and ask him to expound a chapter. If only you'd had some notice, I'll swear you'd have been able to say something decent. As it was, you were bound to make a fool of yourself. When Dafydd called you forward I assumed you knew about it but as soon as you started I could see you were unprepared. I think you were brave to try what you did, what with you not expecting it. I wish I knew as much Scripture as you, and you're not short of common sense. But there's one thing you lack and that's what the English call cheek. What's the Welsh word for cheek?'

'*Haerllugrwydd*,' I suggested.

'No that's arrogance in the English,' Wil said. 'I mean cheek. I'd say *boch* in the Welsh.'

I nodded my head, agreeing that *boch* was the better word.

'It's not quite brazen-facedness, although they're similar. 'Cheek, in my opinion, is a fine art. Every man ought to cultivate some measure of it. Cheek is not as vulgar as impudence; it's a higher order. A mule is impudent in that he isn't shy, but a mule isn't cheeky. A bantam cock is cheeky, but he's not impudent. Cheek is self-confidence, when you've nothing to be confident about. I'm trying to explain myself clearly but I've got the same problem you had, I've not prepared my ideas. I'm not saying that cheek is good in itself, but it's a means to an end. Many a good man lived and died without the world knowing anything about him, just because he lacked cheek, while others who had nothing more than cheek got right to the top of the tree. A man with cheek doesn't believe anybody is better than himself unless they prove it. A man with a retiring disposition won't get on in this world. But he might do well in the next, because the Almighty puts value on humility. He knows it's such a rare thing.'

I nodded in agreement, encouraging him to go on.

'But, as we have to live in this world,' Wil said, 'I think cheek should be cultivated. Ninety-nine out of every hundred men are duffers. But more often than not cheek will stand in for talent and knowledge.'

He stopped as he realized what he had just said.

'I don't mean to say that you don't have talent, Rhys. Let me try and explain. Think about two men. One with talent but no cheek, and one with cheek but no talent. I'll give you an example. Two travellers who call on the old Gaffer yonder. There's Mr Davies, who's long-headed, quiet, always dresses the same and understands the grocery trade perfectly. He never tells lies, and accepts it when my father says he has no order to give. Then there's Mr Hardcastle. He has no more in his head than a mouse has, but he buys a new suit of clothes every three months. He's all pockets, cuffs, collars and rings. He's impossible to insult and he won't take no for an answer. He's learned a dozen or so set phrases, most of them lies, that he reels off exactly the same way each time he calls. He's sure to get an order, because he's cheeky, and father's a duffer. But d'ye know what? If the gaffer's away I give Mr Davies a thundering good order because he's true to nature. As to Mr Hardcastle, I'd like to spit on his white waistcoat. But Mr Hardcastle is a man for this world, because most shopkeepers are duffers. But that's my point. If you want to get on Rhys, you must cultivate cheek. Your talent and your knowledge will be worthless without some cheek.'

I hung my head but Wil hadn't finished with me yet. Now he started to develop his argument by quoting scripture.

'The Good Book gives you lots of examples of this. Now, I'm not much of an authority on the Bible, so if I'm wrong, you must correct me, but John was cleverer than Peter. But who became the master? Just fancy Peter's cheek, he stepped forward to preach at the very next meeting, after playing that dirty trick and everybody knowing he'd done it. That's the coolest bit of *haerllugrwydd* I ever heard of. If John had done anything half so shabby, he'd have been too ashamed to open his mouth again. And there's that woman from Samaria who came and asked Christ to cure her son.'

I knew Wil was thinking of the woman of Canaan and her daughter but I decided not to correct him.

'She wouldn't be put off, because she had plenty of cheek,' he went on, 'and she got just what she wanted. I've often thought that woman would have made a first rate commercial traveller. She'd never leave a shop without an order.'

He cocked his head on one side and looked me in the eye. 'I'm speaking without notes in a cheeky impromptu way, so am I making clear what I mean by cheek?'

I felt he was being more than clear, so I nodded for him to go on.

'You won't get on if you're nervous, and cheek is the perfect cure for nervousness.' He leaned towards me. 'I am going to tell you the rules of being cheeky.' He paused for effect.

'Never blush,' he said. 'When you say something silly I've often seen you redden up like a girl, right up to your ears. It isn't manly. If ever you slip up pretend that what you've said or done is the best thing in the world. Nine out ten folk won't even notice that you make a mistake if you keep cool and carry on. Never sit by the door at public meetings. Always find a seat near the front, and when you stand up make sure you're on tip toe. You're not as tall as me, Rhys, and I'm none too tall myself. Make sure everyone knows you're there. Whenever you get the chance speak up, and don't be afraid to interrupt. Make sure you learn by heart at least twenty stock phrases you can use for any subject; after that all you need to do is vary them a bit. Then you'll always have something to say, even if you can't think of anything new. But make sure you do speak. I've seen many a dull man stand up and accidentally say something good. All the other duffers have immediately noted him down as a genius.'

I grinned as he rushed on in full flow.

'When you go to a public meeting make sure you shake hands with any reporters, both before and after,' he said. 'But keep up your dignity, and you'll be well written up. There are some who write reports about themselves but it's not true to nature, so avoid it.'

I must have looked quizzical, for he stopped for a moment as if waiting for me to object. But I kept quiet.

'I know what you're thinking, Rhys,' he said. 'Wil Bryan is just telling me about the way of this world. It's not the way of religion. But hear me out and I'll show you there's more of this sort of thing going on in religion than you've realized. You've got two things against you. Firstly your voice isn't strong, and secondly you're too weedy. Now it's not in your family to grow stout, but you'll find thinness a disadvantage. Just imagine a thin man telling you something in a squeaky voice then picture a solidly built man saying exactly the same thing in double bass voice. Which is going to impress you the most? The duffers will hear the fat chap as a great man, and the thin guy with the weedy voice as a snob. But I'm drifting away from my text, which is the art and practice of cheek. The English always beat us Welsh people hollow for cheek. You'll never hear an Englishman say he can't do something. If you were to believe him there's nothing he can't do. The duffers will take him at his word. Often you'll find Jack Jones, who's a pretty good sort but doesn't know it himself, touching his hat and taking pleasure in watching John Bull steal his bread and cheese. What's John Bull's great secret? I'll tell you, its cheek. Now do you understand?'

I nodded silently at him but he wasn't yet sure I knew enough so he continued his lesson.

'A man without cheek looks worse than he is,' he said, warming to his topic, 'while a cheeky man looks better than he is. Now I hate a humbug and I like a man who's true to nature. But there's a risk that a man who has no cheek will look less than he should. Even so, you need something more than just cheek. Cheek is handy, and cuts the mustard with many people. But if it's all you've got, then you'll be found out by the wide-awakes. At least, that's what I think. And when you want to seem eloquent, remember what Lord Broughton said. The secret is preparation, preparation and more preparation. Never try to speak in public without preparation, not unless you are full of cheek and have learned a set of phrases that will serve the occasion.'

He paused and looked and looked down before continuing.

'I'm sorry but I'm not quite square with the guv'nor ... that clock incident you know,' he said. 'Otherwise I'd ask you over for supper in in instant. But, things as they are, I can't. So cheer up old boy. Take what I said to heart and stop looking so fed up.'

With that he left me, calling back over his shoulder, 'So long.'

I was glad Wil didn't know that I'd had a week's notice to prepare, and his words hadn't comforted me, they had made me worse. I was glad to escape from him and go home. I didn't realize, though, that I had escaped from Wil's frying pan only to fall down into the hot coals of the fire.

When I got in, Miss Hughes had left some supper for me on the table, and Abel sat smoking in his arm-chair. Miss Hughes had already retired. I sat down near him, thankful that Abel didn't know about my breakdown, but also fearful he would be sure to find out before long.

As I finished my food he asked me about the prayer meeting. Who was there? How did the meeting go? Who took part in it? And so on. I answered briefly as possible. I suspected, from what I saw as a half-sarcastic smile that kept flitting across his face, that someone had told him what had happened.

Finally, he came to the point. 'How did you get along with your discussion of a chapter?' he said.

'Someone has told you,' I said. With that my feelings overcame me and I burst into tears.

'What's the matter with you?' Abel asked, when I finally managed to compose myself. 'All I know is that Dafydd Davis asked you a week since to prepare something for tonight's meeting. What's happened? Why are you so upset?'

I poured my heart out and told him all about my disaster. He listened in silence.

'Never mind,' he said, when I had finished my tale. 'You'll look back on this experience and see it as a blessing.' And he broke into song, to a popular English tune I recognized as *Banks of Sweet Primroses*. 'There's many a dark and cloudy morning that turns out a sun-shiny day.'

He stopped singing and smiled at me.

'Now,' he said. 'Tell me, what do you think of preaching as a vocation?'

'I used to think about it,' I said, unable to keep a mournful tone out of my voice, 'but now I know I'll never be able to do it.'

'Don't be ridiculous,' returned Abel. 'Every good carter started out by overturning in his dray once or twice as he learned how to drive his horse well. And we all had an occasional stumble before we learned to walk. You took quite few tumbles before you became sure-footed. You would never learn to swim if you give up the first time your head went under water.'

He looked at me, smiled and waited. Finally, I had to smile back despite my dismal feelings.

'The first step in any useful life is often a stumble,' he said. 'And the greatest success usually follows an early failure. I've thought for some time that you were thinking about taking up preaching. That's why I encouraged you to attend so many services and meetings. If I didn't think you had it in you, then I'd have told you long ago.'

He looked at me in silence for a moment.

'If you've set your mind on the ministry, don't let anything get in your way. There is no more honourable calling. If I could start my life over again, I would try to become a preacher and make my life of real use. I prefer the word preacher to parson, minister or pastor. Preacher carries in it the idea of a pulpit and the religious influences which made Wales what it is. There's a sacredness about the title preacher that inspires me. When Wales confuses the function of a preacher with that of a clergyman then we will have lost something precious. When I was young, the deacon used to announce, 'We expect Mr Elias to preach here next Sabbath,' but now you often hear them say, 'The Reverend Peter Smart will minister here next Sunday.'

He shook his head.

'What I fear is that their reverence is for the Reverend, and not for the preaching skill of Peter Smart.' He said. 'No earthly title expresses the veneration in a Welshman's heart for the true preacher. Long may it continue that such love should be earned in the pulpit. We should give our preachers the best education, and they should go to college, to develop their natural talent. But an education alone won't make a man a preacher. He must win the congregation's respect for his preaching. Only the other day I read in the newspaper a self-opinionated individual rebuking Wales for having too great a respect for preachers. But there's no higher compliment he could pay the old country. I often fear our churches now let anyone preach who offers himself, and that respect for the preacher is being lost. I've often wondered what makes a good preacher. His duties acquaint him to the highest happiness attainable on earth, and give him the best preparation against the terrors of death and the world to come. In this world he gets the best respect that man has, and when he enters the world eternal, the King Himself will welcome him as a good and faithful servant. Even the most successful shopkeeper is a beggar in rags beside a true preacher. Who recalls the names of those rich carousers in castles, sixty years on? Nobody. But the names of great preachers live on in the hearts even of those who never heard their actual voices.'

Abel reached over and poked the fire. The coals flared, lighting up his face, and I could see the deep sincerity of his feelings being reflected through the fire in his eyes.

'I don't want to discourage you,' he said, 'but you need to be sure of your real motives. If you're not actuated by the purest intentions you would do better to go and hang yourself. I have great sympathy with someone who wants to preach but who's stuck dumb by the awful responsibility of the work. If you eye the pulpit just to feed your ambition, so that people honour you, then God will frown upon you. You will make yourself lower than the devils and an object of derision for thieves and murderers. Remember what one English poet said of such a man.'

He took a deep breath, sat quietly for a moment to compose himself. And then began to recite from memory.

> Among the accursed who sought a hiding place in vain from the fierceness of Jehovah's rage and to avoid the searing displeasure of the Lamb, a place was kept among the most wretched, vile and contemptible for the false priest. There his conscience felt the foulest bite of the undying worm.

He felt so strongly that I should only have pure motives for becoming a preacher that he spat out the last words. He sighed and gathered himself together before saying any more.

'I have often thought Paul must have experienced a sort of electric shock when he said, "I bring the urges of my body into subjection lest when I preach to others I should be cast away."'

He looked me straight in the eye.

'I've no wish to scare you into setting aside your intention to preach,' he said. 'I want to help you if your motives are pure. It might help you understand yourself if you study the first preachers, the apostles. They weren't perfect in their intentions any more than we are. But their love for their Master was genuine. I don't doubt that. Remember what Peter said. "To whom shall we go?" he asked on behalf of all the apostles. And his answer was his Master. "Thou hast the words of eternal life, and without Thee we shall be without words, we shall have nothing to say." He was quite sure there was nobody worth speaking about except Christ.'

Abel had a kindly, fatherly look in his eye, as he continued.

'Rhys my boy,' he said. 'Take care you know your mind. If it is selfishness which pushes you to preach, that interest will soon burn out, and you'll become a burden to yourself and everybody else. You'll be on a treadmill of commitments in places where they accept you rather than have no preacher at all on the Sabbath. But if you are inspired by the fire of Heaven, then your motivation won't falter. You'll find sinners huddle around you to warm their shivering souls and bask in the warmth of your message. But there's no more pitiful being than a preacher who is scorned by God for being materialist and earthly.'

The fire was dying down, and Abel's face sank into the shadows with only a single candle to light his it.

'Make up your mind from the start, Rhys,' he said. 'If you want to become a preacher you must devote yourself completely to the work. You cannot keep a shop as well. The stock of souls a preacher looks after is too important to give you any spare time to look after the stock of a shop. I will do what I can for you. I'm not poor but neither am I rich. I may be able to help you with some money, for you will need money. Young preachers are usually badly off. It must be difficult for a student, no matter how large and warm his heart, to get along on an empty pocket. How useful he would find a ten-pound note from one of the wealthy, but they rarely bother to offer one. And if they do, they proclaim the fact throughout the length and breadth of the country at the Monthly Meeting and brand the poor fellow as a beggar. I find such behaviour scandalous. It's no wonder deserving youths bear their hardship in silence rather than see their name blazoned abroad as the recipient of a few pounds. Don't expect preaching to be a paying business, in the worldly sense. You'll only be disappointed. There are many better ways of making money. You sometimes hear it said that preachers are avaricious. To my mind that is a libel, and is put about by those who are money-grubbers themselves. Most preachers, who depend on preaching for their livelihood, live hand to mouth. It's true that there's a special Providence watches over the most deserving of them. Sometimes God lets them find favour in the hearts of rich young women who take pity on them. Rhys, if you want to become a preacher you must watch and pray against idleness and self-will. I don't know what went wrong at tonight's meeting, but consider whether you were more interested in winning honour or in helping the brethren to understand the word of the Lord.'

Abel had understood my inner thoughts almost as well as I did myself. I had been more interested in gaining honour than in passing on the message of our Saviour.

CHAPTER 33

More of Wil Bryan

Wil Bryan's practical comments and Abel Hughes's serious and encouraging advice had left me more uncertain than ever. I resolved to give up the idea of preaching, and I prayed every day to be freed from my desire, even though I secretly hoped God would ignore my prayer. I felt as if two minds lived inside my head. One wanted to preach more than anything else in the world; the other just kept telling the would-be preacher to give up being so silly. Yet my heart wanted the preacher to win.

If Dafydd Davis had left me alone I might have accepted the sensible advice to forget my ambitions, but he did not. I had considered all the advice offered to me and decided that real enemy was my own ego. Abel Hughes had warned me against it, and the more I thought about it the more I was sure that my ego had a finger in all my problems. I decided I would not do anything public to further my preaching cause unless I had first destroyed the power of my ego by introspection.

When I told Dafydd Davis, I thought he was going to burst out laughing, as I watched a broad grin spread across his face.

'Your intention is excellent,' he said, 'But you couldn't think of anything more selfish. In twenty years' time you'll be no better off if you stick to it. You can't destroy your ego by doing nothing. It's only by doing your duty that you'll subdue your ego, and bring it to task. The more you chase after it the more it will hide from you. You won't kill it by retreating into yourself, you'll have to call it out and crucify it. But don't be surprised if you find your ego is still alive even when you get as old as me. Killing your ego is like a conjuring trick I have heard about which is done by some entertainers in England. They take hold of their hair with their left hand and use their right hand to smite off their head with a sword, or seem to. But the next minute up pops their head, back in place. When I first heard that story I realized that was just what I had been doing with my ego. Some days I felt I had forced its head onto the block, and cut it off, but the following day it'd be back, as strong as ever. If you do nothing until you've killed your ego you will do nothing. The best way is to neglect it and devote yourself to God's service. The Gospel apprentices you to doing good. And an apprentice you will remain in this world. You don't become master of the business until you cross to the next. I often doubt my own motives, but when I can't rise to higher ground, I try my hand at a little good, just to spite the devil, and show him I want none of his friendship.'

Dafydd was trying his best to help, and I listened to what he said. I understood that by taking part in a public meeting at the request of the more experienced brethren I was not indulging my ego, but rather following their guidance. In that way I could share the responsibility for my development with them. The more I practiced, the easier it became to speak. I didn't suffer another breakdown like the one which had so devastated me at Thomas Bartley's house. I began to acquire at least a small ability to speak at the meetings, although it often proved hard for me to do. The little skill in speaking that I acquired became a source of great comfort to me, and I would often find myself humming, a tune as I left a meeting.

How could it be sinful, I asked myself, to enjoy a thrill of silent pleasure when Dafydd Davis or another elder gave me a word of praise? When preachers stayed at Abel Hughes's house, they seemed to enjoy their meal more if the meeting had gone well. If knowing they had earned their meal by the quality of their preaching made them feel better, that was good enough for me.

Step by small step I found myself taking on the role of a candidate for the ministry. But I felt I was putting on a bridle which anyone could tug at. If I stayed out late, then before someone else did I would ask myself, 'What do you want, out at this time of night?' If I was amused enough to laugh, then I would worry I might have laughed too loudly. If I was fortunate enough to speak to a young woman, which I occasionally did, then I felt as if the whole town was watching me and judging the propriety of my behaviour. I was losing my freedom, and I felt obliged to step up to officiate at any prayer meeting if I was asked. I was becoming public property.

Everybody seemed to want to advise me. But the advice I got was so wide, varied and conflicting that it only confused me. First, I was told that if I wanted to preach I should take it slowly; next, I was told that if I wanted to preach I should get on with it and waste no time. I was advised to read as much as possible and not waste my time going to prayer meetings and also told that I should read less and get about more. Someone would advise me to keep up with literature, politics and every new book I could get hold of, as this would prepare me to be a modern preacher. But others warned me to leave such things alone and spend all my spare time reading the Bible, as this was the most important trait of a good preacher.

'Whatever you do,' one adviser said, 'don't go to college to be spoiled.'

'You'll have to go to college, or you'll never be worth anything,' said another. 'Even if you learn nothing, people will respect you for going.'

'Be free and easy with everybody,' said yet another self-appointed mentor. 'I hate a stuck-up preacher.'

'Remember to be reserved and don't give people chance to gossip,' said one well-intentioned old lady.

I met up with Wil Bryan one evening.

'I've been getting lots of conflicting advice about how to become a preacher,' I said and told him the examples I've mentioned above.

'You need to use your common sense, Rhys,' Wil said. 'And if you haven't got any common sense then forget about preaching. You'll have to mind your Ps and Qs, and keep your sense of proportion; you're acting a like rooster stepping through snow for the first time. You need to be true to your nature, because grace never goes against sinless nature. There must be a verse somewhere about it, although I can't recall it. I'll quote old Cromwell to you. He said. Trust in God and keep your powder dry, and he wasn't a duffer. If you follow everyone's advice, you'll kill yourself. We'll all be shaking our heads and wailing, Alas poor Rhys. Just be civil to everyone, but only take advice from the wide-awakes.'

As ever, Wil talked good sense, and after speaking to him I felt better about my situation.

I resigned myself to being seen as a candidate while I waited for my case to be put before the *Seiat*. In my heart I really wanted to become a preacher but I felt young and inexperienced. I wanted to prove to myself, and to the deacons who supported me, that I was ready. I didn't want to find both I and my supporters had been wrong, and so end up sorry.

To be honest, I also wanted to avoid having to preach a trial sermon in the *Seiat*. Quite often candidates for the ministry were asked to preach in *Seiat*, to show what they were made of. This is an unnatural way to test a young man's capacity and fitness. Why ask him to preach to a congregation of critics, not to spread the Word, but just to show off his ability? I resolved to do nothing to provoke such an ordeal. Better to remain a potential candidate than be put through such a proof. There were many chances to show the brethren that I was suitable for the ministry without exposing myself to such a disadvantageous situation.

I had another reason to delay the matter. I wanted to be sure that my desire was real and my motives pure. Abel Hughes had mentioned to me that he knew young men who were plagued with a preaching fit, but with the passage of time realized the ministry was not for them. I worried that I might be having just such a fit. If this were the case, then it would pass naturally.

I had a strange feeling that if my motives were pure, then perhaps the Lord would send me a sign, even though I reasoned such a thing might be impossible. Still, I couldn't suppress a vain ray of hope. I often find I yearn for the impossible.

Months passed, but my preaching fit continued. I used every chance I got to talk with visiting preachers, hoping to learn from them how they had felt when they were a candidate. But they could tell me little that I had not already experienced. I persistently hoped they had met with something I had not considered. My imagination conjured up a whole range of terrors that lay in wait for me if my vocation was not well founded. Despite all this soul-searching, as far as I knew I was not moved by any false intentions.

I constantly worried what people thought of me.

'Whom do men say that I am?' I kept asking myself. 'I have set my mind to preaching but I do not actively seek a license. If I have a desire to preach I should be able to reveal a soul of fire and let my ardour speak out.' I felt it was useless for me to try to act this way, because the memory of my misguided youth disqualified me. I mentioned my misgivings to Abel Hughes.

'I've never expected a young man to be much good at counselling or speaking to a mixed congregation,' Abel said. 'He's not an experienced elder. I think it's unnatural, and I doubt if any good comes from it. I'd rather see a young preacher half drowning than see him paddling safely near the bank. And when a youth of twenty imitates an old man it also grates on me as much as if an old man of eighty were to squabble over a game of marbles. It's a sign of weakness in either case.'

My attempts to address meetings in the houses and small chapels of the vicinity felt dreary and moralistic. I think this was because of the restrictions I placed on myself. If I was filled with zeal, I forced myself to cool down. I did not want to appear self-assertive. I had once seen a young preacher chatting casually with the congregation when he came to old Betty Kenrick.

'Well, old sister,' he said. 'Do you know Jesus Christ at this time?'

'I hope so,' Betty said. 'And I did so long before your father was born, you young sprog.'

I don't endorse Betty speaking so nastily to a young man who was a stranger to her, but there is a moral to the encounter. I suspect that young man didn't feel quite as comfortable at the end of the *Seiat* as he had at the start.

I enjoyed helping out in small country chapels when they had no preacher. Then Dafydd Davis spoke to me.

'Rhys,' he said. 'I think it's time for me to put your case as a candidate for the ministry formally to the *Seiat*. What do you say?'

I was filled with dismay. I wondered if I should back out, but my heart urged me to go on and preach. What was clear, though, was that I couldn't stay a potential candidate for ever. If Dafydd put my cause forward, I knew I would be aiming high. I would be putting myself above the rest of the church and taking on the very responsibility that I dreaded. I fancied I heard a quiet voice whisper in my ear, 'What hast thou to do to declare my statutes?'

I prayed for clear vision, but it didn't come. How could I seek to preach if I had no sign to prove my calling? But I couldn't bear giving up my ambition to preach. It seemed inexplicable that I didn't understand myself. If I couldn't understand myself, how could I expect others to understand me? Did Dafydd have a clearer estimation of me than I did of myself? I decided to follow his judgment and let things take their course.

'If you think I'm ready, then put my name forward,' I said.

Some days later my cause was brought before the weekly *Seiat*. I'm not going to give a verbatim report of what went on. Sufficient to say that many questions were asked of me, and I replied as I felt without attempting to paint myself in any different light from the truth. The meeting then asked me to withdraw while they discussed my merits.

I stood outside the chapel, waiting for the verdict. Had my answers made people think I was not up to the task? I did not expect my application would be easily accepted. Indeed, I almost wished it wouldn't be, so that the matter would be finally put to rest. At long last they called me back in.

'The meeting has agreed to refer your case to a full monthly meeting, Rhys,' Dafydd said. 'Some of the brethren will be asked to look into the matter and take the mood of the whole church.'

I bowed my head in thanks. It was good that I wasn't asked to speak in reply, for I hadn't a word to say. My thoughts were in turmoil as I left the chapel and set off back home.

During this memoir I have written a lot about Wil Bryan. His friendship has been a great influence throughout my life, and I was glad to see my old pal at the *Seiat* that evening. He was not a regular attender, because he did not have a natural inclination towards religion, even though he was a full member of the church. And I admired his generous spirit, open heart, shrewdness, and sharp, ready tongue so much that I overlooked his numerous failings

I was glad to see him at the *Seiat* when my cause was discussed, as I knew he would give me an honest account of what happened while I was outside. I feared he was indifferent to religion, and this had almost driven me away from him, but I valued his friendship too much to throw it away. I believe he was also fond of me, although he would never admit the fact. There was probably no other living person who took a greater interest in my welfare than him. It had grieved me of late that Wil was becoming less and less regular in his attendance at chapel. His parents seemed to have drifted away, and without their influence he had not felt any need to come.

As we left the meeting I was waiting for Wil, instead of Wil for me.

'Just the thing,' said he. 'I wanted to talk to you.'

'I knew you'd tell me what happened, Wil,' I said. 'What did they say after they turned me out?'

'If I give you a verbatim report it will only upset you,' said he. 'But what tickled my fancy was seeing the Old Scraper insisting that you had to preach before the *Seiat*, so that they could see what sort of stuff was in you. Abel stood up and said that would be fine if you had just arrived from America, and no one knew you, but they already knew you perfectly well, so that was the end of that. The only other thing which stood out was that the old thoroughbred Thomas Bartley put up both hands at the voting and when challenged apologized for having to vote for Barbara, because she'd stayed at home with a bad go of the rheumatics.'

I couldn't help smiling at Thomas's enthusiastic support for my cause.

'Tonight, Rhys,' Wil said, 'you've got to the point I have long been hoping for. You've made my conscience easier tonight than it's been for a while. I know I led you astray. That night we nearly hanged Jones I dreamt your mother came back to tell me off. She frowned at me, and I'll never forget the look on her face. I've never been easy about what I did to you since. But tonight you and I are at a junction I knew we would one day come to. We've travelled together a long way, but we're bound for different destinations. From tonight we head different ways. Have you heard about what happened over yonder with my old folk?'

'Heard what, Wil?' I said. 'I don't understand.'

'It's all up back there,' he said. 'Everybody'll know before the week's out.' He shook his head as if trying the clear it.

'I can't stand it,' he said. 'I told you my father was a bit of duffer. I used to think he was coining it and a clever operator who knew a bargain. But when I found out how things stood, I realized just how big a duffer he is. I've seen it coming for a while. I've never been able to get him to change. He's stuck in a rut and won't listen. If he'd been a mule he would insist on crossing a field of clover to browse in the hedge on thistles and rubbish like that. And what do you think are the consequences?'

He looked at me with a deep sadness in his eyes.

'I don't know,' I said.

'Why others have eaten all the clover, Rhys,' he said. 'There's nothing left, not even hedge rubbish. All he can do is voluntary liquidation and starvation. I've got to get out.'

'Where will you go?' I said.

'I don't know,' Wil said, a touch of bitterness edging his voice. 'Next week I'll come of age and I'll have as much to my name as I had twenty-one years ago. I've not had much more schooling than you but I fancy I'm not stupid. I've always I kept a close watch on human nature; it's the best trick for someone who's not had much education. But I made a big mistake in not studying my bread and cheese. I'm neither a gentleman nor tailor. I've not been behind the counter enough to learn how to serve, not that I'm that way inclined.' He smiled at me.

'My great joy has always been to drive a horse,' he said. 'I didn't care if it was a load of bread or a load of young girls, as long as I had a horse to handle. I can manage the reins as good as any man. But next week, Huw Bryan, provision dealer, won't own a horse for me to drive. And there's too much of a difference between driving your own horse and driving somebody else's'.

'You could find another job,' I said.

'As what?' he asked. 'Can you see me as a gentleman's servant? I'd rather break stones, and that's the meanest job I know. I couldn't stomach taking cash for having to put my hand to my hat all the time. So what can I do? How do I merit my bread and cheese? It's a novel question for me, and I don't know the answer. You know how I was brought up, I wanted for nothing except good advice. I always had a jolly dinner set before me. But how'll it be next week? I just don't know.'

'I've never seen you so down in the mouth before Wil,' I said. 'You've left me lost for words. How did things get so bad?'

'It's too long to tell,' he said. 'I'm sorry from my heart for the gaffer, and I don't want to be hard on him. But it's his own fault. If he'd only kept to his own business, things might have gone all right. The old man was always a bit greedy. And once he'd made a bit of money, someone encouraged him to speculate. For a year I've been begging him to stop, but he wouldn't. He's been tipping up fifty pounds a month. How could he keep that up? If he'd taught me how to make a living I shouldn't mind so. If I had been my own father I'd have brought myself up much better. The town folk will probably call me selfish for running out, but I can't bear the disgrace. And there's Suzie, poor girl. How can I look her in the face now? She's just lucky there's nothing definite between us.'

'This is a great shock, Wil' I said. 'Your help and sympathy have been precious to me over the years but I've never known you need sympathy yourself. Will you take one piece of advice from an old friend?'

'What's that, old man?'

'If you go, and no matter where to, please get a ticket of membership. Then when you're settled in a new home, enquire for a chapel and send on your ticket to the deacons. I am so afraid you'll go wrong Wil. Please promise me to take care of your soul.'

'I'd hoped you wouldn't mention this,' Wil said. 'It's been on my mind for a long time to talk to you. If I asked for a ticket it would be an act of pure humbug. I've put on an act for too long. There isn't the least spark of religion about me. Do you remember your mother once telling me there was an old man in my heart, and I made fun of her?'

I nodded without speaking.

'Well your mother was right,' he said. 'She saw my depravity even if she put an odd name to it. I'm afraid I'm gospel-proof, as every verse tells against me. I've not read the Bible for years because the only verses I saw spoke against me. I haven't killed anybody. I haven't wronged anybody. I don't drink, but still I've been left behind. What have I done? Lots of little things. I've learned comic songs instead of the Bible and gone to the billiard table more often than to the Lord's Table. I've poked fun at everybody and everything. I've poked fun at Williams of Pantycelyn's hymns by making up parodies. If a preacher in the chapel has come near to bowling me clean, I've stuck out my bat and been ready. But all they've ever done is bowl me wides. I wasn't brought up like you. Father made me go to chapel every Sunday. But there was never any talk of chapel, or religion afterwards. Father treated me as Ned the blacksmith did a piece of iron. He'd drive me to chapel on Sunday and put my conscience to the fire, then on Monday he'd dowse me in the water-trough. That's why I've got as hard as a horseshoe.'

'Wil ...,' I began.

'Don't interrupt,' he said. 'You're going to tell me repent and make a fresh start. I know what to do; I just don't feel I can do it. A man can't repent as if he is simply signing the pledge. True repentance needs a change of heart; that's what the Bible says. It's full of verses against me. I feel that I want to repent, but I'm being carried along as if in a crowd of people, and can't help myself. Your mother, the Good Lord bless her, gave me lots of good advice. You remember you were upset when I called her Old Ten Commandments.'

I nodded in silence, trying to stop a tear welling in my eye.

'She was always telling me what I should do.' Wil said. 'I knew she was right and resolved to do as she told me, after I'd had my fling. But I've taken too big a fling and I can't come back. I'm gone past feeling; nothing in the world affects me anymore. I may be young in years but I'm old in insolence and inflexibility. I'm tired of myself but I'm not repentant. I only feel remorse, not repentance ... not what I believe repentance is.'

'Wil *bach*,' I said. 'Thou forgettest that God is ...'

'Oh, don't talk!' he cut me off. 'You're going to tell me God is merciful, that I should pray to Him, and so on. I've already tried that in the quiet of my heart, and it felt like sponging. I know I've offended

God with my parodies of old Pantycelyn's hymns, for I'll bet the Almighty and old Pant are great chums. He'll never forgive me for what I've done, so let's drop it. Good night my old friend.'

He gripped my hand and pressed it firmly, then turned and hurried away before I could say anything more. I resolved to seek him out in the morning and to try to change his mind.

Early next morning the delivery lad from Hugh Bryan's shop brought me a note. It was addressed to The Rev. Rhys Lewis.

I opened it and read the following.

> Dear Old Fellow,
>
> So departs Wil Bryan. As the old song goes, it may be for years, or it may be forever. Keep along the path on which thou hast started, and profit by my bad example.
>
> Yours truly.
>
> Wil
>
> **P.S.** I have taken the liberty of being the first to address thee as Rev. I trust thou wilt maintain the title well.

CHAPTER 34

Thomas Bartley on Education

What makes a friendship? Is it similar interests? For two people to be friends do they have to have similar natures? Do friends have to share a viewpoint? I suspect that none of these ideas really describes a friendship. Mutual admiration is not a basis for friendship; there may be admiration without attachment, and closeness without approval. I have known individuals who will enjoy a friend laughing at them while not accepting it from anyone else. Perhaps friendship is an honour bestowed by the heart that is separate from any instinct of the soul.

Wil Bryan is totally different from me. We are unlike each other in disposition and ideas. But when he left, my heart was downcast, and I shed secret tears. Until he went I never realized how close-knit we were. I missed his company for months afterwards, and his absence left a great void in my heart.

His prediction about his father was proved true within a week. But, as I had nothing to do with that sad event, I will not comment on it. Once he had left I didn't hear anything at all from my old friend. I took this as a bad sign, as I recalled him once saying that if he ever left home, nobody would hear from him unless he had good news to send or had captured a wild elephant or a fought a tiger.

I don't think anyone should start an autobiography unless he intends to talk more about the people he knew than himself. A man who talks only about himself is boring. I have learned a great deal from watching how other people behave and noting their strengths and weaknesses.

The life of any ordinary young preacher does not change much from week to week. To keep describing it would not be particularly interesting to anyone but himself. But I said in my first chapter that the events of a commonplace life are so ordinary that no one bothers to write them down. I have read thousands of verses and popular sayings that illustrate the sentiments and encounters of the common people. Most are not poetic or outstanding, and their authors are unknown. Someone must have thought of the phrases Good Morning and Good Night. But who were they? There is nothing inspired about these common terms, but they convey a universal human feeling. The common people use these exact words every day in all places and settings. Yet we don't get bored with them or accuse their users of being trite. If the weather is fair, a thousand mouths will call it a fine day and think it the most original remark to make. A particular man may say it is a fine day twenty times and never feel he is repeating himself. A hungry man does not get fed up with the loaf which is put on his table three times a day. But if you stuff him full with a Christmas feast, once a week would more than satisfy him.

Nothing much out of the ordinary happened to me that might not have also happened in the life of any other young preacher, and so I intend to skip a whole year of my life. I do not think a detailed account of that time would be interesting.

Every young Calvinistic Methodist preacher must have lost sleep when he knew two emissaries of the *Seiat* were coming to cross-question him the next day. And most young preachers have probably been disappointed by the encounter. Most examiners are less alarming than they are imagined to be. And many must have found the questions asked were much easier to answer that they expected. How did they feel after preaching their first sermon? If they had put their heart into the job, then they would be sure to feel drained. They must have all found that a sermon imagined on paper was very different from the way it sounded when delivered from the pulpit. And they must all have found all those bits they had overlooked in the writing, which became obvious during the delivery.

I certainly found that my sermon was thin on substance towards the end, and finished rather raggedly and abruptly. Many a Sabbath night, in my bedroom, I have felt humiliated at how much more I thought of those who admired me than those who would not believe me. I often fell in my own estimation when I went to preach and no one came to listen. I despaired of ever getting to a point where I could exclude all selfish concerns and embrace the desire to serve God and benefit my fellow men. I hated having to raise the matter of the tithe when required to in my sermon, and felt belittled when I realized that I began to automatically work it into my text. I did not feel myself any different from my fellows who had not acknowledged a vocation as I had.

I began to see the *Seiat* in a different way, now I had to deal with it as a preacher. I must admit I viewed the hallowed and ancient institution in a new light. I knew that everyone present at the session was either a preacher or deacon, but I soon found that they were not the angels I had expected. The more I came to know the elders of the *Seiat*, the more I realized they were just like everyone else and had the same weaknesses as myself. They ate and drank like other people, and they could laugh heartily. Some would confer in whispers while one of the brethren was leading a prayer during the service. And some of them lost their tempers. I had previously thought highly of them, believing them to be spiritual and devotional. It was hard to retain this view when I saw brethren staying in the chapel house for a smoke while a brother completed the prayer which opened the meeting. When I got home after a service I found I was on better terms with myself if I reflected on the notion, 'we were all made from the same clay and all have our own weaknesses.'

I did discover that my best and truest friends were also the ablest and holiest members of the *Seiat*. It was the least faithful of the members who most discouraged me. When I preached to the county ministers, those I feared most proved the most considerate and cheering, and those I had most looked up to turned out to be the most patronizing and contemptuous.

Now that I had to preach Sunday after Sunday, I found I was beginning to do the work mechanically, and I was disappointed to find that my preaching did not stop my tendency to sin. The sacred calling placed new temptations in my path and drew out sinful tendencies that had previously been dormant.

I sometimes felt that my preaching created effects that were more useful to other people than they were to me. I knew I was not as sanctified and spotless as some people took me to be. I thanked God that my congregations were unaware of the uncertain state of my heart, but I did nothing to enlighten them. Indeed I caught myself thinking well of men whose insight and ability led them to agree with me, while judging those who differed as lacking judgment.

Many a time after a flat and disappointing Sabbath I vowed to give up preaching. Then after a particularly happy one I felt I was fulfilling my destiny. I still felt a sense of selfishness and depravity but began to get hints that convinced me my efforts were welcomed. At such times I would pray using the verse, 'Thou hast put gladness in my heart, more than in the time that their corn and their wine increased.'

These were the ordinary features of every young preacher's experience. I could write a whole chapter on them, but what would be the point? They are so common that nobody thinks them worth writing down. I had thought to describe them in detail, but as I see this autobiography growing in size, I have decided to leave it to someone else.

I preached regularly every Sunday for about eighteen months. I was now a full member of the Monthly *Seiat* and had passed the entrance examination for Bala College. I had not stood out academically but I had done my best. My poor mother, in her day, had thought she had done well for me by allowing me a whole twelvemonth's schooling. Now I had to fight every step, knowing that I had not absorbed much knowledge from the strokes of Soldier Robin's cane.

My master, Abel Hughes, showed me much kindness and went out of his way to encourage me. I dreaded mixing with young men of good education. And if Abel had not kept pushing me I would never have dreamed of going to college. When the exam results were published I was listed in the middle of the class, and after that I could not think of giving up.

I hadn't put much money aside. I spent most of my earnings on books and clothes. I didn't have enough money to pay the college fees, but Abel Hughes had promised to help me. I trusted that my master would do as he said. He had become my bosom friend, and he repeatedly promised to help me in our private talks; however, he didn't mention his intentions towards me, even to his own sister. When Abel did a kindness, his regard for the feelings of the receiver were such that he would go to great lengths to conceal his charity from everyone else. I often saw him hand out alms to a beggar, whilst speaking of something else so as to divert the beneficiary's attention from what he was doing.

One August night, about a fortnight before I was to go to college, I was preparing for the journey. I was feeling a little fidgety. I'd never before spent more than two nights together away from home. I had shut the shop, and Abel was sitting on the sofa near the parlour window. He seemed weary and a little sad.

'We must talk about you going to college,' he said and then noticing I had put my hat on asked. 'Where are you off to?'

'I've promised to call round and see Thomas Bartley.' I said.

'Will you be long?' Abel asked.

'I don't think so,' I said. 'Would you like me to stay in, sir?''

'Not on my account. I just don't feel myself tonight, somehow.'

'I'll stay,' I said. 'I can go to Y Twmpath tomorrow instead.'

'No, you must go if you have promised,' Abel said. 'There isn't much the matter with me. I'll be better directly, and I expect Marged any minute. Off you go. Doubtless Thomas Bartley will be waiting.'

As I was going through the doorway he called after me.

'Wait a minute. You never know what may happen,' he said. He went to the cupboard and took out his cashbox. He unlocked it and drew out some bank notes. I thought he was about to hand them to me when he stopped.

'What's the matter with me?' he said. 'I'm being childish. There's a fortnight yet. Away you go Rhys. Don't mind me and haste thee back.'

As I walked up the lane to Y Twmpath I couldn't stop thinking that Abel had been acting strangely that evening. I decided that I would get back early to check he was all right. But once seated in the Bartley's kitchen it wasn't so easy. Thomas cast a threatening glance at the ham hanging from the beam and quickly insisted I must stay for supper.

'The best welcome I can give you is a ham and egg tea,' he said. 'Even a prince couldn't ask for better.'

Of course I had to accept his kind offer, and soon we were sat at the table with high-piled plates in front of us.

'Mighty nourishing food is ham and eggs,' Thomas said, 'Mind you, it has to be the right quality. I wouldn't give a fig for this American stuff.

Who knows what they fatten their pigs on? I don't know how those town folk dare eats eggs. My cousin Ned told me that he'd stayed in a respectable house in Liverpool, and the maid brought in a dozen boiled eggs and put them in the middle of the table. The family would break open one after another until they found one or two that were fit to eat. The girl was carrying the bad ones out as fast as she could. But they thought nothing of it. Ned said that was what they did every day. Well Barbara's taken these eggs from the middle shelf, between the plates over there. They were laid fresh today and by the game hens.'

He took a mouthful and savoured it before speaking again.

'So you've made up your mind to go to Bala then Rhys?' he said. 'You know what? We'll be miss you, won't we Barbara?'

Barbara nodded.

'Yes, to be shuar,' Thomas said. 'I've not been to Bala nor anywhere else that way, and I don't know nobody from there except two men who come on fair days. They sell stockings on the High Street, and they seem to be decent enough. I'd like to go to Bala at least once in my life. I hear they have a lake that a man walked over once when it froze up. When he found out what he'd done, I heard he died on the spot. I once heard James Pwllfford recite a poem about Bala. Said it was written by Robin Ddu. I don't quite remember it but it went something like "Bala went, and Bala'll go," or something like that. You'll get to hear it when you get there, no doubt. My father used to say that if a thing was safe it was as right as Bala clock. You'll have to look out for Bala clock when you get there. D'ye know what? If Barbara and me can find a cheap excursion I wouldn't mind coming down to look you up one day. You'll enjoy that won't you? I'm shuar you'll be glad to see us? Pitch into that food, lad. I don't think you eat enough. There's always a hundred welcomes for you here. Are there many students down at Bala learning to preach?'

'They don't teach you how to preach at Bala,' I said.

'What's that you say? They don't learn you how to preach there?' Thomas said. 'Just as well because I've heard some of them come over here and I found nothing to my taste about them. I'd rather hear William Hughes of Abercwmnant than the best of them students. But I'm not much of a judge. So what do they learn if they don't learn to preach?'

'They learn languages, Thomas,' I said.

'Ha ha!' he laughed out loud. 'Languages indeed! Tell me what languages?'

'Latin and Greek,' I said.

'Now I see,' he said. 'They want to go as missionaries so that they can preach to the Africans. That's it, isn't it? But you don't want to go out to the Africans, do you?'

I shook my head.

'I thought not.' Thomas said. 'So why do so few of them go out to preach to the Indians after they've learnt their languages in college? I hear there are scores of foreigners who've never heard anything about Jesus. That's an awful pity. What's the point of learning the language if they don't preach in them? It's like me being apprenticed to a shoemaker and then never making a shoe afterwards. You haven't finished your meal, surely? Take another cup of tea, Rhys. But it's the languages I'm talking about. What did you call them? Latin and Greek? Those are the languages of the Africans and Indians, aren't they?'

'No, Thomas,' I said. 'Latin and Greek aren't the languages of the Africans and Indians.'

'Whose language are they then?' he said.

'They're the languages of old people who've been dead for centuries.'

'Dead men's languages?' Thomas said. 'Why in the world would you want to learn the languages of dead folk? Are you making fun of me, like your brother Bob used to?'

'I'm telling you the honest truth, Thomas,' I said. 'They learn the languages for the treasures they contain.'

'Well now, this is the queerest thing I've ever heard,' Thomas said. 'I always thought a language was something you spoke. So what's the Africans' language? Surely they must, learn that or they won't be much good as missionaries.'

'The language of the Africans isn't taught in college, Thomas,' I said. 'The missionaries have to go to the Africans themselves to learn it.'

'Well, I never heard such a thing before,' Thomas said. 'They learn the languages of people who are dead and don't learn the languages of people who are living. But, since we're on the subject, what else do they learn?'

'They learn mathematics'.

'And who is Matthew Mattiss, and what may he be?' Thomas said.

'It's how to measure and weigh and make all sorts of calculations, and things of that sort,' I said.

'That's handy enough,' Thomas said. 'Perhaps that's why so many preachers turn farmer or shopkeeper. What else do they learn there?'

'English language and history,' I said.

'Well if a man doesn't know a bit of English in these days he's bound to be left behind,' Thomas said. 'And history's interesting enough. One of the best I ever heard at history was James Pwllfford the tailor. When I went out drinking in public houses I loved to hear that man talk. And today there's nothing I like better than a bit of history in a sermon. When Barbara and I've forgotten everything else, we always keep a grip of the story a preacher tells. But I don't see those college boys are any great shakes at telling a story. William Hughes, of Abercwmnant beats them every time. Last time he was here, he told a story about a little girl who was dying, and I won't ever forget it. I couldn't stop myself crying as he told it. I'm glad they learn history in college. But some of them don't seem that good at learning. A lad of a preacher came here who'd been three years in college so he said, but I couldn't make head nor tail of what he said. He spoke about something called a mechanism of unity, or something. I couldn't get any sense from it. But I knew I had something to ask you. What sort of living do you get there? Is it pretty good?'

'They don't give you a living, Thomas,' I said. 'Every student must provide for himself.'

'But how do the lads get along?' Thomas said. 'Are they given so much a week to live on?'

'Oh, no,' I said. 'They have to find their own food, drink, lodging and washing. They can go out preaching and they have to live on what they earn from that.'

'If I never go to Caerwys fair again, that's the weirdest thing I've ever heard,' Thomas said.

'They don't learn to preach there,' he said. 'They don't learn the language of the foreign heathens, only the language of some old dead folk. They don't get paid, and everyone's living on what he gets given for preaching even if he starves. And the only useful thing they learn is history and that other thing ... what did you call it? Matthew something? To be shuar, Matthew Mattis. Why on earth do you want to go there, Rhys? Do they learn anything about Jesus Christ there? I didn't hear you mention that.'

'I'm sure they do, Thomas,' I said. 'But the place is as strange to me as it is to you.'

'If I were you I'd go on a month's trial and take plenty of food with me,' Thomas said. 'That must be why all those lads who come from college preaching looked half starved. It's no wonder after what you've said about how they run the place. Well I live and learn. I always thought that college must be a nice place, although I wondered why the boys looked so pallid and dejected. I used to think they were just a bit nervous, and by Monday morning they'd be over it and fine. They must have got a better living there once, because I remember John Jones of Llanllyfni preaching. He was in college then, and his two cheeks glowed like a rose. Tell me, Rhys, if you go a couple of months without getting an offer to preach, what's going to happen to you?'

'I'll just have to trust in Providence,' I said.

'God helps them as helps themselves,' Thomas said. 'I knew a man around here a while since. He was a bit of a believer but the most careless about his affairs I ever met. He was always talking about trusting in Providence. He died in Holywell workhouse. I wish you hadn't told me what kind of place that college is. Once you've gone there Barbara and me'll be always worrying if you're getting enough to eat. As I see it, you're leaving a good place and moving to a country where they live hard, I don't see the game is worth the candle. I wouldn't mind so much if they only learned you to preach there. But you know what's best for you, Rhys. It's not my business to interfere. But if your mother was alive I don't think she'd want you to go. What does Abel say? Is he for you going?'

'Oh yes,' I said. 'Abel is keen for me to go.'

'Well, Abel's a regular caution,' Thomas said. 'And I've never known him make a mistake.'

'Talking about Abel,' I said, 'reminds me, Thomas, that I should be going. Abel's not so well tonight, and I promised to be back soon.'

'I'm right sorry to hear that,' Thomas said. I hope it's nothing serious. I don't know what'd become of us in that chapel if anything was to happen to our old sergeant major. We'd be all of a mess. When your mother was alive I felt it was as good a sermon to hear them talk. They never spoke of any mechanism of unity, just about Jesus Christ and heaven. I'd sit here a-taking it all in. I was like a sow in the barley. I never got tired of hearing them, and I never wanted Abel to go. I'll tell you what I used to do. It might have been a sin but if I saw Abel coming up the lane I'd turn the clock-hand back half an hour. I never told your mother; she wouldn't have approved I know. I won't keep you, if Abel's out of sorts. Remember us to him. Good night; Rhys. And if you're determined to go to college then come round and take a flitch of bacon with you. We've got plenty to spare. You're always a hundred times welcome here. We'll have quite enough left. Good night.'

I was worried about Abel and glad to get away. I wondered what Wil would have made of my chat with that old thoroughbred Thomas Bartley, as he called him. My mind was full of memories as I hurried homewards. I thought of how Bob could always smooth the wrinkles from mother's careworn face when he told her of his visits to Thomas Bartley. He could imitate the old shoemaker so perfectly he would make mother angry with herself, because she'd have to laugh at Bob's comic descriptions. There are some moments in the life of every man when he seems demented; had I been watched that night, striding past the Hall Park, my face must have seemed strange as I laughed and cried at the same time.

Now, with the hindsight of years, I have realized how much Thomas Bartley had to do with the main events in my life. But little did I realize as I walked back from Y Twmpath that I was to face yet another trial.

It was barely an hour and a half since I had left the Corner Shop. As I walked down High Street I met Jones, who had been looking for me.

'Come quickly Rhys,' he said. 'Abel Hughes has been taken badly ill.'

He may have said more but I didn't wait to listen. I ran as fast as I could to my dear old master's room, wishing that I had not left him that night.

He was lying back on the sofa where I had left him. Doctor Bennett, the works doctor, was sitting on the chair next to him. Miss Hughes stood at the head of the sofa making desperate efforts to hide her distress. She was supporting her brother's head with her left arm. Her face showed great tenderness for the only man she had ever loved with all her heart. She had a glass of cordial in her other hand and was offering it to Abel's lips. He seemed unable to sip it. Two other women neighbours were in the room, but I don't remember who they were.

I would not have believed that a man could undergo such a change so quickly without being assaulted. Abel had sunk into a helpless inert mass. The glory of his spirit had left him. He was like a mighty tower whose foundations have been struck by lightning, his glory all departed. Just two hours before his face had beamed with reason, inteligence and geniality. Now he looked like an imbecile in his cups. His tongue, which had always spoken in a sensible and instructive way had lost its skill. His speech was the inarticulate sound of a strident deaf-mute. He was completely paralysed except for a frantic twitch of his right arm. He didn't notice me come into the room at first.

When he saw me he was clearly distressed. He started to cry like a child and kept pointing to me and then to the cupboard with his right hand. He tried to speak but could only make harsh noises. I knew what he meant, but I couldn't bring myself to say what I thought his intended. He tried again and again to make himself clear but failed. The doctor asked me if I could guess what he wanted, and I told a lie. I said I didn't know. Everyone could see that Abel wanted to say something to me. I knew what is was, but I couldn't tell the doctor and Miss Hughes it was that my master wanted to give me some banknotes from the cash box. They wouldn't have believed me and might have thought I was trying to take advantage of my master's stroke.

I knew with as much certainty as I write these words right now, that he still had all his intellectual faculties but had lost the means to speak, and that he wanted to help me go to college. He tried many times to talk to me, and when he could not make any sense he broke down in tears. The doctor suggested that I left the room, as my presence was upsetting my master. But I found it hard to leave him.

He was the tenderest, most devout, finest man I have ever known. I could have set his mind at rest by explaining what he wanted to do, and I well knew that my future might depend upon it. But I couldn't do so without throwing doubt upon my intentions. I prayed he might be granted strength enough to speak. But as I sat with him he was visibly weakening, and I lost hope he would ever be able to speak to us again.

We struggled to carry him upstairs and get him into bed. The doctor tried every means to revive him but without success. He hadn't completely lost the use of his right arm so I sat by his bedside his hand in mine. He lay for hours, as if in a happy sleep. If I tried to remove my hand he would stir uneasily.

'He might stay like this for days,' Dr Bennett said. 'There's nothing more I can do. I'll come back in the morning.'

The doctor left, and I persuaded Miss Hughes to retire and get some kind of rest.

'There's nothing more you can do for him,' I said. 'I'll stay with him while you get some sleep.'

She insisted on sending Jones into the town to fetch an experienced nurse to stay with me to watch her sick brother. The night was warm, the room was quiet, and the 'experienced' nurse fell fast asleep.

Dr Bennett had told me that he had no hope that my dear old master would recover, and I agreed with him. But, if only to put my master's mind at rest, rather than for any selfish purpose, I prayed earnestly to God that his tongue might be loosened, if only for a minute.

Did God hear my prayer? If I said yes, who would believe me? But I sat watching for some two hours, while the nurse slept on. The breathing of my beloved benefactor was so light and soft that I feared he had gone. I gently let go of his hand. As I did so he awoke as peaceful as a child in its cot. He looked up at me and spoke clearly. What he said I have never repeated to any living soul. I told no one because I feared that Doctor Bennett would say it was impossible and I had been dreaming. Others might say I was making up the story for selfish motives. It no longer matters, as it was so long ago. I decided not to use his words to gain my own ends. Instead I have treasured them in my heart as a testimonial of how true he was to me in his last moments. A moment later his spirit crossed the great gulf.

In the whole chronicles of Death, I know of only One more perfect, who entered its dark portals with such perfect, deep-founded and pure belief.

CHAPTER 35

Troubled Times

I remember when a storm felled a grand old oak, with its roots sunk wide and deep. The earth around was torn apart, so that all the neighbouring oaks were less secure. The nearest ones felt the worst shock of the great tree's downfall, though many others were deeply scarred, so that even several seasons' breezes, rain and warmth didn't quite heal their wounds.

The death of Abel Hughes was just such a ground-shaking event. His passing deprived the town of a man who had been respected even by the men who loafed on the street corners. Abel was a good man in so many ways. The town's tradesmen lost an exemplar who could trade with the world without telling lies and still earn an honest livelihood. I hope he was not the last of such old-fashioned, trustworthy people. But it was the chapel and the Methodist movement that felt his loss most keenly of all.

The Methodists couldn't imagine their cause without Abel. My poor simple friend Seth always called our chapel Abel's Chapel. When Abel moved on to the next world the *Seiat* members felt their sanctuary had lost its spiritual life. There were not more than a dozen members who had known the Big Seat without Abel sitting in it. Almost everyone, except the really old folk, had recited their verses before him in the Children's *Seiat*, and most of the congregation had been received into full membership by Abel Hughes.

Abel had known the secular and spiritual dealings of every family who were connected with the Chapel. Over the years he had visited every Methodist house in the town to sit by the sick and needy or to offer counsel and prayer. The older folk of the parish felt they could share their worries with Abel in the sure and certain knowledge that their secrets wouldn't be betrayed. He'd been a trusted pastor to the Chapel folk, because they knew he'd tell the truth in public and in private. He never held back for fear of being told to mind his own business or of reducing contributions to the collection. He believed that the truth must stand, at a time when too many of us are ready to trim it to our own vague form. We do not always accept what the Bible says, that 'They knew that they were naked.'

If we recognize truths which we think shouldn't be spoken, then we dress them up in aprons of our own devising rather than accept their natural state. Some are boastful of their honesty and brag about how they always speak plainly, but their fondness for telling the truth and speaking plain is often a mask for impertinence and rudeness that stems from their ignorance and bad manners. For such individuals, truth is like a knife. They will speak only that truth which kills their opposition. In many chapels, even to this day, you will find a religious butcher and religious executioner. The religious butcher enjoys hacking his fellow religionists into four quarters and a head, then displaying them on his stall. The religious executioner seeks to hang his opponents immediately and have done with the matter.

Abel could wield a metaphorical knife, but he was neither a butcher nor an executioner. He used the knife of truth to spare life, not take it away. If he saw danger, he never hesitated. He brought home to the individual the ineffable value of his soul's health. He would explain that to secure that health the patient must submit to a severe operation. And those who had been under his hands became his warmest and closest friends.

Those of us bred in the chapel from childhood thought Abel Hughes too sharp and severe when we first met him. As we grew and matured our opinion of him softened. In our childhood he seemed a like a sour green crab-apple that set our teeth on edge, but once we were grown he became a great, yellow, ripe, round apple that was sweet in the mouth. As Thomas Bartley said, 'Abel Hughes did not often make a mistake.' I have often seen ardent and determined chapel members change their minds as soon as they discovered that Abel didn't agree with them.

John Llwyd would rise to his feet and elaborate hotly about some complaint or other in *Seiat*. Listening to him you would be convinced that religion had died out in the land, and that certain personalities in the church were guilty of every imaginable form of iniquity. Then Abel would stand up, and with no more than a dozen soothing words he'd clear the air and still the uproar. He would go quickly to old Betty Kenrick or Thomas Bartley to ask them to talk of their experience. And within minutes everyone had quite forgotten about John Llwyd and his scolding.

Wil Bryan detested John Llwyd, and nothing pleased him more than seeing Abel give the Old Scraper 'a good sitting on'.

'Didst thou see how Abel quelled Old Scraper's bonfire just by spitting on it?' Wil said to me as we sat in *Seiat*. 'That was the smartest bit of work I've seen in a long time.'

Abel knew how to use his secret bradawl of truth to deflate a pretentious windbag. He would never speak of it afterwards, but I suspect that these exploits gave him some inner pleasure. I would sometimes see him sitting at home in his corner by the fire, with a smile of satisfaction spreading across his face, as though he were enjoying reliving some past event.

Abel was strict. He couldn't tolerate an irresponsible religionist, but he would sympathize with good intentions, whatever the person's shortcomings and defects. I never met anyone like him with such skill at reading a human heart. He had studied his heart all his life and often said it was most deceitful. That insight equipped him to understand and guide a young man fighting temptation and doubt. He understood toil and trouble. He could make allowance for inexpertience and encourage everyone he thought had some good in them. He could join in spiritual joy and empathize with the sorrow of the old and tired. It was only indolence, negligence, hypocrisy and cant that he would not tolerate.

I had lived with him as an apprentice, and so knew him better than most. I never saw him take pride in his own virtues, but if he saw any trace of those virtues others, he would beam with pleasure. He set himself such high standards that he was always aware of his own failings, but almost seemed to envy some people who, I thought, didn't compare to him. He had an authority in the church that was well-deserved and that no one dared to question.

I write these reflections long after his death, and I must admit that just after he passed away less noble thoughts filled my mind. I had lost my most valuable friend just when my future depended greatly on his support. I am ashamed to admit how selfish I was. I saw all my prospects destroyed, and no one sympathized with me. They all spoke of the loss Abel would be to the Cause and to Miss Hughes.

'Poor Miss Hughes.'

'What'll Miss Hughes do now?'

'Miss Hughes, poor thing, is alone in the world, now she's lost her brother.'

'Who will Miss Hughes get to look after the business? That boy's going to college. Surely he could stay to help Miss Hughes, if he had any feelings.'

'Surely, Rhys Lewis won't leave Miss Hughes in her trouble. He should be ashamed if he does.'

That was how people talked. They all thought about Miss Hughes, but no one considered Rhys Lewis. Why? Because no one knew that Abel had wanted me to go to college. He hadn't not told anybody except me that I wouldn't want for money as long as I was away, and that I should think of the Corner Shop as my home. Now he was dead I felt alone and unfriended. It's no wonder I was bitter.

I knew I was selfish, but I couldn't help lamenting the upset to my plans. I thought I would have to give up the idea of going to college. I would have to stay and take over the business. And I was acutely aware that Abel had told me not to even think about keeping a shop and preaching as well. If I stayed to run the shop, I must stop preaching. As I thought about my situation through my heart sank. I had a positive dislike of business, and Abel had encouraged my aversion to trade. It just wasn't fair. For a long time before he died he had given me a lot of spare time. I did next to nothing in the shop. As long as I worked at my books Abel let me study. Now all that liberty he had given me was to be wasted, all my efforts had vanished with the wind. And the more I thought about my situation, the less happy I was with my lot.

Miss Hughes had always been kind to me, even when I was at my most mischievous. I owed her lot. She was a simple, innocent old lady who shared none of her brother's intellectual gifts, only his kindness and fidelity. She had never been interested in the philosophical questions that Abel and I used to talk about. I don't think she knew anything about the type of knowledge her brother had acquired. She saw no difference between preachers. To her they were all good, and she held them all in equal regard. Every night as she went to bed she read a chapter of the Bible and then went to sleep. On the Sabbath she would thumb through *Y Drysorfa*, the Methodist magazine. But she opened it at random and quickly nodded off while reading it.

She knew nothing about the business and not much more about her brother's circumstances. But she was a good woman. She kept the house clean and beautiful, and her hospitality to everyone Abel brought home was sincere and convivial.

Abel's death came as a shock to her. She was distraught and her distress elicited deep sympathy from the many folk who came to comfort her. We had so many well-intentioned visitors that I had to resort to asking one, a sensible woman neighbour, to look after Miss Hughes. She was in danger of being confused or even killed with kindness.

I carried out the funeral arrangements to the satisfaction of everyone. I only asked Dafydd Davis to advise me. I was in a sort of dreamy absent-minded state. Everything I did, I felt as if Abel was at my side, and I was doing everything on his instructions.

It was a sad day when we buried him. Most of the town came to his funeral, and as I stood by the open grave I compared the small gap in the churchyard where they were putting poor old Abel with the large gap he had left in the town, which I doubted would be filled.

As Dafydd Davis and I walked back from the churchyard I imagined I heard my old master calling after us. 'Thank you, Rhys,' he said. 'Thank you, Dafydd. Ye both did well.'

We could only reply. 'We've only done our duty to thee. It was the least thou didst deserve.'

Dafydd Davis came back to the shop, and we went into the kitchen. The women were with Miss Hughes in the parlour and had comforted her while the men attended to the burial.

I had hoped that Dafydd would sit in Abel's old arm chair. He didn't. Instead he sat in the chair he usually occupied when Abel was alive. Abel's old chair stayed empty, and beside it his pipe lay on the hob, where he had left it four days earlier.

We didn't speak. I think we both expected Abel to join us. It is hard to accept the final exit of someone who has been a part of your life for many years.

We talked of inconsequential things, as people do after a funeral. Presently Dafydd raised the topic I was dreading.

'What do you intend to do?' he said. 'Is it wise, under the circumstances, to go to college?'

'I can't answer you,' I said. 'I don't want to think about it just now.'

''No one would blame you, for not going,' Dafydd said. 'What with Abel being taken so suddenly, and Miss Hughes left all alone. She knows nothing about the business. I think people would think more of you if you didn't go to Bala. You could always wait a year and see how things turn out.'

He spoke persuasively and from his heart, but what he said upset me. I'd not expected Dafydd Davis to encourage me not to go to college. I was hurt and poured out my anguish.

'Dafydd Davis,' I said. 'If I don't go to college now I never will. I will think carefully about the matter. If I decide it is my duty to stay, then I will give up preaching forever. But if I see my duty is to go to college, as Abel wished, then nothing will prevent me. But tonight I do not know where my duty lies and I do not want to talk about it until I do.'

'Pray for light, then,' Dafydd said. 'The Lord will guide thee.'

He got up. 'I must be going, but I should speak with Miss Hughes first.'

We went into the parlour where Miss Hughes was sitting with the sensible neighbour for company. I hadn't had much chance to talk to her since her brother's death, and in the midst of her grief she had left everything to me. When I tried to ask her what to do, all she would say was, 'You know best.'

When she saw Dafydd and me she began to cry. I felt myself also give way to tears. I felt as bereft as she did at the loss of Abel. It was some time before either of us could speak. Dafydd waited patiently until she was composed before he spoke.

'Dafydd Davis,' she said, finally getting her tears under control. 'Thank you for coming to see me.'

'I'm sorry about your loss,' Dafydd said. 'How will you manage?'

'Rhys has done very well,' she said. 'I've always liked him.' She looked at me. 'And he well knows it. When he first came here he was so wicked, and Abel was so strict. I used to take his side against Abel. You won't go to that old college and leave me alone, will you Rhys?'

I was glad that Dafydd answered for me. 'I suggest you talk of that another time. Miss Hughes, when you're both not quite so upset. We will all miss Abel, and if there is anything we can do at the chapel to help you, then do tell me.' With that he left.

I felt wretched that evening. I sat by the fire in a sort of reverie. The old clock, which Abel always wound, had stopped. No one else had thought to set it going again. With Abel gone, so many things he had done for us were now left undone. If Providence didn't intend me to go to college I was not meant to be a preacher. Abel himself had told me that no young man should think of taking up the ministry unless he first went to college.

Abel had been right about most things, and I didn't doubt that he was right about this too. If I stayed with Miss Hughes, I would have to take over the running of the business, as Jones was no more than a sort of useful shop fitting. I would have to spend all my time running the shop. I would have none spare to read or to write sermons. I could keep shop or I could preach; I couldn't do both.

But I couldn't afford to go to college now Abel was gone. He had promised to provide for my education but died without being able to tell anyone else about the arrangement. I couldn't hope to win a scholarship. Those would be won by the clever, well-off young men who had got a good early education. Some of the students who visited to preach, had told me that they were able to live on very little at Bala. Perhaps I could live on even less than they could? But I didn't even know how much money I had. There were a few shillings loose in my pocket, but all the money I had saved was in my purse. How much did I have? Would it be enough?

I took out my purse out and emptied onto the table. I carefully counted my money back into my hand. I had six pounds in gold with a further ten and sixpence in silver. As I was holding this small pile of coins I heard Miss Hughes and her companion coming along the passage. They must be coming to wish me good-night before going to bed. I quickly stuffed my worldly wealth into my pocket and put the purse aside. I didn't want them to think I was thinking about money on the day of Abel's funeral.

They came in and wished me good night before retiring to bed.

'Don't you stay up too late fretting about Abel,' Miss Hughes said. 'He would be the first to say that he's gone to a better place.'

When they had gone, the house was still and quiet. I was racking my brain trying to work out what I could do. How quickly and completely my situation had changed. Just a few days before I had a plan to become an educated preacher and the means to achieve it. Now I had nothing. I don't know how long I sat there worrying and guessing about the future. I felt imprisoned by the room and the circumstances and was not getting any nearer deciding what to do. The street had fallen silent. All I could hear was the sound of solitary footsteps passing slowly round the corner of the house. It must be the policeman on his patrol, I thought as the same step sounded three or four times over.

I would not be able to sleep if I went to bed. I felt too worried and sick at heart. I decided that a breath of fresh air would help me think more clearly, so I slipped quietly out of the front door, and carefully locked it behind me.

The night was clear and lit by a full moon. It wasn't cold, although there was a refreshing light breeze blowing on my face. The street was filled with the deep silence of the grave, as if the whole town was dead.

I wandered down Chester Street and across towards King Street, as if I was going somewhere in particular, which I wasn't. I passed a little cottage with a light in its upstairs window. I knew the little girl of the family who lived there was very ill. Yes, I thought, it's worse for her than for me. Her parents can't just go to sleep to avoid their sorrows and their worried thoughts.

Going on across High Street I heard the rumble of a barrow in the distance. I recognized the sound of Ready Ned who always worked the night shift. His job was to empty the privies and dispose of their contents. I decided to go up the High Street to avoid meeting him and his malodorous load. A white cat glided, wraith like across my path, startling me until I saw what it was. As I got to the top of the town I saw a slightly built short man slouched against a church gates. He had a soft hat pulled down low over his eyes. I took him to be a weary, hard-up old tramp.

'Good night,' I said as I walked passed but he didn't reply. I wasn't surprised, if he was fatigued and empty-stomached why bother to reply to a greeting from a well-fed member of a cold-hearted world. I reasoned he was probably thinking what's a good-night if you don't give me something?

I walked on and left the town behind me. The lane was deserted and the only living creature I met was old Duke, the mule who belonged to William the Coal. I heard the click of his hobble before I saw him. He was on the other side of a low hedge, grazing in a field. I knew that Duke was of a roving disposition, so William would chain him by the leg to stop him wandering off. Duke was browsing busily. I watched him in the moonlight and saw him shake his head with great dignity, as if debating some weighty matter with himself. Then again, he might just have been troubled by flies. He stopped eating as he heard my footsteps and stood with his mouth open mid-bite, perhaps wondering why William was coming to fetch him to work so early. His ears went up like a double note of veneration. Then, seeing I was not William, he went on grazing. I left him to his meal, my mind flitting over all sorts of subjects, but always coming back to my options. I had a deep desire for knowledge, and an urge to serve God and man, but everything was pushing me back behind the shop counter. Was I doomed to spend my life selling worsted, flannel and calico? But did that really matter? What if I did spend my life in the Corner Shop? There were many young men, far better qualified than me to take up the ministry and preach the Cause.

I stopped and looked up at the infinite, star-studded, sky over my head. I fixed on one bright star. Would it matter if that solitary speck of light faded into the eternal dark? Who would miss it? And yet, as I stood transfixed by its lovely lustre, how could I doubt that even such a small part of the Great Lord's design mattered.

How beautiful the luminous moon looked, in the glory of her radiance. But the Lord had created clouds which sometimes hide that beautiful glow. When a cloud passed before the moon it would hide her completely, and the world would be plunged into darkness. But if I was patient enough to wait, then the cloud would clear away and gentle Luna would beam as brightly as ever.

If a cloud can pass from the moon, can it not also pass from me? Everything is possible for God.

I was deep in such thoughts when I thought I heard footsteps behind me. I looked back but couldn't see anyone. I decided to turn around and go home but had hardly gone a few paces before I saw a man rise up from the hedge side and walk towards me. It was the tramp I had passed on the road. But now he was moving towards me in a purposeful way and his hat was no longer hiding his face. He was striding towards me as if he had some evil intent. Should I turn and run? But what if he had a gun? I decided my best course was to be bold and to face up to him. As we got closer I recognized him.

'You mustn't think me too proud to speak just now, Rhys,' he said. 'Just because I wouldn't answer you. It's not that I'm above owning my relatives but I take care not to lower myself by talking to all sorts on the streets.'

'Uncle,' I said, for it was no other than James, my father's brother who I had always called The Irishman. 'Do you remember what I told you the last time we met?'

'You said good night,' he said.

'I'm not talking about meeting on the street I'm talking about that night in garden of Garth Ddu,' I said.

'Well, just wait a minute,' James Lewis said. 'My memory's not so bad as a rule. What was it you said, that that you'd give me a sovereign next time you saw me. How could I have forgotten that?'

'You know that what I told you,' I said, 'If you ever showed you face around here again I would hand you over to the police. I'll do it too.'

'Codswallop' he said, his contempt showing in his voice. 'I you want an accurate shot never use a double-barrelled gun. And a revolver's no good for anything except close range. I'm your uncle, your father's brother no less. Who will be disgraced if you give me to the police? James Lewis or Rhys Lewis? What do I care about disgrace? I care nothing. But I know a proud young chap who wouldn't like it. I don't want to quarrel with you; it's not right for relatives to fall out. Why don't we let bygones be bygones? I hear old Abel has gone to settle his account. That old screw'll have as much to answer for as I have.'

'Just you look here, uncle,' I said, squaring up to him. 'I'll fight you, even if you kill me, but I will not let you be disrespectful of my good dead master.'

'Well, well,' he said. 'I didn't mean to hurt your feelings. But it's a good thing for you that Abel has gone. You'll be the boss now. That old girl knows nothing about the business, and that idiot Jones knows even less. You can make your fortune now. And when you do, don't forget I'm the only relative you've got left in the world. I've been a bit unlucky lately. I haven't taken much game for a while, and I had a close shave last week. I was nearly nabbed and had to fight to get away.'

'I won't listen to your ungodly talk,' I said. 'I'm going home.'

'I don't want you to take me into the shop, like. That wouldn't work for either of us. But I need some cash or I'll starve. Perhaps you don't have much with you tonight, but I can call over to see you late some night, since you're to be boss and you'll have the key to the cash box.'

'I'll see that you never set foot inside Abel's house,' I said. 'And I'm as poor as you.'

'That's your own fault,' he said. 'If you hadn't been taken in by the balderdash you mother ladled out to you, you wouldn't need to be poor. If I'd had your chances, I'd have a chest full of money by now.'

As he spoke about my mother, I felt a deep rage rising in me. I flexed my hands and made as if to throttle him. He backed away as I shouted at him, and may God forgive me my hostile words.

'You scoundrel,' I shouted. 'Say another word about my mother and I'll tear you limb from limb. She brought me up to lead an honest life.'

My uncle backed away a yard or two and looked at me in amazement. He fumbled in his pocket and I wondered if he had a gun. But I wasn't afraid and I moved towards him. I was quite prepared to give up my life to defend my mother's reputation.

We stood face to face for a minute with neither of us speaking. Then he grinned at me.

'It's good to see you've got bit of the family pluck in you,' he said. 'I thought you were a chicken. But after tonight I'll think a hundred times better of you. I'm sorry if I said anything wrong about your mother. She was a good sort, in her own way, and she did me kindness at times. Why do you always want to quarrel with me? Let's be pals. That's where your father was better; he was as cool as a turnip, always. I'm sorry if I've offended you, but I really do need help, I'm stony broke. I haven't a copper to buy a spot of grub. And I know you won't want me to get into trouble stealing.'

'I don't want anything to do with you,' I said. 'Show me which way you're going and I'll go the opposite way. I won't walk a step with you.'

'Agreed,' he said. 'Give me your small change and I'll leave you now.'

I was seized with an urge to be rid of him at once. I emptied my pocket of the coins, knowing I had but a few shillings loose among the copper.

'Thank you, nephew,' he said and walked away. I set off back home.

My mind was made up. I couldn't stay in Mold to be plagued by this hateful wretch. He had the upper hand. He knew my weakness. I couldn't denounce him without bringing disgrace on myself. Fortunately, he didn't seem to know that I preached. If I went away to college in Bala he would lose track of me. And he wouldn't dare ask after me.

Providence had brought me face to face with my vagabond uncle that night, and had invited me to follow my dream. I had been given the sign I needed. There and then I resolved to go to college, come what may. I couldn't change my family connection, but nobody would know my history among the rest of the scholars. Possibly some of them might also have backgrounds they would prefer that people didn't know.

I felt happy, now that I had made my decision. I was in a good frame of mind as I passed old Duke, who had eaten his fill and was now standing drowsing. He was nodding by the hedge, with one leg resting limply and his head bent low. He was quite still, as though he too had resolved the point at issue in his discussion. I'm sure Duke had a more interesting story than mine, if only he'd been able to tell it.

'Good night my old friend,' I whispered, and walked down towards the darkness of the town.

I walked rapidly down the High Street to the Cross, unlocked the door of the Corner Shop and let myself in as quietly as I could.

I lit the gas and saw my purse lying on the table. I picked it up and found it empty. Now I remembered stuffing all my wealth into my pocket. I had given everything I had to the Irishman.

I had made my decision to go to college, but now I hadn't a single penny to pay my way. I stood on the middle of the kitchen floor, and remembered how many times Abel Hughes had told me to put my trust in God. Surely the Lord was testing me to destruction. I sat down, laid my head between my hands upon the table, and cried like a baby.

CHAPTER 36

A Well-known Character

I closed the last chapter with my memory of the lowest point in my life. I was friendless and lonely. I had no family support, and everything conspired to make sure that I would never achieve my only aim in living. I had fallen out of favour with God. All my belief in religion and my attempts to work within it seemed to lead to hypocrisy and pretence. I knew I was a tolerable preacher and would get better, so why was God placing so many obstacles in my way? All I had really wanted to do since I grew up, was to become a preacher. But, having preferred study to money-making I was left abandoned. I could do nothing without money, and through my own carelessness I had made myself as poor as a chapel mouse. Because I cared so little about money I had never learned to look after it. I wanted to work for the Method-ist cause but had not the wherewithal to start me in my vocation.

It seemed so unfair that the many townsfolk who were rolling in riches never thought of serving anything but their own interests. I could hear Wil Bryan's words echoing in memory: 'Those with pockets full of money are nothing but intelligent pigs. Surely the Good Lord doesn't set much store on money, or He wouldn't have given so much of it to dunderheads.'

I had become too dependent on Abel Hughes, so God was stripping me of all outside help. Was He inviting me to throw myself on His Mercy? Was I presuming too much to set off to college with nothing but the clothes I stood up in and my few books? I thought of the man Thomas Bartley told me about who had totally trusted in Providence only to die a pauper's death in Holywell workhouse.

What else could I do but try my best to complete the work I had begun? If God wanted me for a preacher, then He would make it so. If I failed it was clear I wasn't worthy.

First thing next morning I told Miss Hughes that I had decided to go to college. She was horrified.

'I'd never have believed you could be so cruel,' she said. 'And I've been so good to you ever since you came here.'

'I thank you for that,' I said. 'And I do not want to be cruel to you. It is just that I am called to be a preacher.'

'I'll increase your wages by four times if you will only stay and run the shop,' she said.

I shook my head. 'If I don't go to college now, then I will never become a preacher.'

'What if I should give you a quarter share in the business? You'll be made for life,' she said.

'I thank you most gratefully for your kind offer, Miss Hughes,' I said. 'But I must follow heart and try my best to become a preacher.'

At this she burst into tears. 'I've always been kind to you, Rhys Lewis,' she said. 'You are an unfeeling wretch to abandon me in my hour of need. How can you be so hard-hearted, ungrateful and selfish as to force me, Abel's sister, onto the parish? After all that Abel has done for you. You care only for yourself. You know I have no knowledge of the business, and without your help I will be homeless within a quarter.'

I listened to her in silence. I was almost overwhelmed by guilt at the truth of each of her accusations. I had been afraid that she would admit she knew nothing about brother's business undertakings.

'Calm yourself, Miss Hughes,' I said. 'If you give me some time to look into it I may be able to offer you some advice by tomorrow.'

'If I am to do without your services, I can manage without your advice,' she said.

I didn't say anything as I left the room. I now see that was rude of me, in her distressed state. But she had pierced my heart with her accusation of selfishness. I didn't walk out, though. I went to the shop, and with Jones's help we worked all that day and most of the night to work out the state of the business.

Miss Hughes did not ask what we were doing and did not seem to care. When Abel died she handed over all his keys to me and did not speak of the business again. She seemed so upset that she was ready to die to be with her brother.

I didn't stop until I had taken an inventory of all the stock. Abel did not give his customers credit, so I was quickly able to total the shop books up to date. Twenty-four hours later I had a pretty good idea of the extent of the estate my master had left. As I sat down to enter the last item in the ledger, I saw Jones slump on his stool, rest his head on the counter and fall fast asleep. The poor fellow was quite exhausted.

To complete my stocktake I investigated every cupboard, chest and drawer in the building. Had Abel been alive I would never had been so bold, but Miss Hughes was quite helpless. I believed my dead master would want me to see to her welfare, so I made a thorough search.

I opened a drawer in the oaken cupboard in Abel's bedroom and found a stash of private papers. As I looked through them I felt the Devil at my shoulder. At the bottom of that drawer was a roll of banknotes. I heard the Devil's voice clearly.

'Jones is snoring and Miss Hughes is the sitting room,' he said. 'Abel told you that he intended to give some of these notes, and as they are stuffed in a bedroom drawer there will be no record of the number now Abel is dead. If you were to take some of them it would be no more than Abel would have given you freely. In a way you own some of these already. Even if you just took one it is less than Abel would have given you. Remember you haven't got a penny to your name. It wouldn't be theft, as Abel intended you to have them. You can't go to college without money, so if you take some from this hoard you will put it to good use.'

The Devil can be very persuasive when he tries. But I was alert to the Old One's attempt to subvert me. I drew on the armour of prayer, watchfulness and the Word of God that my mother first clad me in, and turned to face down the Devil. I carefully counted the money, put it in the cash box and added the full amount to my total.

Now I had finished my self-imposed task, I went through to talk to Miss Hughes. My conscience was easy and my hands clean and honest. I had lived up to the teachings of my dear mother, and that meant more to me than any amount of money.

Miss Hughes was cool and uninterested, but that didn't stop me telling her what I had been doing.

'Miss Hughes, you did not need to remind me of your kindness towards me,' I said. 'I have never once forgotten it. You think me hard-hearted for leaving you and going to college. But you must think I am honest, or you wouldn't have trusted everything in the business to me. I do not think you have any idea of your financial position now my master has died. I am surprised that so shrewd a man as Abel had not told you about his means and I am even more surprised that he did not make a will. I did not ask your permission but decided to take stock of your wealth. I have worked out that, after paying all his creditors, my master died owning property – including the stock, money on the books, in the bank and in the House – that comes to about fifteen hundred pounds. This will support you comfortably, assuming you live to old age. My advice, which you may take or reject as you wish, is that you sell the stock and business. I know a trader who would willingly buy it from you. My staying on to run the business is out of the question. I am resolved to go to college. If you could only consult my old master, he would assure you that I am doing the right thing.'

While I spoke I could see my words melting her sourness like sun on a snowy roof. First she looked incredulous, then a great tenderness came over her face. I knew she and I were great friends again.

'I'm sorry I said those things to you, Rhys,' she said. 'I didn't know what I was doing. Please forgive me; I always liked you. You have much more sense than I do. Poor Abel used to tell me, when you were a boy, that you could twist me round your little finger. I'll take your advice and do as you say; if I get someone else in your place, he will only rob me. I've known for a long time that you wanted to go to Bala, and I won't try to dissuade you. You'll be in your element there and have all you want.'

'Thank you,' I said.

'But must you go next week?' she went on. 'Can't you make it a fortnight? Now what would you like for your dinner? Shall I stew some kidneys for you?'

'Simple woman,' the Devil whispered in my ear. 'Ask her for the money that Abel promised you.'

'I will not,' I told the Old Man. 'I value my independence, and I won't ask her for a penny piece, although I know as well as you that she would not refuse me if I asked.'

She knew no more about the college than Thomas Bartley did. She thought it was next door to heaven, not a place where the students had to pay to lodge, eat and drink. Thomas and Miss Hughes were not alone in thinking that streets of Bala flowed with milk and honey and that, once I got there, I would want for nothing. Not a single member of my church had the least objection to my going to college. The monthly *Seiat* unanimously wanted me to go. But only Thomas Bartley had asked me how I would support myself there. The only man, who understood the difficulties facing a poor lad who set out to go college was Abel Hughes, and he was lying cold in his grave.

I had challenged Providence to provide. Had the Good Lord accepted my challenge? I would find out in due course. It was my duty to do as much to help Miss Hughes as I could before I left. With the help of one who understood such things, I set up the sale of the business to the man who was anxious to take it over. After all was settled I reckoned Miss Hughes, was worth about fourteen hundred pounds, a figure quite close to my original estimate and quite enough to keep her comfortably for the rest of her life. The buyer had agreed to take on Jones as part of the fixtures. This deal took a load off my mind, as I now felt I had compensated Jones for the pain I caused him on the night that Wil Bryan and I almost hanged him.

The Devil kept tapping me on my shoulder as I was packing up my books and clothes. 'You're a fool, Rhys,' he said, 'to give up a good place, turn down a generous salary, and miss out on the opportunity to become a prosperous trader. You must be mad.'

'What does it matter?' I said to the Devil. 'Dunderheads can have the business and money for all I care. I am going to college and I am going to be educated and make some sort of living as a preacher.'

My plan was simple. I challenged Providence to see that I did not starve. I knew if I told my friends of my poverty, they would help me. But I didn't want to beg.

I had no commitment to preach on the Sunday on the Friday night before I was to leave for college the following Monday. I had refused to take one as I thought I might need the time to prepare. I could have earned a fee for preaching and I was sorry I hadn't done so. Wil Bryan had always called me poor and proud, saying I'd inherited this stupid attitude from my mother. He might have been right from a worldly view, but I prayed that I'd keep my independence, something which I greatly valued.

On that Friday night Providence seemed set to humble me completely. I realized that if I wanted to pay my train fare and lodging I would have to try to borrow a sovereign with no hope of paying it back. Who could I ask? There was only one man whom I would dare to approach: Thomas Bartley. I knew the old thoroughbred would have a sovereign in my hand the moment I asked for it. And he was so ingenuous and kind that he would be sure to preserve my dignity during the act of borrowing. I accepted I had to ask the favour of Thomas but I put it off to the last minute. I wanted to give Providence a chance to take care of me.

My careful planning was interrupted by a knock on door of my room. Miss Hughes came in.

'Rhys,' she said, 'William Williams, the deacon at Blaenycwm, is downstairs and he wants to see you.'

I rushed down to the kitchen where William was sitting by the fire.

'Can you come over to Cwm to preach this Sunday? He said. 'The Minister we had booked has let us down.'

'Why?' I said. 'Is he ill?'

'He didn't give us a reason he just said he wouldn't be able to come.'

I waited a moment or two before I said anything more. I wasn't pleased to hear of a man breaking his engagement in such an offhand manner, but I didn't want to seem too eager.

'You do know that I'm going off to Bala, first thing Monday?' I said. 'I have to pack my books, and sort out my affairs and it's quite a way to Blaenycwm.'

'But it will be your last to chance to preach for us for a while, and the folk so enjoy your sermons,' William said. 'And we'll make sure that someone gives you a ride back home on the Sunday night.'

After a little more prevarication I allowed myself to be persuaded. I had already realized that if I had to live from preaching I would quickly have to learn how to bluff when negotiating employment.

Providence was smiling a little at me. I felt quite cheerful that Sabbath night as I was borne home with half a sovereign in my pocket. I had some money, even if it wasn't quite enough to avoid having to ask Thomas Bartley for a loan of a further sovereign.

Thomas and Barbara had arranged to come to the station on Monday morning to see me off. As I sat down to the excellent breakfast Miss Hughes had prepared for me I realized that Thomas might not have a sovereign in his pocket. The more I thought about it the less likely it seemed that the old cobbler would carry gold with him. If I wanted a loan than I would have to go Y Twmpath and ask him. There were only a couple of hours before the train went, so I began to hurry my food.

'Why are you eating so fast?' Miss Hughes asked. 'Aren't you enjoying your food?'

'Just you remember, Rhys,' she went on, 'I'll expect you to spend your Christmas holidays with me. Don't be too proud to come. I'll keep your bed for you, although I will have moved and be living in Y Bwthyn by then.'

'Thank you, Miss Hughes,' I said.

I felt that Providence was at last beginning to take the work of providing for me more seriously.

'Did Abel owe you any wages?' she said.

'No,' I said. 'He gave me my earnings in advance and had paid me up to last Saturday.'

'I know you'll have all you want at college, but perhaps a little pocket money might come in handy. Here's five pounds for you, if you'll take them.'

I could have shouted Hallelujah. I welled up with tears in my eyes, and in order to hide my feelings I coughed as if a bread-crumb had gone down the wrong way.

'Thank you very much, Miss Hughes,' I said. 'You will never know just how grateful I am for your kindness.'

'I'm just pleased that you'll let me help you, Rhys,' she said. 'After all you have done for me since Abel died.'

I didn't need to rush over to Y Twmpath now. Providence had spared me the ordeal of having to beg a loan from Thomas Bartley. I was now well set up and felt as merry as a lark.

Miss Hughes and I parted on the best of terms. And, to tell the truth, I did something that I had not done since my wicked days when I had wanted a shilling. I kissed her wrinkled cheek. The kindly old soul burst into tears.

'Make sure you write and tell me how you're doing,' she said. I assured her I would. I left The Corner Shop for the last time and set off down Chester Street towards the station.

As I walked down the street I felt happy for two reasons. The first was that Providence was clearly showing its approval of my decision to go to college. The second was the warm affection demonstrated by so many friends who had come to the station to wish me farewell. Not least amongst them were Dafydd Davis and Thomas and Barbara Bartley. Whenever the Bartleys travelled by train they would be waiting on the platform at least an hour before the train was due. I arrived at Mold station fifteen minutes before the train time, but Thomas was worried.

'So you're here at last Rhys,' he said as I crossed the footbridge to the platform. 'You know you're within an ace of missing the train.'

Barbara was sitting on a large hamper on platform, agreeing with every word of the advice her husband gave me by nodding her head. Thomas spoke unceasingly for the fifteen minutes we waited for the train, so that Dafydd couldn't get a word in edgeways.

The train puffed under the road bridge and hissed to a halt by the platform. I shook hands with all the friends who had come to see me off, and with Barbara, who seemed too tired to get up from the hamper. However the moment I was seated in the carriage, she jumped to her feet. Thomas took hold of the hamper and hoisted it up onto the seat next to me. He leaned over and whispered.

'It's for you, that is. Now you take care of it, and, think on, if we hear of a cheap trip to Bala, Barbara 'n I will be coming down yonder to see how you are.' And before I could say anything to thank him he was off down the platform, with Barbara leaning on his arm.

I was overwhelmed. The gift was so unexpected and yet so typical of Thomas Bartley. I was sure the hamper contained much of interest to my hearty appetite. But there was a fellow traveller in the compartment, so I didn't try the package's weight or sniff it. I didn't want to give the impression that I had no idea what was in the basket.

We were whisked through Llong, where I caught a last glimpse of the River Alun, and onto the main line for Corwen. As we clattered rhythmically along I weighed up my travelling companion. Whenever I travel by train and have company in the compartment, once I have been with them a while I begin to imagine that I ought to know them. This is, of course, a delusion. I wonder if I automatically classify faces and, when I am with strangers I have been looking at a while, pigeonhole them into groups I know. Do I think I should be able to group the individual into the class he belongs to? I'm not sure, but I felt I recognized something familiar in my fellow-traveller, even though this was the first time I'd seen him.

He looked a few years older than me. His skin was pale, and its whiteness contrasted with his jet-black hair and eyebrows. His clothes were homespun, and he had the look of a Caernarfonshire Welshman. He wasn't reading the book he held in his hands; he was staring out of the window with a sad expression. He didn't seem to be interested in the passing landscape, and I surmised he was thinking about his home, his family or worrying about an uncertain future.

I wanted to speak to him, but he was so engrossed in thought I didn't feel it polite to disturb him. Although I felt he was a Welshman I decided to speak to him in English, to see how he responded.

'The weather is delightful, is it not?' I said.

'Yes, it is,' he said with a strong Welsh accent.

With that brief exchange he showed no interest in extending our conversation. I was sorry about this, as I liked the look of him and felt that I would like him more if I got to know him.

We sat silently, each absorbed in his own thoughts, until the train reached Corwen. That was where the line ended and so I would have to find some other transport to complete my journey to Bala. I unloaded my precious hamper and was retrieving my box and tea-chest of books from the guard's van when I felt a light tap on my shoulder.

'Mr Lewis, is that your hamper, sir?' a cheerful male voice enquired

'Yes,' I said. 'Why do you ask?'

'I only want to take care of you,' the man said. 'Is there a strike on? There's only two of you students come today, not really enough to make up a good load. That's the way with students. Always doing things piecemeal when they could club together and make a decent job of it. Do you have anything more than these two boxes and the hamper?'

At first I didn't know what to make of the man. He was a burly, bold-looking man, and had a cheerful face to match his voice. I couldn't guess if he was a butcher, a farmer or a horse-dealer. But he clearly wanted to transport me and my belongings to Bala.

'How do you know I want to go to Bala?' I said.

'Even if I hadn't read the address on your box,' he said. 'I would have recognized you for a student at once. I can pick out a student and a Methodist preacher out of any crowd. I'm so used to them, sir. I spotted the other one and packed him onto the coach as soon as he got off the train.'

There's a wonderful man for you, I thought. I didn't know I looked like a scholar. How can I? I've not even got to Bala yet. But I'm not sorry he's recognised me as a student.

I followed the man as a dog does its master. The folk of Corwen seemed to know him well. They called out to him, addressing him either as Mr Edwards or Rice. Rice sounded like the stuff you make puddings with, so I wasn't sure if it was his real name or a nickname.

The other student he had already collected was sitting in the back of the wagon. I was surprised to see it was the young man who had shared my compartment on the train journey. What a pity we hadn't discovered that we were both going to the same college. How was it we hadn't recognized each other as students, but Mr Edwards had spotted us at once? I decided that we were both as dense and unaware as each other.

While Mr Edwards was loading my luggage onto the coach I weighed up his horses. I could see that there was little danger of them running away with us. At first I couldn't decide if they were young horses which had not yet built up a solid covering of flesh, or old horses which were fading away. I was not well acquainted with the qualities of horseflesh but I fancied from the sharply defined bones showing through their hides that they were fading away, not growing into their skins. I confirmed my suspicion with a closer inspection of their behaviour.

Young horses, I thought, would not be experienced enough to use the wait for a nap. Both these were fast asleep, so they must be old hands.

One of them was looking as if he was smiling in his sleep. Perhaps he was dreaming of a time when he had been fed on oats, but the other kept starting awake with a look of terror in his eyes. I wondered if he was dreaming of the tanner taking aim at his head with a gun. As I was musing about the skinniness of the horses it suddenly struck me that I'd heard that Bala students lived on very little, so perhaps Bala horses didn't eat much either. By now my fellow passenger was seated in the carriage, once more lost in contemplation.

Mr Edwards did not want to set off back with such a meagre load. He spent some time inquiring, searching and haggling until he came across a couple of old women whom he managed to persuade to join us for the trip. The carriage being full, I climbed on dickey next to him.

I'm sorry we're a bit late setting off, Mr Lewis, 'He said as he winked at me. 'But we needed a bit more ballast, to make sure we ride safe.'

Then I witnessed the most marvellous transformation I had ever seen. Mr Edwards cracked his whip and shouted some sort of guttural noise, rather like a curse. It had an instant effect on the horses. The poor brutes came to life at once. It was clear that their fear of the driver was such that they would rather have dropped stone dead on the roadside than refuse to comply with his orders.

'They are excellent beasts to go, Mr Edwards,' I said.

'That depends on who's driving them, sir,' Edwards said. 'The students complain it's impossible to make them move. But just watch.'

Once again Mr Edwards yelled out that fearful guttural sound and laid on with his whip. The horses strained forward, panting with fright in the way animals do at the sudden burst of a thunderclap.

'I am the man, sir,' he said, 'who rents out horses to students for their Sunday appointments. And if they would just do as I tell them, the beasts would go fast enough. Much too quiet, those students are. All my horses can tell a student from a normal man. They know students are preachers, and take advantage of their good nature. It's not good being too squeamish, sir. Not if you want horses to get a move on.'

He turned back to the horses and yelled in a fearsome voice. 'Get on you Devils.'

He turned back to me.

'D'ye see how they step out, now? Where are you going to preach next Sunday? You'll need a horse. Just you come and see me on Friday night. I'll see you right.'

I shook my head. 'I don't have an engagement.' I said.

'What? No invitation to preach?' he said. 'Don't worry you're sure to have one by Sunday. Half the students aren't back yet, and there'll be lots of letters asking for preachers. Just you see. I know about these things. Sir. Have you been to Bala before? Where are your lodgings?'

I eagerly drank in all the information and advice that Mr Edwards freely gave me as we drove the fourteen or so miles from Corwen to Bala. He told me the full history of the family I was going to lodge with. And with only a little prompting from me he described the main personalities of the town.

Before I reached Bala I knew who lived at Rhiwlas house, at the Big Bull, the Little Bull, the White Lion, Plas Coch, and the Post Office. I could list the names of all the chapel deacons and all the doctors, both of divinity and of medicine. But Mr Edwards delighted in telling me about the students. He knew every one personally, which county they came from and who they lodged with.

Of one student he said, 'He's a cure,' of another 'He has nothing at all in him,' and of the third, 'He's a bit of a swell.'

He told me many stories, and every one involved his horses. Mr Edwards was an entertaining fellow, and I have never before learned so much in so short a time. He certainly took a deep interest in the students, but I couldn't decide if he was a religionist himself. I thought it too rude to ask. His closeness to the chapel people and the Cause, combined with his knowledge of the college lecturers, made me suspect he was. Yet listening to him drive on his horses, calling them his devils or his demons, made me wonder if he was really of the brethren. His character seemed to be flamboyant, but in his own way he seemed to be eminently serviceable to Methodism.

Little did I guess just how much I would have to do with Mr Edwards while I was in Bala.

I was so engrossed with him that I forgot all about my fellow-traveller. But Mr Edwards did not. As we were coming towards the Tryweryn bridge over the River Dee, he looked over his shoulder.

'Mr Williams,' he said, 'where are you going to lodge?'

Williams gave the same address as I was heading for.

'There's lucky, then. You're both going to the same place. I'll just set these ladies down on the bridge.'

I was pleased to learn that my taciturn fellow-student was going to be living in the same house. I had felt a great interest in him during the journey. A few minutes later we were sitting in a small and sombre parlour, with the housewife, who was a joyous, kindly, little Welshwoman, preparing tea for us.

'You're the only students to come to Bala today,' she said, 'but they'll all be here within the next week, or a fortnight at the latest.'

When two men of similar belief and aims discover that they will be living together for some years they soon develop a mutual accord and trust. Mr Williams and I got to know each other within a half hour. By the time the rest of the students arrived in force we were already firm friends. Mr Williams was from Caernarfonshire, and he soon confirmed what I had suspected from his face. He was a serious, straightforward and honest young man. I was happy to have found someone who understood me and had followed the same path as me. We could converse about our difficulties without fear of being laughed at.

Williams was a few years older, but I quickly found that I knew more English and more about the way of the world. For that I am beholden to Wil Bryan and the town of Mold where I was brought up. But I soon found he was the better divine, and he was an infinitely better preacher than me then and remains so today. Those Caernarfon boys are rare hands at preaching. I feel that the more English the place one is nurtured in, the worse preacher one makes. Williams measured up to exactly what I had hoped my fellow lodger would be.

Abel Hughes always took care I dressed well, and the day I went to Bala I wore a good suit of the best black worsted. While Williams was talking to me, I saw that he noted my clothing and looked impressed. We took a stroll to look over the town and lake, and came back to an unlit hearth. The Bala folk do not light their fire as early in the year as we do in Flintshire. We sat down to get to know each other better.

'Mr Lewis,' Jack Williams said, 'I'm afraid we are unsuitably matched. I am a poor lad. My mother is a widow and depends on me. I was greatly troubled during our journey if I was doing the right thing in leaving her. But it is clear from your suit that you are from a respectable, well-to-do family.'

Before he could say another word I exploded into laughter.

'Mr Williams,' I said. 'I'm a bit of a bard. But do you know my nom de plume? It's Job of the Dunghill. And I'm sure you recognize how just how poor he was.'

I gave him a short summary of my family history (without mentioning my father or my Uncle James) and explained my limited resources. Williams looked far more at ease when he learned of my poverty.

'So you are as poor as I am?' he said. 'Despite your heavy hamper?'

'I most certainly am,' I said. 'My old friend Thomas Bartley gave me that hamper as a surprise parting gift. I have no idea what it contains and I was not expecting it. Will you help me carry it into the house so we can inspect its contents?'

With that he helped me fetch the hamper into the parlour, and we looked inside. It took us many days to finally reach the bottom, so well had Thomas and Barbara packed it with culinary delights. Our hearts were gladdened by the good things in the hamper, and throughout our stay at college we never lacked sustenance for a day.

We had both placed our trust in the care of our Master, and He did not disappoint us.

CHAPTER 37

Thomas Bartley's Visit to Bala

I left Mold with little idea of college life. I knew that all the students were preachers, and I expected them to be staid, serious, sad young men. As they came together from all parts of Wales I imagined they would enhance and deepen each other's individual gloom. I pictured a term as like attending a four-month funeral service for the dead languages they studied. Quite what benefit I expected from that I cannot really explain.

Fortunately, my expectations were much mistaken. The students turned out to be just like any other bunch of lads who could relax and enjoy harmless fun without compromising their consciences. If Wil Bryan had been there I'm sure he would have noted there was no humbug about them, and they were true to nature. Piety is not melancholy, and there is an enormous difference between sincerity and sanctimoniousness. I soon found how natural, carefree and unburdened by guile the students were.

Two birds, the crow and blackbird, wear coats of the same black as favoured by student preachers. The solemn crow croaks and the jolly blackbird sings, but I'm not convinced that the crow gives the Creator greater glory, even if young crows do seem to outnumber young blackbirds.

I wondered what Dafydd Davis would think if he could hear and see us students? Would he think we were too carefree, and so doubt whether we had really been called to preach the gospel? I'm sure if he'd been there watching us we wouldn't have done anything which didn't fit into his idea of dignified. But he wouldn't have seen the real boys, only the side they showed when in company. I concluded from this that only a student ever really saw another as he really was. You can only be natural and spontaneous among like-minded fellows. The presence of a critical Dafydd Davis would make any student draw a veil over his light-hearted side, or perhaps even drive him to pretend to attitudes he didn't have. Every society has its Dafydd Davises who enforce their conventions on the rest of society. Perhaps I can explain this by describing how I have seen animals behaving. I have seen a flock of sheep and their lambs frisking on the side of the hill and playing about in enjoyment. Then a Dafydd Davis approaches in the form of dog. Their play ends at once. You also see it in the birds. The birds in the wayside hedges warble sweetly until a passing traveller stops to listen to their melody. Then the warblers fall silent to avoid attracting his attention. Such is the effect of a Dafydd Davis.

Think of the Sunday School trips you have been on. Often in June the scholars of the town's Sunday School are taken for a trip into the country. Both old and young come together, and after they have eaten their picnic on the grass you see some of the youngsters silently slip away to amuse themselves. And much fun they have, until some pious and revered old man strolls their way. They may know him well, like him and think highly of him, but nevertheless his appearance will dampen their sport. This is another effect of a Dafydd Davis.

No man is ever fully himself except when he is by himself. When he is being watched he will lay out his stall to conform to the notions of some Dafydd Davis or other. It follows that a man only really knows himself when he is alone.

The public and private faces of the students of the college at Bala were quite different from what I anticipated before I joined them. And when my old friend Thomas Bartley paid me a visit he saw the student preachers in a whole new light.

I had been at the college for about two months when Thomas decided to pay me a visit.

I had been preaching at Trawsfynydd on the Sabbath. On my way back on Monday I visited the Rhyd-y-Fen pubic house, where I had a cup of tea and few chunks of oaten bread and met with two friends who had been preaching, one at Llan Festiniog, and the other at Lampeter-yr-Gwynfryn. It was between one and two o'clock in the afternoon when we got back to Bala.

I went to my lodging and I approached the door to the parlour I smelt a strong smell of pipe tobacco. As I opened the door I could hardly believe my eyes. Through the haze of smoke I saw Jack Williams sitting opposite Thomas Bartley, who was in my chair. They were both smiling as if their faces would split in two. Even though I knew Thomas well, I still thought he looked comical. He was wearing his best blue dress coat but what stood out was the enormous shirt collar he had on. That collar was prodigious. If Thomas had blackened his face with burnt cork he could have passed for a Christy Minstrel.

He only wore his great collar on special occasions. I remember my brother Bob saying 'Thomas Bartley is off to fetch coke again'. This was a reference to the way in which carters would decorate their wagons with crepe when hauling coke for sale. If only I could have asked that collar to tell its history. I'm sure it must have been on some famous outings. When Thomas wore it, as he would do on the day of his club feast, it was as if the collar went to the dinner and Thomas just tagged along to keep it company. The collar was more important than its wearer and made its entrance long before anyone noticed Thomas.

Thomas looked striking. He had a high crown, a long, sharp nose and a chin which dwindled deep into his neck, giving his head the aspect of a triangular problem from Euclid. But Jack Williams couldn't keep his eyes off that outrageous collar.

I must admit that, even though I had seen it many times before I couldn't help admiring it. Thomas had the look of a man at ease in my easy chair. I smiled broadly to see him there. As I came in he stood up.

'Well my boy,' he said, 'how art thou, after these hundreds and thousands of years?'

'Right well, Thomas,' I said. 'And all the more surprised and pleased to see you here in Bala. What brings you here?'

'To be shuar,' he said. 'I was in the middle of feeding the pigs, about six o'clock this morning, look you, when I took it into my head to come and see you. Who'd have thought Bala was so far. It's a goodish step from there to here. I thought there was a train all the way, but when I enquired they said Corwen was the last station. Whatever, I was lucky enough to meet Mr Williams there at Corwen. He recognized me from seeing me on Mold station when you were going away. He sorted me out and got me a lift with lot of students, and we had a real pleasant chat, didn't we Mr Williams?' Jack nodded in agreement. 'Wonderful smart boys they were too,' Thomas went on. 'Where've you been so long, Rhys? Mr Williams told me you'd been out preaching somewhere yesterday?'

'I was at Trawsfynydd, Thomas,' I said.

'Trawsfynydd you say? Is Mathew Llewellyn still there? He's a rare one. If I were to get into trouble, it's Mathew Llewellyn I'd ask for advice. Did you hear of him when he was at Ruthin, Mr Williams?' Jack shook his head. 'No? I'll tell you, then.

'This is as true as the Paternoster. There was a man there at the time of the Assizes who was up for stealing bacon. They'd employed Macintyre to prosecute, and this chap had Mathew Llewellyn to defend him. Well Macintyre was laying it on the man's case, and it was looking pretty black. Then up comes Mathew's turn. He calls a butcher to the stand and asks what is meant by bacon? "A pig's sides, salted and dried," says the butcher. "To be sure," says Mathew. Then he calls the shopkeeper on and, asks him, "Was the meat you say this man stole, dried and salted?" "No it wasn't," says the shopkeeper. "Then it's a false indictment," says Mathew, and wins the case there and then. He's a rare 'un, is Mathew. Are any of his family still in Trawsfynydd?'

He didn't wait for me to answer, but stood up and tugged at his great collar.

'D'ye know what, boys?' he said. 'It's awful close in here. Can't we open a window a bit? It's no wonder you both look so pale. There's not a breath of air here. You might's well live in a box as in a fiddling little room like this. You keep your door shut and all you've got is a table some chairs and books. You'll be bound to lose your health. If I was in this place for two days together I'd die.'

He opened the window wide.

'There,' he said. 'That's more like it. We just need a puff of wind now. And how art thou, Rhys? Dost thou like thy place? Are there plenty of provisions here?'

'I've done all right so far, Thomas,' I said. 'How are things with you? How's Barbara? Why didn't she come with you?'

'Barbara's only so-so, to be shuar. She's troubled something shocking with the rheumatics in the legs. She'll be glad to see me back, I can tell you. But she asked to be remembered kindly to you. This is the first time I've been away from home in twenty-five years.'

'What do you think of Bala, Thomas?' I said.

'I haven't seen much of it yet,' Thomas said. 'But what I've seen looks like a town stuck in the middle of a field. Why don't they cut those trees? Ain't the crows a nuisance? I never saw such a row of big trees right in the middle of the street before. Do they not have a Town Board here?'

'The Bala people are proud of their trees, Thomas Bartley,' Jack Williams said.

'Indeed so, Mr Williams,' Thomas said. 'They might be handy on fair days to tie cattle to. But they struck me as odd when I saw them. Rhys? Are you going to take me out see the town? I haven't much time, you know, I have to get back to Barbara. Have you got time?'

'I think I have,' I said. 'I'll show you as much as I can. Have you had something to eat?'

'Yes in the name of goodness.' Thomas said. 'I had an uncommon hearty dinner with Mr Williams here, enough for any man.'

'Good,' I said. 'I'll have a quick wash and then show you around.'

'A wash! Why dost thou want to wash?' Thomas said. 'Thou'rt as clean as a pin in paper. There's not a speck on thee. Art thou getting a bit stuck up here?'

Williams laughed while ran away to perform my ablutions. Jack followed me to my bedroom, threw himself on the bed, and rolled about, laughing.

'Rhys,' he said, 'Mr Bartley is the most original character I've ever met. The boys had a sovereign's worth of fun out of him between Corwen and Bala. They asked me to tell you to keep him here as long as you can. Perhaps we could smuggle him into the class, eh? That'd be a real treat.'

'I'm not sure that would be the right thing to do,' I said. 'To be honest, it's a bit a nuisance to have to show him around. I wouldn't have minded so much if he'd left that enormous collar at home. The whole town will be staring at us.'

'Rubbish!' Williams said. 'That collar's priceless, it makes him interesting. I'll come with you and skip the mathematics class this afternoon.'

'Will you, indeed?' I said. 'I'd been thinking about offering you five shillings to come along to share the shame with me.'

Thomas was reloading his pipe when we got back to the parlour.

'Is Mr Williams coming along too?' he said. 'That's good. But just a minute Rhys. I haven't seen you take anything into your mouth while I've been here. Have you had anything to eat?'

'Yes, thank you, Thomas.' I said. 'I stopped for a meal at the Rhyd-y-Fen.'

'Rhyd-y-Fen, where's that?' Thomas said. 'Is it far?'

'It's a public house half way between Bala and Festiniog,' I said.

'What? Do they let you preachers go into pubs?' Thomas said. 'Well there's no harm in that in my view. I always thought Abel Hughes was too strict on such thing. So let's be off, boys.' He lit his pipe.

'Perhaps you shouldn't smoke as we walk the town,' I said.

'Why on earth not? Are the folk of Bala all stuck up?'

'There's no harm in smoking, Thomas,' I said. 'But in Bala respectable people don't do it in the street.'

'Is that so?' Thomas said. 'And I heard they were keen smokers. But, whatever, let's go and see what we can see. There are three things I want to see. Bala Lake, Bala Clock and the Bala Green. Your mother used to talk a lot about Bala Green. And my father used to say that a safe thing was as right as a Bala clock.

'We'll go to the lake first, Thomas,' I said. I wanted to get through the town as quickly as possible in the hope no one would see us.

But Thomas wasn't to be hurried and stopped to look at everything. He stood in the middle of the road with his hands under his coat-tails and his hat tilted back.

'Wait a bit Rhys,' he said. 'Let me catch my breath lad. Those trees look funny, stuck there in the street.'

He turned and spotted a public house. 'Now there's a slap-up pub,' he said at the top of his voice. 'What's it called, Rhys?'

'The White Lion,' I said softly. I was hoping that Thomas would take my hint and lower his voice.

'Oh, the White Lion,' he said, his voice sounding even louder.

People stopped and stared at us. The shopkeepers came to their doors, children crowded around us, and I felt that they were all staring at Thomas's great collar and odd appearance. Perhaps they expected him to start acting the clown and turn somersaults in front of the hotel. I didn't know what to do for the shame. I was annoyed with Jack

Williams who seemed to be enjoying the spectacle and was sticking close to Thomas's side. At last Thomas moved on, and as he did he spotted the curious children.

'Whatever's the matter with those, children?' he asked, turning to face them.

'What are you gawping at?' he shouted. 'Didn't you ever see a man before? You're the strangest lot I've ever seen in my life. I've heard tales of Bala children. If you don't get away, I'll put my stick across your backs, that I will.' He waved his stick at them, and the children backed away. He turned back to me.

'What's your hurry, Rhys?' he said. Then he turned to Jack. 'Is there just the one street in this town, Mr Williams? I don't see anything special about it. The shops aren't much to speak of, and the whole place looks quiet. I'd always thought Bala was full of chapels, churches, clocks and schools.'

We walked on but Thomas had spotted another pub.

'D'ye know what, Mr Williams,' he said. 'There's another awful nice pub. What's the name of it?'

'The Bull Mawr,' Williams said.

'Now that's a queer name for pub, Mr Williams?' Thomas said. 'Why not Y Tarw Mawr? Do the folk of Bala talk like they do in Buckley? A bit of the Welsh and a bit of the English, all jumbled up.'

Before Jack could answer him Thomas had spotted Mr Edwards, who was standing in front of his house smoking.

Thomas crossed over to him and Williams followed. I tried to walk on slowly in the hope they'd follow me.

'Hullo, Squire,' Thomas said to Mr Edwards. 'Can you give me a light?'

I kept moving for a few steps and then looked back. Mr Edwards and Mr Bartley were doing a good impression of a pair of pigeons mating. The peaks of Thomas's great collar and Mr Edwards's eyes were dangerously close and the bowl of Thomas's pipe was held against that of Mr Edwards's. Rice Edwards was puffing his cheeks out as if he was blowing a bugle. Thomas was drawing his cheeks in and panting heavily as the pair struggled to light his pipe. Jack Williams was holding his sides in silent laughter at their performance.

Clearly Thomas was ignoring my plea not to smoke in the streets. Indeed he seemed to be enjoying himself; I could hear him whistling. I speeded up to try and encourage him out of the town.

'Take time, my boy,' he called after me, 'The end of the world hasn't come just yet!'

I felt as if everybody was staring at us. I was getting mad with Williams who seemed to be encouraging Thomas to hob-nob with Mr Edwards. Now Thomas had lit his pipe he seemed happy to amble along after me. I walked ahead quickly. I could hear him still talking at the top of his voice, even though he was some way behind me.

'That's a Baptist chapel, did you say, Mr Williams?' Thomas shouted. 'Not much of a place, is it? Don't suppose they go down well here? I don't like their way of doing things. All that dipping folk under water. How would my Barbara go on with her rheumatics and the pains in her legs? It wouldn't do for her to be pushed under cold water. To my mind that baptizing looks too much like killing a pig. I'd much rather the Methodist way. Although my father was Baptist. It's all down in my dad's Bible and all our names are.'

Then I heard him shout after me. 'Hi, Rhys,' he said. 'Wait a minute. You look as if you're trying to lose us.'

I felt I could tolerate my old friend's bizarre appearance and the attention he attracted if only he'd stop shouting. I was glad when we finally got out of the town. But there was a fresh problem looming. We were some hundred yards or so out of town when Williams gave me a dig in the ribs. I looked ahead to see one of our teachers taking his customary stroll. He was coming straight towards us.

Out of the frying pan into the fire, I thought to myself, and contemplated trying to pass him with just a lift of my hat. But Thomas had other ideas.

'Here, you boys,' he said. 'Who's that man coming towards us? He looks like a master. I think I know him.'

'Yes he is to be sure,' Williams said at once.

'I thought so,' Thomas said. 'He looks a proper man sure enough. I hear he's very clever, and knows lots of languages. I've heard he's the best of them all when push comes to shove. I've only heard him preach a couple of time but I liked him. I could understand every word he said. He gave me time to think. Not like John Hughes of Llangollen, he kept rushing on without a pause and leaving me behind. What luck meeting him. I must have a word with him, so I can have something to tell Barbara when I get home.'

'He's a busy man, Thomas,' I said. 'Perhaps we'd better just wish him a good afternoon.'

'No danger,' Jack Williams chipped in. 'You can be sure he'll be glad to speak to you, Thomas Bartley, you being a visitor to Bala. And if you ask him I'm sure he'll let you visit the college, then you'd have so much more to tell when you get home.'

'To be shuar,' Thomas said

I could happily have choked Williams, and he knew it full well. It was no use trying to dissuade Thomas, for Williams was clearly going to egg him on. I was dripping with sweat. Williams, though, could hardly hide his amusement. Even if Thomas Bartley not been with a couple of students, I knew our respected teacher would have noted his bizarre attire, and although he was a truly great-minded man I'd never noticed much sign of a sense of humour about him.

Thomas didn't wait for me to introduce him, he took his hat off, and strode forward.

'How are you this long time, sir?' he asked. 'I haven't seen you since the Secession over yonder, and that's years ago, but you look well, sir.'

'This is Mr Thomas Bartley, sir,' I said. 'He's one of our members who has come to see Bala.'

'Thank you,' our Teacher said. 'I am pleased to see you, Mr Bartley. I hope you like Bala.'

'I've only seen one street so far, sir,' Thomas said. 'But I fancy it's a fairish place.'

'How is the Cause going on with you, these days, Mr Bartley?' the master asked him. 'You suffered a great loss with the death of Mr Abel Hughes.'

'Quite well now, sir,' Thomas said. 'We were all higgledy-piggledy for some time after Abel died. But it's coming pretty straight, all things considered. When are you coming over to preach to us again, sir? I'd like to hear you again because I can understand every word you say. I wish you'd teach these young preachers to talk more plain. Sometimes they're too deep for me and my Barbara. There was one of them came lately and I couldn't make any sense of what he said. He kept talking about mechanisms and unity or something like that. I can't really remember exactly. Me and my Barbara couldn't make either horse-hair or hobgoblin of what he said. I told Dafydd Davis that I'd tell you sir, if I saw you while I was in Bala.'

'Well, Mr Bartley,' the master said. 'I've spoken a deal to them on the subject of speaking plainly. What we need is someone, like you, to give them a word of advice. And keep giving it until they listen. It would do them good.'

'To be shuar, sir,' Thomas said. 'I wonder sir, if you could see your way to let me see the college where you teach them?'

'Certainly, Mr Bartley,' he said. 'Perhaps Mr Lewis will bring you to class at five o'clock.'

'Thank you very much, sir,' said Thomas, 'And a good afternoon to you'.

We had hardly left him when Thomas turned upon his heel and walked back towards him.

'Beg pardon, sir. But do you have such a thing as a match about you?' he shouted. 'To be shuar I don't know how I came to leave home without one.'

I tried not to listen and was afraid to turn and look. I was so embarrassed that I wanted to sink into the earth. Williams was silently splitting his sides as Thomas came back to us.

'He hadn't one.' Thomas said. 'He said he doesn't carry any, or he would have given me one and welcome. To be shuar I'm bound to get a light somewhere, before long. Is there a house anywhere? He's a decent man, that master of yours. I'd give a crown for letting me come into college to see you at work. I'll have so much to tell Barbara when I get home.'

I owed Thomas Bartley so much that I felt quite guilty for wishing that he would set off for home at once. Now he had permission to visit the class, I was afraid that he might accidentally humiliate me. It would have sounded inhospitable if I had warned to him that if he came to college he wouldn't be able to get home that night. In Mold I might have enjoyed the fun, but in Bala I felt wretched. I felt that he would be judged as if he was my father.

I did my best to put on a cheerful face, but Thomas noticed I was upset.

'You look a bit down in the mouth, Rhys,' he said. 'Are you annoyed about something?'

I shook my head. Williams was fully enjoying the entertainment. He and Thomas Bartley were as close as a whip and top. He was eager to show Thomas the sights and he seemed delighted with the matter-of-fact way Thomas accepted them. As we stood looking down the beautiful stretch of water for which Bala is widely famous, Thomas was not impressed.

'This lake wouldn't make a bad sea, for a picnic.' Thomas said. 'There must be lots of fish in it. What fly would you use? A Coch-y-Bonddu perhaps? It looks a good place for rearing ducks.'

He didn't want to walk on to Llanycil churchyard.

'All churchyards are the same,' he said. 'And they only make me think of Seth. Let's go back to Bala to see the clock.'

'I've never seen a clock in Bala, 'Jack Williams said. 'I think it must be an imaginary tale. Neither Rhys nor I have managed to find it.'

'I see,' said Thomas. 'So it's a bit of a sendup, like when folk say that the best thing for mending bruises is snail's foot oil?'

I tried my best to delay our return in the hope Thomas would be too late to visit the class, but Jack kept him bang on time. He made sure we got back to our lodgings by half past four. He had already ordered tea to be laid ready. I felt ashamed of myself when I saw the meal he'd ordered. He was making Thomas Bartley welcome, something I should have done myself. Fortunately, Thomas hadn't realized I wasn't involved. He tucked in with gusto. I felt ashamed at my meanness and was glad he hadn't noticed.

'You know what boy?' Thomas said. 'You live like fighting cocks. But you deserve it, because a man needs to be well fed if he's going to give of his best.'

Thomas hadn't guessed that the meal Jack had arranged was so much better than our normal fare. It was a veritable club feast, but it was over in few minutes, and Williams insisted that we set off for class at once. I suspected him of wanting to show Thomas off to the rest of the boys before the Master arrived.

I thought quickly. 'Thomas wants a smoke first,' I said.

'To be shuar,' Thomas said, 'If there's time.'

'You take as long as you want, Thomas,' I said.

Jack Williams kept reminding Thomas of the time as he puffed away at his pipe and made sure that we arrived in the classroom of the dot of five o'clock. The class was for study of the Greek Testament. We freshmen did not yet understand Greek, but we listened carefully to the exposition in a language we were still learning.

The whole body of students were there and met us with a deafening cheer as we arrived. It was clear that Thomas Bartley's fellow travellers from Corwen to Bala had been spreading word of his enormous collar.

I'm sure the cheers were for his mighty collar, because when Thomas gracefully bowed to acknowledge the greeting and as his great collar flapped it got another great cheer. He sat down, between Williams and myself as the applause died away.

Williams stood up and made an announcement.

'Gentlemen, this is Mr Thomas Bartley, a friend of Mr Rhys Lewis ... '

Before he could say anything more the Master came, and the room immediately fell silent.

'There's a wonderful lot you are,' Thomas whispered in my ear. 'And you're all so much alike, all except that man with the crooked nose over there. He looks a card.'

Thomas nodded to the Master as if he were an old friend. His nod was courteously returned but I saw as the Master turned his face away the back of his neck was flushing bright red.

For the next twenty minutes an explanation of the Greek Testament continued, most of it in Greek. For the first five minutes Thomas paid careful attention, looking like an adjudicator at an *eisteddfod*. For the second five minutes he seemed to be paying less attention, and after the first quarter of an hour he murmured softly in my ear. 'Will it be much longer?'

I placed my finger to my lips, urging him to keep quiet. He subsided into his great collar and I began to worry that he might begin to snore. The rest of the students kept casting furtive looks at him, sitting between Jack Williams and me. They were making faces suggesting that they too were expecting Thomas to begin to snore.

The Master couldn't help noticing and perhaps he was also afraid that Thomas might doze off noisily. He brought the class to an early close and spoke to us in English.

'Perhaps we'd better stop there,' he said. 'Mr Lewis has, with my permission, brought a friend with him to this evening's class. This is an unusual thing, and should not be taken as establishing a precedent. But I felt that Mr Lewis's friend might give you some advice about your preaching.' He looked at Thomas who was once more alert and paying close attention.

'I was observing, Mr Bartley,' he said now speaking in Welsh for Thomas's benefit. 'That you might give these gentlemen a word of advice. As you observed earlier the young men of today need a deal of talking to. Will you say something to them, Mr Bartley?'

'I'm not much of a hand a speaking, sir,' Thomas said. 'But I'll do my best. I've heard much about Bala, sir, before Rhys came here. His mother and I were great friends, and she brought me to religion. I knew nothing before she explained it to me. She was a wonderful woman and I told her, many times, if she'd happened to belong to the Ranters, she'd have made a champion preacher.'

At this point the whole class cheered.

'Wait a bit now,' Thomas said as the noise died down. 'What was I going to say? Oh, yes. When Rhys came to you, I determined I'd come over and see Bala, someday. This morning as I was feeding the pig ...'

This caused another loud cheer.

'I said to myself, now's the time to go,' Thomas said. 'From Corwen to Bala I got a ride with some of the young preachers here, and I was surprised, sir. I always thought students were poor things, with their heads tucked under their wing and half starving themselves. But I never saw a more decent set of lads. They wasn't a bit like preachers, they were so powerfully witty. D'ye know, sir, Mr Williams here,' he put his hand on Jack's shoulder, 'can do an impression of you that true to your life. If I shut my eyes I wouldn't know it wasn't you speaking.'

The applause broke out again, but Jack didn't join in. He blushed to the roots of his hair. I must admit I wasn't sorry to see him put on the spot. He'd done the same to me many times in the course of the afternoon. Thomas looked puzzled by the acclaim, as if he wasn't sure if he had made a good point or a big mistake. He hesitated for a moment then gathered himself together.

'Honestly sir,' he said. 'It's as true as the Paternoster.'

He got another round of applause for this and, reassured, he went on.

'But I must tell these fine young men, to their faces, sir,' he said. 'They're not as clever at preaching as they think. I'm a bit dull, as I was old in coming to religion, and I've only heard a few of them preach. Perhaps they weren't the best. When you preach, sir, you must speak plainly. But to tell the truth I couldn't make horsehair or hobgoblin out of what some of them students said. And my wife Barbara couldn't follow them either. They didn't talk enough about Jesus Christ, and heaven sir. A man like me has a pretty fair grip of that. But they spoke more about mechanisms or the like. I'd no more idea than a mountain goat what they meant. Rhys told me you don't teach them to preach, sir. That's an awful pity. I know you're wiser than me, but if I was you, sir, I'd make them preach before you. One every week and when he'd done you should show him where he'd gone wrong and if he didn't learn better you should give him the sack. These boys expect to make their living by preaching in Welsh. It's no good learning the languages of people who've been dead for years if they can't preach in the language everybody understands. That's my view, sir. Perhaps I'm wrong, because all I have is a grip of the letters. I'm glad to see your school, and I'm pleased that I gave half a sovereign to the little man who came about collecting to support it. He told me we got all our crowing cocks from Bala. And now I can't hear the young fowl in our yard without remembering his words. It's a queer enough clamour young cocks make, sir, if there isn't an old 'un among them to set a pattern. But they come little by little to tune in lovely with enough practice. I takes an interest in fowl, sir, as Rhys will tell you. And the worst thing is chicks that you can't tell if they're cocks or hens. If they don't show pretty quick which they are, I chop their heads off. Well, I'm glad from my heart to see you all getting on so well, and I hope you'll forgive me taking up so much of your time.'

With that he sat down to long cheers and loud applause.

'What's the meaning of these cheers, Mr Williams? 'I heard him ask Jack. 'Did I speak middling tidy?

'You spoke capital well,' Williams said.

'Well, Mr Bartley,' the Master said. 'I hope the young men attend to your pointed observations, and act upon the valuable advice you have given them. When next a student preaches to you, take careful note whether they have improved. If they do not show clearly that they are a hen or a cock, let me know, Mr Bartley. I may well have to cut their heads off.'

The room erupted in a tumultuous ovation as the Master shook hands with Thomas Bartley and left the room. As soon as he had gone, one of the students locked the door.

'What's going on now?' Thomas said.

'I don't know,' I said. And I really didn't, but something unusual was going happening. Then Dylan Hughes from Aberdaron stood up. He was the boy with the crooked nose that Thomas had picked out earlier as a bit of a card.

'Friends,' Dylan Hughes said. 'The talk of mechanism that Mr Bartley mentioned is not the only fault we students are guilty of. There is a close connection between our obsession with mechanism and the matter I wish to bring before you. A brother from Flintshire, who was returning from a preaching engagement this morning caused a valuable horse of Mr Rice Edwards's to fall. This was because of inexcusable carelessness and an acute lack of equestrian skill. The horse fell and broke its knees. This action has occasioned great loss for Mr Rice Edwards, and inflicted dreadful pain on the horse. We shouldn't look lightly upon this sort of act and so I propose that we enquire into the case. We must place our brother upon trial. I will take the role of judge. Mr Vernon Powel will be prosecutor, and Mr Rhys Lewis, who comes from the same county, will defend him. I also appoint Mr Thomas Bartley foreman of the jury, and Mr John Jones as interpreter.'

'Is he serious or is this a bit of a joke?' asked Thomas.

'It's all in jest,' I said.

'Ho, I see. It's all in fun then.' Thomas chuckled to himself.

The trial began quickly. I won't tell every detail but will summarize it.

The accused looked dejected, just as an accused man should. Dylan Hughes sat in the teacher's chair on top of the table. He put a white handkerchief on his head to look like the judge's wig. Thomas Bartley took his duty as foreman of the jury most seriously and paid careful attention to the pleadings.

Vernon Powel made an excellent prosecutor, he was quick-witted and eloquent. He called several character witnesses to attest the trustworthy nature of the horse and its undoubted agility. He asserted it was highly unlikely to stumble onto its knees unless its rider was negligent.

No matter how hard I cross-examined I couldn't shake their evidence of the animal's general health and soundness of limb. I had shaken off the restraint I had felt all afternoon, and threw my heart and soul into the defence of my fellow Flintshireman. But it was a bad case to defend, as every witness spoke out in favour of the horse.

The arguments went on for an hour and a half. The witnesses all refused to speak English, and the judge refused to hear any evidence in Welsh. This forced Mr John Jones, whose command of Saxon was the poorest among us all, to interpret everything that was said. This caused much amusement.

I summed up for my client as best I could, although I was conscious that I hadn't got a leg to stand on. My only hope was to try to engage the sympathy of the foreman of the jury. But my legal arguments were systematically demolished by the judge as he summed up. I submitted one last desperate plead to allow the accused to make a final statement in mitigation to the jury before they retired to consider their verdict. This was granted.

The defendant, who had remained silent through the whole proceeding now stood up and spoke to Dylan Hughes.

'I submit there is not case to answer my lord,' he said. 'I hired a mare from Mr Edwards, not a horse.'

Thomas stood up and shouted 'A bad indictment indeed. No case to answer.'

All the students erupted into laughter. Some of the lads were stretched out on benches, overcome with merriment, whilst others rolled about the floor. Thomas Bartley climbed onto a bench and waved his hat about. He was shouting with all his might, as if he were at an election. The meeting broke up in paroxysms of laughter.

I had the great difficulty in preventing Thomas stopping random passers-by to tell them the tale, as we went back to our lodgings. He would keep stopping and shouting out with laughter.

'That was every bit as good as Mathew Llewellyn of Ruthin,' he kept repeating. 'That was the jolliest meeting I ever went to. The first bit was boring, and I couldn't follow it, but that mock trial was a hoot.'

Finally I got him back to my lodgings.

'Where's Mr Williams got to?' Thomas said. 'He looks very like your brother Bob, don't you think? What are you going to do tomorrow night? I wish I could stay for a week, but I must set off for home. Barbara will be wondering where I've got to.'

'I'm afraid you're far too late for the last train back to Mold,' I said. 'You'll have to stay the night and set off in the morning.'

'Oh my dear Lord,' Thomas said. 'How will Barbara go on, left on her own all night?'

'I'm sorry,' I said, 'but there is no way you can get back tonight.'

'I wish I'd brought my Barbara along,' he said. 'Even if she is a bit off-colour.'

At the moment Jack Williams arrived. He had three of the other students with him, and looked pleased when I told him that Thomas was staying the night with us.

Six of us crammed into the small parlour for supper that night. Thomas enjoyed the meal, and the guests enjoyed Thomas Bartley. I have already gone on too long in this chapter to add a full account of the conversation. Enough to say that the boys enjoyed themselves hugely. But Thomas would now and then let out a quiet sigh, showing that he was worrying about Barbara being alone back at Y Twmpath.

We had to rearrange our sleeping arrangements that night. He slept in my bed and I bunked in with Williams. Thomas was up a dawn the next morning. He came into William's room shouting.

'Time to get up. It's nearly the middle of the day.'

He gave us no peace until we got up. Thomas wanted to catch the first train from Corwen. By six o'clock he, I and Jack Williams were crossing Tryweryn bridge aboard Rice Edwards's carriage.

As we stood on the platform awaiting the train Thomas took me aside.

'How does your pocket stand, my son?' he said.

'I'm not hard up yet, Thomas,' I said.

'Here you are,' he said, handing me a sovereign. 'Take a loan of this forever.'

'Bless you Thomas Bartley,' I said. That was neither the last nor the only sovereign Thomas gave me while I was at Bala.

'Mr Williams?' Thomas said. 'You must come to visit Barbara and me, and spend a week at Y Twmpath.'

'Thank you indeed, Mr Bartley,' Jack said.

The train arrived, and Thomas set off home to tell Barbara all about Bala and the college. And what a tale he had to tell. Now Thomas thought he knew all about the students. But I could tell from his question, 'What have you got planned tomorrow night?' that he thought he had taken part in an ordinary evening.

Little did Thomas know that a mock trial happened perhaps once every two or three years. The part of the evening he had found boring and called the most miserable thing on earth was what we normally did. The long hours and hard labour involved in study, the fear and anxiety of spirit committed to understanding yourself, and the eternal questioning of your own ability that every student knows were not things that occurred to his innocent soul. He had a simplistic impression of collegiate life. In this he was not alone; I have since heard similar observations from many people who should know better. Only one who has been a student knows the real cost of education.

CHAPTER 38

A Fortunate Encounter

I was as interested in learning as any other young man who came to Bala, but I never won any prizes during the four years I was there. I wasn't especially gifted, and the few months I went to Soldier Robin's school hadn't given me much of a start. I just couldn't compete with young men who were well educated before they joined the college. And I had to earn my keep, which meant preaching.

If I didn't preach I didn't eat. I couldn't survive without meals, and so I took up preaching dates every Sunday. My Sabbath journeys were often long. I would travel to any chapel with a twenty-five mile radius. I went to Trawsfynydd, Festiniog, Tanygrisiau, Maentwrog, Rhydymain, Corris, Aberllefenni, Machynlleth and everywhere in between.

Llanfor was only a mile up the Corwen Road, but I only once accepted Edward Rowlant's invitation to go there. It was so close to Bala that if a student was preaching there a dozen of his fellows would come to the Llanfor meeting instead of going to Sunday School at Bala. And each would bring his own critical tape measure.

One good friend of mine, preaching at Llanfor, joked about Adam's uncircumcised appendage. He was never allowed to forget that remark as long as he remained at Bala. What if I made a similar stupid attempt at humour? The next morning it would be pinned up on every noticeboard in the college. But I will not speak of the notice-boards of the old college, even though they were wonderful to behold.

My Sabbath journeys took two-and-a-half days a week out of my study time. I would spend Saturday morning planning and organizing. The afternoon would be spent on the back of one of Mr Rice Edwards's old sixteen-handers. Sunday was spent preaching, and Monday morning used to travel back to college. It would often take me most of Monday afternoon to recover from the bumping and jolting of the ride.

Those boys whose parents who could afford to support them could spend Saturday and Monday at their books. These disadvantages joined forces with my natural lack of talent, to stop me from distinguishing myself in the examinations.

However, the effort my brother Bob had put into instructing me helped. I could read and write both Welsh and English, and I made every effort to attend classes regularly, so was never at the bottom of the class. I consoled myself by thinking of myself as unextreme: neither at the top nor the bottom, but somewhere towards the middle. I flatter myself that I still walk a middle way even today.

I may have not made a mark on the college, but the college definitely made a mark on me. I learned thousands of things I didn't know before, and even now I cannot underestimate the value of that knowledge. College opened a new world for my mind, and, even though I only managed to explore its middle regions, it was a great benefit to learn that it existed. I was now able to see with my own eyes the beauty of a leaf upon the water.

It was worth going to college, if only to discover how much there is to know. College shook the dust out of my mind and rubbed off the rust it had gathered at home. I had thought that I stood out in our chapel for my natural insight, and that only Wil Bryan had been brighter than me. This gave me an inflated opinion of myself, but I soon found I was in no way out of the ordinary. Many of my fellow students could fit me in their waistcoat pocket.

I got the benefit by rubbing up against many who surpassed me in every way. No young man can spend four years in college and come home again without improving himself. My time at college was the most blessed and happy period my life. I look back on it with the sweetest of memories. I tied many knots of friendship there which neither time nor distance have undone. I only have to close my eyes to see the faces of my dear companions. But where are they now?

A few left without finishing, but most of them completed the course and are scattered up and down the world. Several became pastors of flocks and are doing useful work, some are famous names in the ministry. Some get by as best they can, preaching here and there on the Sabbath and not doing much during the week.

As the time drew near when I would have to leave college, the issue of what was I going to do became important. We all asked ourselves the same question. We had given up our old occupations, and were now so out of practice that we could not return to them. Some had comfortable homes to go back to, or wealthy family who would support them. But those of us without such blessings found ourselves in a serious fix. Such was my case. Miss Hughes had been extraordinarily kind to me during my four years at college. She had invited me to her home every holiday. But once I had finished my education I could not expect her to continue to give me free board and lodging. Even if she offered, I couldn't in fairness take advantage of her, be a gentleman idler in the week, and just go about preaching on Sundays.

My fellow lodger Jack Williams was in the same quandary. We had many serious talks about what we were going to do. Sometimes he could be quite jocular.

'It seems to me,' he said to me one night, 'that if you want to be a Methodist preacher you should look around for an old gal with plenty of cash? Look at us. We'll be leaving Bala within the month, and how can we earn a living? I'm very good at wearing a black frock coat, but four years of college have spoiled my hands so much I can't go back to working the land. You, Rhys, can post an advert in the *Liverpool Mercury* saying: "Wanted: a young man with four years college education, knows a little Latin and Greek and a lot of Divinity, seeks a position as a draper's assistant. Can preach well. Salary immaterial but needs Saturdays and Mondays off to facilitate his Sabbath journeys."'

'As for me,' he went on. 'I will have to become a ticket collector on the railways, or go out to Africa as your friend Thomas Bartley suggested. Perhaps you should try and creep up the sleeve of the Bishop of St Asaph, and I will do likewise with the Bishop of Bangor. I wouldn't be hard for two thin lads like us to creep up a Bishop's wide sleeve. But would we both have to go and study for another four years at Lampeter before the English Church would give us a living? Despite the fact we're both better preachers than most vicars. What do you think? Have you a better plan?'

I couldn't help laughing at Jack's vision of our future, despite my uncertainty about what I was going to do when I left Bala. The question was becoming serious.

'If we have to go back to our old jobs what was the point of spending four years studying here?' I wondered.

We were both hoping to find work of a religious nature but neither had heard any hint of a chance to take over supervision of a chapel. We had spent four hard years studying to master the religious work we felt called to, and the idea of having to go back to our old jobs was disheartening. I couldn't see any other options for us, but we were both determined not to sit about doing nothing after we left college.

Williams was a better speaker than me, and I thought him the best preacher in the college at that time. He had twice been asked to preach in Bala during his stay: a certain indicator of a bright future. But the Bible says that the last shall be first, and so it was for me. Just a couple of weeks before finishing at college I received two letters.

Getting up early is a talent I do not have. My brother Bob had to start work early, but Mam had to call him a dozen times to get him out of bed every day. He never got out of bed without her calling him a dozen times. He could, however, stay up at night as long as you liked. I am just like him. Jack Williams, though, had a flair for early rising.

The morning those fateful letters arrived I came downstairs at eight o'clock. Jack had gone out for a walk. On the parlour table I found two envelopes. I recognized the handwriting on them both. One was from Miss Hughes, the other from Eos Prydain.

I opened the letter from Miss Hughes first, as I always gave her priority. Inside the envelope was another letter, written in a strange hand. It was written in English and read as follows:

A Fortunate Encounter

Old Bailey, Birmingham
Rhys Lewis, Esq,
May 1st, 1879

Sir,

This morning a man named as John Freeman passed away in the prison I administer. Six weeks ago he was found guilty of poaching and sentenced to three months' hard labour. He was not strong when he arrived and soon took cold. He rapidly took a turn for the worse and, realizing he was dying, asked to speak to me privately. During our conversation he admitted that his real name was James Lewis. He asked me to inform you of his death, which I promised to do if and when it took place. He specifically asked me to tell you that everything he had previously told you was a lie. He did not know your address but believed you would get it if I sent this letter to a Miss Hughes of Mold.

I have fulfilled my promise to the deceased. We have not yet buried him, as we have been short of coffins and I did not expect him to die so soon. We hope to be able to bury him soon.

Yours truly,
J.F. Breece
Governor, Old Bailey Prison, Birmingham

I was confused. I read and reread the letter. My Uncle James had been the cause of many of my troubles, and I detested him but as I read of his dreadful end, and what he had told the prison governor, I felt emotions I do not want to write down. I looked out over Tegid Street with the letter in my hand. I didn't see the houses, instead my mind flashed back to my first meetings with my uncle when I had named him The Irishman. For almost half an hour I stood staring out of window while the meetings with my uncle and their consequences replayed in my mind.

Mrs Owen, my landlady, laid the table for breakfast and said something to me, but didn't hear what she said and I don't remember answering her. Then Jack Williams came back from his walk and broke my reverie

'Hey, you Seventh Sleeper,' he said. 'What's the matter with you? Have you had bad news? You look as miserable as if you were standing by your *Nain*'s grave. '

I tried to look cheerful as I sat down to breakfast. While I was eating I opened and read the letter from Eos Prydain.

This is what it said:

Bethel Chapel, New Street, Mold
May 1st, 1879

Dear Brother,

We understand your term at Bala is almost complete. You know the history and the situation of Bethel Chapel as well as we do. The Cause suffers for need of someone to take it forward, since the death of your old master, Abel Hughes.

    We feel that our children and young people do not get the level of care and attention that they should. We have been thinking about appointing a pastor. Last week we, the undersigned, brought the question before the congregation and suggested your name as someone whose college course was nearly complete and knew us well. The idea was met with general approval. We did not take a vote, not having yet got permission from the *Seiat*. However, we decided to tell you it is our aim to apply to the *Seiat*, and fully expect that they will approach you, unless you are promised elsewhere. You need not fear that anyone will think less of you because you are still a young man. We hope to see you in a few weeks, so that we can discuss the matter further. Until then we send you our kind regards and wish you every success.

    Yours on behalf of the church,
    Dafydd Davis, Alexander Phillips (Eos Prydain)
    Deacons. Bethel Chapel, Mold

I passed the letter over the table to Williams. His joy on reading it could not have been more if it had been addressed to him. My call to take up the pastorate of the chapel I was brought up in was quite unexpected. I realized it was a great compliment, and, if I had not received the other letter, I would have thought it a matter for great rejoicing. But in the context of that other letter it was sad news. I felt my spirit sinking within me. I wrote at once to my old friends, Dafydd Davis and Eos Prydain, and thanked them for their kind letter. I added that I would be coming back to Mold in a few weeks' time.

Having sealed the envelope and addressed it, I told Jack what I was going to do.

'Jack,' I said. 'Don't mention this to the boys or anybody else, because there is no way I can accept it.'

'You're taking nonsense,' he said. 'I'm going to rush out and tell everyone. What's the matter with you? Are you off your head? How can you refuse that which you most wished for?'

'I have a skeleton in my cupboard,' I said. 'I can't talk about it. I might be able to tell you one day, but not now while I am dispirited and sad. I know you would willingly share my burden, but today you cannot help me. I must go away for a few days, this very morning.'

Jack had a tender heart

'My dear fellow,' he said. 'I've realized for some time that there was a secret unpleasantness in your life, and I have no right to ask you about it. What I do ask is, How can I help you?'

'First do not tell anyone about this offer, as I cannot accept it,' I said. 'And, if you could, please go over to Rice Edwards and ask him, if he has a carriage to spare, to send it after me along the Corwen Road. I intend to leave at once to save time, in case he has nothing available.'

'I will do as thou askest, my dear friend,' Jack said.

'Perhaps I can explain all this to thee someday.' I said.

I took my top coat, and what little money I had and set off towards the station at Corwen. Williams, dashed away to order a carriage without questioning me further. It was a long trek to Birmingham and would take me all day. But I was tired of pretending about my family and living in fear of discovery.

I had not got far before Mr Edwards caught up with me. He drove me to Corwen as fast as he could go but we just missed a train. I had a long wait for the next one.

Once on the way to Chester I welcomed the solitude of the carriage compartment to allow me to reflect on what was happening, without having to make conversation with fellow travellers.

Many things passed through my mind. I kept rereading Mr Breece's letter. Could it a forgery my uncle had written to torment me? But what purpose could such a forgery serve? I couldn't think of any.

If the letter was true, there was a chilling implication to the sentence, 'He specifically asked me to tell you that everything he had previously told you was a lie.' It was those words which had convinced me that I couldn't take up the call to become the Minister of Bethel. I was amazed that the chapel should have made such an offer, with more than half the members knowing the full history of my family. But, I reflected, over twenty-two years people forget things, and, because of my meetings with my uncle, I knew far more about the matter than they did.

My family's history was not my fault, but were the sins of my father to be visited upon his child in my case? I was afraid they would be. Was Providence calling me back to Mold just to feed me the sour harvest that my ancestors had sown? How could I accept the chapel's call? But then again, how could I turn it down? I had nowhere else to go, unless I emigrated to Australia or somewhere just as far away.

I felt myself the innocent victim of misfortune. Was I exaggerating my terrors of the past, fearing something that would never happen? I vowed that I wouldn't sleep until I had confronted this matter.

My plan was to visit Mr J. F. Breece, to see if he really existed. If the letter was honest, then it was possible my uncle might have told the writer far more than he had put in his letter.

Whatever happened my journey would not be in vain. I would finally resolve this matter one way or another. If my worst fear was realized, then I couldn't accept the call to lead Bethel church. Indeed, if what Uncle James had told me was indeed a pack of lies, I might be forced to flee the land of my birth. I had tried to keep my conscience clear with God, and no reasonable soul would blame me for my father's sins, but they would pity me, which was far worse. My pride wouldn't let me become an object of commiseration and pity. I had the moral courage to bear any disgrace which I instigated myself, but how could I atone for sins in which I had played no part? Yet the chapel folk would say that blood was thicker than water. This matter must be laid to rest.

I knew nothing about Birmingham, never having been there before. The weather was wet, and the continuous drizzle dull and heavy. Fate was against me, for I missed my connection at Chester and had to wait two hours. I would arrive in Birmingham late and was afraid I wouldn't be able to see Mr Breece that day.

It was nearly ten o'clock in the evening when the train got to Birmingham. I had dozed off before we arrived at the big, bustling town. I was wakened from my dreams by the lights of the station and noise of the crowd of passengers bustling through the station, even at that time of night. Was I too late to call on Mr Breece?

I decided I would not be any worse off by trying to find him that night and made my way to the cab stand. Before I could get there a sprightly young fellow jumped out saying, 'Want a cab, sir?'

'Yes I do,' I said. 'Can you take me to the Old Bailey Prison?'

The young man opened the door to the cab.

'Certainly sir,' he said. 'I know it well, sir. Better to be outside than inside it as the worm said to the blackbird that was about to swallow him.' He closed the door and away we went.

After the quiet of Bala the rattle of carriages along the streets was deafening. I was astounded at the endless flow of people milling about. Within a few minutes I saw hundreds of faces I had never seen before. Each with their own story and purpose, which were as strange to me as mine were to them.

Though there were many lamps along the street they showed up the dirty fog rather than lit the way. Perhaps the smoke which had risen from the chimneys during the daytime had now settled back, with a fine rain to keep it company, to add to the misery of the city.

Many large businesses were closed and in darkness, but the lights of the small tobacconist shops, the public houses and the gin-shops made them seem more attractive than they would have been in daylight.

Every vault and gin-shop we passed had people going in or coming out even at that time of night. I saw a soldier in red coat reel out of one pub with a bonnetless woman in a red shawl clinging to him. From another I saw a lame man in such ragged clothes that he had to hold his money in his fist for safekeeping as he struggled towards the bar. I couldn't tell if he was young or old.

Looking into one public house as we rattled passed I saw a man leaning back against the doorpost, his chin resting on his waistcoat, and looking down as he if were counting the buttons of his breeches. At the door of another I saw foppish young man in a frock coat which was buttoned up to his throat as if hiding a multitude of sins. He was sniffing at perfume from a handkerchief as if he could find no better enjoyment.

I saw a multitude of hideous faces that night, looming out of the fog, lit only by the light of the taverns they haunted. They looked as if their owners had been locked in dark cells for the last fifty years and left to half starve. Some were as filthy as if they had escaped up a chimney, whilst others were so emaciated that they could have escaped through a key hole. I quietly thanked God I was Welsh, red-cheeked, healthy and honest.

As the cab drove on the lights became fewer. Soon there was nothing to be seem but vast warehouses, dark, looming and silent. There were hardly any people walking these streets, and the only sound was the rumble of the wheels and the steady clop of the horse's feet. Then I heard someone whistling a familiar tune. The whistler seemed to be keep pace with the cab so I stuck out my head to listen and realized it was the driver. He was whistling the old Welsh hymn tune, Caersalem. It was not a melody I had expected to hear in an English city. The tune took me back to Bethel, and I could hear the words 'Thanks be to Him, For remembering the earth's dust' echoing in my memory. This cabbie must attend a chapel, I thought.

By now we were moving though a very gloomy part of the city. Was I being foolish trying to see Mr Breece so late at night?

The lights of the cab shone onto a high, black wall. It stopped in front of a wide gateway which was closed by a great wooden door, completely studded with nail-heads. Beside the door a large lamp hung from a bracket fixed to the sturdy wall.

'Here we are, safe and sound, sir,' the cabbie said, opening the door for me. He was standing with his back to the wall light, which shone in my eyes so I couldn't see his face. He looked at me and then jumped back as if startled.

'Well hello, my Old Hundredth,' he said. 'And how are you keeping?'

He stood back under the light, so I could see his face. My heart jumped as recognized my old pal, Wil Bryan.

Before I could speak, a small door, set within the larger one opened. A tall, round-shouldered man, stepped out and the door slammed shut after him. He strode passed without looking at us, keeping his eyes towards the ground. But we both saw his face clearly in the lamplight.

Wil waited until he was out of earshot and then said. 'I'll be damned if that wasn't old Nicklas o' Garth'

'Thou'rt right, Wil,' I said. 'That was Nicklas sure enough. Please, for my sake, will you follow him and find where he goes? I'll do what I have to do here and, no matter how long it takes, I'll wait for you to return.'

'At thy service, Rhys my old pal. I always wanted to be a detective,' Wil said, speaking in Welsh. He jumped up onto his cab and drove off after Nicklas.

I stood watching him until his lights faded into the fog, then I turned back to the prison door. I rang the bell as hard as I could.

But it will take another chapter to tell what else happened on that strange night.

CHAPTER 39

Wil Bryan in His Castle

I felt perplexed and dispirited. The sudden appearance of Wil Bryan and Nicklas of Garth Ddu only added to my confusion. The vigorous clamour of the doorbell faded away, and the sound was replaced by steady footsteps, each stride accentuated by a jingle of keys, the badge of office of a jailor.

The door opened and the bright glare of a lamp shone in my eyes making it impossible to see the face of its holder.

A man's harsh voice rang out. 'Who are you? What do you want?'

'My name is Rhys Lewis. Is Mr Breece, the governor in?' I said.

'He is.'

'Can I see him?' I asked.

'If your business is important enough, you can,' he said.

'I have come in response to his letter,' I said.

'Then come in and explain yourself.'

My guide led me into a small, square room. It was sparsely furnished with a table and two chairs.

'Wait here,' the man said, locking the door behind him as he left.

I was shaking with fear at the thought of being called to explain myself to the Governor of the Old Bailey. I knew I must speak to him to find out what had really happened, but it made my mission no easier.

A memory of the only other jailor I had ever met flashed through my mind. I could see Mr Prichard, the keeper of Flint prison, giving me a look which would make even the most innocent tremble in their shoes. His face had showed a seething authority and his sharp, wild eyes had looked right through me to my very back bone.

Almost everyone who was committed to Flint jail, except Ned James, was terrified by Mr Prichard's hostile stare and overpowering voice. When Ned was sent down for a second time Mr Prichard was not pleased to see him back.

'Well, Ned, Ned, Ned.' He shouted each repetition of Ned's name twice as loud as the one before. 'Why have you come here again?'

'I never was in any place in my life that I couldn't go to back to,' Ned said in a quiet calm voice, to annoy Mr Prichard as much as possible.

If the custodian of our small Flint prison was such a terrifying individual, how much more frightening would the keeper of the Birmingham Old Bailey be?

The door opened, and I stood up with my knees knocking. The gatekeeper beckoned me to follow him and escorted me to the presence of Mr Breece. My fear was groundless. Mr Breece was not anything like Mr Prichard. He was small, refined and innocuous-looking. He had obviously invited me into his private quarters, for his wife was sitting knitting in what seemed to be the sitting room. Mrs Breece was a large, well-built lady, of pleasing aspect. She made her husband look even smaller with her presence.

As I came to the door Mr Breece stood up to welcome me. He gave me a kindly look over his gold rimmed spectacles and offered me a seat which I gratefully accepted.

'Thank you Mr Gloom,' he said to my guide. The man nodded in acknowledgment and withdrew from the room.

'You are Mr Lewis?' Mr Breece asked.

'Yes, sir,' I said. 'I beg your pardon for disturbing you so late.'

'Don't mention it! Don't mention it!' he said. 'When there's duty on hand, I never consider the time.'

'Excuse me, Mr Lewis, but are you a clergyman?'

'I am sir,' I said.

'I guessed so,' he said. 'Will you take a glass of wine with us.' He turned to his wife. 'Mother would you mind fetching us some glasses?'

'Please don't trouble,' I said. 'I am of the Methodist calling and do not take drink, thank you. I do not want to intrude on you for too long. My errand is simple. This morning I received your letter informing me of the death of a man named James Lewis in this place. I have come to find out the circumstances as best I can.'

Mr Breece's expression changed. He gave me a keen, searching look. 'Yes,' he said. 'I wrote to you and thought no more of the matter. Was he your father?'

'No he was not,' I said, and felt glad I could say so. 'He was a relative of sorts but I can assure you he was not one I was proud of. If you would be good enough to tell me, did he say anything more than you put in your letter? I have good reasons for asking this, but it would be no use or interest to explain the circumstances to you.'

'Yes, I quite understand,' Mr Breece said assuming his previous cordiality. 'To the best of my recollection, I repeated everything he told me in the letter. Do you have you many relatives, Mr Lewis?'

'As far as I know he was my last living family,' I said.

'Really?' said Mr Breece, with a look of surprise on his face.

'I understand you buried him today, as you said in your letter,' I said.

'No, we have not yet buried him,' he said. 'But are you sure that he was your only relative, Mr Lewis?'

'On my oath,' I said as I saw a look of doubt in his eyes. 'As far as I know, he was the last of my family.'

'That's odd,' said Mr Breece, 'but we are constantly misled. You being a clergyman, I willingly take your word, but this morning, just before I was to order the body to be placed in a coffin, I had another visitor. The man told me he was a brother to the deceased.'

Was my father still alive? I felt a shiver of fear run through me.

'I must admit that he looked nothing like James Lewis,' Mr Breece went on, 'He was a strange character, but seemed well off. He requested to be allowed to finance a suitable coffin for his unfortunate brother. He put down a five-pound note to cover the costs. How could I refuse him, sir? I always think that, when death steps in the law must give way. I will not punish a dead man. That would be fighting against the will of Almighty God, sir. I ordered a good coffin to be made for the dead man. And it is very good coffin. Indeed, it's a pity to put something so expensive in the ground. The man who paid for it must have loved the dead man dearly. If you had been here a few minutes earlier you would have seen him, sir. He has only just left. Quite a strange character.'

My heart leaped at these words. I had seen the character and knew him as Nicklas of Garth Ddu.

'I am much obliged to you, Mr Breece for your kindness,' I said, getting up to go. 'I apologize again for bothering you so late at night.'

'Don't mention it,' The Governor said. 'These things happen. Would you too like to see the coffin? I'm sure you'll also be pleased with it.'

'That would be good of you, sir,' I said.

Mr Breece pressed the bell by his elbow. Within a minute the man who had shown me in appeared.

'Gloom?' said Mr Breece, 'has coffin No. 72 been screwed down yet?'

'The carpenter is just about to do it, sir,' Mr Gloom said.

'Take this gentleman to see it,' Mr Breece said.

'Thank you,' I said

'Don't mention it, sir,' Mr Breece said. 'Goodnight, Mr Lewis. You're very welcome.'

Mr Gloom led me across a wide courtyard which was open to the foggy night air. He unlocked a door which opened onto a long corridor, took me through a series of locked doors and then down a flight of stone steps into the dark depths. At the bottom we went along another long corridor. I followed Mr Gloom, seeing only the light of the swinging lantern he carried. There was something about the atmosphere of this prison's strong, locked doors and damp walls which made me feel I was being taken down to the underworld of the dead. Only my guide, the Governor, his wife and I were alive in those dark, dismal surroundings

Finally, we reached the mortuary. Its ceiling was low, the walls were bare and dank as if soaked in a hundred years of snail slime. An odour of death hung thick about, and there wasn't a breath of fresh air to be had; the dead didn't need to breathe, and the living didn't linger there. Following my guide into the chamber I imagined rats were gnawing at my boots and brushing between my legs. I told myself to stop imagining things, then I heard my guide curse and kick at one of the vermin. I too kicked away the rats, whether they were real or imaginary.

I hadn't eaten much that day, and I began to feel faint. I wanted to go, but I hadn't come this far to not see for myself. At the far end of the long and narrow room was a board table. The 'nice coffin' lay on it, and a man in shirt-sleeves the stood over it by the light of candle. He had a paper cap on his head and, hearing our footsteps, looked round with the expression of a man caught robbing a grave.

Mr Gloom explained who I was and why I was there, and the carpenter then explained all the most excellent features of the coffin. I must admit I wasn't interested. What I wanted to see was the body it contained.

'If I give you a shilling, will you unscrew the lid so I might see the deceased for one last time,' I said.

'Certainly, sir,' the carpenter said grabbing at the coin I held out.

I watched as he removed the screws. I couldn't get the idea out of my head that my Uncle James had faked his death, and it was part of a deep plan to escape from prison. To tell the truth, I half expected my uncle to sit up and laugh in my face, as the joiner took out the last screw and lifted the lid.

But it didn't happen. To my great relief James Lewis lay there in the same old clothes he wore when I last saw him alive, but now he was as dead as a doornail. The man who had ruined my father, inflicted misery on me and my mother, spent every farthing of the money I had saved up to go to college and committed every evil he could, was now powerless and still, brought low at last by the Great Leveller.

I touched his hands and his forehead. They were as cold as the surrounding walls. But the Devil had set his mark on my uncle's face.

I had only seen three other dead faces previously, Seth's, my mother's and Abel Hughes. I thought of the pleasant cheerful look on Seth's face as he lay in his coffin. I remembered the serenity of my dead mother and the repose of Abel Hughes. The look on my Uncle James's face showed that he had found the pangs of death horrible. He might have been my uncle, brother to my father, but I doubt that a worse man had ever been placed between four boards. Looking at his tortured face I felt a degree of awe and pity. I knew this was a fitting end for such a degraded and sinful man.

My clothes were sticking me with cold sweat. But I as I looked down I heard myself chuckling at the thought that he would never again torment me. Whatever other troubles might be in store for me, I was at last free of the demon who had caused me so many nightmares.

'Thank you Mr Gloom,' I said. 'Would you escort me outside, please?'

I hurried away from the scene. As soon as I was outside the gates of the Old Bailey, I took a long, deep breath. 'O blessed liberty,' I said quietly to myself.

The streets were silent and still. I walked to and fro before the gates waiting for Wil Bryan. I didn't see another living creature as I paced, like a soldier doing sentry duty, waiting. I walked and walked, thinking of Bala, and how I longed to be back there.

I thought of Jack Williams, snug in his bed. What would he have thought if he had known where I was and what I was doing? I'm sure he wouldn't have slept a wink for worrying about me.

Fortunately the rain stopped and the fog cleared. The moon shone out in the sky, and I was glad to see her. As a child I used to think the Welsh people owned her. Now I knew her as an old friend, and I believe she knew me.

Wil was a long time coming. I feared something might have happened to him and that he wouldn't come at all. I kept getting pangs of hunger, but I put them aside, and thought through what had happened in my mind. Now I could see God's hand guiding me through each distress. But why had He brought me here? My thoughts were tangled, and I couldn't see a way forward. Wil was so long coming. Then I remembered Mam would say, 'Every wait is a long one' and took comfort.

I listened for the rumble of wheels in the distance, and at each hint listened more intently. Was it Wil? No, the rumble went off in another direction. I heard a church clock strike twelve. Then I thought I heard footsteps on the pavement. I bent my ear to catch the sound. Yes, someone was coming. He was walking quickly and whistling as he went. To avoid looking suspicious I walked towards the man, intending to return to my post after he had passed. As I got within forty yards or so of him, he started to sing a duet I knew well from my childhood. It was called 'All's Well,' and had a series of questions and answers.

'Who goes there?' he sang.

'A friend,' I sang back.

'The word?' He sang.

'Good Night.' I sang back.

The voice was Wil's and the sound of it healed my spirit.

'Well, old soot-in-the-soup, art thou tired of waiting?' Wil said in Welsh. 'Thou must excuse me for not bringing the cab, but the nag was dead tired, so I fed him and bedded him down in the stable. It isn't far to walk to my crib, and we can catch up. I can see by the set of thy jib thou art in some sort of wrangle. What brought thee here? I've been thinking about thee so often and hoping that Providence would bring us together again. But, my weary pilgrim, tell thy tale.'

'Before I explain all, Wil,' I said. 'Didst thou discover where old Nicklas went to? '

'Yes, and I got a tanner for doing so,' Wil said. 'It's hard to follow a chap in a cab without being noticed so I drove up straight to his nabs, asked him to step in. I made as if I meant to give him a lift for nothing. The old boy took the bait: '65 Gregg Street,' he said, and when I put him down he gave me sixpence. The house is only a two-minute walk away. I'll show thee. But what's the matter? What's it all about? Now spit it out.'

It was easy to explain to Wil why I was in Birmingham. He knew more of me and my family's history than anybody else. I gave him a brief account of what had happened to me since he had left Mold, and he listened with deep interest. I trusted him completely and I thanked Providence for our meeting. If I hadn't met him I would never have found out where Nicklas was staying, then one-half of my errand to the town would have been left unfulfilled.

We walked, arm in arm. I didn't know where we were going but Wil guided me through various streets, often turning to right and left. As I finished telling him what I had seen in the Old Bailey, he spoke softly.

'Here it is,' he said.

We in a narrow, quiet street. The houses were high and, judging from the number of windows, contained many tenants. There were shutters upon the lower windows.

'Here's the house,' he whispered. '65 Gregg Street. This is where old Nick went. Shall we knock on the door and ask if supper's ready?'

Now we had reached the place I was overwhelmed by fear and curiosity. The occupants seemed to have retired, but Wil pointed out a streak of light above the shutters of No. 65. We walked as stealthily as cats towards the window. As we stood close I could hear voices inside. Wil put his right hand on my shoulder and his left foot on the low windowsill. He reached to his full height, and tried to peep over the top of shutters. He was too short.

'You're taller than me,' he said. 'You have a go.'

I went up, and was found I could see into the room. My heart beat so fast that I thought my head would burst. I could see a bed at the far end of the room with someone lying in it. I couldn't see his face, because Nicklas was standing between me and him. Nicklas was pouring from a bottle, into a glass. He bent forward to pass the glass to the man in the bed. I craned forward, struggling to see his face. Just as I thought I would be able to make it out, I felt a strong grip on my arm, pulling me down from the window sill. I looked down and saw the dark form of a tall, powerful policeman holding me firmly.

Before I knew what to do I was standing on the ground and my wrist clicked to the loop of a pair of handcuffs, the other was quickly attached to Wil. The officer didn't speak as he secured us and within a seconds or two we were trapped. The policeman kept a tight hold of my coat collar as he checked the number of the house. I nearly collapsed with fear but Wil quickly recovered his self-possession. He spoke before I did.

'Officer,' he said. 'You are a smart fellow, I must give you that.' He looked ruefully at the handcuffs. 'We've always been a pair, ever since childhood.'

He started to protest to the officer, but was cut short.

'Be quiet and march,' ordered the policeman. We did as we were told and the officer walked close at our heels like a dog herding cattle. All he said to us was 'right' or 'left' if we came to a street corner.

Wil spoke quietly to me in Welsh.

'This is a bad day's work,' he said. 'We've made a right mess of things, but it's no use arguing with a Bluecoat. I must speak pure grammatical Welsh or he'll understand us. How can we get out of this? Have you any ideas? Try not to tremble, an innocent man has no cause to quake with fear. You know we're as innocent as William the Coal's mule. (By the way, is old William living, and does he still keep blaming Satan?) Perhaps we can blame the Devil. How can we explain it? Our Bluecoat here will swear lots of things when we appear in court tomorrow morning. What do you think?'

'All we can do is tell the Truth and take the consequences,' I said. 'But, once I get free of this man I must go back to that house.'

'The magistrates won't believe the truth,' Wil said. 'If we say that we only wanted to see who was with old Nicklas in the house there, they won't believe us. There are many different ways to tell the truth. If Bluecoat doesn't tell them a pack of lies, I don't see how they can do much to us. We might get fourteen days I suppose. That would be a shame for us two innocent lads, I suppose. I'd hoped we'd have a pleasant night, remembering old times. I've thought about trying to bribe Bluecoat but he's so quiet I can't judge him. If we pretend to be drunk it will only be five shillings and the costs. Do you have any plan? You're so quiet. You shouldn't give up hope. Say something but don't use any English words in case Bluecoat understands us. We need to have our story clear. What if we said we were after courting the servant girls? There's bound to be servants in a house like that. But they might ask their names. We could say Ann and Margaret. But what if they asked the colour of their hair? We could say black but where would be if their names turn out to be Maud and Cecilia, and they have red hair? No, that won't wash. I'm terribly sorry for you. I don't care for myself, one of my mates will look after the nag. But what of a Methodist preacher locked in the Bridewell? It wouldn't go down well in Bala. You'd lose your preaching slots right away. You can't say your real name. You'll need an alias. What about if you were to pretend that your name was Melltrathraneorosllanerchrugog? They wouldn't know any better. I'll need a different name. I will have to take a Bardic name, in order avoid the shame. That's not a bad rhyme is it? See I really am a poet, so it will be version of the truth. Have you still got nothing to say?'

Indeed, I was upset to join in his conversation. Would Wil take matters so easily if he knew my real worry, that my father was still alive and that I was afraid he would come back and disgrace me at college and in Mold.

I was still wondering what to do when Wil began to talk again.

'I can't see any way out of this scrape,' he said. 'Appearances are against us. Our fate rests on Bluecoat's testimony. Perhaps Providence has decided to make sure all your family have the blessing of going to prison for a time. Your father and uncle were quite at home there. And your brother Bob, who I think was one of the best lads ever, he had a spell inside too. And now, perhaps it's your turn. Don't forget even St Paul and St Silas spent some time in prison, and we are as harmless a pair as they were. And how did they get out? Wasn't it by singing psalms and praying? Well, if you pray I'll sing until the walls fall down. Take heart we'll get out yet.'

Before I could say anything a great explosion of laughter erupted from the police officer. He spoke to us in Welsh with a strong Mold accent. 'Well my boys. What were you really doing at that house?'

Wil answered him in Welsh. 'Hello there John Jones, brother from the land of my fathers. Are you going to open those cuffs for the sake our shared language? Welsh is as Welsh does.'

The policeman unlocked the handcuffs while Wil poured a torrent of praise over him. He called him a 'trump' and an 'old brick' told him he was 'A1.'

'We were just curious about who old Nicklas of Garth Ddu was meeting at the house and trying to catch a glimpse of the fellow,' Wil said. 'Now constable will you let me stand you the cost of a good dinner?'

'No,' said the officer. 'This Bluecoat doesn't take bribes, and he won't be rewarded for doing his duty. Now go home like good children.'

'You're true to nature and an honour to your country,' Will said. 'You should be promoted to Inspector at once.'

We left our captor on good terms and in much improved spirits.

'D'ye know what?' Wil said. 'I'll never again say all Bobbies are humbugs. There are some good ones among them. I think it's worth getting into a scrape now and again just for the pleasure of getting out of it. I've only been caught by a Bluecoat once before. I knew a girl around here, there was nothing agreed between us, you know, we were just extra good friends. Then one night I took her home. She invited me in and I stayed for some time, longer than I realized. Well it was eleven o'clock, when we heard the mistress coming down from the sitting room. Instead of introducing me the girl shoved me into a pantry. It was frightfully close fit. I could hear the missis order the girl to bed, and locking the front and the back doors. I didn't know then but she'd taken the keys with her to bed. I heard them both going upstairs but I hoped the girl would come back and let me out.

I nearly smothered but I managed to get the pantry door open. There was no light, the fire being as dark as the black cow's belly. I was stuck what to do, so I sat and waited. Some long time later I heard the girl creeping down in her stocking feet. I've never been more pleased to see a candle. I was in a hurry to get out. It wasn't right to stay in somebody's house on the sly like. I was sorry for the girl. She told me that her mistress had the keys and that she couldn't let me out. But I had to try to leave, even if I had to hack a hole in the wall. It wouldn't be true to nature to stay in that house all night. I asked the girl if it would be easier if I went out the front parlour window. Yes, indeed she said in a delightful Welsh accent, she being a good Welsh girl. She left the candle on the table, and we went to the parlour. The moon was shining through the window and lighting the room. There was a flower stand by the window and in my rush I knocked over a pot and smashed it. Fair play to the girl, she told me she'd blame the cat for it.

I don't think the lower part of the window had been open for years. I got it up some ten inches and it stuck tight. I had to try to squeeze though feet first. I was about halfway out when I stuck tight as wedge. I thought I'd be there till morning but then I felt someone tugging at my legs. He pulled me so strongly that the all the buttons popped off my vest. It was a Bobby who had rescued me. When the girl saw the policemen holding me she burst out crying. I hadn't realized she was so fond of me. Anyway, I said don't cry, Gwen *fach* (Gwen being her name). I'll come and see you just as soon as I get out jail. That made her cry ten times worse. I never saw her again. But this is the point. The Bobby knew full well I'd done nothing wrong but he wanted five shillings to let me go. After a bit of bartering I got him down to half a crown. Those Bluecoats don't get much of wage so I expect they must make up their pay with jobs of this sort.'

At this point I struggled to suppress a yawn as I struggled to keep pace with him.

'Are you tired?' Wil said. 'You're not as spry as you used to be? Have you got a touch of the rheumatics? It isn't far now.'

'The nearer the better,' I said. 'I'm really weary. But I have to get inside 65 Gregg Street. How do you think I can do it?' I then told him what I had seen just before the officer a caught us. 'Before I leave this town I have to find out who was in the bed. It's clear that Nicklas doesn't live there. He had his hat on, as if he were about to leave. You understand my worry, don't you?'

We continued to discuss the matter as we walked on to Wil's digs each thinking about the problem. Then Wil spoke.

'I have it,' he said. 'Dost thou recall I told thee not to be in a hurry to put on a white tie? Well, I've changed my mind. Thou must put one on tomorrow. There are folk around here who call themselves town missionaries. They keep going about and looking up the sick or ungodly, to try and do good. They have a knack of sniffing out anyone who's ill. I was sick for four days, just the once since I got here, but they visited three times while I lay abed. There's two things about them that annoy me. They expect you to believe right off, without giving you time to think about, and they puff the Gospel up too much. They're not like the old chapel folk who think the Gospel doesn't need exaggerating. They think if you want to know about the Good Book you'll come to chapel to ask for it. These town missionaries are like patent medicine salesmen. They advertise every day, and at every house drop off a leaflet offering miracle cures. They're never worried about their sins, not like your mother, old Abel, and others in the chapel at home, who were really pious. They're always as jolly as if they'd never sinned. They're probably good people, because they don't want to do anything but good. But I can't abide their endless being happy. And they expect everybody to be the same. If the angel Gabriel had sinned as much as I have and then been forgiven he'd be down in the dumps now and then, even though he lives in heaven. These town missionaries never are. But then everyone respects them and lets them go into their houses to give them advice. That's my plan. Thou speakst English well, so thee can go to 65 Gregg Street and kill two birds with one stone.'

He stopped outside a house. 'Here's my crib,' he said. 'Don't expect too much. I don't keep a butler.'

Wil took a key from his pocket and let us in. Once the door shut we were in total darkness. Wil struck a match. On a little table beside us, I saw a candlestick. Wil lit the candle.

'I must be the last home tonight,' he said. 'Or they'd be a lot of candles here. This house is for anyone and everyone. Come upstairs but try not to make a noise for everyone else will be asleep. There are eight of us living here, and we each have our own room. The landlady, her daughter and the servant live here too, but we don't know where. Here's my room. The best thing I can say about it is that it's clean. Make thyself at home while I get us some food. Thou canst wash over there. Thou'rt not going to eat in my house without washing after thou hast been handling that old rogue's corpse.'

The room was only about four yards square, but it contained a bed, a cupboard, two chairs, a round table and many other necessaries. The table was set with a clean white cloth, a cup and saucer, two plates and two knives and forks. There was a fire lit in the grate and beside it a kettle and a coffee pot.

'I see thee taking stock,' Wil said as he took off his coat. 'What would thou like tea or coffee?'

'Well, Wil *bach*,' I said. 'Is this what thou hast come to?' I could hardly hold back my laughter.

'Come to what?' Wil said. 'One room is true to nature. Every creature God ever made can only live in one room at a time. It's pure humbug to have lots of rooms. One can only be in one at once, it's the only physical possibility. I'm doing pretty well for myself, as I'll tell thee in due course. Now say the word. Tea or coffee?'

'Tea,' I said.

'I'll join thee,' Wil said, unlocking the cupboard, taking out his stores and skilfully making a meal.

'Thou couldn't have a better woman for my landlady,' he said. 'I often don't see her for a week at a time. If I want anything, I write my order on that slate, leave the money on the mantelpiece. When I get back it will be ready on the table. I never used to lock the cupboard, when I first came here. But my landlady would sometimes take a loan of my things. I'll tell you how I caught her out. I noticed the tea went down rather quickly, so I caught a live gnat and locked it in the caddy. When I next opened it that gnat had flown. That was a positive proof. But it was my own fault. She's perfectly honest as long as I lock the cupboard.'

As he was talking Wil was down on his knees, toasting ham upon a fork before the fire. The meal was ready in minutes.

'There is a drawback,' he said. 'I only have one cup and saucer so thou shalt take the cup while I use the saucer.'

We did just that, and I have never enjoyed a meal more than that night. Once we had eaten I asked Wil to tell me his history.

But I will need another chapter to tell you about it.

CHAPTER 40

The Adventures of Wil Bryan

'What made me leave home,' Wil said as we sat by his fireside drinking our tea, 'was pride. I was used to driving through the streets like fury to impress the girls. I couldn't bear the humiliation of my father's bankruptcy. I'd saved a little money but I didn't have enough to emigrate. I had enough to come here to Birmingham, where I expected to find a job within a few hours. It wasn't like that. I was lost and lonely among all these people. I was afraid to ask for a job because I didn't have a trade at all. All I could do was drive. I did nothing until I was about to run out of money, and then I quickly realized that pride wouldn't fill my stomach. I started to hang around the stables hoping to get offered a job before my money ran out. I was quite well dressed, and I still had a bit of swagger about me. The cabbies would touch their caps to me, as if I was someone. But, finally, when I had to sell the gold watch-chain my mother gave me when I was eighteen I felt desperate.

'I kept going to the stables. I think the cabbies thought I was a gentleman's son who'd had a row with his father. They were very respectful. But they could see I was hard up, and they'd argue over who should stand me a drink, expecting that I would throw them a fiver once I made it up with my father. I had to pawn my overcoat, but by then I'd made friends with the owner of the stables. He would shake my hand and try to find out where I was from and how I came to be broke. I kept up the mystery and let him wonder until the day I had to take my watch to the pawnshop. I went down to the stables and asked the gaffer for a job as cabby. He thought I was joking and laughed at me. But a couple of days later one of his men was taken sick with congestion of the lungs. I asked to take his place until he was well, and, still thinking it was a joke, the boss let me. They all lined up to laugh at me as I drove the cab across the courtyard and the gaffer laughed the loudest of all.

'But I was laughing up my sleeve and hoping the sick man would take his time recovering. The rest of the cabbies were soon saying that the young swell, as they called me, could handle a horse as well as the best of them. I had a good run that day and for the next week, and by the end of the week the gaffer offered me a wage. He still thought I was doing it for a joke, but he could see I was good at the job.

'I was mixing with the cabbies and soon dropped into their bad habits. I kept going with them after work to share two penn'orth of ale. I wasn't as used to the drink as they were, and so one day I took far too much and fell off the dicky of the cab and landed on my head. They carried me back here and put me to bed. I lay sick and fevered for four days, and that's when town missionary came to visit. He could tell from my speech that I had been brought up well and so he gave me some good advice.

'He pointed out to me just how much the average cabby spent each year getting drunk and damning his soul. It was a goodish sum so I decided that I wasn't going to keep pouring that sort money down my red lane, just to make my head ache. I changed overnight from being a regular drunken terror to a teetotal miser.

'As I began to save a bit I found I liked having money again. I got so I wouldn't spend a penny. Last thing every night I'd reckon up my money. Within a few weeks I had a few pounds. I put them under my pillow at night and carried them inside my vest during the day. I lived in fear that I'd be robbed. But I dared not put the money in the bank because I'd need to tell the bank manager my name.

'I'd eat only bread, butter and tea. I'd put sixpence in my purse rather than buy some meat for my supper. My money kept growing. Anyway one morning I was running a bit late as I tacked up the horse. Two cabbies were standing behind me waiting for me to finish when it happened. My vest was unbuttoned, and my purse fell out. It spilled fifteen or so sovereigns on the yard. The others nearly fainted with surprise. Now they were quite sure I was a gentleman's son worth thousands. They asked me why I had taken up such a strange hobby as cab-driving.

Well, of course they told all the others, and the next day the gaffer again confronted me about my past. He knew I wasn't robbing him, because I handed in more money than any other man in his employ. But I still wouldn't tell him my history, I just told him I liked the life. Anyway, to keep up with the story I bought a nice suit, with good deep pockets. And, now I was respectably dressed, the customers picked me out, and would give me an extra tip.

'By now I had more money than I could safely carry about. I bought that lever lock for the box over there, and screwed it down myself. It cost me four shillings and sixpence, and I spent eight pence on a gimlet, screws and a screw driver. Now I could enjoy myself counting my money when I came home at night. And I greatly regretted how much I had wasted drinking that two penn'orth of ale.

'My conscience kept whispering that I was a humbug and wasn't being true to nature. I'd shut her up by thinking of all those pious old Methodists who used to groan when they had to part with a shilling. I had stood in my father's shop and watched their shoulders fall with a groan as they paid their money over. Now I sympathized with them.

My conscience fought back, saying I was no better than in my drinking days, just richer, but I said I would set up on my own and not stay someone's servant.

'I've always loved horses, and if I understand anything really well it's them. Well I soon knew every horse in the town, and their good and bad points. I knew a chap who had an animal that had a good nature with a willing spirit, but he was starving the beast. He was always drunk and forgetting to buy feed for the animal. Many a time I'd give the beast a chance at my own horse's nose-bag out of pity. The horse had the same name as your brother. He was called Bob, and he got to know me as well you do. I'd be driving towards him, and he'd stand stock still in the street, as if he were expecting something. But poor Bob got worse each day until he was so weak he could hardly stand. He was so spiritless that if someone fired a gun right next to his ear he wouldn't flinch.

'One day while he was next to me in the cabstand, his owner having left him to go to the pub. He started shivering as if he was going to collapse. A crowd gathered around him expecting him to drop down dead. I pulled him out of the cab but he couldn't walk. His owner came back and one of the cabbies suggested that it would be best to put him out of his misery there and then. But before they could do anything I offered to buy Bob for a sovereign, just as he was. The fellow sold him to me there and then before going back to the pub with the cash.

'You remember how I used to get on with Mr Edwards who bred horses over in Caerwys? Well he had shown me how to treat a sick horse. I threw a rug over his back, asked a mate to hold him and ran to a chemist's across the street to buy a bottle of a patent tonic he'd re-commended. I was scared the horse would die before I got back, for I knew he was starving. He was gaping like a man dying of hunger.

'When I got back Bob was quiet and listless, but he was still on his feet and breathing. Once of the bystanders asked me how much I'd sell his skin for? I ignored him, and as Bob opened his mouth to gape I poured some of the physic down his throat. I asked some of the other cabbies to rub his legs to help his circulation. They thought it was a bit of a joke but they did it to humour me. Within ten minutes Bob was starting to revive and taking notice of what we were doing. There must have been a hundred people gathered around, watching and laughing like they were at a show. Then an Irish cabby, who was rubbing one of Bob's forelegs yelled out the Bob was trying to bite him. The crowd roared with laughter and gave Bob three cheers. Well, within half an hour I had Bob eating a bucket of nice warm mash, and the crowd were all shouting Hooray.

'The man who'd sold Bob to me came out of the pub and couldn't believe the change in the horse. He wanted to go back on the bargain but the crowd booed him and told him I was a smart fellow who knew how to treat a sick horse. They didn't know I'd learned the secret from Mr Edwards of Caerwys.

'Well, I hired a stall in a livery stable and tended that horse. I fed Bob well, exercised him gently, and he got better every day. He wasn't an old horse, he'd just been ill-treated. By the time he was fit I'd spent about five pounds on him and I had a strong, fit horse. I gave my master a week's notice and bought a cheap second-hand cab. Then I set up on my own. Bob had grown back into his skin, and his coat shone so well that the lads asked me if I'd been using black stove polish on him. I was famous as a horse doctor and got plenty of cab work. The man who'd nearly killed Bob and then sold him to me when he looked like dying, sounded off at me whenever he saw me. I told him it was his own fault for mistreating the poor beast. The more I earned, the more money I wanted. I got a bit of local reputation for being a bit of a vet, but all I thought about was making money.

'Are you tired of my story?' he said, noticing I was looking a bit bored.

'Yes, Wil,' I said. 'If thou hast nothing better to talk about than bragging about making money, then perhaps it might be better to say nothing. Thou art nothing like thyself anymore.'

'Have patience while I get to the point,' Wil said. 'Do you put the moral at the start or the end of thy sermons? If thou starts with the best bits, thou'rt not worthy of the pulpit. One night, after a good day's work. I treated myself to a quarter of a pound of sausage for supper. I took out my money and counted it. I had forty-eight pounds stored in my box, and I owned my own horse and cab. Well, that sausage put me in a good mood. I was started to sing that old tune the 'Black Flower'. I got to the line "How fares my father, mother dear, How is the state succeeding?"

'I was suddenly overcome with a deep sense of regret. I started to cry like a baby. I got to thinking of my mother and what a selfish young devil I had become. There I was, only interested in scraping up money and I didn't know why I wanted it. I felt a religious longing for home come over me. I hadn't written to the old folk since I'd left home. I didn't know if they were starving or even alive. Thou art not being true to nature in what thou doest I told myself, and then I fell to crying again. That night I wrote to gaffer, asking him how he was getting on and how much he still owed.

'I went out to post the letter that night. I was afraid I might change my mind if I left it to the morning. But after I dropped the note in the post box I felt I had become Wil Bryan again and stopped being just a money-grubbing cabby. I can't tell you how good it felt to see my old self was coming back. I needn't have been worried, though; I hadn't changed my mind by the morning. I was impatient for a reply. My mother wrote back by return post. She said my father was too cut up to write, but I knew she thought the old man would write something nasty and drive me further away. Old Huw Bryan had never been tender-hearted. My mother begged me to come back to Mold and said how pleased she was to hear from her prodigal son. Calling me a prodigal son annoyed me; his father was wealthy and gave him half an estate, which he wasted so ended up in rags with a job feeding pigs. My father went bust, and I never saw any of his money. And I didn't have to resort to pig-feeding, nor had I any intention of turning up at home in rags.

'Mam told me the old boy had been four hundred pounds in debt when he went bust. The creditors agreed five shillings in the pound and he'd managed to pay that off. Now he was getting along and had stopped speculating. Then the old girl played a cute trick. She told me that Suzie was still single. The gaffer wouldn't have thought of using such tactics. Mam showed her canniness when she mentioned Suzie, and she was right. My heart leaped at the thought of going back to that girl, but I controlled my feelings. I wrote back saying that I wouldn't come back to Mold until my father had paid off every farthing of his debt. I told her I was in a good place but I didn't tell them I was a cabby – and thou mustn't tell them Rhys. I promised that I'd help them pay it all off. I've sent them over two hundred pounds clear' he said passing me a slip of letter, 'Here's a receipt for ten pounds the gaffer sent me this morning.'

I read the note put it back in the envelope. 'This is addressed to Mr Walter Bateson,' I said. 'Not to you.'

'That's the name I use here,' Wil said. 'It's why I can't put my money in the bank. No one in this place knows my real name. I don't want them to take me for an Irishman or a bankrupt's son.'

'Is this really worthy of thee, Wil?' I said.

'What's the harm in it?' Wil said. 'Everyone of note in Wales has a Bardic name. Look at Rev. John Blackwell, he called himself Glan Alun, and nobody thinks any the worse of him. Why shouldn't I call myself Walter Bateson? What's in a name? A rose by any other name and all that. And I've kept my initials I'm still yours truly, W.B. The old folk don't like it but, even though I've felt my old self come back, I don't know how to throw off my new name. I have to stick with it until I can go home.'

'I'd heard thy father was paying his debts,' I said. 'But I didn't know thou wert helping him. It's creditable of thee. But thou wouldst do better by going home to assist thy parents in person. I am so pleased to see thee again, Wil. But thou hast greatly changed. I've never heard thee talk so much about money and...'

'Hold on,' Wil interrupted me. 'I know that I've lost my way and I've not much to say that's worth hearing. But thou must remember that I am just starting to come back to myself. I'm not there yet. I haven't reached the real W.B., and when I do I'll come back home.'

'But Wil,' I said, 'thou hast not spoken of religion or chapel. Dost thou not go to service?'

'I won't lie to thee,' Wil said. 'I don't like the church. I went once to the Congregationalists here and sat by the door. Their minister is a Welshman, by the name of Price, and they kept advertising on posters how good a preacher he is. I went along out of curiosity, and his text was Morgan o' Dyffryn's old one, the one about the little foxes. Anyway, as I listened to him I spotted that he was just translating Mr Morgan's sermon and claiming it for his own. So I cut and ran. A man who steals someone else's sermon is no better than a man who steals a sovereign. In fact he's worse, because he's paid to preach, while the thief of the sovereign gets three months for his work. I didn't go anywhere else after that. Then by accident I decided to drop into the Wesleyan chapel one Sunday night. I liked way the minister prayed, but his congregation didn't stop talking, not even during the prayers. I never before saw such a thing. He preached about Peter after he'd made a mess of everything, and I was getting interested, but then he ran Peter down in a shocking way. He said a man can get religion and then lose it. It all depended on the man himself. If that's the truth, then it's goodbye to Wil Bryan. I decided if he could make such a mess of drawing a moral from Peter's denial, which I knew a lot about from Abel's teaching, then how could I trust him about things I knew nothing about? I didn't go there again.

'Then a couple of weeks back I found the Cause had a Welsh chapel here. I went to it but it's not like Capel Bethel at home. There were a lot of swells sitting around the big seat. There were a few Abel Hughes's dotted around the congregation, but the swells were in charge. A young chap preached to us, and by the sound of him he was from Bala. I was beginning to wonder if a new sect had taken over religion. It seemed to have taken bits from everywhere. It had the style of the Church of England, the smartness of the Congregationalists, the spirit of the Wesleyans, and the doctrine of the Calvinists. I like the style of the English Church. I like the way they don't look about them or talk to each other during the service, but they are awfully ignorant. The Congregationalists are extremely clever, but there's too much of politics and the *eisteddfod* about them. And they all have a *nom de plume*, although I can't criticize them for that, as it would be the devil finding fault with sin. The Wesleys are ardent, warm and jolly, but they're dreadfully clannish and all pray in the same way. We old Calvinists (I feel I'm still a sort of honorary member) are the John Bull of Wales. We are a fat, unwieldy chap who finds it hard to move. It's no use trying to tickle us, we are too thick-skinned. We move in our own time, but when we do move we are like an elephant. Nothing can stop us and we'll pull any load you give us. But we're like Duke, William the Coal's mule. There's no stronger mule in the county but he won't take a step unless he wants to, and the only thing that will move him is William's goad. The other mules would have a bunch of hazel stuck over their heads to keep the flies away but Duke didn't care about flies. Only the goad affected him. If they do a post mortem when he dies they'll find his skin's like a pepper box. But I've seen Duke draw twelve hundredweight of coal to the top of the bank, when he was in the mood. The old Calvinists are just like him. They have enough power, but no go. They're too serious. Every service is like a funeral. Now if you could take the best points of them all and put them into a new denomination, then I could go with that. What do you think?'

'I think that the real Wil Bryan is coming back,' I said, 'Thou hast not lost thy old pertness. But rather than found a new sect wouldn't it be better if we tried to combine all these religious virtues thou hast mentioned in ourselves? What would thou think about starting a new life? Thou dost well to pay off thy father's debts, but what about thine own? Thy soul must settle its account if thou wilt avoid a dread future. I urge thee to think about thy religion.'

'I expected thee to say something like that,' Wil said, his voice sounding sad. 'I'd have been disappointed in thee as a preacher if thou hadn't tried to save my soul. I do believe thou art seeking my good, but I don't know how to answer thy question. I would be lying if I said I didn't value religion, but I'm not ready for it yet. I said the same to the town missionary. He asked me how would it be if I had to leave this life early – if I fell off the dicky of my cab and was killed. It would be too late then to repent and try to save my soul. I've thought more about religion since then, and it's higher up my list of priorities. It's just that I'm not ready yet. I'm still a young chap but I'm getting tired of singing comic songs. I've always managed to be jolly, but I wouldn't say that I have ever been happy. I know there has always been a stink of corruption in my heart.'

'I am glad thou findest the smell annoying,' I said. 'And I'm pleased that thy soul yearns for purification and true happiness ...'

'I don't want a sermon,' Wil interrupted. 'I've heard thousands of them. What I need is solid common sense. I don't go to chapel and have no chum to talk to about these matters. That's not true to nature. The chaps I mix with every day have nothing in their heads and think only of beer. I've never found real religion. I don't think it's possible a man can find the real thing and then lose it. The old chapel at home gave me a sort of religious inoculation and saved me from going too bad. But it hasn't convinced me. Dost thou see what I mean?'

'We were both brought up religiously from childhood,' I said. 'And despite our upbringing we both strayed from the narrow path. But I've always hoped that thou hadst not lost thy inoculation and wilt return to the way.'

'But thy inoculation took better than mine,' Wil said. 'I need another one before I will be safe.'

'Go to the Doctor, then,' said I. 'Thou wilt find Him at the Chapel. Thou spotted a Welsh chapel. I don't want to suggest that other denominations are not as good as ours, but our upbringing stops us getting much from them. We get more from the Calvinists. Why can't thou go to chapel regularly? Thou'll soon make friends there. Thou hast a knack for introducing thyself. Thou wilt make a new friend to help thee.'

'I'd like to be there, every Sunday,' Wil said. 'But if I went regularly the minister and the deacons would ask my name and where I live. I would have say William Bryan and give the number of this house or be a humbug. Then the minister would come here and ask for Mr William Bryan. My landlady would tell him no one of that name lives here. And then what would he think? To give an alias in chapel would feel like trying cheat the Almighty. I can't do that. I could my change my lodgings, but Walter Bateson would still be the registered owner of my cab. If I don't find a way out of this mess then Wil Bryan will not take his seat in chapel. Mark thou my word.'

He stood up and stretched. 'Look at the time,' he said. 'It's a quarter to three. If thou art going to be fit to visit the sick tomorrow, thou must get thee to thy kennel.'

It was a small step to bed, and I was glad the journey was so short. I slept soundly.

The following morning I was in that confused state between sleeping and waking and couldn't make out if I was handling bacon or smelling someone shaking me. Then I woke up fully and found Wil shaking me and the smell of bacon and coffee filling the room.

I rubbed my eyes. I felt everything that had happened had been a dream. But the room was exactly as I remembered it, except there were now two cups and saucers on the table instead of one.

Wil and I spent the next hour or so, talking over what had transpired, and then we began to plan the day.

CHAPTER 41

The First and the Last Time

'Who was that other chap with Old Nicklas?' Wil said. 'If thou wants to know, then thou'll have go to that house. If I were thee I'd forget about it. How wilt thou be any better off knowing? But if thou'rt determined, I'll borrow thee a white choker to wear around thy neck.'

'I have to know?' I said.

'Right, I'll borrow a white kerchief for thee,' Wil said. 'And while thou'rt decking thyself out as a town missionary I'll go and fetch Bob. I intend to take today off and spend it with thee.'

Wil had always dominated me when we were lads. I felt I was in his hands once more, and I would have to wear the white neckerchief and take his advice. I was desperate to find out the identity of the other man. Was it my father? Had my Uncle James lied about his being dead? I had to know, and if I were to miss this opportunity I would never forgive myself.

Wil was soon back, and he had borrowed a trap. 'I don't want to be hailed by fares today,' he said.

I'd heard a lot about Bob the previous night but I was too worried about my forthcoming adventure to take much notice of him when I saw him in daylight. I had to say something to Wil, though.

'Bob looks to be in good condition,' I said.

'The other cabbies call him Lazarus.'

Wil's plan was to drive me to Gregg Street and leave me there. He would return after half an hour to fetch me. Then we were to spend the day together and catch up on old times. But the plans of men can easily be overruled by Providence.

We were within about a hundred yards or so of where we had been caught and handcuffed the night before when Wil reined in the trap. He whispered to me in an excited tone of voice.

'There's that Bobby who nabbed us last night. And he's ordering us to stop,' he said.

The officer was indeed signalling us to stop. Wil as upset as I was myself.

'Rhys Lewis,' the Bluecoat said. 'Get down from there.'

I did as he ordered me. I tried to keep up a bold front but my legs were trembling and I felt cold as if the blood was draining from my face. Wil jumped down beside me and threw the reins onto Bob's back. 'I'm with thee whatever happens. If we've got to go to court we'll go together.'

We stood before the office and waited out fate. Then officer's face dissolved into a smile.

'Why are you so worried?' he said. He smiled again. 'Don't be alarmed. Do you not know me, Rhys Lewis?'

I shook my head.

'Wil Bryan, don't you know me?'

'Yes, I do,' Wil said. 'You lent me a half a pair of handcuffs last night.'

'That's quite right, Wil,' the officer said. 'But don't you recall I've also given the loan of my cane to your backside, more than once?'

Wil looked hard at the policeman for a second or two.

'Well I never,' he said. 'If I'm not mistaking you for a wooden bedstead it must be Sergeant Williams. No wonder you turned out such a trump last night. And how are you, my old A1? Can you get a day off today and join us?'

'I might be able to, Mr Bateson,' Sergeant Williams said.

Wil looked sheepish. 'Every Welshman needs a bardic name, you know,' he said.

'I didn't know cabbies were noted for being bards.'

'Hush now,' Wil said. 'Least said soonest mended. I feel like I'm back in Mold here with Rhys Lewis and Sergeant Williams. All we want is William the Coal, Duke and that old thoroughbred Thomas Bartley and we'll be complete.'

My memories of Sergeant Williams were not the most agreeable. He made me feel uneasy. But he soon dismissed my fears as I explained my problem. He offered to help me by introducing me to the landlady of the house.

Wil jumped back into the trap and drove off. The Sergeant walked with me to 65 Gregg Street and knocked at the door. It was opened by a well-built, masculine-looking woman. She obviously knew the Sergeant.

'This minister wishes to call to see the sick man,' he said.

He then left us, and woman took me towards the room I had tried to spy on the previous night. She opened the door and escorted me inside.

'Here's the Minister come to see you,' she said.

My heart was racing. This was an unpleasant task I had to face, but I couldn't shirk it. I saw before me the man I had seen the night before. He was sitting up in bed. I summoned up all my courage and greeted him in English.

'Good day to you sir,' I said. 'I hear you are sick. How do you feel?'

Now I could see the man's face, I recognised his likeness to my Uncle James and my brother Bob. Memories of his history swarmed through my mind as I waited for him to answer.

He said just a single word. 'Bad.'

'What hope to do you have of recovery?' I asked him.

He shook his head sorrowfully and didn't speak.

I asked him about his thoughts and expectations but he would only shake his head in reply. I tried to guide his mind to God and the mercy He extends to even the greatest of sinners. I recited as many of the Biblical promises of forgiveness as I could recall but he only responded by shaking his head with an air of profound misery and deep despair.

His failure to respond left me struggling to find anything more to say. An image of the bedroom at Y Twmpath formed in my mind. I heard my mother's voice as she lay on her deathbed, saying, 'If ever thou dost meet him, and who knows but thou wilt, remember he is thy father. Try to forget his sins, and, if thou canst can do him any good, then do it.'

As her words echoed in my mind my thoughts jumped back to the night Seth died and the meeting I had with my uncle by the Hall Park where he told me about my father. I heard my brother Bob whispering the dark history of my family. He'd told me how my father took a downward path, wasted money and treated my mother with great cruelty. I'd been forced to stuff the bedclothes into my mouth to stop crying out loud as Bob told me how Mam had to stay away from chapel because my father blackened her eyes. How could she pray for the man who struck her while her own blood had not yet dried on her apron? I hated the wretch then and was glad I had never seen his face.

Now I stood by his side and I heard my mother's words as if she was speaking them for the first time. 'Forget his sins, and, if thou canst do him any good, do it.'

My father had been a strong man but now he lay a helpless husk. I could hardly grasp that I was looking at my father. I could smell the tang of whisky as evidence of how he had arrived at this pitiful state. He and his brother James had run their course almost neck and neck. Should I tell him who I was? Would it do any good? Was it wise?

I have never seen a man so wretched. He had abandoned all comfort and hope, and was sinking into unfathomable darkness. My allusions to the promises of Scripture only seemed to push him further into those obnoxious depths. The verses I quoted, seemed to terrify, even though I meant them to console him. He reacted to them like old acquaintances that he shrank away from. As I was trying to comfort him he was inching towards the wall, trying to get away from me too. As he listened he became agitated, as if the fires of hell were already burning his heart within him. He clutched tightly at the bed clothes. Then he would become quiet, as if he had forgotten I was there and was intent on taking a long journey down into himself. Then he would come back to himself and look around wildly. Seeing me still there, he would move uneasily towards the wall.

I felt my company was a burden to him, and that he would like me to go. He kept reaching out his hand towards a whisky bottle on the little table by his side. Then, seeing me sitting with him, he would pull back.

I could see his life was nearly over. I'd done all in my power to help him understand the seriousness of his condition. I'd laid out the guidance of the Gospel, and how it offered hope to even the worst sinner to the very last. I'd told him of those who recanted at the eleventh hour and were saved. I'd reminded him of the thief on the Cross ... but I hadn't been able to stimulate any religious interest in him.

'Would you like me to pray with you?' I said. He refused resolutely. What more could I do for him?

He was taking little notice of anything I said, and realizing I couldn't help him I got up to go. But my mother's words kept haunting me as if she was repeating them from another world. 'If thou canst do him any good, do it.'

I would not be doing my best for him if I didn't speak to him in Welsh, and say who I was. I could tell him that my mother had forgiven him for his brutal behaviour towards her. It might be the only forgiveness he would ever know. I decided to reveal myself and prayed silently that it would affect him for his good.

'Robert Lewis,' I said in Welsh; 'Do you know who I am?'

He started at my question and for the first time stared at me. His eyes were marvellously bright, like two lamps lighting his way into the darkness of despair. I could see he was struggling to find a memory of me

'I am your son, Rhys,' I said. 'Father, you will be glad to hear that before she died my mother forgave you everything.'

My words were brief but they pained him more than anything I had previously said. He couldn't have reacted more strongly if I had thrown a bucket of fire on him. The effect of my words was fearful: he writhed and twisted in awful torment. He shrieked with fury. I repented a thousand times that I had spoken out.

'Get out of my sight,' he screamed. 'Go away. Go away.' He backed away as through I were a viper. He pressed himself close against the wall as if trying to push through it to escape me.

The landlady was alarmed by his howling and rushed into the room. She glared at me like a furious lioness defending its cub.

'What are you doing to a sick man?' she shouted. She looked as if she was about to sink her nails into my face. I was too upset to try to explain to her, and instead I fled out of the house in fear of my life.

I felt that unclean spirits had come into hither to my mind to torment me. If only I had been blessed with the second sight of Ellis Wynn o' Glasynys then I could have the avoided the pangs of misery I suffered from meeting my dying father.

My visit had only lasted twenty minutes or so, but it was the blackest time of my life. I didn't feel the grief that a son should feel when seeing his father in such a wretched state. This was because I'd never had any love for the man. Instead I experienced a feeling of pure horror in my heart. Seeing him made me wretched, and the only comfort I could draw from the meeting was that I had carried out the last wishes of my mother, to the best of my ability.

I went to meet the Sergeant and Wil Bryan. They were both waiting for me and I told them the result of my visit.

'I warned thee that no good would come of meeting him,' Wil said. 'I told thee to drop the idea.'

Now I had done what I needed to do, I was impatient to get back to Bala. My final examinations were to take place the next week. But, seeing that the Sergeant had something to say to me, I waited. The Sergeant took me to one side.

'Rhys,' said he quietly. 'Have you anything to conceal from Bryan?'

'Nothing,' I said.

'Good,' he said. He turned to Wil. 'Well boys, where shall we go now?'

'I'm for getting back to Bala as soon as I can,' I said.

'Thou'll not go from here today if I have to chain you by the leg, like William the Coal does with Duke,' Wil said. 'Anyway, there's no train for at least an hour and half.'

'That's true,' said Sergeant Williams.

'I know a hostel where we can get something to eat and have a chance to talk,' Wil said. 'Will you both join me?'

Sergeant Williams agreed, so I did likewise. Wil drove us to a hotel where I made but a very poor meal. I was too busy listening to what Sergeant Williams had say. I have recorded a summary of what he said that day and note that he made me promise to keep what he told me strictly confidential.

'It's years since I last saw you, Rhys Lewis,' the Sergeant said. 'It was the night I came to your house to arrest your brother Bob. I'll not forget that night as long as I live. I knew Bob was innocent, but it was my duty to arrest him. Bob and I were great friends, and I knew your mother well. As we left the house two men set upon us as we were leaving the courtyard. They were your father and uncle. I made the other policeman promise not to report the attack. They wanted to give Bob a chance to escape, but he wouldn't take it. I met the owner of the Hall the next day, as he was going to Church. I told him that I knew for certain that Bob, John Powel and Morris Hughes were innocent, and that it would be a mistake to lock them up.

The Squire took my advice badly. He swore at me and called me an interfering fool. I told him he ought to rush to Church to pray, as his soul needed to seek redemption for his sins. But from then on I knew that my fate in the town was sealed. The old scoundrel did everything he could to get me thrown out of office. Do you remember the slaughter of his pheasants on the night Bob was sent to the county jail? The colliers were blamed but it wasn't them who did it. It was done by two men of far greater daring than all the colliers put together. Bob knew it, and so did your poor mother. After what he had done I wasn't going to tell the owner of the Hall who they were. If I'd seen his house on fire, and could have dowsed the flames by spitting on them, I wouldn't have done it. He treated the town and me worse than any dog. I had a bad time after Bob was sent to prison. Most folk hated me, although what happened wasn't my fault, and I couldn't stop it. Before the riots I had many friends, but they shunned me and the other policemen afterwards. I wasn't sorry to move away. I came here and have lived here in middling comfort since.

'I bumped into your father, quite accidentally, about three years ago. He was scared when he saw me, for he remembered that I knew he'd had been guilty of something worse than poaching. But I told him not to worry. I wouldn't say anything. I'm not such a fine policeman, am I?

'I felt I an obligation to your mother and to Bob, so I wasn't going to rake up old stories. I met him many times after that before he became a total slave to the drink. I would visit him at his lodgings for a chat and to pick up news of Mold. He and your uncle often went back to raid the squire's game. They didn't hide what they did from me, as I'd said didn't care if they stole every pheasant on the place. I still owed the squire an old grudge. I never liked your uncle, but I got along well enough with your father. We shared a hatred for the squire. Your uncle didn't care whose game he stole, but your father took a special pleasure in saying about his prey, "These are the Hall owner's birds, and they cost him ten shillings a head."

'Your father and uncle systematically plundered the estate for years. And if you put me in the witness box, I couldn't deny under oath that some pheasants might have ended up on my table. After all I was a friend of your father's. Yes I'm a fine policeman, aren't I? But eating those pheasants was splendid sauce for my old grudge. I wondered how they had managed to avoid capture for so long; then one day I found out.

'You remember Nicklas o' Garth Ddu? Well, he managed their expeditions and gave them a hiding place. Nicklas had long been a dealer in game, and he'd done business with half the poachers in the kingdom. He'd made a lot of money, and your father and uncle were regular suppliers to him before he retired. Your father persuaded him to buy Garth Ddu, and it became a safe haven for him and your uncle ever after. The two kept in touch with old Nicklas. I'm sure you know that no one in Mold thought old Nicklas was quite on the square. But your father told me that the old man was a good thirty-seven inches to the yard. He was their scout, and he enjoyed the work. He walked the old paths through the Hall Park and Bryn Coch at all hours of the night. No one suspected him, as they thought him mad. But he knew exactly where the keepers were watching every night of the year.

His housekeeper, old Modlen, reported everything that happened in town to him. Your father used to laugh about the jolly nights they spent at Garth Ddu after a big haul. But that's all done now. Nicklas sold Garth Ddu about three months ago. He's living down here now. He still looks just the same as he did when I knew him in Mold. He's looked after your father. Once he dies, Nicklas will be off the next day.'

'Thank you Sergeant,' I said. 'That's helped me understand my history better. You've shed light on those parts of it I thought would always have to remain dark.'

Now I had definitely finished my business at Birmingham. I was in a hurry to return to Bala.

The Sergeant and Wil came with me to the railway station. As I got into the carriage Wil spoke to me through the carriage window.

'If I'd known thou wert were going to rush off so quickly,' he said. 'I'd not have let thee waste time sleeping. I haven't said a thousandth part of what I want to. I feel like preacher who's been told to shut up when he's just got into the swing. This sort of thing isn't true to nature. When I finally pay off the old man's debts and get back to Mold thou'll be long gone and the minister at Llangogogoch or somewhere just as remote. And I'll still be without a chum.'

'Thou can't be sure of that, Wil,' I said as the engine sounded its whistle ready to move off. 'I've had a call to the pastorate of Bethel, and now I see nothing to prevent me accepting it.'

Wil's face split into a joyous smile as the train puffed slowly forward. 'Pact?' he said. 'Bye bye, and remember to be true to …'

His final word was lost as the train gathered speed but I knew it was nature. I had heard him use the phrase hundreds of times.

Had I known that was the last time I would hear his voice or see his face, my heart would have been even sadder than it was. For all his failings, Wil's wit, honesty, and great fidelity had carved out a place in my heart from which he can never be ousted. I still sadly miss him.

As the train was speeding back to Wales I made every effort to forget the past, and to think only of the future. I had had a great shock, and my mind was still disturbed. I was dreading the forthcoming examination. I was bound to earn a lower ranking because of the preparation time I had lost with my trip to Birmingham. I hoped my tutors wouldn't think I had been lazy, going away when I should have been studying, but I couldn't have done otherwise, whatever my shortcomings.

I couldn't help thinking about my father's deplorable condition and his impending death. But I now had a calm conscience, knowing that I'd done my best for him. I fancied I could hear my mother's voice.

'Do not grieve, my son,' she said. 'Thou hast done thy duty by him, as I myself did mine. It is between him and God now.'

My journey to Birmingham hadn't been in vain. My meeting with Wil Bryan was a blessing. Before I left he had given me his word that he would go to chapel, and I trusted him. Wil didn't consider any man who broke his promise to be true to nature. And I was finally purged of the nightmare that had haunted me since childhood.

Now I could get on with the work of preaching without fear that my name would brought into disgrace. But I was still worried about the exams. I was sure to cut a sorry figure in the examination hall.

But when I reached Corwen I felt quite nauseous. I was so disoriented that I thought I was at the wrong station. My limbs trembled, and I was afraid that people would think me drunk.

I had to walk back to my lodgings, and by the time I arrived I was struggling to stand up. I managed to open the door and remember Jack Williams rushing forward to shake my hand, but then I collapsed and recall nothing else.

I woke up in bed. It was daylight, and when I tried to stand up I was too weak. Jack Williams was by my side.

'Well my lad,' he said. 'How dost thou feel?'

'What's the matter with me?' I said. 'Who's been beating me? Where have I been?'

'Be quiet,' Jack said. 'You've been very ill for the last ten days.'

'What day is it?' I said. 'When do the Exams begin?'

'They're over, since yesterday,' he said. 'Thou wilt not be either top or bottom this time. Thou must try and keep still. Thou hast suffered a heavy fever. Thou hast been raving by day and night about Wil Bryan and some Sergeant or other. But thou art well on the road to recovery now, and I'm heartily glad of it.'

There was a quiet knock on the bedroom door.

'Here's Dr Hughes,' Jack said. 'Well, Doctor, he's finally talking some sense at last.'

'Has he got tired of talking of Wil Bryan?' asked the doctor. 'About time.'

Hughes was a popular man. He was skilful and lively with just a single fault: he'd never send a bill to a student. He joked with me a deal that day until I asked him when I should go home.

'You must first go to the sanatorium at Jericho,' he said, 'and stay there till your hair grows.'

I felt my head and it was smooth. My hair had been sheared away during my treatment. How I mourned it. I was prouder than I realized.

It took weeks of convalescence before I was well enough to go home. Jack Williams was incredibly kind to me. He stayed a fortnight with me, during which I told him the gist of this history which I have now nearly finished writing.

No living soul but he and Wil Bryan know the full story of my life. If this autobiography ever sees the light of day I will have already travelled the unreturnable way, but its contents will not be any surprise to those two.

CHAPTER 42

The Minster of Bethel

Now I will have to end my Autobiography for similar reasons to those that decided me to begin it. I knew I was getting weaker when I began to write. But I wanted to write the history of my years as the minister of Bethel. When I began, I intended my account of those years to be the most important part of my work. I now know I will be unable to do that and regret that I took so much time writing of less worthy topics.

I thought hard before I took on the pastor's role in the church I was brought up in. I was afraid I wouldn't be up to the job, even though I knew the congregation were accommodating and kindly individuals. I didn't need time to make myself at home; I went back to Miss Hughes's cottage in my home town to lodge. Only the responsibilities of the job were new to me. It is not for me to say how well I adapted to my duties, but I can say that I devoted my entire heart to them. I wanted to be the best minister I could. Even to accept the office, I felt, was proof of lofty aspiration. But I often felt abashed when I couldn't match my own expectations. I learned that the best way to handle responsibility was to pray more. If I was going to fail, I wanted to make sure it was not because of lack of effort or carelessness. I worked hard, but I don't claim credit for it. I couldn't help myself.

My small stipend was enough to meet my needs. I didn't want much, and I took comfort in the fact I wasn't paid so much that I felt unable to earn it. Had my pay been higher, then I would have felt I didn't deserve it. As it was, it was small enough to avoid anyone reproaching me for accepting it. If there had been objections I would probably have refused it completely; I still had that streak of my mother's unreasoning independence about me. But no one ever queried my remuneration, so I tried to do my duty and give satisfaction to those I served.

The harder I worked the easier I slept at night. Work calmed my mind. If my hands were idle my old enemy, the despair of low-spiritedness would attack me. I have had nothing to complain about since I came here, and the few times I have been concerned I managed to hold my tongue. The monthly *Seiat* had quickly proposed me for ordination. Dafydd Davis and Eos Prydain gave me much help and encouragement along the way, and I met with nothing but kindness from both the elder congregation and the young people.

About two years ago. I noticed that this kindness seemed to be increasing. If I had to travel as little as six or seven miles, Dafydd Davis would insist I borrow his horse. Miss Hughes made sure I had warm and comfortable clothing to wear, and Thomas Bartley kept insisting I ate more ham and eggs, 'To build you up,' he said.

I also noticed that other folk kept reminding me that I should look after myself. All this interest in my welfare bothered me, and I wondered why it was happening. It finally dawned on me that my health was failing. Now I understood the meaning of the looks and the attitude of my friends. I'd never been strong, and, although I hadn't noticed it, my congregation had seen my strength was deteriorating. Others saw the danger long before I did. My spirits sank within me

The doctor tried to cheer me up, saying it was no more than a passing weakness.

'All you need is a change of air,' he said.

'Where shall I go?' I said. 'I like the seaside. Should I go there?'

'I suggest you go to Trefriw and take the waters.'

I understood his concern. He knew that visiting the sea always made me sad. It made me think of voyaging to a distant shore. To go the seaside would focus my thoughts on the loosening of my earthly bonds; I would think of far off places and of travelling to the Unknown.

I met several old friends at Trefriw that summer. Some even pretended to be astonished at seeing me so much better. They would comfort me and rejoice in my company. They helped me forget myself, but underlying their joy I could hear undertones of serious concern. I told them how I envied their sprightliness and vitality

I felt much better after my time at Trefriw and began to enjoy the innocent fun which accompanied taking the waters of the Well. I thought I was taking a turn for the better and I felt pleasure at the thought I would soon return to my work.

Back at Bethel my friends were delighted at the improvement in me. I preached on the following Sabbath without feeling the least weary. This made me so happy: I was cured and back doing the job I loved.

However, a few weeks afterwards I found things getting hard again. I was constantly weary. I was persuaded to go again to Trefriw. This time it was winter and I was the only visitor in the village. The weather was cold and wet. I stayed in my room for four days and felt I was getting worse. I went back to Mold in worse health than when I left.

I was afraid the doctor didn't know what was wrong with me, and I began to search the newspapers for quack advertisements. I soon discovered the declarations were lies and the endorsements imaginary. I had to face the fact that my physical condition was deteriorating. Preaching was getting more difficult each Sunday.

If a kindly deacon expressed concern about my condition it depressed me. At first I refused to accept help, but as I got worse I accepted it gratefully. It is now over a year since I last preached. I think I would have continued for longer, but I decided to seek a second opinion.

That doctor told me the truth. I was not long for this world. He told me to give up work immediately.

Should a doctor always tell the full truth? I insisted he tell me, and I must tell you I wish I had not asked. If you are ever put in the position of wanting to know the truth about your prospects it is better never to ask. Once I knew, I wished the doctor had withheld the truth from me.

The truth was terrible and drove my already low spirits to more frightful despair. I didn't speak to anyone for some time afterwards. I developed a fierce craving for life that I had never before known. I felt cheated by that on which I most depended. For days my mind raged against doctors, fate, Providence, and even God.

Every day I saw men older than me who were sturdy, strong and broad-chested. I heard them cursing, getting drunk and fighting. They thrived while I nursed a chest like a rickety basket. Why had God arranged things in this way? What was the Divine Purpose behind it all? My plans were frustrated, and I tasted despair.

I read several sermons about death, the other world, and similar subjects to try to understand. But in my circumstances I found them cold and soulless. I knew that if I only had the strength I could preach a much better sermon about the reality of facing death. It was weeks before I discovered how to submit to that which I could not change. My future was inevitable and so I gave up the struggle. Then, when I was resigned, I saw things from a new perspective.

Subjects that once fascinated me, like politics and literature, lost their allure. Why I had ever taken any interest in them? My studies contracted steadily until I could think only of my spiritual fate.

The truths I had once taken great pleasure in preaching only made me sink me deeper into the depths of unspeakable sorrow.

Then, with a grace granted from Heaven, I began to master my melancholy. I recognized God's hand in the matter and threw myself into His arms. In acceptance of His Will I caught occasional glimpses of an ineffable happiness that I had never experienced before I was stricken.

I would fall into silent raptures about my impending demise and feel a powerful longing for the perfection of the spiritual world. I began to envisage my body and its weakness as a thing quite separate from my essence, and I would laugh at it. Then I would subside into a pleasing peace, and reflect on the many disagreeable things that my breakdown would save me from. If I continued to live I might be overcome by some temptation that would have disgraced me and my calling. I would thank God for the mercy of allowing me to die young, and then I gave way to morbid and pointless brooding.

I had a strange daydream. If Providence was determined to take me in the middle of my days perhaps I could live my life over again in my own mind. If I relived my whole life I would effectively double it.

If my strength allowed, I could spend a few hours every day going over and recording the main events of my life. This would stop me brooding on futile subjects and save me eating myself away before my time. Perhaps writing my autobiography might do me good. I experimented until I found a position to lie in that was fairly free from pain and enabled me to write this book.

It is the work of a serious man, even if it contains various amusing incidents. But what's wrong with that? If I've spent too long describing Wil Bryan, I have addressed some of the great questions of life too. If I hadn't, the fire would have been the best place for this manuscript.

I wish I could write something more cheerful about Wil Bryan. However, I have heard nothing from him for some time. In his last letter he told me he had finished paying his father's debts and he was still attending the Welsh Chapel, but he had not yet got back to his real self. I wrote back, but my letter was returned with the note, 'left without forwarding address.' That was months ago, and he has not written to me. Has he gone with the tide to start afresh overseas? I have no idea, but I feel sure he will turn up safe one day.

On her death-bed my mother asked me to repay the Bartleys for their kindness to her. I have never had the chance. Indeed, they have increased the debt of kindness to both of us. Their benevolence to me has been endless, and their sympathy with my illness precious. Their comprehension is limited, yet, simple as they are, I envy them. They are well, both are happy and look likely to survive for many years yet. Both their heads together are unable to read a single verse of the Bible but they enjoy their religion, and draw great strength from it. They are so close and so well matched that I believe they will die on the same day. I cannot see how either Thomas or Barbara could possibly live without the other.

If anyone takes the trouble to read this history, they may wonder why I dwelled so long on dishonourable family matters. Perhaps they will ask, in Wil Bryan's words, 'Is this true to nature?' But if a history is true, how can it be different? Nobody is left to be hurt by it once I go. But don't be sad that I am the last of my family. I'll join them soon.

As I look over what I have written I notice I have left out some things that I would have liked to have dealt with. And some things I have deliberately omitted. But it is unlikely I will be able to revise this version, because I have found writing the later parts extremely difficult.

I hope any reader finds it less of a burden to read than I have found it to write. If you should find it hard to read, dear reader, then you can do as I am doing now and lay it aside to rest a while.

The End

TRANSLATOR'S POSTSCRIPT

Why Translate a Victorian Novel about Mold?

I was born into a world dominated by three sisters, the children of Caroline Blackwell. Annie (born 1888) was the eldest, Jenny (1890) the most adventurous, and Sophia (1894), the youngest, was my maternal grandmother. The three, all born towards the end of the nineteenth century in the Welsh border town of Mold, were brought up speaking mainly Welsh. The Welsh word for grandmother, *nain*, is the only name I ever called Sophia.

Their father, Joseph, was the eldest of eleven. In 1878 he was working as a tinplate roller at Alyn Tinplate Works on the Denbigh Road when he met Caroline Griffiths (born 1862). As a girl Caroline had lived with her father John Griffiths and her mother Ann at 34 Maes-y-Dre, Mold. There they were neighbours of Daniel Owen and his family, who lived at No. 53. They attended the prayer meetings he held both in Maes-y-Dre and later in Pownalls Row.

Caroline met Joseph Blackwell when she went to work as a tinplate polisher at the Alyn Works, fell in love and married him. They moved into a two-up, two-down terraced house in Pownalls Row and had five children. Their elder son George (born in 1886) became a tinplate cutcher at Alyn Works. Annie married Joseph Tarran, a miner from Buckley, while Jennie and Sophia joined a small Welsh diaspora in Higher Broughton, Salford, near Manchester, and went into service before they, too, married; Jennie married a tram-driver called Jack Duckworth, and Sophia a railway worker called Harold Woodcock, and they both settled in Salford. Joseph and Caroline's younger son, Teddy Griffiths Blackwell was born in 1897.

Both George and his father Joseph died in accidents at the tinplate works, leaving Caroline a widow with four surviving children. In those times, before the introduction of Social Security, Caroline had only one asset – the two-up, two-down terraced house which she rented – and somehow she had to use it to keep the whole family.

She made it work for her by turning her front room into a shop. She bought groceries in bulk and sold them on in small quantities to the families living around her, including Daniel Owen, whom she described as a kind and God-fearing man.

Looking back at what she achieved with her family, her strength and tenacity amazes me. She had major disadvantages: she was illiterate and she spoke no English, so she couldn't even read the Welsh she spoke at home. She had never been taught arithmetic and knew nothing of book-keeping, yet she succeeded in running a successful local shop for the next forty years. As she had never been taught how to write, she invented a system of picture writing for herself, and used it to keep track of her business activities. It was a system of notation that she alone could read, but it did everything she needed. She earned enough to bring up her children and live to the ripe old age of 86. Caroline Blackwell died in 1948 when I was one year old, and unfortunately I have no memories of her to visit. But I remember her daughters well, they all still live where I wander in the fields of childhood memory, where they remind me about her, her life and her pride in the success of her childhood neighbour, Daniel Owen.

When I was a child I stayed with my *nain* in her little terraced house in Salford every Friday night, while my mother and father went to the cinema. I loved those cosy evenings sitting in front of the open fire with her. She sang Welsh nursery rhymes to me and told me tales of her childhood and the hard life of Nain Blackwell in the little market town of Mold.

The three sisters all kept in touch, writing to each other and visiting when they could. Annie or Teddy would read out their letters to Caroline, who never learned to read anything other than her own system of notation, the secret of which died with her. When the Great War came, Teddy, Jack and Harold served in France, Jack and Harold with the Manchester Pals, and Teddy with the Flintshire Regiment. Jack returned safely but died in the terrible 1918 flu epidemic; Teddy was reported missing in action but eventually came back shell-shocked; whilst Harold developed Parkinson's disease, returned to Salford an invalid, never to work again, and died young. Soon after the end of the Great War both Jenny and Sophia were widowed. And each had a young child to support.

Sophia, who inherited Caroline's flair for business, got a job in a bakery and confectioners on Great Cheetham Street, Salford. She went on to become manageress of that shop and bought a house close by. And my great aunt Annie still lived near Mold when I was a child, and I visited her and great uncle Joe regularly. I spent every childhood school holiday in and around Mold, where I had many relatives who Auntie Annie took me to visit, and I got to know the places and characters that had shaped my family.

Despite being an author with many best-selling books to my name, I am dyslexic. It is a gift I have learned to manage, nurture and use to advantage, since it encouraged me to become a physicist. As a youngster at school I was constantly told I was thick and didn't pay enough attention. I failed the eleven plus and was sent to a secondary modern school in Prestwich, Manchester, where my family, including Nain, was then living.

I was extremely lucky to be taken under the wing of John Hywel Roberts, a young Welshman who had just qualified as a teacher and at one time had struggled with his English, being a native Welsh-speaker. I was educated long before dyslexia was identified and so didn't expect, or get, any special treatment, but John Roberts noticed a considerable mismatch between my verbal reasoning and musical ability on the one hand and my written work on the other; he also quickly picked up that I had a basic grasp of Welsh. He encouraged me to develop my music, which later translated into making the leap from reading and playing a piano score, to learning how to type out the shapes of words I could not spell. He inspired me with a love of history by his beautiful storytelling during history lessons, and he took it on himself to teach me how to read Welsh. (I couldn't really read English at that time, so this was a great act of faith.) He taught me how to relate the shapes of Welsh letters to sounds and helped me to read the words like a music score. He kick-started my academic career and gave me a new perspective on the technique of reading that I adopted and developed. He also encouraged me to think about going to college, and in time I went on to university, where I earned a B.Sc. with first-class honours in electronic engineering and then a Ph.D. in solid-state physics.

As part of my undergraduate engineering course at university I had to study either Russian or German. By that time I had developed a system of reading using symbol recognition (a strange echo of Nain Blackwell's solution to the problem of reading), although, unlike her, I used a system of shape-to-sound reading that relied on the standardized symbols of written words. The shapes of German words looked so similar to the shapes of English words that I thought it would cause me confusion with my English reading. Russian words were quite different in shape, so I opted to study them. My Russian tutor was a charming woman who approached her task with great pragmatism. Her students didn't need to learn how to speak and write in Russian; they were going to be examined in translating Russian technical papers. To achieve this she taught us a system of translation she called boilerplating. The idea is simple: you first look up the meaning of every word from the dictionary and write it above the Russian word. Next you sort the order of the words, using the rules of grammar to sequence verbs, nouns, adjectives, etc. This results in a clunky but sensible rendering of the text. Finally you rewrite it in more fluent English. I can still read out Russian text, as I have occasionally demonstrated at literary festival events in support of PEN International, and I can even produce readable translations, given enough time.

When Nain died I inherited her few books. Among then was a copy of *Rhys Lewis* which I have kept on my bookshelf ever since. When I inherited it I believed it to be a first edition. Then, in 2013, I went to the Welsh National *Eisteddfod* in Denbigh with my old teacher and friend Dr John Roberts, who had recently retired from Glasgow University. As we walked around the *Eisteddfod* field (*y maes*) and went to see the award of the Daniel Owen Memorial Prize to Bet Jones, I told John of my interest in Daniel Owen and how I regretted not being able to read the book I inherited from Nain.

John told me he'd heard about a modern English translation of Daniel Owen's *Tales of the Fireside* (*Straeon y Pentan*) that I might enjoy. We went along to the Welsh Books Council shop and found a copy, which I bought. I did enjoy it, and found the tales of Victorian Mold took me back to childhood Friday evenings, listening to Nain's fireside tales.

As I drove John back to his Welsh home we talked about Daniel Owen and his writing. I asked if there was a modern translation of *Rhys Lewis*, as I had the copy which had belonged to my Nain but had never been able to read it. He said he didn't know of a modern translation, but then he asked me:

'Why not sit down with your dictionary and read it?'

'I struggle with dictionaries. I don't know the English, Welsh or Russian alphabet, and, being dyslexic, I can't learn them.'

'But you can use a computer,' John said. 'Have a look at Bangor University's Online Dictionary, which lets you search online. You've told me how you do boiler-plate translation. Boiler-plate it and read it. You can if you want to.'

I realized he was right: I did know how to read *Rhys Lewis*. So I went home, downloaded the iPad app from Bangor University and was able to find the words I didn't know and set about boiler-plating.

If I wanted to read that book I would have to translate it myself – but I didn't want to subject the precious copy I inherited from Nain to the severe manhandling my mechanical method of translation required. I needed a less precious copy to work with, so I went to my favourite second-hand book shop, at the Old Post Office in Blaenau Ffestiniog. I consulted the charming woman who runs it, Ms Elin Jones, and asked if she had any early editions of *Rhys Lewis*. She came up with a Hughes and Son first edition published in Wrexham, like Nain's copy. Then she said, 'I think I've got an earlier edition, if you're interested.'

Translator's Postscript

I didn't know there had been an earlier edition, and was amazed when she produced an edition that had been published by J. LL. Morris of New Street, Mold. I bought both copies. Then I started to research the publication history of *Rhys Lewis*, which I have outlined in the Preface to this book.

The Morris edition has a list of subscribers' names and addresses added as an appendix, so I checked it, hoping to find Joseph Blackwell. But I should have realised that he couldn't read and write, and certainly couldn't have afforded to spend four weeks wages on a single book. I did, however, notice that Mr David Davies, Manager of the Alyn Tinplate Works where Joseph worked, had bought a copy. I now know that Nain's copy is not a first edition, and she probably bought it second-hand, after becoming established in Salford.

I decided that if I was going to read *Rhys Lewis* I would make sure I read its earliest version, the Morris edition. Then, having painstakingly boiler-plated the text, I was so impressed by the story that I decided to rewrite the boiler-plate translation into modern English. Throughout the four years the whole process has taken I have tried hard to stay true to the story and to the spirit of Mold that I learned from Nain Woodcock and Nain Blackwell. Translating this important novel has been a labour of love to celebrate the memory of my family roots in the town of Mold and to enable me to pass on part of our family history to my children and grandchildren.

Robert Lomas
Gorwel, 3 January 2017

ACKNOWLEDGEMENTS

I thank my *Nain* (grandmother), Sophia Woodcock, née Blackwell, for teaching me my nursery rhymes in Welsh, for telling me inspirational tales of her girlhood in Victorian Mold and for introducing me to the work of Wales's greatest novelist, Daniel Owen.

I also thank a young teacher, fresh out of training in Aberystwyth, who, on his first teaching job in a secondary modern school in Manchester took a young, dyslexic eleven-plus failure under his wing and taught him to love history, to find joy in music and to read Welsh. Everyone has an inspirational teacher in their past, and mine is Dr John Hywel Roberts, who began as my teacher and went on to become my friend. Without his encouragement I might never have become a scientist or a writer, and most certainly would never have learned to translate Welsh.

And I thank a young girl from Mold who asked me on a date to the Savoy Cinema in Chester Street well over fifty years ago, and who is still by my side as my wife. She shares her birthday with Daniel Owen, loves his work and has an encyclopaedic knowledge of Mold. She warned me it would be massive job to translate *Rhys Lewis*, but has constantly supported me over the four years my self-imposed task has taken.

Finally I thank Elin Jones, who runs Siop Lyfrau'r Hen Bost in Blaenau Ffestiniog and who found me my copy of the J. LL. Morris subscription edition of *Rhys Lewis*.

Other books by Robert Lomas:

Freemasonry for Beginners
The Lewis Guide to Masonic Symbols
A Miscellany of Masonic Essays
The Lost Key
The Secret Science of Masonic Initiation
The Secret Power of Masonic Symbols
Turning the Hiram Key
Turning the Solomon Key
Turning the Templar Key
The Secrets of Freemasonry
W.L.Wilmshurst's *The Ceremony of Initiation* Revisited
W.L.Wilmshurst's *The Ceremony of Passing* Revisited

The Man Who Invented the Twentieth Century
The Invisible College
Freemasonry and the Birth of Modern Science

Mastering Your Business Dissertation

Co-authored:

With Chris Knight
The Hiram Key
The Second Messiah
Uriel's Machine
The Book of Hiram

With Geoff Lancaster
Forecasting for Sales and Materials Management